About th

Evie Woods is the pseudonym of Evie Gaughan, bestselling author of *The Story Collector, The Heirloom* and *The Mysterious Bakery on Rue De Paris.* Living on the West Coast of Ireland, Evie escapes the inclement weather by writing her stories in a converted attic, where she dreams of underfloor heating. Her books tread the intriguing line between the everyday and the otherworldly, revealing the magic that exists in our ordinary lives.

www.eviewoods.com

x.com/evgaughan

instagram.com/evie.gaughan

tiktok.com/@eviewoods.author

THE LOST BOOKSHOP

EVIE WOODS

ONE MORE CHAPTER

One More Chapter
a division of HarperCollins*Publishers* Ltd
1 London Bridge Street
London SE1 9GF
www.harpercollins.co.uk
HarperCollins*Publishers*
Macken House, 39/40 Mayor Street Upper,
Dublin 1, D01 C9W8, Ireland

This paperback edition 2024
22
First published in Great Britain in ebook format
by HarperCollins*Publishers* 2023

A catalogue record of this book is available from the British Library

ISBN: 978-0-00-860921-4

Printed and bound in the UK using 100% Renewable Electricity
by CPI Group (UK) Ltd

To all the book lovers

Prologue

The rainy streets of Dublin on a cold winter's day were no place for a young boy to dawdle, unless that very same boy had his nose pressed up against the window of the most fascinating bookshop. Lights twinkled inside and the colourful covers called to him, promising stories of adventure and escape. The window was packed with novelties and trinkets; miniature hot-air balloons almost reached the ceiling, while music boxes with mechanical birds and carousels twirled and chimed within. The lady inside spotted him and waved him in. He shook his head and blushed slightly.

'I'll be late for school,' he mouthed through the glass.

She nodded and smiled. She seemed friendly enough.

'Just for a minute,' he said, having fought the urge to go inside for all of three seconds.

'A minute it is.' She was behind the counter, taking more books out of a big cardboard box. She glanced over at his untucked shirt, his mop of hair that had managed to evade a comb for quite some time and mismatched socks. She smiled to herself. Opaline's

Bookshop was a magnet for little boys and girls. 'What class are you in?'

'Third class in St Ignatius,' he replied, craning his neck to look up at the wooden airplanes suspended mid-flight from the vaulted ceiling.

'And do you like it?'

He scoffed at the thought.

She left him leafing through an old book of magic tricks, but it wasn't long until he approached her desk and began looking at the stationery.

'You can help if you like. I'm sending out invitations to a book launch.'

He shrugged and began mimicking the way she folded the letters and stuffed them into the envelopes with a little too much enthusiasm. He wrinkled his nose with the effort, changing the constellation of freckles that spread out to his cheeks.

'What does Opaline mean?' he asked, pronouncing it with far too many syllables.

'Opaline is a name.'

'Is it your name?'

'No, I'm Martha.'

She could tell that he wasn't satisfied with that as an explanation.

'I can tell you a story about her, if you like? She didn't like school very much either. Or rules.'

'Or doing what she's told?' he suggested.

'Oh, she especially didn't like that.' Martha smiled conspiratorially. 'Here, you finish jamming those letters into envelopes and I'll make us some tea. A good story always begins with tea.'

Chapter One

OPALINE

London, 1921

I let my fingers run along the spine of the book, letting the indentations of the embossed cover guide my skin to something tangible; something that I believed in more than the fiction that was playing out before me. Twenty-one years of age and my mother had decided that the time had come for me to marry. My brother, Lyndon, had rather unhelpfully found some dim-witted creature who had just inherited the family business; something to do with importing something or other from some far-flung place. I was barely listening.

'There are only two options open to a woman your age,' Mother pronounced, putting down her cup and saucer on the table beside her armchair. 'One is to marry, and the other to find a post in keeping with her gentility.'

'Gentility?' I echoed, with some incredulity. Looking around the drawing room with its chipped paint and faded curtains, I had to admire her vanity. She had married beneath her station and had always been at pains to remind my father, lest he forgot.

'Must you do that now?' my brother Lyndon asked, as Mrs Barrett, our housemaid, cleared out the ashes from the grate.

'Madam requested a fire,' she said in a tone that showed no inflexion of respect. She had been with us for as long as I could remember and only took orders from my mother. The rest of us she treated like cheap imposters.

'The fact of the matter is that you must marry,' Lyndon parroted as he limped across the room, leaning heavily on his walking stick. Twenty years my elder, the entire right side of his body had been warped by shrapnel during the war in Flanders and the brother I once knew stayed buried somewhere in that very field. The horrors he held in his eyes frightened me, and even though I didn't like to admit it, I had grown fearful of him. 'This is a good match. Father's pension is barely enough for Mother to run the house. It's time you took your head out of your books and faced reality.'

I clung tighter to my book. A rare first American edition of *Wuthering Heights,* a gift from my father, along with a deep love of reading. Like a talisman, I had carried the cloth-covered book, whose spine bore the duplicitous line, tooled in gold, 'by the author of *Jane Eyre*'. We had come across it by complete chance at a flea market in Camden (a secret we could not tell Mother). I would later discover that Emily's English publisher had permitted this misattribution in order to capitalise on *Jane Eyre*'s commercial success. It was not in perfect condition; the cloth boards were worn on the edges and the back one had a v-shape nicked out of it. The pages were coming loose, as the threads that sewed them together were fraying with age and use. But to me, all of these features, including the cigar-smoke smell of the paper, were like a time machine. Perhaps the seeds were sown then. A book is never what it seems. I think my father had hoped my love of books would instil an interest in my schooling, but if anything, it only fuelled my loathing for the classroom. I tended to live in my imagination and so, every evening, I would race home from school and ask him to read to me. He was a civil servant, an honest man with a passion for learning. He always said that books were more than words on paper; they were portals to other places, other lives. I fell in love with books and the vast worlds they held inside, and I owed it all to my father.

'If you tilt your head,' he told me once, 'you can hear the older books whispering their secrets.'

I found an antique book on the shelf with a calfskin cover and time-coloured pages. I held it up to my ear and closed my eyes tight; imagining that I could hear whatever important secrets the author was trying to tell me. But I couldn't hear it, not the words at least.

'What do you hear?' he asked.

I waited, let the sound fill my ears.

'I hear the sea!'

It was like having a shell to my ear, with the air swirling through the pages. He smiled and held my cheek in his hand.

'Are they breathing, Papa?' I asked.

'Yes,' he said, 'the stories are breathing.'

When he finally succumbed to the Spanish Flu in 1918, I stayed up all night by his side, holding his cold hand, reading his favourite story. *The Personal History of David Copperfield*, by Charles Dickens. In some silly way, I thought that the words would bring him back.

'I refuse to marry a man I've never even met purely to aid the family finances. The whole idea is preposterous!'

Mrs Barrett dropped the brush as I spoke and the sound of metal on marble churned my brother's features. He loathed any loud noises.

'Get out of here now!'

The poor woman had very unreliable knees and it took three failed attempts before she got up and left the room. How she managed to refrain from slamming the door behind her, I will never know.

I continued with my defence.

'If I am such a burden to you both, I will simply move out.'

'And where on earth do you think you would go? You have no money,' my mother pointed out. Now in her sixties, she had always referred to my arrival in the family as their 'little surprise', which would have sounded quaint had I not been aware of her loathing for surprises. Growing up in a household of an older generation only compounded my urge to break free and experience the modern world.

'I have friends,' I insisted. 'I could get a job.'

My mother shrieked.

'Damn and blast, you ungrateful brat!' Lyndon growled, grabbing my wrist as I attempted to get up from my chair.

'You're hurting me.'

'I will hurt you far worse than this if you do not obey.'

I tried to free my arm, but he held fast. I looked to my mother, who was making an intense study of the rug on the floor.

'I see,' I said, finally understanding that Lyndon was the man of the house now and he would make the decisions.

'Very well.' He still held on to my wrist, his sour breath in my face. 'I said, very well.'

Meeting his eyes, I again tried to pull away. 'I will meet this suitor.'

'You will marry him,' he assured me and slowly he released his grasp.

I smoothed down my skirts and tucked my book under my arm.

'Right. That's settled then,' Lyndon said, his cold eyes looking somewhere just beyond me. 'I shall invite Austin to supper this evening and all will be arranged.'

'Yes, Brother,' I said, before retreating to my bedroom upstairs.

I searched the top drawer of the dressing table and found a cigarette that I'd stolen from Mrs Barrett's stash in the kitchen. I opened the window and lit the tip, taking a long slow inhale like a femme fatale from the films. I sat at my dressing table and let the cigarette rest on an old oyster shell I had picked up at the beach last summer, a carefree holiday with my best friend Jane before she herself got married. Despite the fact that women now had the vote, a good marriage was still seen as the only option.

Looking at my reflection in the mirror, I touched the nape of my neck where my hair ended. Mother had almost fainted when she saw what I'd done with my long tresses. 'I'm not a little girl any more,' I had told her. But did I really believe that? I needed to be a modern woman. I needed to take a risk. But without any money, how could I do anything other than obey my elders? That was when my father's words returned to me … *Books are like portals*. I looked again at my bookshelf and took another long drag of my cigarette.

'What would Nellie Bly do?' I asked myself, as I often did. To me, she was the epitome of fearlessness – a pioneering American journalist who, inspired by Jules Verne's book, travelled around the world in a mere seventy-two days, six hours and eleven minutes. She always said that energy rightly applied and directed could accomplish anything. If I were a boy, I could announce my intentions to do the Grand Tour of Europe before getting married. I longed to experience different cultures. Twenty-one years old and I had done nothing. Seen nothing. I looked again at my books and made my decision before I finished smoking my cigarette.

'How much can you give me for them?' I watched as Mr Turton examined my hardbacks of *Wuthering Heights* and *The Hunchback of Notre Dame*.

He was the proprietor of an airless shop that was in reality just a very long corridor without any windows. His pipe smoke gave the air a viscous quality and my eyes began to water.

'Two pounds and that's being generous.'

'Oh no, I need much more than that.'

He saw my father's copy of *David Copperfield* and before I could stop him, he began to leaf through the pages.

'I'm not selling that one. It has … sentimental value.'

'Ah, now this is interesting. It is known as the "reading edition", as Dickens would have read from it at his public readings.' His bulbous nose and tiny eyes gave him the look of a badger or a mole. He sniffed out the valuable book like a truffle.

'Yes, I am aware,' I said, trying to snatch the book back from his greedy paws. He continued with his appraisal, as though he were already selling it at auction.

'Sumptuously bound in full polished red calf. A charming edition; ornate tooling in gilt to the spine; all page edges gilt; original marbled endpapers.'

'My father gifted me that book. It is not for sale.'

He looked at me over the rim of his glasses, sizing me up. 'Miss …?'

'Miss Opaline Carlisle.'

'Miss Carlisle, this is one of the best-preserved examples of these rare issues I have ever handled. '

'And the illustrations by Hablot K. Browne. You see his pen name, Phiz,' I added, with pride.

'I could offer you fifteen pounds.'

The world fell silent, the way it often does the moment before a life-changing decision. On one path lay freedom along with the unknown. The other was a gilded cage.

'Twenty pounds, Mr Turton, and you have a deal.'

He narrowed his eyes and his lips betrayed a grudging smile. I knew he would pay, just as surely as I knew that I would devote my life to getting that book back. As his back was turned, I slipped my *Wuthering Heights* back into my pocket and left.

That was how my career as a book dealer began.

Chapter Two

MARTHA

Dublin, nine months ago ...

When I first arrived at the redbrick Georgian house on Ha'penny Lane that cold, dark evening with rain dripping from my jacket, I hadn't planned on staying. The woman on the phone sounded less than friendly, but I had nowhere else to go and very little money. My journey to Dublin had begun a week previously and from the other side of the country, at a lonely bus stop just outside the village. I don't know how long I sat at the bus stop, if it was cold or warm, or if anyone passed me by. All of my senses were dulled by one overwhelming urge – to leave. I couldn't see out of my right eye, so I didn't see the bus eventually pulling up. My whole body felt numb, but when I slid off the stone wall, my ribs complained. Still, I wouldn't let my thoughts go back there. Not yet. Even when the driver got down to help me with my suitcase and looked at me as though I had just escaped from a secure facility, I wouldn't let my thoughts go back there.

'Where to?' he asked.

Anywhere but here.

'Dublin,' I answered. Dublin might be far enough. I watched the countryside slide past my window. I fucking hated those fields, the small towns with a school, a church and twelve pubs. The greyness of it, pressing in on me. I must've started to doze off, because I jumped, thinking he was on top of me again – my hands protecting my face. I didn't know what to protect. He was too quick. And when he found the poker, it all fell away from me. Everything. Every hope I had. Every naive, stupid hope. I learned something in that moment; you're on your own in this world. No one is coming to save you. People don't suddenly change, say they're sorry and begin to treat you with respect. They are a jumble of hurt and pain and they will take it out on whomever they can. I had to save myself.

~

'Just a coffee and a toasted cheese sandwich please,' I said to the waiter, picking the cheapest item on the menu.

I'd had no luck online, so I grabbed a local newspaper and began searching for jobs. One week staying in a hostel and I was already running out of money. That's when I saw it: *Housekeeper. Live-in*. I dialled the number and the very next day found myself on the steps of a very grand-looking house, knocking on the glossy black door. Madame Bowden, as I was told to address her, was like no one I had ever met. Like a character from some historical TV drama, she wore a feather boa and diamond earrings. Within five minutes, she had already regaled me with stories of her days in the Theatre Royal, dancing with the Royalettes and acting in some old plays I'd never heard of.

'People call me eccentric, but then I call them boring, so it's all relative. What's your name again?'

'Martha,' I repeated for the third time, following her down the stairs to the basement. She had a walking stick and while she made a big production of it, she seemed agile enough. I guessed that she was probably in her eighties, but she also seemed timeless – an actress who had chosen a character to be frozen in time.

'Now, the last girl was very happy here,' she remarked in a tone that warned me I should feel likewise.

It was so dark, I couldn't make anything out, save for the half window close to the ceiling, where I could see people's feet walking past at street level. She flicked a switch using her cane and, following a moment's blindness from the large bulb in the pendant lamp, I could see a single bed in the corner with a wardrobe on the opposite wall. Beside the door was a small kitchenette and just outside, a door led to a tiny bathroom with a shower. The lino on the floor was curling at the edges and the wallpaper similarly obliged, but I immediately felt a sense of safety. It was mine. A space I could call my own. I could close the door and not have to worry about who might beat it down.

'Well?' Madame Bowden asked, arching an eyebrow.

'It's lovely,' I said.

'Of course it is. What did I tell you.'

'So, do I have the job?'

She narrowed her gaze, taking in my dishevelled appearance. I thanked God for what must have been her very poor eyesight, because she didn't seem to notice my battered face or, if she did, it didn't put her off.

'Oh, I suppose so,' she capitulated. 'But don't get carried away, I'm hiring you purely by default. No one else showed up. Can you believe that? That's the trouble with your generation. Entirely unwilling to do an honest day's work. It's all "tikkity-tok" these days, expecting money for nothing.'

She was still talking as she walked away from me and up the stairs. I carefully sat down on the bed and listened as the springs played like a broken accordion underneath me. Still, it didn't matter. No one would ever find me here. I set the clock for 7 a.m.

Apparently my new employer expected a 'fine dining experience' in the morning, at which point I was to conjure a Michelin-star breakfast out of whatever was in the fridge. I would think about that later. I fell into a blessed sleep without even changing my damp clothes or closing the blinds.

I sat up the minute I awoke. Why was it so bright? Where was I? And why was my alarm ringing? One by one, my mind slowly answered these questions and I looked down at my old jeans and baggy jumper. I wasn't sure exactly what the uniform was for being a housekeeper, but it probably wasn't this. I opened my suitcase and pulled out a long, grey knitted dress. I could hardly recall throwing it in there, but some part of my brain must've thought to grab things I wouldn't need to iron. I quickly pulled off my jumper and was just unzipping my jeans when I saw the bottom half of two legs walking in front of the basement window at the side of the house. I held my breath until I saw the boots, brown suede with laces. They weren't his boots. I watched, holding my jumper over my bra, as they paced up and down and in semi-circles. What the hell was he doing? I felt my anger rise. With no small amount of resistance, I managed to push the window open and stick my head out, with my arms resting on the windowsill.

'Excuse me?'

No response. I cleared my throat loudly. Still nothing.

'Can I help you?'

'I highly doubt it.'

I was surprised to hear an English accent. I had begun to think the feet were not attached to a body at all. I still could not see his face, but already I could read snippets of him. It was something I'd always done, reading people, even though it got me into trouble sometimes. This one seemed distracted, searching, unhappy.

'What are you doing here?' I continued my conversation with his shins.

'I hardly think it's any of your business. What are you doing here?'

'I *live* here!' I said, wishing I'd pulled the blinds in the first place. 'So you can do your Peeping Tom act somewhere else.' My voice was shaking a bit. I didn't feel up to having a confrontation with a stranger, but I also wanted my privacy. I could hear his boots scuffing the dirt and next thing I knew, he was sitting on his haunches, his face looming in front of me. It didn't really match the voice at all, which was all sharp edges that you could cut your finger on. There was a warmth in his brown eyes, or were they green? Hazel, perhaps. His hair kept falling in the way. But his features held the quizzical look of someone who would challenge every word you spoke.

'Did you just say Peeping Tom?' he asked, clearly amused. 'Have you time-travelled from the eighties?'

I wasn't sure which I disliked more, being ignored or mocked. His grin was annoyingly infectious and it revealed some imperfect teeth, which I read as the result of a short-lived passion for sports. Football, I think. Blocking a penalty kick, he'd been hit in the face. I smiled, then immediately stopped.

'Look, if you don't stop stalking me or whatever it is you're doing, I'm going to phone the police.'

He raised his hands in surrender.

'I'm sorry. Look, my name is Henry,' he said, offering me his hand to shake.

I stared at it and watched as he sheepishly retracted it.

'I wasn't peeping in your window, I promise. I'm ... I'm looking for something.'

Likely story, I thought.

'What did you lose?'

'Um …' He looked around him at the waste ground between Madame Bowden's house and her next-door neighbour, messing up his already messy hair with his hands. 'I didn't lose it exactly …'

I rolled my eyes. He *was* a Peeping Tom. Or whatever. A perv! That was it. I was about to tell him when he blurted out a word I hadn't expected.

'Remains! I'm looking for the remains—'

'Oh Jesus Christ, did somebody die here? I knew it, I knew there was a weird vibe about this place. I got a feeling as soon as I arrived—'

'No, no. God no. Not those kinds of remains.' He stooped his head low to make eye contact with me again. 'Look, I know this looks sketchy, but I promise you, it's nothing bad, it's just difficult to explain.'

For a moment, we said nothing. Him crouching by the gable wall, me half hanging out of the window, standing on a kitchen chair. That's when I heard the bell.

'What was that?' he asked, trying to peer inside.

I looked around and saw a very old-fashioned bell with a wire running away into the ceiling. By the looks of things, I was in my very own real-life version of *Downton Abbey*. I turned back to him. Henry.

'Do me a favour. Whatever you're looking for, go look for it somewhere else,' I said, and shut the window firmly in his face.

Chapter Three

HENRY

I sat nursing a pint of Guinness in the same pub as the day before and the day before that. I even had my preferred stool at the bar, tucked away in the corner. 'Tainted Love' played in the background, and I tapped the beat with the tip of my shoe against the wood of the bar.

Sometimes I feel I've got to – TAP TAP – *run away, I've got to* – TAP TAP.

I was reading over my notes from the day before:

In the course of your life, you'll spend six months looking for missing objects. An insurance company did a survey once that suggested the average person misplaces up to nine objects a day, meaning that by the time we turn sixty, we'll have lost up to 200,000 things. When it comes to books, how many paperbacks, manuscripts, handwritten drafts have been lost or forgotten throughout history? The number is infinite. How many forgotten libraries remain hidden, like the Dunhuang Library on the edge of the Gobi Desert, sealed up for a thousand years and discovered, quite by accident, by a Taoist monk who knocked down a wall whilst leaning against it and smoking his cigarette. Behind it, he found a mountain of ancient documents, piled almost ten feet high, containing scripts with seventeen different languages. Who is to say what treasures are yet to be rediscovered, what lost things are waiting to be brought to light?

At least, that is what I reminded myself as I spent yet another night in the bed and breakfast I couldn't afford, writing up notes in my journal about the bookshop that didn't exist. Had it ever existed? All I had was a letter from one of the world's most successful rare book collectors to its owner, a Miss Opaline Gray, discussing a lost manuscript. And where had I come across such an unusual piece of correspondence? In the only room in the world where possibility became reality – an auction room. I had spent years looking for the one, the big discovery that would make my name in the world of rare books, and this was the closest I had ever come.

I should've been on a flight back to the UK days ago. I took another mouthful of 'the black stuff', as the locals called it. Motivation comes in all shapes and sizes and my motivation for staying in Ireland was to avoid looking like a complete failure. That was what everyone expected – including me. If no one takes you seriously, how can you ever hope to do so yourself? I blamed my father and had no qualms about it. My very first memory of him was one of betrayal. He'd told me to stand up and 'perform' with my new toy microphone. It must have been Christmas and he had some of his mates over. I sang some songs, who knows what, but all I remembered was his laughter – the way it almost resembled a wolf snarling when he was really drunk. The others joined in and my cheeks burned so much I hardly noticed the hot liquid running down my legs.

'He's pissed himself!' my father wheezed, falling off the chair with amusement.

I can't recall what happened after that. My mother must have come and rescued me. But from that point on I was always tagged with the reputation of being a cry-baby; too sensitive. It didn't help that my sister Lucinda came out of the womb with her fists ready for a fight. He respected her. In fact, we were all slightly intimidated by her. And so my position as the runt of the litter was firmly established.

Until I found that Rosenbach letter.

Suddenly, I became a man of destiny, as though all of those years missing out on vital stores of vitamin D by ensconcing myself in libraries would finally be vindicated. I ended up spending so much time reading books in the library that everyone thought I worked there and eventually, I thought so too. It reached quite remarkable levels of self-delusion when I began telling the other staff how to perform their duties. When my mother found out she was furious.

'All that money I spent on your fees! You haven't even sat one exam, Henry!'

Yes, but I had used the money to attend courses at the London Rare Books School, so it wasn't all for nothing. I had a trade, even if no one else saw the extreme love of old books as a trade.

Still, I had never actually followed a lead like this … I was hardly Indiana Jones. Lucinda once told me I was about as adventurous as a bucket. Well, who was the bucket now, eh? I laughed, the drink clearly going to my head. I'd spent weeks at Ha'penny Lane looking for any sort of clue, some sign that the bookshop had existed once. A dark shadow like the kind left behind on the carpet when you move the sofa. But I had come up empty-handed.

Until the girl.

Where had she come from? She had stared at me with the most piercing blue eyes I'd ever seen. I stared back. She looked angry. No; she looked afraid, I realised. She had the palest skin, but her round cheeks had a pinkish glow. She failed to conceal a nasty-looking black eye under a long bleached fringe. The whole effect was like that of an angel fallen on hard times. I had wanted to keep on talking to her, but what could I say? Have you seen a missing bookshop? Is it possible that your house has consumed it? Are you free for dinner? When she slammed the window and turned away, still clutching her jumper over her chest, I could see a vast tattoo all over her back. Not a design as such, but lines and lines of tiny script, like the Dead Sea Scrolls.

We had only spoken for a matter of moments, but I was certain that she was the most intriguing woman I'd ever met. Annoyingly however, she stayed true to the pattern of most women who met me and took an instant dislike to me. Still, maybe she knew something about the bookshop, so I would have to dig deep and find any modicum of charm to get her on side.

~

Two hours later I found myself back at the B&B, standing in a narrow hallway made narrower still by the claustrophobic wallpaper and the framed portraits of at least five popes. Orange flowers seemed to leer out at me and the swirling brown carpet offered no respite.

'Are ya back for your tea, love?'

Nora had the look of Hilda Ogden but with the thickest Dublin accent I'd ever heard. She was the kind of person who'd seen it all. Standing with one arm folded and a cigarette held in a limp hand, she looked as though nothing would surprise her. I envied people like that. If there was a nuclear explosion right now with bricks and mortar falling around our ears, Nora would probably still be stood there with her cigarette, rollers in her hair, wondering who'd made that racket and then getting on with frying some eggs for tea.

'No thanks, Nora. I ate pie and chips at the pub.'

I had never met anyone so concerned with my diet and most of our conversations ended with anxiety over my weight – there generally being not enough of it for her liking.

'Oh good, that'll stick to your ribs.' She nodded approvingly. 'And you'll have the full Irish in the morning,' she told me, in no uncertain terms.

I nodded politely and began heading up the stairs to my room with the frilly curtains and shiny bedspread, but despite the decor, the house had felt immediately like home. Not my home, of course. But the concept of being at home. Perhaps it was Nora's way of making you feel as though she'd known you for years. As though you were part of the family, which, from what I could tell, consisted of three Jack Russells and a husband called Barry who remained safely out of sight.

'He lives in that shed,' she'd said, as she showed me the shared bathroom on my first night, replete with an avocado suite. The sound of a hammer hitting wood had echoed up from the backyard. 'If I could just get him to sleep out there,' she had said, with an indulgent sigh.

'There's a letter for you by the way,' she said now, fishing it out of a pocket in the front of her apron. 'From the council. Looks official. I didn't read it,' she added hastily, confirming that she had.

Chapter Four

OPALINE

As the gangplanks were lifted and handkerchiefs fluttered in the air, my heart was a mix of excitement and trepidation. Having spent a cold and sleepless night on a mail train to Dover, I had countless hours to question the wisdom of my decision to escape to France. There was just enough time to send a telegram to Jane and I bitterly regretted not having the chance to say a proper goodbye to the one person I would miss. I knew not what lay ahead of me, but was keenly aware of what I was leaving behind. My mother would doubtless be distressed at my departure, if not for the loss of a daughter, then surely for the gossip and notoriety that would befall our family name. I was bringing shame to them both, but I had no choice. It was their pride or my future and I could not, would not, sacrifice myself on the altar of their expectations. I had enough schooling to get by, or so I thought, and would soon realise that the university of life was an altogether harsher education.

As I stood on the deck, I put my case by my feet and looked out at the horizon. Many of my fellow passengers had already installed themselves on reclining chairs to avert seasickness, but not I. I held on to the railings and began imagining all of the adventures that lay ahead, without a practical thought as to how I would survive alone in a foreign country. A blur of activity caught the corner of my eye and before I knew it, someone was making off with my case. I cried out but my voice was lost on the wind and while he ran, I stumbled along the smooth wood of the deck. Quick as lightning, another man brushed past me and chased down the gangway and apprehended the thief – a young boy of twelve if he was a day. He brought him back by the scruff of the neck, the case in his other hand, and in a heavily accented voice, asked me what I would like to be done?

'I, um, well …' I mumbled, embarrassingly. The whole event had left me in shock.

'I shall report him to the ship's captain, if mademoiselle so desires,' he said, with a touch of dramatic licence. I was immediately conscious of his height; he was well over six feet tall, and his dark features were very striking. Black hair, dark eyes and brown skin. He was unspeakably attractive.

'Mademoiselle?' he repeated, with a slight smile sparkling in his eyes.

'Um, yes, yes, of course.' I turned to see the boy, whose features had suddenly taken on those of a persecuted lamb. 'And what shall happen to him?' I enquired, taking my case back.

'He will be removed from the ship and taken straight to the prison, I assume,' the man said, rather dispassionately.

'Oh.'

'It is entirely your decision, Mademoiselle.'

'Well. I have my possessions back now, so I suppose there's no harm done. And you won't do anything like this again, will you?' I asked, looking at the youngster, who I now noticed was not wearing any shoes and his clothes seemed two sizes too small for him. He shook his head vehemently and like a wild creature, disappeared into the crowd as soon as the man loosened his grip.

'Mademoiselle is too generous,' he said, watching the boy escape. 'Allow me to present myself; my name is Armand Hassan,' he said, bowing slightly.

His name sounded so exotic and intriguing, giving him an instant allure. He was dressed well, but with an air of casual elegance, as though he couldn't help but look well, no matter what he wore. Yet there was something dangerous or secretive in his eyes that stirred a feeling of mistrust in me.

'Miss Carlisle,' I replied, offering my hand and realising too late that I had already given a complete stranger my real name. I had to sharpen my wits and fast.

'*Enchanté*, Mademoiselle Carlisle, and may I say what a beautiful name you possess. I hope I will have occasion to speak it. And often.' He brought my gloved hands to his lips and I swore I could feel the warmth of his breath through the fabric. I quickly averted my eyes and hoped that my cheeks had not flushed. I had hardly left England's shores and already I was succumbing to the charms of a foreign accent like some ingénue. I had to get a hold of myself.

'Yes, well, thank you very much, Mr Hassan, but I must get on,' I said, realising too late that I was on board a ship and had no pressing engagements to speak of.

His eyes twinkled, imagining the warnings I had received about entering into conversations with strange men.

'If I may, Mademoiselle, some parting words of advice; a charming young woman like yourself must be more careful in future. Travelling alone on the continent, the fairer sex will always be at risk from unscrupulous types.'

That was when I regained my composure, shrugged back my shoulders and raised my chin.

'Mr Hassan, while you are obviously very well accomplished in the fluency of the English language, you are sorely lacking in your knowledge of English women. We are quite capable of looking after ourselves, thank you very much.'

With that, I swung my coat and walked purposefully into the headwind, almost losing my hat but trapping it with my hand at the last minute. 'The arrogance,' I mumbled to myself, determined not to let myself be lured in – no matter the circumstance.

~

The Hotel Petit Lafayette appeared quite smart on the facade, but as with books, one can never judge by appearance alone. I was led to a stairwell that swirled around an inner courtyard, giving every room a balcony of sorts, which overlooked the dull grey innards of the building. My spirits were lowered still further when the man opened the door to my '*chambre*'. I never had occasion to enter a convent, but I imagined it to be the equivalent of what stood before me: a narrow room with a narrow, uncomfortable-looking bed and no window.

'No, no,' I said, shaking my head.

'*Non*?' he repeated, unmoved.

'No, I'm afraid this is quite out of the question.'

As no response was forthcoming, I elaborated on my theme.

'Your room,' I said, raising my voice and speaking slower, for how else should he come to understand my plight, 'is something akin to a monastic cell! I would like – *je voudrais une chambre plus grande. Avec une fenêtre!*'

Ten minutes later and at double the cost, I found myself in a modest-sized room with a slightly bigger bed. Clearly, my bargaining skills would need refining, but once I opened the long window and saw my view, I put all of my grumblings aside … There, the rooftops of Paris spread out before me, golden in the evening light. I was, quite simply, terrified of what I'd done. Desire and its attainment can provoke strikingly opposing thoughts in a person. Yet I was determined to make a go of it. And there would be absolutely no tears.

~

My first day in Paris was blustery but bright and I held tight to the little map that I had purchased from a street vendor. Paris was as beautiful and inspiring as I'd hoped; every street was more beautiful than the last. The buttery-stone buildings with elegantly tall windows and grey tin roofs looked immaculately chic in the soft sunshine. Walking back along the Quai de la Tournelle, I came across a row of booksellers, or *bouquinistes* as I would later learn, selling all sorts of books, in French and English, magazines, journals and even old posters and postcards. I stopped to browse, wondering at the green metal boxes that held their treasures, hanging on the parapets on the banks of the Seine. They looked like train carriages that had just pulled up overnight, opening their doors to the reading public until nightfall.

I was in heaven, on the banks of the river in bright sunshine, lost in a world of books and foreign accents. That was when I spotted it, *Histoires Extraordinaires*. Bound in cerulean blue, it was a two-volume translation of Edgar Allen Poe's short stories by Charles Baudelaire. I opened the cover to find that it was a first edition, published by Michel Lévy Frères, Paris, 1856–1857. My father was a fanatic when it came to Mr Poe and I too enjoyed 'The Tell-Tale Heart' and 'The Fall of the House of Usher' and so I saw it as a sign. I enquired as to the price of the book, my broken French immediately betraying me as a foreigner. It sounded like one hundred francs too many and after much gesturing (him turning out his pockets to indicate that I was robbing him blind) we agreed a price. I felt drunk with recklessness, spending the little money I had on another book. As he began wrapping the volumes in brown paper and string, I heard a voice I recognised calling my name.

'Monsieur Hassan,' I said, surprised when he, yet again, took my hand and kissed it. I flushed immediately and the bookseller smirked. They then began a conversation in French that I could not follow, but the subject matter soon became clear.

'I see you have purchased my Baudelaire,' he said, with a devilish smile.

'Whatever do you mean?'

'I told my friend here to keep this translation for me, but I see he has sold it to you ... for a much higher price.'

The implication was not lost on me, that I was a silly woman who'd be taken for a fool. I chose to ignore it. 'Well then, it is not your Baudelaire but mine,' I said, taking the package and heading back towards my hotel.

'At least allow me to offer you dinner tonight, as a felicitation for your excellent bargain,' he said, his long strides easily catching up with me.

'No thank you, I cannot accept such an unsuitable invitation. We are strangers.'

'Oof,' he said, mockingly taking a dagger to the heart. 'But we are not strangers and it would seem that you are alone in Paris ...'

'I'm not alone,' I said, defensively. 'I'm staying with my ... aunt.'

'Ah, I see,' he said, nodding and almost admitting defeat. '*Alors*, if you change your mind, Mademoiselle Opaline,' he added, handing me his card. 'I will not forget this slight easily but, fortunately for you, I have a forgiving nature.'

With a tip of his hat, he disappeared down a side street and I was left standing there, feeling furious. He was an infuriating, pompous, arrogant man. And I loathed him. And yet I put his card in my pocket rather than throwing it in the Seine.

That evening, I wrote one of the postcards I had bought at the bookstall to my Jane. I knew I could trust her to keep my whereabouts a secret. The thing about Jane was, you could hear her laugh before you ever saw her. She adored the outdoors, which Mother declared 'unladylike'. I missed her terribly, but writing to her closed the distance between us, if only for a short while. I tried to keep my tone cheery as I filled the postcard with statements that ended in exclamation marks. *Paris is glorious!* Not very original, but still. I fancied that perhaps one day she might come and visit if I were to remain. When I looked at the money I had left, I wasn't so sure. I had to find a position doing something. I resolved to visit the library the next day and see what I could find out there.

As I undressed for bed, I pulled the card that Monsieur Hassan had given me from my pocket.

Armand Hassan
ANTIQUAIRE
14 Rue Molière
Casablanca
Maroc

So, Monsieur Hassan was a book dealer from Morocco. That explained his exotic good looks, if you liked that sort of thing, which I was determined I would not. The romance books I read were littered with stories of young women falling for fast men like him. I put the card away, in my case this time. When I should have ripped it up and thrown it in the bin.

Chapter Five

MARTHA

Working as a housekeeper for a woman of 'advancing years' with serious delusions of grandeur was not where I had seen myself ending up. But I kept telling myself that this was a stopgap, just until I got myself sorted. Whatever that meant. After a couple of days, I found myself quickly settling into a routine. I realised then it was exactly what I needed, for I was still in shock. Unlike the movies, you don't just leave your home, your marriage and everything you knew and simply start a new life. There is a bit in between where you're just breathing – like a drowning man who clings to a rock. You know you're alive, you can move, even speak, but something is missing.

So I performed my tasks. I woke in the morning and prepared breakfast for Madame Bowden (a boiled egg and English muffins with thick-cut marmalade). After I'd cleared up, I made her bed and tidied her room while she dressed, then I lit the fire downstairs. The house was old and chilly – she had refused central heating; said that the pipes would destroy the aesthetic. She had fiercely strong opinions about everything, which honestly baffled me. Mainly because I couldn't remember ever having an opinion on anything. My father had the only opinions that mattered in our house. My mother never spoke at all. Nowadays, people would call her non-verbal, but when I was a child, the people in my village called her other names.

Madame Bowden, on the other hand, read the papers aloud, contradicting every opinion piece and making speeches about what she would do if she was in charge. I largely ignored her, getting on with vacuuming the carpets and doing the laundry. She was not unkind but not exactly friendly either, which suited me just fine. I ate my dinner in my little basement room every evening, mostly beans on toast, and took to walking along the river late in the evenings, when the office workers had gone home and the city was quiet. Well, quieter at least.

It felt like I was thawing out after a very long winter. Every day I felt my muscles relax a little more and even when I went shopping for groceries in the supermarket, I hardly checked behind me to see if he was following. Until the day Eileen, Madame Bowden, decided to succumb to 'the ruination of the twentieth century' and ordered a television. I was busy in the kitchen making her lunch (poached salmon and baby potatoes) and when I took her tray into the living room and saw a man walking through the front door, I dropped the tray and stood frozen to the spot.

'Ah, sorry, love, I knocked but the door was open,' he said, clearly mortified and struggling with the heavy package.

I kept staring at him, trying to trust my eyes. *It's not him*, I kept repeating silently; *It's not him*. I recovered as quickly as I was able and began to clear up the mess. My hands were shaking so badly that he offered to help. I couldn't even look him in the eye, I was so embarrassed.

The following morning, Madame Bowden asked me to give a good dusting to her study, a small room on the first floor facing the street. It had gorgeous flowery wallpaper and a writing desk beside the window. The other walls were fully shelved and, just like a library, were filled with books.

'It's time for a good spring clean in here,' she announced and directed me to take down each and every book and with a damp cloth, wipe the dust off every single one.

'No, not too damp!' she warned, then gave me a dry towel to remove any moisture afterwards.

While the task seemed overwhelming at first, I soon developed a method to make things easier. I took one shelf at a time and brought all of the books to the floor, placing them on an old sheet. I put a cushion under my knees and carefully wiped each and every book. Some of them were very old and threatened to come apart in my hands. Others were in foreign languages I couldn't understand. Madame Bowden must have been highly educated, I thought, envying her. Books and I never really got along. No, that wasn't right. Books made me nervous. Always had done. For as long as I could remember, I'd had this kind of reaction to them. Almost like they were a threat to me. I preferred to read people. People were easier than books. My mother taught me how to read a person's story without them ever having to utter a word.

Like Madame Bowden: I knew she was afraid of getting senile and that was why she was so angry with the world. I knew that my mother was carrying some emotional pain that she didn't have words for. And I knew that the English man outside my window was in love with a woman called Isabelle. For the longest time I assumed everyone could do this, but it was only when my friends became angry with me for finding out their secrets that I saw it was a gift belonging to me alone. Or a curse. The real curse was how I couldn't read my husband after I fell in love with him. They say love is blind and for me it was truer than for most. So I never saw the violence coming. Come to think of it, neither did he, or I would have sensed it. What made him change? Was it me? Something I had done wrong?

His favourite taunt was to yell at me, 'You think you're special, don't you!'

And he was right. I did. Not in a vain way, but in the kind of way where you think you're meant to be something greater in this life. That your path will somehow lead to something better because you're really good at something or you have a destiny. Well, he didn't like that. Nobody liked it, in fact. And so I learned to hide these thoughts. I hid them so well that I'd forgotten where I put them. Because now, I didn't think I deserved any better than this. A battered face, a broken marriage and a job cleaning someone else's beautiful home. I knew I didn't deserve better, but somewhere inside, I still hoped. That's what was making me miserable: the hoping. I realised then that I would have to give up one or the other, happiness or hope.

Chapter Six

HENRY

'The thing is, 11 Ha'penny Lane is, um … well, it's here,' Mr Dunne said, pointing to the patch of waste ground that stood between number 10 and number 12. 'Or rather, it's *not* here. Here's where it isn't,' he said, disguising a snigger with a hearty cough.

An official from the planning office, he had reluctantly agreed to a site visit after weeks of my incessant phone calls.

'Okay,' I said. He seemed to be waiting for me to say something else. 'But you've seen the maps I sent you, the ones showing the shop to be right here?'

'Yes, I've seen the map, Mr Field, but as I explained on the phone, there are no official records for any building registered on this site. Apart from this,' he said pointing to the house next door.

'But this is number 12.'

'Exactly. There is no number 11.'

'But just because it's a house now, doesn't mean it wasn't previously used as a shop. The ground floor I mean.' I was warming to this idea. I hadn't a clue about historic buildings, but people used to conduct commerce from their homes, surely.

'Even so, it doesn't alter the fact that there is no number 11,' Mr Dunne said, losing interest. 'Have you tried speaking to the residents?'

'I'm sorry?'

An articulated lorry was slowly making its way down the street, meaning we had to shout to be heard.

'They might know something about the area's past,' he roared.

'What, a past of disappearing buildings?' I said.

Mr Dunne simply looked at me as though there was something not quite right about me and stepped back, in case it was contagious.

'Is this some kind of prank?' Mr Dunne checked his watch. 'I'm already late for my next appointment so I'll have to leave you to it,' he said, jangling his car keys in a very pointed manner. 'Good luck with'—he gestured to the space between the house—'all of it.'

Yes, I get it, I thought. *I'm on my own.* The idiot who came all the way to Ireland to find a bookshop that doesn't exist.

He left, but I couldn't move. I stared at the facade of number 12 and then at number 10 and back again. I wasn't sure how long I'd been standing there when I noticed the front door of number 12 opening. It was her, the fallen angel, looking as unimpressed with the world as she had done the other day, leaning out of the window. There was something about her, perhaps it was just the sight of another lost soul, looking for something they knew should be here, but wasn't.

'Excuse me! I wonder if I might take a moment of your time, Miss?'

She halted mid-stride and turned to look at me, as though she would make me regret my entire life if I didn't make the next words from my mouth worthwhile.

'What is it?'

'I – well …' Brilliant. Ten out of ten. She carried on her brisk pace.

'Can I buy you a coffee? I could tell you all about it—'

'I can buy my own coffee, thanks.'

'Look, I'm not some kind of weirdo—'

'That exactly what a weirdo *would* say.'

I struggled to find the words that might make her turn around. As a last resort, I went with honesty.

'I need your help!'

She stopped, her head dropped and she paused for a moment, as though deciding something.

'There's a café through here,' she said, pointing to a narrow cobbled street through an old archway.

As I followed her lead, I reintroduced myself as Henry. Henry Field. Exactly like that, as though I were a key member of MI5.

She kept her name to herself, making an altogether better spy.

~

'So, you found an old letter that mentions a book no one's ever heard of, hidden in a bookshop that doesn't exist.'

'That's about the size of it,' I agreed, before taking a mouthful of coffee and inadvertently giving myself a frothy milk moustache. It was kind of liberating, this honesty business. For so long I had hidden my findings for fear someone else would uncover the lost manuscript, but I knew this girl, Martha (as she eventually told me, no surname), wouldn't have the background knowledge or the interest to steal my discovery.

'Have you thought about seeing a therapist?'

'Hah!' I hadn't expected her to be funny, her whole countenance was so serious up to that point. She was wearing makeup, which went some way towards covering her bruises, but she still winced from the cut on her lip when drinking her tea. I did the honourable thing and pretended not to have noticed.

'I know it existed, I have the address on the letter-headed paper, even if the council has no record of it.'

'And how do you think I can help? I've only been here a few days. I don't know this city at all.'

'Oh, I just assumed. You don't own number 12?'

At this she laughed heartily, then just as quickly her features fell back into their strained expression.

'Madame Bowden owns number 12. I work for her.'

'Oh, I see, as some kind of assistant?'

She did not answer straight away and I immediately regretted prying. What did it matter? It was just something you say.

'I'm her housekeeper.'

'Oh.' *Oh? Can't you think of anything else to say, idiot?*

'Well, thanks for the tea, I'd best be off.'

She was up and heading for the door before I reacted.

'Maybe we can do this again?' I called out.

But she never turned back, just waved a hand and headed back out on to the busy street.

Chapter Seven

OPALINE

Paris, 1921

I started early the next day, enquiring about jobs wherever I saw a sign that read *offres d'emploi*. It rapidly became clear that no one wanted to hire a young English woman with no skills to speak of, broken French and no experience of commerce. The naivety of my plan, or rather the lack of it, filled me with panic. I wandered the streets aimlessly, blindly hoping for a sign. I let myself be swept along by people who knew where they were going and crossed the Seine on the glorious Pont Neuf. I raised my eyes to the spires of the Notre Dame cathedral, thinking of Esmerelda and Victor Hugo. I reached inside my satchel and rested my hand on the Baudelaire. Even feeling the book under my fingertips calmed me. I couldn't explain it, not even to myself, but books gave me an unflinching sense of stability and groundedness. That because words survived, somehow I would too.

As I walked the drizzled streets, feeling as though I were about to give up, I came across a bookshop called 'Shakespeare and

Company'. There was something reassuring about seeing that name. The doorway was blocked with boxes, and I saw two women just behind them, arguing over where to put things. They spoke English, and while one had an American accent, the other was unmistakably French.

The window gleamed with a luminous display of books – a rainbow of colourful calf bindings, woodcuts and intriguing title pages. The familiar feeling of excitement and curiosity I always had looking in the window of a bookshop pricked my skin. *Don't buy anything,* I warned myself, as I craned my neck to look inside.

'Give me a hand, will you?' said the shorter of the two. She was dressed in a tweed jacket and skirt and reminded me of a scout leader, someone you obeyed unquestioningly.

I rather awkwardly took the other side of a large box she was holding, which had the weight of a small elephant.

'An occupational hazard,' she said, amused by all my huffing and puffing.

'I'm afraid I don't have much in the way of muscles,' I replied.

'Is that an English accent I detect?'

I nodded and introduced myself.

'My name is Sylvia. Sylvia Beach.' She gave a firm handshake. 'Well, you're in the right place. We stock English language novels.'

'You mean, you own this shop?' I asked rather stupidly. It was just that I had never heard of a woman running her own bookshop before.

'And all of the debt that comes along with it!' she laughed. It sounded like a bark and was quite infectious. I found myself laughing along, even though I wasn't entirely sure what we were laughing about.

'I don't suppose you're hiring?' I blurted out, hoping I didn't sound too desperate.

Miss Beach leaned back against some boxes with a thoughtful expression on her face.

'Am I hiring?' she asked, rhetorically.

'Do you have experience working in a bookshop?' asked the other woman, who reappeared from inside the shop.

'This is Miss Monnier, she owns the shop across the street,' Miss Beach explained.

Unlike Sylvia, her dark eyes looked me over suspiciously and I instinctively knew she found me wanting.

'Not particularly,' I confessed. A look passed between them. Perhaps they had seen this before, a naive girl searching for her Parisian dream. 'I earned my passage here by selling a first edition Dickens and here, look,' I said, taking the Baudelaire from my satchel. 'I bought this from one of the *bouquinistes* along the Seine.'

Miss Beach took it carefully in her hands, gently opening the cover and checking every page.

'It's important to count every page,' she said quietly. 'The earlier in print history you go, the more likely you are to discover missing pages.'

'Is that so?'

'Yes, we call the period before the 1800s the hand-press period, when paper was a much more valuable commodity and people tore pages from books for their own use. Well, this is a nice find. Congratulations.'

'Thank you,' I said, taking it back.

'You have an eye for quality, and any young woman who can trade her way to the continent in books clearly has a flair for the business. How about I take you on as an apprentice, teach you what I know about books?'

I began to gush effusively when she held her hand up to halt me.

'I can't pay you well and the hours might be long, but you will learn much and make some important contacts.'

'Oh, Miss Beach,' I gasped, 'I'm quite unaccustomed to being speechless, but this may just be a first.'

'Good. Can't stand sentimentalism. Now, you can start by helping us with these deliveries.'

'Start now?'

'Well, is there a better time than the present?' she asked, in that matter-of-fact tone I would come to depend upon, more than I could ever have known.

~

Shakespeare and Company was a fascinating place to be. The shop itself had the quiet warmth of all bookshops, with dark wooden shelves worn soft over the years and that unmistakable scent of paper and leather. But Sylvia, who was merely a few years older than me, was something of a mother hen to a bohemian family of artists and writers, offering them a refuge, a lending library, a literary social club, a post office and (she hoped) a publishing house. She had befriended an Irish writer by the name of Joyce and was so passionate about his writing that she intended to publish his debut novel, *Ulysses*. It was a very great risk, as the work was so avant-garde, the author feared it would be suppressed for ever. Nor did it help that the manuscript itself was three times the length of an average novel, which would be astronomical to print.

On my very first day, I must have behaved like a child given the keys to a toy shop. I found my attention being pulled hither and thither by books of every age, every subject and binding. I couldn't help but wonder who they had once belonged to? Where had they travelled from? What is the scent?

'You shall be no use to me if you insist on behaving like a customer, Opaline,' Sylvia announced sharply, and over the following days I made a concerted effort not to be swayed by every interesting book I saw, which was often.

She was determined that I should learn the business from the ground up. I began by lugging books around and shelving them carefully, as well as serving customers as best I could. On quieter days, whilst dusting the shelves or the books themselves, she explained the finer details of being a book trader.

'Now, an old book isn't necessarily rare, Opaline. A book becomes rare when it's both hard to find *and* highly sought after. And it's not just books that are valuable to collectors; manuscripts, prints, etchings, archives – even letters. Especially letters. Anything that will feed the insatiable curiosity that surrounds the greatest minds.'

I must have looked unsure because she stopped what she was doing for a moment and turned to face me.

'Not convinced?'

'I just, I'm not sure why someone would want to collect someone's letters. How could they even be sure they were authentic?'

'Very good question, we'll make a literary sleuth out of you yet. Who's your favourite author?' she asked.

'Easy,' I said. 'Emily Brontë.'

'Right, well, isn't there anything you'd like to know about Miss Brontë other than the fact that she lived a quiet life on the moors?'

I thought about it for a moment. There were many questions I had, like did she ever fall in love? Was she happy or sad?

'What I've always wondered, I mean, the one question that always frustrated me is whether or not she began writing a second novel before she died and if so, what had happened to it?'

'There you are then. Now you have your question you can start searching for the answer.'

Chapter Eight

MARTHA

'Well, *that* was mortifying,' I muttered to myself, as I let myself back into the house.

'What are you talking about?' Madame Bowden called, startling me. She was stood in the doorway of the parlour, cigarette in hand, mischief in her eyes.

'Oh, nothing, I didn't realise I was talking out loud,' I said, taking off my jacket.

'Well, your face is the colour of beetroot and I'm bored, so tell all.' She took me by the shoulders and led me into the room as though I were one of her guests.

'I-I just, there's this guy …'

'A man, why didn't you say!' She laughed, her eyes widening with pleasure. She pulled back the curtains and scanned the street. 'Where is he?'

'He's nowhere. He's gone. It's not important. Is there anything you need before I get started on dinner?'

'It's cocktail hour, Martha, and I still don't have a drink in my hand,' she announced with that put-on upper-class accent she used when she had company.

'It's three in the afternoon,' I said, hardly bothering to keep the judgement out of my voice.

'Exactly,' came the reply, so I went to the kitchen to 'fix her a martini', whatever that meant.

As I was searching through the bottles for one called martini, my mind wandered back to my old life. I hadn't had any contact from my parents, but then again, they didn't know where I was. Even if they did, they probably wouldn't bother. They were embarrassed by me. My mother would fold her arms and look out the window when I tried to talk about Shane. I assumed she was ashamed of me – not because I married a violent man, but because I didn't listen to her when she warned me off him. My father already acted like I didn't exist, so life would not have changed much for him. Except maybe at the pub – there was bound to be talk. He would hate that. Which made me smile in a vindictive way. This was what they had made me. All of them. I was so lost in my memories I hardly remembered what I was meant to be doing. I still hadn't found any martini, so I just sloshed a measure of gin into a tall glass and threw in a slice of lemon. Then I knocked it back myself and poured her another.

'Coming!' I called, hearing Madame shout my name. I almost threw the drink on the table beside her.

'So, this man, was he attractive?'

Yes.

'It wasn't like that, he was looking for an old bookshop that used to be here. I don't think he was all there, if you know what I mean.'

'A bookshop?' she said, her eyes glazing over, probably from the gin. 'How amusing.'

'Is it?' I took her ashtray and emptied it into the fireplace.

'I'll tell you a little story,' she began, crossing her feet on a cushioned footstool in front of her. 'When I was the grand dame of Ha'penny Lane in the eighties … ah, the parties we used to have.

That was with my third husband, Vladimir. He was a Russian mathematician, which sounds boring, but, my girl, he was anything but! He served the best vodka and caviar. People came from every walk of life to our parties.'

I pulled a J-cloth from my pocket and began wiping some invisible dust from the mantlepiece. I'd hardly had any interest in listening to her stories when I first arrived, but now I was curious. It was possible that both of us were softening a little at the edges. We had nothing in common, but we were starting to realise that maybe we weren't such bad company.

'Anyway, there was one particular evening, midsummer, or was it midwinter? Well, either way … no, it was winter. I remember there was frost on the pavement. One of the guests arrived late and she was very shaken indeed. As she warmed her posterior by the fire, she told us of how she had got out of the taxi and walked into what she thought was our house. But when she got inside, she realised that it was a bookshop – a small, old-fashioned little place, full of charming old books and knick-knacks. Anyway, she came back out on to the street, turned around and poof! The shop was gone and there was my front door again. Of course, we all thought she was on something – so many people were in those days. But isn't that funny how it happened again?'

I felt a chill run through me. I didn't like ghost stories and this was starting to sound like one.

'Well, not exactly. He just said he was looking for one.'

What *had* he said? This house must have been attached to it or something. I shook my head vigorously and got up to prepare her dinner. When Henry had asked for help, it reminded me of the person I used to be – open, giving. I should probably tell him this story; maybe it would help him in his search, or at least give him a clue. But helping people only seemed to lead to trouble and regret these days. So I decided I would keep it to myself and keep my blinds closed.

~

It's funny how people complain about boredom. God, how I ached for a boring day when I was living with Shane and his unpredictable moods. A day where the worst thing you could expect was that nothing much would happen. But now that I had it, I wasn't sure what to do with it. My routine was taking up less and less time as I grew more accustomed to it and I found myself with some free time in the afternoons. Madame Bowden, not being one for tact, dropped as many hints as she could that my clothes were 'uninspiring' and 'depressing'.

'It's the uniform of the invisible!' she scolded, putting a hand across her eyes.

I looked at my jeans and jumper in the long bathroom mirror and frowned. They seemed fine to me. Maybe a little old. I studied my face then. The bruising had healed and was almost invisible now. If you didn't know better, you'd say it had never happened. Then the images rushed through me like a speeding train: cowered in the corner, back against the kitchen cupboards, screaming for him to stop. I put the flat of my palm against the wall to steady myself. The trick was not to remember; not to let the fear catch up. Always look ahead, keep busy.

I looked again at my clothes and saw that small town, the curious neighbours, the guards that did nothing. I suddenly wanted to burn everything I owned that came from that place. It was time. With my small wage packet (cash in hand, no sense bothering the tax man, she said) I took myself down to O'Connell Street and into Penneys. It was wall-to-wall denim. That woman would put me in a maid's outfit if I came back with more denim. I decided to start with new underwear and picked out a cotton bra and knickers. It felt strange, having this time to myself, money in my pocket and no one to please but myself. I looked around almost feeling guilty. It was the middle of the day and here I was acting like … what? A free woman, I supposed. Just then, I felt something I hadn't experienced in a long time. It was like my heart was smiling. So I moved on to the shoe department and picked out some black slip-ons. Then I spotted some black capri pants and I hooked them over my arm to bring to the changing rooms. I found a white blouse that looked sort of professional and I even bought a red hairband with white polka dots! I was so impressed with myself and my good eye that I threw caution to the wind and picked up a new backpack, so I could get rid of the duffle bag I'd had since secondary school. I tried everything on and put my old clothes in the duffle bag. I took the tags up to the till, just like you'd see in the movies, and felt the thrill of starting my life right there.

I stuffed my old belongings in a bin outside and walked around the city for a while. I bought a takeout coffee and a doughnut and strolled through Stephen's Green. The weather was mild and I became aware of how much lighter I felt in myself. I walked with my arms relaxed, not tight around my chest as they always used to be – always on alert. I watched the swans in the pond picking at the bread people threw in and heard the clap of wings when a flock of pigeons were spooked from their perch. It was like coming out of some kind of coma, I thought, because now everything sounded clearer and looked brighter. That old hope returned to my stomach again, as I saw students of all nationalities sitting on the grass; discussing intelligent things, I supposed. Maybe they were just talking about parties they were going to, but either way, it was a life I'd never tasted and the hunger in me was nearly overpowering. I did something I never thought I'd dare and stopped in the library on the way home. My courage almost left me at the door when I realised I hadn't been inside one since I was a child and even then it had been the travelling library. This was a big, busy building with a revolving door that saw much use. I caught my reflection in the glass, a new woman in new clothes, and took a deep breath.

Once inside, I wasn't sure what to do. Everyone seemed to know where they were going – heads bowed over open books. It was so quiet but, my God, you could *hear* how smart everyone was. It was terrifying. I spotted an older woman at the reception desk and asked her if she had any information on going to university.

'Adult education?' she asked.

'I suppose, yeah.'

Without any further conversation, she got up and took some leaflets from a Perspex shelf behind her.

'You'll find everything you need here.'

That was it. She'd moved on to the next person and I was quietly relieved that I'd got what I came for without making a show of myself. That's when I spotted a book I'd heard so many people talking about: *Normal People* by Sally Rooney. I loved the title and for the first time in for ever, I thought this book might speak to someone like me. Someone who felt anything but normal. I picked it up and made to put it in my handbag.

'Excuuuuuuuse me!' came an unsettling shout from the librarian.

I halted as though I'd been stopped by the guards and looked every bit as guilty.

'I'll need your library card to check that out,' she insisted, at a volume that seemed unnecessary, given we were in the quietest building in Ireland. I felt my cheeks going red. I didn't know what to do.

'Library card?' she repeated, her hand outstretched.

'Um, I don't have one,' I mumbled, conscious now that

everyone was looking at me. This was where having notions above your station got you.

'Well, you'll have to fill out this form then,' she sighed, as though my visit had set her life's progress back by about ten years. I could read the frustration in her body language, the way her wrist flicked and her neck tightened. I could see her as a dancer when she was younger, but something must have happened, an injury, and now she was here. Resenting every minute of it.

'I'll just leave it so,' I said, putting the book back on the counter. I had never felt so utterly stupid. I didn't even know how to borrow a book from a library – how was I ever going to get into college? I stuffed the leaflets into my bag and was about to leave when I saw him. Henry.

Chapter Nine

HENRY

'Is everything okay?'

I'd heard the commotion and was quite surprised to see Martha, still with that defiant expression, having something of a disagreement with the librarian. Having spent so long in libraries myself, my sympathies tended to lie with the staff, but not today.

'Fine, thank you,' she replied, tugging the strap of her bag on to her shoulder a little too vigorously, whereupon it snapped and dropped all of the contents to the floor.

'Oh, let me,' I said, bending down to help.

'It's okay, I can manage,' she stage whispered. 'I just bought this,' she said, looking somewhat forlorn.

I wasn't sure what to say to make it better.

'Buy cheap, buy twice,' I said, in case there was any doubt that my chosen Olympic event would be sticking my foot in my mouth.

She rolled her eyes as I picked up the leaflets and left her to gather her personal effects.

'Oh, you're thinking of going to university? Cool,' I said, flicking through them.

'You really think so?' she asked.

'Yes, of course. Especially as a mature student, I think that's ...' I looked at her face as she stood up and held her hand out in order for me to return her leaflets. 'Oh. You were being sarcastic.'

It was possible she might have smiled at that, but only fleetingly.

'Apologies. None of my business. Quite right.'

She sighed heavily.

'No, I'm sorry. It's all just a bit—'

'Can you keep the noise down please?' the librarian whisper-shouted at us. 'People are trying to read.'

'Give me a sec to grab my stuff,' I said, motioning for her to stay where she was, as though she were a car with a dodgy handbrake.

Once outside, she seemed much happier, but still very guarded towards me, which was fair enough.

'So, are you still looking for your lost manuscript?'

Her tone made it clear that she didn't see it as the life-changing search I knew it to be.

'Very much so, yes. Actually, I came across an old catalogue that was printed by Opaline in the 1920s. It's really quite fascinating—'

'Opaline? What a beautiful name,' she said, and I stupidly felt glad that I was the cause for the smile that spread across her face.

'Yes, it's unusual, isn't it?'

'And what happened to her?'

We stepped through a stone archway which led into something of a secret garden, right in the middle of the city, with marble statues and a fountain, which was currently empty.

'Well, that's what I'm trying to find out. I'm hoping it will give me a clue as to what happened to the bookshop.' And the manuscript – that was where my interest truly lay. I would make my name, then return home to London a success and show

Isabelle that marrying me wouldn't be a 'last resort', as she had put it once.

She took a can of Coke out of her giant bag and pressed down hard on the top so it wouldn't spray everywhere.

'Do you want to sit down for a minute?' she said, pointing to a bench positioned neatly in front of a miserable flowerbed. 'I'm not really in a rush to get back. Turns out being a live-in housekeeper means you're on call 24/7.'

I was only too delighted. It seemed her first impression of me had thawed somewhat. That's when it dawned on me why her company mattered so much. I was lonely. My whole life I had been quite comfortable with the lone wolf lifestyle, but I felt like a total outsider here.

'So what's with the obsession?'

'Obsession?'

'With this manuscript?'

'I don't think I'd call it an obsession.'

'Erm, you seemed pretty obsessed outside my window the other day.'

'Oh, right. I suppose I did a bit. I'm writing a PhD proposal about lost manuscripts and why we're so fascinated with them.'

'Are we?' she questioned, scrunching up her nose, then taking a large gulp of her Coke.

'Come on, surely you can see the appeal? Look at Harper Lee, for example. All those years assuming that she had only written one novel.'

She looked at me askance.

'*To Kill a Mockingbird*?' I said, in case there was any confusion.

'Oh right, yes.'

There was an awkward silence in which I realised that being an expert in rare books and lost manuscripts could sometimes be construed as quite boring.

'Of course, there's Sylvia Plath's second novel, *Double Exposure*, which mysteriously vanished after her death.'

'Who?'

'You're not much of a reader, are you?'

She stole a glance at me then, a mixture of spite and hurt in her eyes. I really had a knack for pissing her off.

'Okay, listen to this. Let me tell you the story of Walter Benjamin. He was a writer, intellectual, genius of a man who also happened to be Jewish living in Nazi-occupied Paris. He didn't have the right papers, so he had to trek south with other refugees, across the Pyrenees and into Spain.'

'That's awful,' she said, turning her whole body to face me.

'But there was one thing slowing him down on this perilous journey – a heavy black suitcase containing his manuscript. Speaking to a fellow traveller, Benjamin said that the contents were more valuable than his own life.'

Her face was so animated, as though she were on the journey herself.

'What happened to him?'

'Well, when he arrived at the border, Benjamin was informed by Spanish authorities that he would have to go back to France. He knew it meant certain death, so that night, he swallowed a bottle of morphine.'

'Jesus!'

'Indeed.'

'And what about the manuscript? Did he give it to someone?'

'After his suicide, there was no trace of the black suitcase. The manuscript has never been recovered.'

She shook her head and looked to be almost on the verge of tears. And just like that, she was bitten by the same bug. The unrequited love for what might have been, if not for these cruel acts of fate. I had told the exact same story to Isabelle and yet her only response was that she'd never had a properly good holiday in Spain.

'So, for all we know, someone could have published it under their own name?'

'Hmm. I'm not sure which scenario is worse – having lost the work for all time, or having it stolen by someone else.'

I would develop that idea in my paper when I got home.

'There are so many more stories like that one – rumours of hidden books, forgotten drafts in shoeboxes or novels burned by the author's family. Poor old Hemingway's wife had his novel in a briefcase that got stolen from a train station in Paris!'

Paris. Paris. The lost generation. I wondered …

'What is it?' she asked, sensing my thoughts as they formed.

'Oh, maybe nothing. It's just I can't seem to find any other records of Opaline Gray and now I'm wondering if she spent any time in Paris.'

She took out her phone, which I thought was rather rude but one can only capture attention for so long.

'Is this her?'

'What?'

She shoved her phone in my face, showing a grainy black and white photo from an old newspaper clipping.

'Who is it? What did you do?'

'Well, Mr Fancy-Pants Scholar, I googled the words "Opaline", "books" and "Paris" and found this.'

I looked closer, hardly daring to believe my eyes.

'This is Ernest Hemingway!'

She grinned like the proverbial cat, but did not meet my eyes. I read the caption underneath: 'Sylvia Beach, proprietor of Shakespeare and Company, shop assistant Opaline Carlisle'. There she was; a young woman with dark cropped hair, halfway up a ladder with a book in her hand, Hemingway by her feet.

'Carlisle? Oh my God, this is huge.'

'You're welcome.'

'Oh gosh yes, of course, thank you.' I moved to hug her but she jumped away from my clumsy attempt and I immediately felt her reproof. 'I'm sorry, I just, you've no idea how much this means.'

'I think I do,' she said, then grabbed her phone back and picked up her bag. 'Anyway, I better go.'

Chapter Ten

OPALINE

Paris, 1921

The weeks swiftly became months and, quite without realising it, I began to feel at home in Paris. I had become a part of Sylvia's little patchwork family and my position at Shakespeare and Company became permanent, or at least I hadn't been told otherwise. I rented a demi-pension, a room with half board that was close to the shop. On the weekends, having eventually permitted myself to succumb to his charms, I met Armand. He took me to the hidden corners of the city, like the flea markets in Saint-Ouen where rag and bone men who scoured through the garbage of Paris at night sold their wares. He called them *les pêcheurs de lune*, moon fishermen, which made me smile because I knew that I was caught in Armand's net and the more I fought it, the tighter his hold on my heart became. Jane, in her letters to me, had encouraged the romance: '*What was the point in flitting off to France if not to take a lover!*'

One bright morning at the end of the summer, when the city was quieter as the locals retreated to the countryside, I was working diligently in the shop, shelving the latest books to arrive. Sylvia was in the back having tea with an American writer, Ernest Hemingway, discussing a literary evening they were planning. He was unbelievably handsome and everyone was enthralled by his intense magnetism, but there was something malevolent about him. He adored Sylvia, of course, whose respect was worth more than that of any critic. Still, I couldn't explain it, but I didn't like being in a room alone with him. Once, when I was on the ladder putting books on to a high shelf, I found him staring at me.

'Yes?' I asked, giving him a direct look that I hoped would shame him into looking elsewhere. It did not work.

'You ought to be careful, Missy.'

Missy. Honestly.

'And why is that?'

'All writers are cannibalistic by nature.'

I wasn't sure what he was driving at, but it didn't sound very appetising to my ears.

'Meaning?'

'Keep waving that ass around here, you might find yourself a character in one of my books,' he grinned, openly enjoying my vexation. Honestly, writers could be such egoists!

As I slowly lowered myself down the ladder, Sylvia and another man, a reporter, entered the shop and as quick as lightning, he took a camera out of its case and almost blinded the three of us with the flash.

'There we are, I will have it in our next edition,' he said, and the two men left, discussing Hemingway's bruised fingers, which he said he'd got defending Joyce in a drunken brawl.

'What was that for?' I asked, wary of the idea of my photograph appearing in print.

'*Cosmopolitan* magazine, they're printing one of Ernest's stories.'

I was halfway up the ladder, I thought to myself. *I probably wasn't even in shot*. Besides, Lyndon was hardly a reader of *Cosmopolitan. Nothing to worry about*, I assured myself, and almost believed it too.

~

I decided to surprise Armand with a visit, and on my way to his flat I walked past Les Deux Magots, a café fashionable with writers and artists. Its bright green awning stretched out over the pavement and an intricate ironwork balcony wrapped like a piece of lace around the first floor. I caught my reflection in the window, then, for a moment, I thought I saw Armand. I came to a halt and realised that it was him, sitting at a leather banquette beside a woman with cascading chestnut curls. They sat very close and he seemed to be whispering something in her ear, something that deemed it necessary for him to part her hair back with his fingertips. A shock ran through me like a lightning bolt. I don't know if he sensed it, but he looked up just then and saw me watching him. For some reason, I was the one who felt embarrassed, and I began walking away in any direction. After a few seconds I heard him shouting my name but I did not turn around.

'Please, Opaline!' he begged, catching up with me and grabbing my arm.

'Leave me alone.'

'But you must let me explain.'

I didn't want him to explain. It would either be a lie, or worse, the truth and I wasn't sure I could bear to hear either.

'Christine, she is an old friend of mine.'

I wanted to cover my ears like a child. Hearing her name made everything worse. He wasn't to know it, but I had fallen in love with him like falling down a flight of stairs, and it hurt every bit as much. Suspecting this heartbreak in advance hadn't helped to prepare me for the reality.

'Armand, please spare me the indignity of this.'

It was as though a cloud passed over his face and what remained was something close to clarity.

'You are right, of course. I have humiliated you and for that I am sorry. But you must believe me, my feelings for you are deeper than I have ever felt for anyone before.'

'You might see me as some kind of ingénue, but I know a cheap cliché when I hear one.' I broke away from him and kept walking.

'It's true!' he called out. 'You think it is easy for a man to admit to his feelings?'

I turned and gave him a scornful look.

'It's difficult to explain in English.'

'Do your best.'

'The way you make me feel, it's wonderful but it's also a problem. It makes me vulnerable and that is not something I'm used to. So I flirt with other women to prove … something. *J'en sais rien.*'

'That makes no sense.'

'Not out loud, no. But in my head, I felt like I was staying in control.'

I couldn't think of how to respond. It was such a terrible excuse it must have been the truth.

'What you saw just now, I was ending things with her.'

I looked away, trying to shield my emotions from him. I had my pride, after all. Was he just telling me what he thought I wanted to hear? The human heart does not weigh these cold facts. It sees hope in the impossible, love where perhaps there is only desire. It acts without rhyme or reason. His arms were around me now. I stood motionless as he continued with his soft, comely words, how I was all that mattered to him now.

'Will you come with me? We can talk better at my apartment.'

Of course I would go. I was willing to make believe with him.

~

He lived in an area of the city called Montmartre. We walked under the gleaming white domes of the Sacré-Cœur that kept watch over the city, and followed the cobbled street into a bustling little square. Place du Tertre was like something from a postcard – elegant buildings with shutters rose above restaurants and cafés, and artists lined the perimeter, selling their wares cheek by jowl. He turned the key in the lock of a blue door and we climbed the stairs to the second floor.

Once inside, neither of us seemed sure what to do. A small table and two chairs stood invitingly in front of the long window overlooking the square and he gestured for me to sit.

'I will make us some tea.'

He arrived back at the table with a silver tray bearing an antique silver teapot with ornate patterns and little glasses printed with gold writing, which looked to be Arabic. However, it was the scent of sweet mint that surprised me the most.

'Have you ever tasted Moroccan tea?' he asked.

I shook my head and watched as he lifted the lid of the teapot and stirred a copious amount of thick leaves into the hot water. Then he set about the ritual of pouring the tea into the glasses from an impossible height. My eyes widened as he held the teapot further and further away from the glass on the tray and he tried not to laugh.

'It is the traditional way,' he replied simply, before handing me the glass.

I blew on the surface of the golden-hued tea and let the exotic flavours fill my nose.

Some musicians had begun playing in the square, *gitane* music, with a rhythmic guitar and virtuosic violin. It filled the spaces where our words could not. I had spent the entire time searching the room for somewhere to hide my gaze: the silk rug on the floor, the strange leather slippers by the door that came to a point at the toe, a small wooden table with a gold inlay of Moorish design. Finally, I looked back to him and realised he had been staring at me the entire time. Without breaking his gaze, he stood up, took the glass from my hand and placed it on the tray beside his. Taking my hand in his, he raised me up and I stood so close to him that I could breathe his breath. He bent his head and my lips parted of their own volition. I felt his warm tongue inside my mouth and my only thought was of wanting more. We held each other tighter and I had the sensation that I wouldn't be close enough unless …

'Opaline,' he said huskily, breaking my chain of thought.

'Yes?'

'Tell me if you wish to stay or leave,' he said, his breath heavy. 'For I fear I will not have the chivalry to ask you again.'

All mental activity had ceased. For the first time in my life, my sensuality took the lead.

'Stay.'

The room was narrow, just large enough for the brass bed. A voile curtain fluttered in the breeze from the open window. It was almost dark, save for a low candle guttering in the corner on a table.

All of those years in my adolescence, how I worried that I wouldn't know what to do! If only I had understood that there is no 'knowing'. Only instinct. His body glowed golden in the candlelight, the sweat on his skin like an aphrodisiac to me.

'Did it hurt?' he asked.

'Only a little,' I replied. Pain is the price of pleasure, I had read somewhere once. I was no longer a virgin. The thought startled me momentarily, replaced by a deep sense of having crossed a threshold. We lay there together for hours talking. It was late when he walked me home and I hoped to sneak past my landlady unnoticed.

There was no light, save for the moonbeams softly coming through the tall windows. Every creak on the stairs was like a cannon blast and I bit my lip, praying that no one would hear. When I reached my room, I locked the door behind me and flopped down on the bed. I could see my reflection in the mirror of the dressing table opposite, half ghostly in the moonlight. I grabbed my pillow and hugged it tightly to me. That's when I saw it. My brother's walking cane beside the door.

Chapter Eleven

MARTHA

I began the afternoon by scrubbing the toilet. Madame Bowden had invited some of her old theatre friends around for dinner, or supper as she called it, and she wanted the house to 'sparkle'. There was an edge about her that I hadn't seen before. She was always a bit of a fusspot, but now nothing seemed right for her. She came back from the hairdressers in a black mood, insisting that they had deliberately set her curls too tight to make her look older than she was, and I left her at her dressing table, brushing them furiously into fluffy balls of frizz.

'MARTHA!' She screeched my name and I dropped the toilet brush, expecting to find her collapsed on the bedroom floor.

'What is it?' I said, breathless.

She was sitting at her dressing table wearing a nude colour slip and a silk dressing gown. My eyes were drawn to her neck and chest where the skin was puckered and mottled like a dead turkey at Christmas. I recalled an old nun at school saying that you couldn't make a silk purse out of a sow's ear and I finally knew what she meant.

'I'm missing my pearl earring!' Her eyes openly accused me.

I looked on her dressing table at the jumble of jewels emptied out of their box and back at her. She had one pearl earring in her ear and the other was in her hand.

'It's in your hand, Madame,' I said flatly.

'I know it's in my hand, you halfwit, I'm looking for the other one!'

I took a deep breath. If I didn't need the money so badly, I'd tell her where to shove the other one.

'It's in your ear.'

She reached up, feeling nothing but soft flesh.

'Your other ear.'

I leaned against the door frame. I had all the time in the world.

She felt the cool pearl and gave what could almost be described as a look of shame, if you didn't know her better. Madame Bowden had too much pride for that.

'Well, now that you're here, you can help me get dressed. Don't forget, the caterers are coming at four, so be sure to give them a hand. And you did put the silverware out and give it an extra going over?'

No apology for basically calling me a thief; not that I had expected one. I took the dress off the hanger (a silver sequin gown that looked like it belonged to Liberace) and ended up bending my body for her to lean on, like a climbing horse, as she stepped into it. I could feel the shakiness in her arms vibrating through my frame. She had a sharp tongue and a quick mind, but her body was letting her down. I felt some sympathy for her then. It was strange to see her like this. She always gave the impression of being too fabulous to care. Perhaps she was a talented actress after all. Eileen Bowden was just like everyone else. Afraid.

Following a stand-off over what I should be wearing for the event, in which she produced an actual maid's outfit, I wore my new blouse and a black pencil skirt that she happened to have in her wardrobe. It was probably the dullest thing she owned. It was too big for me, so I borrowed a large red patent belt as well, which matched my hairband and pleased her enough to let me answer the door. As I had expected, three pension-age women stood gossiping and preening on the doorstep like a couple of old hens. They barely gave me a passing glance as they swept past me in a flurry of feathers and noise. I shook my head and smiled. When I thought of all the days I'd sat in the gloom of my kitchen, staring out at the fields that offered nothing but maybe the odd glimpse of a hare or the bright colours of a pheasant before some farmer shot it, it was hard to imagine that people were carrying on like this. Having fun. Eating well. Getting caterers. It was another world.

I stood with a frozen smile on my face, acting as a human coat hanger. Who even wore fur any more? Finally, it was time to serve the meal and I carried out my duties like someone who had worked in service all their lives – an invisible figure. That was when I realised someone was, in fact, invisible. Madame Bowden. Her place at the table was unoccupied. The women ate and gossiped and laughed at other people's expense, not seeming to have noticed.

'Will Madame Bowden return before dessert?' I asked a little uncertainly.

'I shouldn't think so,' said a woman whose neck was of such girth that she was in danger of being choked by her own pearls, which she now clutched. They all gave each other pointed looks and then, rather rudely in my opinion, began to laugh. Had this happened before? Madame Bowden not showing up for her own party?

'And where did she find you?' asked the other one, in a slim black dress that threatened to fall off her scrawny shoulders. I stopped mid-stretch as I was clearing the table, thinking of all the things I'd like to say. *On the bottom of her shoe!* Where did she think?

'She put an ad in the paper for a housekeeper and I responded.'

'Wonders never cease. What possible use would she have for a housekeeper?' said the third woman, who was clearly the alpha female of the group. She lounged like a cat and smoked a thin cigar.

'I should get myself a nice country girl too. They're less likely to run off after their dreams or whatever it is. Know what side their bread is buttered,' she said, speaking as though I wasn't even there.

I nearly dropped the tray. I was used to people looking down their noses at me, but you'd swear I was Cinderella.

'Actually, I'm working here to fund my way through university,' I said defiantly.

'Is that so?' said pearl lady. 'And what are you studying?'

What was I studying? Why had I opened my mouth! My hands started to feel sweaty. I decided to pretend I hadn't heard the question.

'I'll bring some brandy through to the parlour when you've finished.'

I was seething with anger and shame. She knew I wasn't good enough to make something of my life. They all did. I'd blown everything, made all the wrong choices and landed here, bowing down to these pretentious old biddies. But there was nothing I could do. This was my home now. I couldn't just walk out without a plan. I wished I could, but the shame I felt at being a victim always tripped me up first. It was always there, I felt branded by it. I left them playing cards and getting rip-roaring drunk.

I went downstairs to my little apartment and tugged off my outfit before having a long, hot shower. Wrapped in a towel, I lay down on my bed and saw the continuing education leaflets from the library on the kitchen table. It felt pointless now. Whatever burst of energy I'd had earlier was completely gone. What hateful women they were. No wonder Madame Bowden did a runner. With friends like that, who needed enemies? A feeling bubbled up from somewhere deep inside of me – I just wanted to be held. I missed being held. The only person I'd spoken to since arriving in Dublin (besides my annoying employer) was Henry. Little did he know, he was the only thing I had that resembled a friend. And I couldn't even count on that because he didn't even live here. He'd be gone as soon as he found his manuscript, or whatever he was looking for.

Why was I thinking about him anyway? I felt guilty, or wrong in some way, to be thinking about a man at all after everything I had just been through. But Henry was the polar opposite to Shane; to any man I'd ever met. The way he told me that story about the author carrying his heavy suitcase across the border, his passion for rescuing lost or misplaced things, there was something so endearing about it. And even though I didn't want to admit it to myself, he really was attractive. Sometimes when he looked at me with those hazel eyes, I found it hard to catch my breath. But then I would think, what would he ever see in a woman like me? All he was interested in was the bookshop. Nothing more.

I turned on my side and hugged my pillow. That was when I noticed the cracks in the wall. Had they always been there? Surely I would have noticed them. Three crooked lines of various thickness appeared from behind the wardrobe and spread out like tiny vines creeping along the blue wall. I lay there staring at them. How could I not have spotted them before? And what was going on behind the wardrobe? I got up and ran my fingers over them. They seemed pretty deep and solid, as though they had been there for some time. I tried to move the wardrobe but it was an antique and weighed a ton. For a second, I became aware of breathing; someone else's breathing. I turned around but there was nothing there. I wondered if it were possible to read places, the same way that I could read people. The thought made me shudder. Maybe I didn't want to know what had gone on here. I whispered the name *Opaline* into the walls. Nothing. I shook my head, realised I was being ridiculous and got dressed for bed.

~

I woke in the middle of the night with another line from the story in my head. Like a notification in my inbox, they came to me like that sometimes, whispered into my subconscious mind. I had no explanation for it. I only knew that I had to hold on to them somehow. Writing the words down on paper wasn't enough. So the following day I would go to the local tattoo parlour and have them inked on my back. It was a story that didn't seem to have a beginning or an end, but every time I felt a new line came to me, I would ink the words on my skin along with the others and instantly feel better. No one knew about it, not even Shane. It was a small act of defiance. Something just for me. I'd managed to hide this strange story from the world, but the further along it went, the more I needed to know what it meant and where it was coming from.

Knowing I'd struggle to get back to sleep, I tiptoed upstairs to see what kind of mess the women had left. I didn't want Madame Bowden giving me an earful in the morning and figured I might as well clear up while I was awake. I stepped into the dining room and flicked on the light. I couldn't believe it – the room was in perfect order and not a thing out of place. I quickly reassessed my earlier opinion of Madame Bowden's friends and conceded that anyone who clears up their own mess can't be all bad. I didn't even hear them leave. A quick trip to the kitchen confirmed that they had even washed and dried all of their plates and glasses; there wasn't even a spoon left to be cleaned. Like nothing had happened at all.

Chapter Twelve

HENRY

I did consider ringing the doorbell, but where was the fun in that? I hunkered down and knocked on the basement window of number 12 Ha'penny Lane. I'd spent the past few days searching through online archives and old newspapers for Opaline Carlisle, but with no success. I needed a break and that's the excuse I was telling myself when my feet brought me back to her door. Or rather her window. After a few minutes, the blind flew up and I came face to face with a very angry and tired-looking Martha.

'What the hell?' she croaked, once she'd got the window open.

'Bit early?'

'It's seven in the morning, so yes, I'd say you're a bit early.'

'Oh. Apologies. I just wondered if you might join me for a little excursion.'

'Now?'

What had seemed like a good idea last night when I couldn't sleep had now lost its lustre. I hardly knew this girl and here I was, banging on her window.

'Um, well, whenever you're free really.'

She looked down at her clothes and did that thing again where she seemed to be calculating an impossible equation very quickly in her mind.

'I'll have to get Madame Bowden's breakfast and do some cleaning, but I could be free by eleven?'

'Perfect!' I shouted a little too enthusiastically. I'd forgotten how nerve-wracking it could be, asking someone if they wanted to hang out with you. As youngsters, we do it all the time, making new friends. But when you get older, it feels as though there is so much more on the line – the rejection is so much harder to take. 'I'll text you the deets.' I had never spoken the word 'deets' aloud in my life and wasn't quite sure I had carried it off.

'You don't have my number.'

'Yes, that was a roundabout invitation for you to offer it, Martha. Work with me here!'

An awkward silence followed, which she seemed to relish a little too much.

'Are you … going to give it to me?'

'I might.' She smiled.

Was this flirting? It certainly felt like flirting, but it was hard to tell when most of her body language was on the defensive.

'Here,' she said, putting her hand out for my phone, quickly typing her number in. 'Now, I have to go.' With that, she shut the window and pulled the blind back down.

~

It was like something out of a romcom my mother would watch. My thumb hovered over the 'send' button until I recalled a hack my sister often employed. Count down from five to one and then just do it. I lightly touched the screen, my phone made a whooshing sound and my message was now time-stamped.

Meet me at Pen Corner

I thought it sounded enigmatic … until I got Martha's reply:

Who is this?

It's Henry. The guy who isn't a weirdo.

Oh, that Henry. Where is Pen Corner?

Just get to the junction of College Green & Trinity Street.
You'll see

The only establishment that could rival a bookshop or a library, in my opinion, was a good stationery shop. The Pen Corner, however, was something of a hallowed ground when it came to the humble writing instrument. In full prominence on the corner of the street, the Edwardian building had a tower with a clock at the top which told me I was unfashionably early. The black and gold lettering of the shop sign, along with the mosaic-style glass panels above the windows, held all the promise of a hushed library. I had intended to wait for Martha outside, but my willpower lasted all of two minutes. I spotted a Mont Blanc pen in the window that begged closer inspection.

Once inside, I felt my shoulders relax and my nose picked up that distinctive scent of paper, leather and ink. Glass cases discreetly displayed rows of Parker and Cross pens along with calligraphy nibs, like expensive jewels. Behind the counter were leather satchels that brought to mind Hemingway's lost novel. Would it have been kept inside a leather satchel just like this? That's what every MA Lit student assumed as they strolled around campus with an exact replica slung over their shoulder.

Two or three other customers milled around and as I turned to see if I could find my pen, I saw her, standing in the doorway, unsure of herself.

'Martha, you made it.' Well, no one could say I ever missed an opportunity to point out the obvious.

She just smiled in response and slowly let the door close behind her. 'What are we doing here?'

'An existentialist. I knew it.'

She looked at me askance.

'Just a little humour, no need to be alarmed.' God, why did I sound like such a fucking weirdo? It seemed I had lost all ability to speak like a normal human.

'Can I help, sir?' came a voice from behind the counter.

'Yes! I mean, yes please. I was looking at the Mont Blanc in the window.'

'Ah, Le Petit Prince,' he said, anticipating my taste. The sign of an excellent salesman.

'Why did you bring me here?' Martha asked, when he was out of earshot.

'It's magnificent, isn't it? Although this isn't the place – I mean, we'll be going someplace else after this.'

'Okay.'

She sounded anything but okay.

'Here we are, sir. The Meisterstück Le Petit Prince edition.'

It was beautiful. A burgundy-coloured case with a tiny gold star on the clip.

'As you can see, it's engraved with a quote from the book.'

I read it aloud. '"*On ne voit bien qu'avec le cœur.*"'

'You speak French?' she asked.

'Just a smattering. I spent a summer working in a gite in the South of France.'

'Okay,' she repeated, her eyes widening before she stared at her feet.

'It means that one sees clearly only with the heart.'

I could see that the words struck her in a way that I hadn't predicted. Just like in the park, when I told her the story of the lost manuscripts, she became truly moved by it. I had grown used to the indulgent smiles and nods from 'lay people' when I talked about my passion, but she seemed genuinely interested. I struggled with the instinct to puff out my chest with pride. I don't care what anyone said, quoting Antoine de Saint-Exupéry was impressive in any man's language.

'Shall I wrap it up for you?' said the shopkeeper, interrupting the moment.

'Erm, yes. How much is it?'

'€799 inclusive of VAT.'

I gulped. I had wanted to impress her and now I had backed myself into a financially constrained corner. I didn't know how to get out of it and in the end told him that it was a gift I would buy as a reward once I'd completed my paper. He simply stared at me with the dead eyes of a shopkeeper who knew I would never return.

'But you know what, I will have one of those Moleskine notebooks!' I said, assuming this would erase the entire episode from everyone's memory. Except mine.

Chapter Thirteen

OPALINE

Paris, 1921

I immediately got up, packed all of my books and other belongings into my bag and fled down the stairs. I thought if I could just make it to the shop, Sylvia would know what to do, how to help. I waved away Madame Rousseau's offer of breakfast and pushed the outer door open only to find myself coming face to face with my brother, who was waiting for me. He was not alone.

'Here she is,' he said, a new black walking cane in his grasp. 'You see, Bingley, she is overcome with emotion.'

I stood there, open-mouthed, like an idiot, trying to take it all in. There was my brother, triumphant and relaxed, and this Bingley character looking eager and holding a large bouquet of flowers.

'Well, don't just stand there, man, give her the blasted things before they wilt!'

'Miss Carlisle, I am delighted to finally make your acquaintance,' he said, handing me the blooms.

Still, I said nothing, but gripped tightly the handle of my bag and wondered if I could outrun them.

'Now don't worry, Sister, good old Bingley here bears you no grudge for standing him up on the last occasion you two lovebirds were to meet.'

I couldn't fathom his tone of voice. It was not my brother speaking but some imposter. With endless charm.

'How did you find me?' I asked, finally.

'How do you think? Your dear friend Jane found a picture of you in a magazine and her husband was only too delighted to share it with your proud family.'

He must have seen the look on my face, how foolish I had been.

'Oh, come now,' he said, taking my arm firmly in his grasp. 'We are men of the world, after all. We understand that you needed to spread your wings before marriage. Have one last hurrah. Isn't that so, Bingley?'

'Indeed, indeed,' he agreed, eyeing me up and down as though I were his next meal. He was tall and ruddy with a hooked nose and a receding hairline. They both smelled of brandy, which explained their exaggerated behaviour. Everything seemed outrageously strange – the juxtaposition of my brother and his associate in *my* Paris. I hardly noticed them guiding me towards a hotel.

'Where are we going?' I asked. 'I have to go to work.'

'Work! We have a socialist in our midst, Bingley!' my brother continued in this strange jovial voice that didn't suit him. It was like the wolf talking to Red Riding Hood. 'Of course, I should call you Lord Bingley,' he said, ushering us both ahead of him and into a grand-looking foyer.

'This is all very well—' I began, but Lyndon once again hushed me with his effervescent monologue.

'Champagne, we must celebrate!'

He gestured to a waiter who was serving an elderly couple their coffees in the foyer. I could tell he was insulted by my brother's arrogance, but he simply nodded his head and arranged some chairs at a table for us.

'I shall book my little sister a private room for this evening,' he said, gesturing towards the concierge's desk. 'Must uphold tradition and all that. There will be time enough for you both to become better acquainted after the wedding.'

Wedding? Surely he wasn't suggesting that I marry this stranger. Of course I didn't wish to create a scene in front of so many people so, as he turned to leave, I said in a low voice, 'Lyndon, have you taken leave of your senses entirely?'

'I'll explain everything upstairs,' he said, and all but pushed me down into my seat.

Alone with Lord Bingley, I did my best impression of a mute. He asked if I had enjoyed my time in Paris and I simply nodded and pulled my lips into something resembling a smile. The waiter returned and placed a bucket of ice on the small table beside us. He gently popped the cork of the champagne and poured a tiny amount into Bingley's glass. Naturally, he had to taste it first and the whole charade left me inwardly screaming with impatience. Just pour the damn thing, I wanted to say. I needed a drink.

Bingley clinked my glass and toasted to our future. I smiled again, thinking of how our future would be as long-lived as it took me to escape my brother's clutches. I saw Lyndon, still chatting to the concierge. My mind raced – perhaps I could get them both drunk and slip away unnoticed.

'He's quite the fellow, your brother.'

'Quite.'

'We served together in the army, you know.'

'Oh?'

'A man of rare conviction.'

'Is that so?'

'Why yes, Miss Carlisle. Opaline. I may call you Opaline.'

May you indeed, I thought, wondering how long I would have to endure this charade. A thought struck me of how Sylvia would mock this forced politeness at all costs. If only I were an American!

'You learn a lot about someone's character in the trenches. You have to make unpopular decisions.'

I knew what he was referring to. It had been a bone of contention between Lyndon and my father.

'Yes, I am aware that my brother shot one of his men for cowardice,' I said, no longer able to keep the fake smile on my face. The thought alone disgusted me – killing our own men, purely because their fear got the better of them.

'*One* of his men? Oh, it was at least ten times that,' he said, almost boasting. 'You see, one must set an example when leading men.'

'An example?'

'Earned himself a nickname: The Reaper.' He widened his eyes and I felt a frisson of fear run along my spine.

Just then Lyndon returned, holding a room key in his hand.

'Let's get you settled,' he said, lifting me by my arm.

I felt I had to comply until I could find the right opportunity to escape. We stepped into the elevator while the attendant closed the iron grill and pushed the button for us to ascend. No one spoke a word and I looked down at my shoes. I could see the rip in my stockings from the night before. Armand. Oh, my heart crumpled in on itself like a discarded love letter. I suddenly felt very weary. I longed to be inside the comforting surrounds of Shakespeare and Company, working with Sylvia, cataloguing the books, greeting the customers.

'*Troisième étage*,' the attendant informed us and opened the gate for us.

As we walked down the carpeted hallway lined with tall

plants on either side, I tried to gather my thoughts, but it was pointless.

'Here we are,' Lyndon said. 'I booked you the room next to ours.'

I walked in, about to put my bag on the bed, but came to my senses and turned to leave. 'I can't stay here, Lyndon.'

He stood in the doorway, blocking my path. 'You will do as you are told, little sister.' With a movement I hadn't seen coming, he pushed me so hard into the wall opposite that I smacked my forehead and slumped to the floor, dazed.

As I sat there, he calmly closed the door and left.

~

I'm not sure how long I lay there, hugging my knees on the floor. It could have been twenty minutes or two hours.

'*Ménage*!' called the housekeeper.

I had no energy to reply, but the knocking was relentless.

'*S'il vous plait?*'

I heaved myself up and unlocked the door. 'What on earth ...?'

It was Armand.

He strode into the room and picked up my bag and coat. 'Come quickly.'

'But where ... how?'

'I'll explain after, *dépêches-toi*!' He grabbed my hand and made for the door.

We hurried down the corridor, in the opposite direction from which I'd come, to a back stair. I hadn't time to think, only silently prayed that we would not get caught. He held my hand tightly and, once on the ground floor, we kept to the staff corridor and found ourselves running through the kitchen, where the chefs hardly had time to shout at us before we found a side door on to the street. We ran down the alleyway and crossed several cobbled streets, Armand winding his way through the shortcuts of the city like a street urchin. Past street vendors selling flowers and fruit, under bridges and then out on to a grand boulevard I recognised. We were heading towards Shakespeare and Company.

'Wait, wait!' I panted, out of breath. 'Just … a moment,' I said, grabbing a streetlamp for support.

Armand finally let go of my hand, which he'd had in a tight grip the entire time. Immediately, I felt the loss and as I glanced at his face, his brown eyes scanning the street, the night before came into sharp relief.

'He knows about the bookshop,' I said, 'it's the first place he will look for me.'

'Sylvia wants you to come, she has a plan.'

'You've spoken to her?'

'This morning, I came to your lodging …' he hesitated. 'I couldn't wait to see you.' A brief smile lit his face. 'That's when I saw them take you, so I followed.'

'But how did you know what room I was in?'

'I didn't,' he replied, shaking his head. 'I knocked on every door.'

'Oh.' I was somewhat taken aback.

'Now we must hurry.'

Sylvia was awaiting my arrival at the back entrance. She gave me a quick, firm embrace, then handed me a key.

'A friend of mine has a house outside Paris, near Tours. You can stay there until—'

'You don't understand, I have to leave. Permanently. What I have done, running out on this wedding—'

'Wedding?' Armand repeated.

I opened my mouth to explain but found that I did not have the wherewithal to speak.

'How's everyone at Stratford-on-Odéon today?' Mr Joyce asked in his offbeat manner, poking his head around the door. My heart jumped – he must have wandered through from the front of the shop without any of us noticing.

'There's no time to explain, Jimmy. Opaline must leave the country immediately,' said Sylvia.

After some suggestive winking in Armand's direction, he casually suggested a swift exit to Dublin city.

'I have only ever heard you complain of your country' said Armand, which was quite true. We'd all heard him opine about Ireland's lack of culture and their ignorance at failing to recognise his genius.

'Yes, but I'm a writer. An artist. I am obliged to curse my home. But no,' he said, leaning against the wall and lighting a cigarette, 'I think Ireland could suit you down to the ground.'

I considered it. We spoke the same language. For heaven's sake, it had been part of Britain until that business with the treaty.

'Now that I think of it,' Joyce said, snapping his fingers, 'I've got a friend there who owns a nostalgia shop. A rare gentleman in these times, Mr Fitzpatrick. If you use my name, he's sure to give you a job, might sort you out with lodgings too.'

'It sounds like a bit of a long shot,' I said.

'What other option is there?' Sylvia asked.

And that was that. Joyce was hurriedly scribbling the name and address of the shop, whilst promising to send his friend a telegram, so he could expect my arrival.

What he actually meant was that he would get Sylvia to do it.

Everything got lost in a blur of tears after that. I felt like I was breaking apart and no one was coming to put me back together.

'Now, now, there's no need for all that,' Sylvia said, handing me an envelope with the address and my wages. 'You're a grown woman with a brain in your head, two good arms for carrying books and two strong legs to get you where you need to go.'

'What will you do if my brother comes here looking for me?' I asked.

'Why, sell him a book, of course!'

~

Armand took me to the port and secured a crossing for me. As we stood together, waiting for my turn to embark, he removed a chain from around his neck. The golden, hand-shaped pendant sparkled brightly in the sunlight .

'It is called a hamsa,' he explained. 'In my culture, we believe it offers the wearer protection from the evil eye.'

'Like an amulet?'

'*Exactement*. As long as you wear it, you will always be safe.'

It was time to leave.

'You have my address – it is the safest way to communicate with Sylvia. Your brother knows nothing of me.'

I nodded. I hadn't been aware that I'd been crying. I could now feel my tears drying on my cheek, or perhaps the sea air had caused them to evaporate. He took me in his warm embrace one last time. There was nothing left to say. He crossed the street and did not look back. I felt my heart descending rapidly, like an anchor into a bottomless sea.

Chapter Fourteen

MARTHA

I had no idea why he wanted to take me to a shop filled with pens I couldn't afford. And what exactly was a propelling pencil? There was a sign outside the shop saying they stocked them, but I couldn't bring myself to ask in case I ended up looking like a complete idiot. I remember somebody once saying it's better to keep your mouth shut and look stupid, rather than open it and remove all doubt. Well, something like that anyway. Henry, on the other hand, had no such worries.

'Ah, the old parliament buildings,' he said, pointing to a large cream-coloured building that looked as though it had just landed there from ancient Rome. 'Wonderful architecture, the Palladian style, I believe.'

He just said stuff like that, off the top of his head, as if it were perfectly normal. He wasn't even from here and he knew more about it than I did. I stuck to my rule of nodding in agreement, whilst having no idea what he was talking about.

'Where are we going, exactly? I have to be back to—' I was about to say, *to make her ladyship's dinner*, but I couldn't bear how ordinary and mundane it sounded compared to him. '—to work on my application for university.'

'Fantastic! Then we're going to exactly the right place.'

It was nice to have the distraction. My back was still stinging from the new tattoo I'd had done the day before, adding the lines to the previous ones. It felt good while I was getting it done, as though giving the words permanence was a kind of release, but it hurt like hell afterwards.

We crossed the road, walked through some gates and then in through a giant arched wooden door that had a smaller door within. It suddenly occurred to me that he was taking me to Trinity and I reared like a frightened horse.

'I can't go in here!'

'Whyever not?'

'Because … I don't know, don't you have to be registered or something?'

He looked at me like I was some kind of simpleton.

'Gosh, you're right. I hadn't thought of that. What if we get caught by the police?'

'I've never been here before,' I said, bumping into other people as I turned in circles to take it all in. The cobblestones, worn smooth over the centuries, were like the set of some historical movie.

'Really? I'd just assumed. This is where I've spent most of my time since I got here – beats sitting in the bed and breakfast.'

Imagine, just wandering in here cos you're bored. He inhabited a completely different world to me, that was for sure. Just knowing that he belonged, without question. I tried to ignore the jealousy that made my stomach tighten.

'Down there is the Glucksman Library, the centre for cartographic materials. I've been trying to find a map with the bookshop marked on it, but no luck so far.'

'There's a centre for cartographic materials?' My mind was

blown. All of this existed and I knew nothing about it. 'It's like that movie … Narnia!'

'You mean the C.S. Lewis books.'

I'd done it – I'd confirmed out loud that I was an idiot.

'Exactly, that's what I meant. It's just like that.' There was even a lamppost.

'I suppose it is in a way. It has over half a million maps and atlases down there – a little labyrinth with underground guardians of overhead maps, keeping track of things in case we get lost. Still couldn't find my bookshop though.'

'Your bookshop?' I arched my eyebrow.

'Yes, well, we're not looking for maps today, we're going in here.' He pointed to a sign saying 'Book of Kells'. There was a line of people in front of us, mostly tourists coming to see a very old, very famous book. My skin began to bristle – the only thing more intimidating to me than books was really, really old books. Who knew what kind of knowledge they held, the power they could wield? It didn't make any sense. But with Henry, I felt like a tiny doorway had opened up inside of me and I found myself thinking, *Maybe it wouldn't do any harm to look?*

'I know what you're thinking, who cares about the New Testament, am I right?'

No, he was not right and that's not what I was thinking. My thoughts had flitted back to my first date with Shane (not that this was a date today, obviously). We had gone to the cinema to watch a film about a racing car driver, then went home with a bottle of wine and had sex in his single bed.

'I'm not very religious,' I said.

'Just wait, you'll see.'

He was so excited about going to see some old pages of a manuscript, written by monks hundreds of years ago. I didn't understand it but I kind of liked it. I kind of liked him. But I knew his heart was elsewhere and this was clearly a fun little detour for him, exploring these literary delights before heading back to his real life. It felt bittersweet standing by his side and the feeling almost knocked me over – that sense of glimpsing a life that could have been.

~

And he was right. Once inside, I forgot about everything else. The darkness of the room and the light falling on the pages illuminated them like gold leaf. It felt as though I were witnessing something important, something beyond the fingertips of my understanding yet resonating within my soul.

'It was written in 800 AD by Columban monks on the island of Iona, Scotland.'

I simply gaped and followed the people in front of me, peering into the glass cases that held the manuscripts.

'How did they survive all this time?' I whispered.

A smile spread from his eyes to his lips.

'You're getting hooked now, aren't you?'

I just rolled my eyes, but he wasn't far wrong. Of course I'd seen reproductions from the Book of Kells in books and even on tea towels, but seeing it in real life like this, the intricate drawings and the handwritten text, it was hard not to get sucked into its story.

'It was stolen once in 1007 from Kells by the Vikings. They stripped whatever gold they could from the cover and left what they believed was a worthless manuscript under a sod of turf.'

I couldn't help wondering about the lives of the people who wrote the text, all in Latin. Still, there wasn't much time to ponder as the crowds kept coming and it was time to move on to the Long Room Library.

I don't know what I expected, but my skin flushed with goosebumps at the sight of it. It was like a cathedral of books;

wooden galleries arched upwards from floor to ceiling, filled with leatherbound books. I'd never seen anything like it. As we walked along the central corridor, marble busts lined the way; philosophers whose names sounded vaguely familiar, but I couldn't have said what any of them were known for. Surrounded by all of this learning, it was hard not to feel like, no matter how much you studied, you would never have an inch of the knowledge contained in this room.

'Impressive, isn't it?' he said. I hadn't been aware that he was watching for my reaction.

I turned to face him, ignoring the crowds pushing us ever forwards.

'Why did you really bring me here?'

He took a moment, shoved his hands in his pockets and looked up to the highest mezzanines where conservators were working with gloved hands.

'I wanted to show you that anything is possible.' He stepped out of the way of a group of American students, noisily making their way past. Then he stepped back a little closer to me, so I could feel his breath. 'After that day in the library, I could see you wanted to belong. And I just wanted to show you that you do.'

I stopped hearing the people around us, barely even noticed them filing past. No one had ever seen me the way he just had. And even if they did, they certainly didn't do anything to try and help me. I was lost for words and my throat felt thick with a sadness I'd never allowed myself to feel. He ran his hand through his hair, which unfailingly fell into his eyes when he bent his head, as he was doing now.

'Do you want to grab a pint somewhere?'

I just nodded and smiled as he stood back and cleared a path for me to walk ahead.

He'd found a pub on a small side street that looked as though it hadn't changed its decor in a hundred years. All dark wood with layer upon layer of varnish, smoothed down over the years, and little snugs lit by low-hanging glass pendants. It was quiet enough, just a couple of regulars at the bar, and so we sat in a snug that even had a little door, if you wanted complete privacy. We left it open and ordered two pints of Guinness and two shepherd's pies. A light rain began to fall outside and as the drops hit the windowpane and passers-by took out their umbrellas, I felt a warmth inside that I hadn't felt for a long time. Once our food arrived, we each took a mouthful and both groaned in satisfaction at how good it tasted. I was beginning to feel more comfortable around him, even if sometimes my breath still caught when he looked into my eyes.

'So what got you into all of this anyway?' I asked, eager to know more about him.

He took a large gulp of his pint, as though buying time.

'When I was a kid, my dad used to take me to car boot sales. Massive things, out in some old field in the middle of nowhere. Looking back, he'd probably had me foisted upon him for the day and it was that or the pub. We used to park up with everyone else and spend the day looking at what was usually other people's old tat. He'd call it a treasure hunt, trying to get me excited about it. And it was true, sometimes you would find something pretty special. He liked all the old war memorabilia – medals and that sort of thing – but I still stuck to my books.'

He picked up his fork and carried on eating his pie, but I could tell that something was troubling him. I don't know how I'd missed it before – I was probably so dazzled by his seemingly perfect life. Something had happened with his father. They hadn't spoken in years. I didn't want to push, and sometimes found that if you gave people enough space, they would say the words that haunted them from within.

'He must be very proud of you now, an expert scholar.'

He gave me a look that I hadn't seen in his eyes up to then. It was a look of hurt and anger. He took another long gulp of his pint, holding it there until he'd finished it and caught the waiter's attention for another round.

I didn't say another word and focused entirely on finishing my meal. I excused myself to go to the bathroom and when I came back, the atmosphere had changed. I could tell he was sorry for the mood that had gripped him and I just wanted to touch his hand and say it was okay. I knew. People you loved could hurt you and there was nothing you could do about it.

'When I was fifteen, I picked up an old copy of *Lord of the Rings* in a second-hand bookshop. By then I was already a bit of a dealer.'

I snorted. In my experience, a fifteen-year-old dealer meant something else entirely. I nodded for him to continue and began on my second pint. I hadn't watched the films but had heard that they were based on a series of books.

'I learned the value of the rarer editions and what collectors were willing to pay for them. It was a handy source of pocket money and an easy way to earn it. I'd scour the markets and charity shops for books they didn't know the true value of, then sell them on to the more upmarket antique sellers. I needed the extra cash by then. My father's drinking had grown worse and things weren't great at home.'

His eyes flitted across the room, but I could sense he wanted to get this out.

'Anyway, when I got it home, I had a proper look at it and tucked into the flap of the jacket, I found a letter.'

I leaned forward, drawn into his world of literary treasure hunts.

'The date was 1967, the address was Oxford and the name signed at the bottom was J.R.R. Tolkien.'

'Wow.'

'Indeed. Wow. It was a handwritten note addressed to a little girl who must have sent him a fan letter. I couldn't believe what I was holding in my hands and back then, I had no idea how to authenticate it. So I asked my father if he knew anyone and that was the last I ever saw of it.'

'What happened?'

'He sold it for five hundred pounds.'

'Well, that's not bad, is it?'

'It was worth ten times that. Not just that, it was the prestige of finding it, bringing something lost back to the world. He took that away from me and drank the proceeds.' He blinked quickly, then shifted in his seat.

'I'm sorry.'

'I'm giving you the abbreviated version. My father's alcoholism is like a footnote to every chapter of my life. Sometimes I feel like I'll never be free of it.'

This time I did reach out my hand and placed it softly over his. He gave me a tight smile, then once again signalled for another round. I lost track of the time as we sat there across the table from each other. He was letting me into his world and it felt good to be out of my own for a while. He spoke about the paper he was writing on lost manuscripts.

'Reading the book, that's only the beginning – I want to know everything about it. What I want to know is who wrote the book, when and where and how and why. Who printed it, what it cost, how it survived, where it's been since, when it was sold, why and by whom, how it got here … there's no limit to what I want to know about a book.'

I could tell he was getting a bit tipsy now; his words were crashing together in a haphazard way. I was getting very tipsy myself. I'd forgotten all about Madame Bowden.

'That's the allure of books – it's not just the story between the covers, but the story of where they came from, who owned them. A book is so much more than a delivery vehicle for its contents,' he continued, hands gesticulating wildly. He only stopped talking when he realised I was laughing.

'What? I'm rabbiting on, aren't I?'

'No, it's just, I've never heard anyone so hyped up about … anything! But it makes sense now, why you're here.' I broke off, realising that something was niggling me. 'But what about the story? Don't you care what the book is about?'

'Of course, but when you're a collector, the books themselves become artefacts. Most collectors don't even read them.'

'Well, that doesn't seem right.'

'Says the person who doesn't read books.'

'That's different!' I snapped. He failed to read the change in my mood and kept playfully prodding.

'I don't mean to be the bearer of bad news, but university life tends to involve books.' His smile faltered when he saw my face. I was never one for crying, certainly not in public places, but my eyes were stinging with hurt and I fought to keep the tears in by squeezing my brows together.

'God, I'm sorry, Martha, that was unforgivably stupid of me.'

I felt hot and stuffy in the snug and when I turned around I saw the pub had filled up with people. Now it had become noisy and unwelcoming. I had to get out of there.

'What time is it? I have to go.'

I grabbed my things and he shot up beside me.

'I'll walk you home. If you'd like.'

I shrugged. What difference did it make?

~

As we stepped on to the street, the fresh air made me feel as though I'd drunk double what I had. Instead of the warm, fuzzy glow of earlier, now I felt nauseous and irritable. It was dark and people were heading home from work, so the street was at a standstill, full of traffic and the honking horns of impatient drivers.

'Here,' Henry said, taking my hand and leading me down a quieter side street. The touch of his warm skin had a powerful effect. I felt a sense of safety that I didn't think possible again. I probably should have let go, once we had got around the corner, but I didn't want to. Neither, it seemed, did he.

'I'm sorry if I hurt your feelings, Martha.' He spoke so softly it almost broke my heart.

I had assumed, when we first met, that he had the perfect life. But after he told me about his father, well. Eventually, I made a decision, took a deep breath and told him what I'd never told anyone.

'My feelings? Don't worry about it. There are worse ways to hurt a person, I know that now. I've had two broken ribs, a dislocated shoulder, bruised kidneys and I've lost four teeth.'

Henry looked horrified. I could tell that, despite what he had lived through with his father, there hadn't been violence. If you haven't experienced it, it's easy to fool yourself into believing that it could never happen. That was how people could look through you, how you became invisible. Because your story didn't exist. 'But they're the physical wounds. They heal over time. Imperfectly, maybe, but they heal. It's the constant fear he's left me with. That's the wound that won't heal. I'm not just afraid of him, I'm afraid of life.'

'How—' he began, then stopped.

We found ourselves outside a small church and he gestured to the bench just inside the gate. I smiled. It was the right place for a confession. I may not have committed the sin, but I carried the guilt nonetheless. *How had I let this happen to me*?

'The thing is, you don't really recognise what's happening at the start and by the time you do, it's too late to do anything about it. You think it's a one-time thing. He's so sorry about it, feels terrible. But then it happens again. Next thing you know, it's all you know.'

'You don't have to tell me if you don't want to,' he said.

I realised he was still holding my hand. Or I was still holding his. I could still read him well enough and I knew he would keep my story safe.

'It started during my first year at the technical college. I'd decided to do an admin course and got myself a room in a house, renting with two other girls. I would stay up in Galway for the week, then come home at the weekends. I was still living with my parents then, but mostly I stayed with Shane in his flat. Looking back, I think he was kind of an escape from the atmosphere at home. It was fine when we were in school together. I mean, he was a bit jealous at times, but nothing that made me think he might be any different to any of the other lads.'

The hardest thing about telling my story were the flashbacks – one minute I was here, in Dublin, and then, bam!, I'd be back there, cowering on the floor, trying to protect myself. Had it actually happened, or was it some awful nightmare that I'd imagined? No one could have lived through that kind of abuse, could they? I thought of the day my two girlfriends came home to find me hiding in the wardrobe in my room. I remembered getting out and putting my hands in the pockets of my jeans, so they couldn't see them shaking. I tried to pass it off as a joke, as though I were planning to surprise Shane. I was so embarrassed – I would have said anything to make it look like something other than what it obviously was. He had come up to Galway for the night and I couldn't wait to show him around. But he was moody the entire time, making fun of my friends and acting jealous of every guy in my class. *How did they know my name? Was I flirting with them?* By the end of the night, he was roaring drunk and calling me a slut.

He shouted at me on the street the whole way home from the pub and by the time we got to my door, he had worked himself up into a fury. I shouted back that he had no right to speak to me that way. Next I heard a crack. He had smacked me, open-handed, right across the face. I was too stunned to speak. He took the keys from me and opened the door. I'll never forget what he said as he walked past me.

'That'll teach you to answer back.'

I walked in behind him, stunned into silence. I didn't want to wake the girls. I lay on the bed beside him and didn't even change out of my clothes. He fell to snoring as soon as his head hit the pillow. After a while I got up and didn't know where to go. I was terrified. So I hid in the wardrobe until I heard him leave the next morning. That year, which should have been about my first year at college, became all about Shane and his jealousy. My flatmates knew what was going on. They saw the bruises, even under the layers of makeup. The worst part was, right before the exams, they convinced me to break up with him. And I did. For two whole months, I was free of him. But his father died and I felt so sorry for him. He swore to me that he had changed and was ashamed of what he had done. He said he wasn't himself at the time and I believed him because it was true; he wasn't being himself. That wasn't the person I fell in love with. And so we both believed the story that he had somehow been possessed by a mad fit of jealousy and of course it wouldn't happen again. I failed my exams in the summer and that was the last time I ever went back to Galway. I could see the look in the girls' eyes when I told them I'd got back with him. I think they felt betrayed and confused. How, after getting away from a man who hit me, could I go back? I couldn't bear their judgement. Because they were right, after all, weren't they? His promises meant nothing and I was a bigger fool for believing him.

I was so lost in my memories, I almost forgot where I was or what we were doing. I looked up at him and saw a look of empathy in his eyes. Not sympathy, thank God. I couldn't bear that.

'I'm sorry, I don't think I can do this.'

'It's okay,' he said, about to embrace me but then stopping short. 'Um, do you want a hug?'

I nodded. A lot. Yes, I did want a hug. I never asked anyone for anything, but to have what I needed offered to me like that was a blessed relief.

Chapter Fifteen

HENRY

Holding her in my arms, I wondered how any man could inflict the kind of pain and terror that would fracture this woman apart. That was how she felt in my arms, like broken pieces that no longer fit together. I wondered if there was more going on than she had said, but her poker face was the best I'd seen. Until now. Just then my phone began to ring and she pulled away. I searched in my pocket, trying to turn it off.

'Bloody thing,' I muttered, until I finally got hold of it, only to let it slip through my fingers and on to the ground. We both bent to get it, bumped foreheads and finally she picked it up.

'Isabelle,' she said, reading the name and handing it to me.

I just stared at the screen until it stopped ringing. Isabelle. I'd somehow managed to put her completely out of my thoughts. Like I'd compartmentalised my life in London into a separate filing system in my head. Having spent the most incredible day with Martha, opening up about our pasts in a way that neither of us ever had before, and being in a different country, I felt like a different person. I felt as though I were no longer running, at least for now. My whole life up to this point had been running away from something, losing myself in books and hoping to God that no one would notice the great big hole inside of me where something vital should have been. I looked back at Martha, the vulnerability in her eyes challenging me and my propensity to simply tell people what they wanted to hear, rather than the truth. *She's just a friend,* I could have said. But there was something about her gaze, like she could see right through me.

'Isabelle is my girlfriend.'

'Oh.'

There was a vacuum, which I stupidly chose to fill with more words.

'Actually, I should probably call her my fiancée. I proposed just before I left.'

'Oh,' she said again. 'Well, congratulations!' She smiled with a forced jollity that made me feel even worse.

Why hadn't I told her earlier? I should have told her at the start. Surely that's what a normal person would have done. I could sense her embarrassment, which was misplaced because I was the one who should've been embarrassed. I tried to seek refuge in the thought that lying and not telling the truth were two different things, but even I didn't believe that. She then made a big production out of checking the time on her phone and saying she should get back home. Alone. That point was underlined and in bold. I'd fucked up.

~

I arrived back at my B&B to find Nora watching a quiz show on the telly in the front room. She sat on an armchair with wooden armrests, her ashtray balancing precariously on one while a Jack Russell snored peacefully on her lap. I looked around for the other two, then realised they were sniffing my shoes. He could probably smell where I'd been and how much of an idiot I was.

'Oh, you're back,' she said, despite the fact that I had not made her aware of my departure. She simply maintained an air of familiarity with everyone coming through her house. Like a mother to all of us.

'Do you want a cup of tea or a sandwich?' she asked, slotting her bunioned feet into her slippers.

'I'll make it,' I said. 'You stay where you are.'

She looked at me as one might look upon the face of a saint, which made me realise how little it took to make someone happy and yet how rarely it happened. I rinsed out a brown teapot and set the cups on a tray, with a packet of pink wafer biscuits.

Once she had the tea in her hand and another cigarette lit, she turned her attention to me.

'Come on then, who is she?'

'Sorry?'

She even took the unnerving step of turning down the volume on the TV.

'You've that look.'

'What look?' I asked, immediately trying to change my look, which is a very difficult thing to do when you weren't aware you had a look in the first place.

'I didn't come down in the last shower,' she said, tipping her ash into the ashtray and wriggling into a more comfortable position for interrogation. 'You're a brooder – a bit like himself outside.' She nodded at the shed, wherein I assumed her husband was still hiding. 'He used to be a window cleaner, before he got the pension. Now that might not seem very grand to the likes of you, but there'll always be windows that need cleaning.'

I nodded, because you couldn't argue with logic like that. And there was no point in telling her that 'the likes of me' had to rely on scholarships and student loans, thanks to Father's drinking.

'Anyway, years ago, he had the chance to go into partnership with this fella; said they could tout for more business and get bigger jobs. So, himself starts brooding on it. And brooding and brooding until, well, it was too late. The other fella found someone else who jumped at the chance and they got the contract for half the hotels in the city!'

Just then her husband stomped down the stairs in his vest and trousers and smacked the newspaper down on the hall table.

'For the last time, woman, I'm afraid of heights!' he announced, before shoving his arms into a shirt and storming out the front door. It closed with such a thud that the pictures of the various popes hanging in the hall shook in the most unholy way. We stared open-mouthed at the hallway where he no longer stood.

'He never got over it,' she said, a slightly judgemental tone in her voice, and I wondered what was the glue that held people together. Mutual disdain? Lack of any better idea? 'Anyway,' she continued undeterred, 'it doesn't do any good to brood.'

Perhaps she was right, I thought, as I sipped my tea and the volume on the TV crept up again. What the hell was I brooding over anyway? I came here to find the manuscript, not to develop a crush on another woman. If anything, spending time with Martha was getting in the way of my research. I began warming to this idea because it meant that the blame was being lifted off my shoulders. I took my leave of Nora and went upstairs to my room and laptop. There were two emails. The first from Isabelle:

Answer your phone!

Classic Isabelle style. Direct and to the point. She was a woman who had high standards for herself and everyone around her. She was a life coach and often spoke in rousing statements like *Go big or go home*, or *If it doesn't challenge you, it won't change you!* Was I slightly intimidated by her relentless energy? Maybe, but it's also what drew me to her. She was everything I felt I needed to be.

We had met two years before at my sister's wedding. She was the wedding planner then. Her previous incarnation, as she called it. She seemed to have a new career every few years and was totally brilliant at all of them. I had it on good authority that she was an amazing yoga teacher before that, according to the groom, who could still throw his legs over his head, which was a bit too much information really. I was immediately struck by her confidence, and by the time we waved the happy couple off on their honeymoon, she made it clear that whatever I had in mind, it would be on a trial basis only for her. Much like her careers. She looked at me like someone deciding whether to pick a bruised apple and give it a go. And so I found myself constantly trying to win her over (as much as myself) to the idea that I could, given the right conditions, become a success. Like a houseplant. I knew that if I had someone like Isabelle in my life, everything would be infinitely better, bigger, brighter! I never had anything or anyone in my life that I could feel proud of – that I could say, 'Look what I've got'. Flashbacks of my father's face haunted me, those tear-drenched nights when he tried to convince my mother to take him back. But at times, I just felt so tired. Tired of proving myself. Tired of trying to make someone see something in me that I wasn't even sure was there.

I decided to send an equally punchy reply:

Lost in research! Tomorrow ok?

I opened the second email. It was from a colleague in London who had been scanning Carlisle family archives for any mention of Opaline. There was nothing of note beyond her twenty-first birthday. It was as though she had dropped off the face of the earth. Her brother, however, was very well documented and had been quite high up in the army during the First World War. He'd earned himself a rather grim nickname, 'The Reaper'. It wasn't very much to go on and brought me no closer to the lost bookshop on Ha'penny Lane. Or the elusive young woman who lived next door. The woman who had helped to find out Opaline's real name. I couldn't quite put my finger on it, but I had this weird sense that she was somehow the key to it all. Or perhaps that was the story I had to tell myself in order to stay close to her, no matter the cost.

Chapter Sixteen

OPALINE

Dublin, 1921

'I'm afraid Mr Fitzpatrick died two months ago. We were going to put the place up for sale …'

These were the first words I heard on arriving in Dublin city after a long, uncomfortable train journey from Cork. I was standing in the parlour of a Georgian-style house, with long panelled windows looking out on to a busy street.

'But I've come all this way,' I said, rather desperately. 'You received my telegram?'

The man I was speaking to seemed rather baffled by my sudden arrival into his life.

'Yes. Mr Joyce telegrammed from Paris. He mentioned that you worked in a bookshop, Shakespeare?'

'Shakespeare and Company.'

'Forgive me, but I'm not entirely sure why he would have suggested'—he hesitated for a moment—'that someone such as yourself should come to work for my father.'

I tried to overlook the implication.

'Mr Fitzpatrick was your father? My condolences, sir,' I said, shaking his hand.

He thanked me and it seemed as though our business was at an end.

'I don't suppose I could trouble you for some further information?'

'Of course, if I can be of assistance.'

'Can you recommend a decent hotel room, or perhaps somewhere that I could rent a room at a reasonable rate?'

'You don't have anywhere to stay?' he asked, obviously perplexed that someone with my accent and appearance should find themselves in such a predicament. A middle-class woman, travelling alone with nowhere to stay and very little money.

'I'm afraid I made my departure in something of a hurry.' God only knew what he made of that explanation. I wanted to assure him that I hadn't broken any laws, but that would have only raised his suspicions further.

'Well, it's not much,' he said, before taking a set of keys off a hook by the door and leading me outside, then down the front steps. 'There is a small flat in the basement of the shop,' he explained, as he turned right and stood outside the shop.

I looked at the building with no small amount of incredulity. It was tapered, almost as if it had grown like a stubborn weed between the two houses on either side. He noticed my face, scrunched up in the evening light.

'It shouldn't really be here at all,' he said, mumbling something about planning permission.

Neither should I, I thought to myself. It felt surreal and as though I were strangely removed from myself; a baffled spectator wondering what would happen next. The crossing to Ireland had taken all day and most of the night. As there was no passenger ferry, I'd had to travel on a mail and goods boat that took me to Cork. Once again, I was on a boat with my small carpet bag, running towards freedom. I tried to sleep on a makeshift bed that was in reality just a bench with a thin cushioning on top. I vomited into a bucket and cried into it too. It was nothing like crossing the Channel. This sea was rough and unforgiving. When the boat moored at the harbour, the rain pelted down and the wind threatened to separate me from my bag as it attacked in gusts. One of the boat hands guided me to a small bed and breakfast nearby where I was able to freshen up before taking the train to Dublin.

Matthew Fitzpatrick was a pleasant man who spoke few words, something for which I was grateful at that moment. I was not at my most sociable. I was tired and hungry and homesick for the kind of home I had never known. Any display of kindness might have resulted in an outburst of tears, so I was glad to keep things perfunctory. I gave the narrow facade another appraising look. On the ground floor there was just room for one panelled glass window, which bowed outwards, and an identical yet smaller window on the first floor and a tiny, diamond-shaped window on the top floor which seemed to taper into a point, like the hat of a wizard. The sign above the window was in the art nouveau style, so popular in Paris, with its swirls and flourishes. *Mr Fitzpatrick's Nostalgia Shop.*

The door gave way with a sigh, followed by an elongated creak. Matthew turned to offer an apologetic smile and I waited on the threshold for a moment, giving him time to switch the lights on inside. I heard a click and caught my first glimpse of the shop by the warm glow of a yellow lampshade. The chequer-tiled floor welcomed my feet as I entered the topsy-turvy world of the nostalgia shop. The dark green walls gave one the impression of entering a thick forest, with wooden shelves stretching around the entire room like branches. There were all types of knick-knacks and ornaments, with everything from soaps and hand mirrors to toy soldiers and candelabras. Yet they were of a variety I had never laid my eyes on before – brightly painted and ornately decorated, the gold and silvers glimmering in the soft light.

'It's beautiful,' I said, and meant it. 'Like walking inside a fairy tale.'

He regarded me strangely and it seemed for a moment as though I were looking into the face of a young boy. Gone was the harried man with the hat and overcoat. It seemed he was wearing a disguise also.

'I'm glad you think so.'

Such few words, yet they were imbued with so much meaning. It was as if I had passed some sort of invisible test for him.

'Look, I know you came here to work for my father, but how would you feel about running the shop yourself?'

'Me?' I squeaked. So much for trying to impress him.

'You could rent it. On a trial period. I had considered the idea, but couldn't find anyone suitable. Until today.'

I looked around the shop and felt a ripple of excitement.

'I'm not sure I could afford it, on top of my lodgings,' I said.

'Well, as it happens, the flat is included in the rent. Here, let me show you,' he said, leading the way down the stairs.

I watched the back of his neck, where his blonde hair grew darker. He had to duck as we came to the last step to avoid a beam and he stood back to let me go first. His soft lilting accent as he pointed out the bed and the tiny kitchenette couldn't conceal the myriad questions he must have had about my hasty arrival from Paris. He must have thought me strange; there was no doubting that. And yet, if anything, he seemed intrigued by my presence. It suddenly felt quite intimate, standing there with him, and so, as if in agreement, we both decided to cut the tour short.

'It's perfect. I'm sure I will find everything I need,' I said with a competence I hoped would appear from somewhere in the very near future.

'I don't doubt it. I'll have a tenancy agreement drawn up.'

As we ascended the narrow wooden staircase shining with a high varnish, I noticed that there was a word painted on the riser of each step.

found
are
things
strange
lost
called
place
a
In

'He built it himself, so you'll have to forgive the slightly eccentric nature of the building,' Matthew said, placing his hand on the newel post with a tender look of pride on his face. 'Had the wood shipped over from an old library in Italy. A strange story actually – he took my mother on their honeymoon to a little village in the mountains and they found this abandoned library. It was going to be demolished and my father was the kind of man who couldn't let something that held so much history go to waste. So he bought the building, had it dismantled and put it back together here.'

'Didn't any of the locals wish to keep it?'

'Ah well, that was the thing; many of the villagers believed the library to be inhabited by spirits.'

'Good grief!'

'But of course, that was just superstition,' he assured me.

'I wish I could have met your father. He must have been such an interesting man,' I said, looking with new eyes at the interiors that resembled a puzzle pieced together.

Matthew smiled to himself.

'Eccentric, that's how most people would have described him.' His features failed to conceal the bittersweet memories of his father.

'Some people have no imagination, that's all.'

He seemed pleased with this assessment and presumably felt safe to open up a little more. 'He used to say that he would like people to open this door in the way they would open a book, entering a world beyond their imaginings.' He gave a wry smile, an expression formed by grief and loss.

'He sounds a little like my own father.'

'Is he a book dealer also?'

I shook my head and continued shaking it until I had to shut my eyes tight to prevent the tears from falling. Why had I mentioned Father? It brought reality crashing down around me. Everything that had happened: Lyndon, Armand, escaping on that horrid boat. Truly, I still felt at sea myself. Who was I now? I felt ashamed of my night with Armand and how my father would be so disappointed in his little girl. I must have been in shock. Try as I might, I could not contain it and my shoulders began to shake until I let out a desperate gasp.

'Miss Carlisle, Opaline, whatever did I say?'

Words failed to form. He took me by the shoulders as if to keep me steady, but I fell into his arms and sobbed for what seemed like a very long time. He held me fast and absorbed all of the grief and pain without saying a word. When I finally felt wrung out and my ears throbbed with the sound of nothing but my own ragged breathing, I hastened to pull back from his embrace.

'Please forgive me, Mr Fitzpatrick. I have embarrassed us both with this unbecoming outburst.'

He made no reply but handed me a handkerchief from his

pocket. I wiped my eyes and blew my nose before attempting to hand it back. Our eyes met and we both smiled.

'Perhaps I shall have it laundered first,' I said and released an unfortunate snort of laughter. The giddiness after such an impromptu intimacy.

There didn't seem to be much else to say and I was too worn out to think. He saved me the trouble by acting as though nothing problematic had happened at all.

'I will stop by in a few days to arrange the particulars, if that's agreeable to you?'

I nodded and walked him back to the door.

'Thank you, Mr Fitzpatrick, and again, I apologise for—'

'No need. Grief is a constant companion, is it not?'

He placed his hat on his head and turned to leave.

'Given the history of the place, you'll have to excuse its little eccentricities,' he said, as though it were a mischievous child.

'I think we are well matched,' I said, determined to prove that I was not easily put off.

~

I brought my old carpet bag downstairs to the basement and hung the only other skirt and blouse I owned in the armoire. I lit the stove and boiled some water in a little pot for tea. Except I hadn't bought any tea. I realised I would have to go out and buy some provisions. Suddenly, the weight of everything that had happened and the effort needed to carry on seemed too much to bear. I let myself collapse on to the bed and regretted it, as the springs made a very uncomfortable dig into my ribs. Whether it was luck or courage that I had possessed in Paris, it felt like they had both abandoned me. Perhaps Lyndon was right; I was indulging in childhood fantasies. This was not how the world worked. At best, I would be looked upon as an anomaly. I turned on to my side.

The mattress was bare. I didn't even have a coverlet. I would have to buy that too.

'No tears,' I warned myself, but it was no good. I could already feel them running down my cheeks. No matter how much I let myself believe that I could be just like Sylvia and her partner Adrienne, it wasn't true. They were outliers; they no longer cared for the kind of society that would not accept them. Instead, they inhabited a world of artists and free spirits who chose the vicissitudes of a nonconforming life over the comforts and security of the status quo. And the truth was that they had each other. I had never felt more alone, so far from the only home I knew. I cried myself to sleep that night, with an empty stomach and only my overcoat for warmth.

~

I woke in the middle of the night to the sound of scratching, like a branch against the window. I couldn't figure it out, as there certainly weren't any trees on the street outside. I sat up for a moment and realised it was coming from the shop overhead.

I flicked the switch on the wall, but no light came on. Mr Fitzpatrick the younger had warned me that the building could be 'temperamental'. Luckily, I had spotted a candle on the kitchen table where I had left my purse and so I carefully felt my way across the room to it. My hand searched and found a small box of matches beside it and soon the room emerged out of the shadows. I climbed the stairs, reading the words that Mr Fitzpatrick painted there, *In a place called lost, strange things are found.* I certainly felt strange and out of place. I paused for a moment, wondering what on earth I would do when I found the source of the noise. What if it were an intruder? Then I heard it again, a soft tapping, like brambles in the wind. I took a deep breath and carried on to the top of the stairs.

The shop itself had an air of stillness and anticipation, as though it were waiting for me. The light from the candle reflected softly on the curiosities adorning the shelves. I felt like an intruder myself amongst these things and hesitated to touch anything. Intricately designed music boxes sat atop a glass case full of pocket watches and engraved pendants. A wooden cabinet of long, narrow drawers, the type for keeping botanical drawings, was actually full of old buttons and stamps. I jumped when a cuckoo clock announced the hour from the opposite wall. Three cuckoos. It reminded me of one of my favourite books I had read repeatedly as a child, by Mrs Molesworth, in which a young girl called Griselda and a cuckoo from a clock became unlikely friends. I spoke the opening line aloud: 'Once upon a time in an old town, in an old street, there stood a very old house.'

A collection of Russian matryoshka dolls painted brightly in red and blue peeked out at me expectantly from one of the shelves. I couldn't resist opening one, revealing a smaller doll inside. I opened that too, on and on until I had five dolls, each decreasing in size, all made to perfectly fit inside the largest one. It was exactly how I felt: a fully formed woman, but the little girl inside was still there.

A heavy thud made me turn around with a fright. I held the candle out in front of me.

'Hello?' I whispered, feeling slightly ridiculous. Perhaps a cat had come in through an open window. I walked to the rear of the shop where the noise had come from. There was a modest glass cabinet of books, its doors open and a tome lying on the floor. The temperature was so cold and I was in my bare feet, so I bent to pick it up and replace it quickly. A cursory glance at the cover almost made my heart stop – *Dracula*, by Bram Stoker. A terrifying image of a vampire was on the cover. I looked around the shop. All was quiet now. I replaced the book and turned to go back downstairs when another thud made me jump. Looking back, I saw the book on the floor once more.

'That's very strange,' I said out loud, trying to sound calm. The very fact that I thought someone (or something) was listening confirmed my state of mind. I picked up the book and once again spoke out loud. 'Yes, I think I shall take a book to bed,' I said with a little uncertainty, before bringing it back downstairs with me. I read until the candle extinguished, terrified, exhilarated and unsure whether the book was a warning or an invitation.

Chapter Seventeen

MARTHA

The cracks were getting bigger. I sat at the table eating Weetabix before I had to go upstairs to cook Madame Bowden's breakfast. With every mouthful, I looked up again at the dark lines spreading across the wall like the branch of a tree. There was no crumbling plaster, but a very definite line of growth. A dark material was visible now and I slowly raised my hand to touch it. With a slight tremble, my fingers ran along the ridges and I discovered that the surface I was touching was wood-like. It wasn't even wood-like, it *was* wood. There were branches growing in the basement. I would have to tell her now. This couldn't be good. What if the house was structurally unsound?

'Oh, I shouldn't worry about it too much,' Madame Bowden remarked, having finally made her way down to take a look. 'Old buildings have their quirks. Now I think I shall have croissants for breakfast this morning, Martha. You can pop over to the French bakery,' she said, already turning to leave.

I stood there with my mouth agape.

'But they're pretty big cracks and they weren't here when I

moved in!' I said, unsure she'd grasped the seriousness of the situation. 'Shouldn't you call an engineer?'

She had a wistful look in her eye, as she let her fingertips rest on the cracks. She was touching the wall the way you would touch the soft cheek of a child.

'It was always such a strange little place,' she whispered, almost to herself. 'Oh, Martha, do stop worrying so much, you're giving yourself frown lines.'

'Frown lines?' I asked, perplexed (and giving myself more frown lines).

That was when she spotted the leaflets on the table.

'So, you're going ahead with it then?' she asked, raising her reading glasses that she wore on a pearl chain around her neck and peering at the papers.

'University? Oh, um, yes. You would know this if you'd bothered to attend your own dinner party. Where were you?'

She gave me a filthy look and a hasty reminder that she was still paying my wages and I was living under her roof.

'I can't stand those women.'

'So why did you invite them?'

She walked around the room and wrapped her silk shawl around her shoulders.

'Maybe I wanted to amuse myself; see how you coped with them. By all accounts, you held yourself rather well.'

Did I?

'Hang on, what—'

'I assume you'll fit these studies around your work here?' she interrupted.

'Of course. I'm thinking I might just start with a part-time course.' Shit. I hadn't thought about how to ask her about it. Would I still be able to keep my job? A roof over my head? I tried to quieten my thoughts and read her story. Most of the time you could predict someone's behaviour by their past. Most of the time people didn't change. Most of the time.

I realised she was staring at me.

'Croissants, Martha. And fresh coffee. Chop-chop!' And with that, she went back upstairs.

'So, when did you buy this house?' I tried to act as casually as possible; as if the answer mattered little, one way or the other. I knew if she thought I was fishing, she wouldn't bite. Perhaps it was her acting skills that made her so difficult to read.

'Martha, a person such as myself does not buy a house, one *acquires* a house.'

It took all of my willpower not to roll my eyes.

'Okay, well, when did you *acquire* number 12?'

'Oh, it's hard to say really. I feel as though I've always been here. In fact, it's hard to remember a time when I lived anywhere else.'

I dusted the picture frames on the mantelpiece and picked up the black and white wedding photo.

'It was 1965,' she began, settling down to the cosmopolitan-style breakfast I had laid on the dining table. 'I was a beautiful bride. Many of the guests likened me to Grace Kelly. Oh, you mightn't think so now, but I was a natural blonde.'

A natural liar, I thought. It was hard to tell if her stories were real or mere fabrications of the truth – stories she had picked up along the way and made her own. I looked at the woman in the picture. It was true, she did look like an old Hollywood starlet, but I couldn't see the resemblance at all. The man was tall, dark and handsome with the look of someone who had captured the moon in his pocket.

'He was a pilot,' she said, slathering butter on her croissant.

'Far too old for me, or at least that's what my mother told me. But I was hopelessly in love with him. I thought he was so dashing. He was an American, you know, and to a twenty-something Irish girl, well, he was like Clark Gable.'

She lost herself in the past for a moment.

'He adored this strange little house. But he was a perfectionist, always trying to fix things. You have to understand, old houses have their quirks. Some things are meant to be flawed. Therein lies beauty.'

She was a captivating storyteller. I knew there was a peculiar history within these walls and whatever it was, it must have happened long before Madame Bowden arrived.

'What happened to your husband, if you don't mind me asking?'

'Plane crash. We were only married a year when his plane went down over Gibraltar.'

'Oh, I'm so sorry,' I said.

'Yes, it was a difficult time. That's when I met Archie.'

'Archie?'

'My second husband. He was a doctor from Cork.'

'I thought you said he was Russian?'

'Oh no, that was husband number three.'

'But what happened to Archie?' I realised that this was really none of my business, but I couldn't help myself. Maybe when you got to her age, minor details like this didn't matter any more.

'Archie contracted malaria when he was working in Africa, poor fellow.'

I wondered what had happened to the Russian mathematician – death by numbers?

'What's with all of these questions? I hope you're not planning on bumping me off and getting your hands on my house?'

'Honestly, Madame Bowden, if anyone should be worried about getting bumped off, I think it should be me.'

She stared at me for a moment and I was full sure she was going to fire me for insolence, when she let out an enormous laugh. I really needed to hang out with people my own age.

~

I spent that entire day giving the house a deep clean. It was something I always enjoyed doing, not because I was a fan of housework, but because the methodical action of cleaning was the only way I'd ever found to make my thoughts stop. Thoughts like: I had married a bully, I had wasted my life, and now I could add a new one to the list – I had humiliated myself in front of Henry. Why did I care about his opinion so much anyway? Besides, it wasn't my fault he'd neglected to tell me about his fiancée. But the truth was, I already knew. I could read in his eyes that his heart was tied elsewhere, so why did I act like it was such a big surprise? And why did it even matter? What kind of an idiot would start having feelings for someone when they'd just got out of an abusive marriage? That should have been the end of it. I simply couldn't permit myself to feel anything.

I was exhausted by the time I got downstairs to the basement that night. I brushed my teeth in the bathroom and changed for bed with unseeing eyes. It was only as I pulled the covers down and flopped into bed that I saw it. Where the lines in the wall had been, there now emerged a shelf. With one single book on it. Standing upright. I looked around the room, for what, I don't know. I almost felt like saying out loud, 'Can anyone else see this?' I was afraid to get out of bed and so I just stayed there, frozen for a minute. Nothing else happened, not a sound came. I had no idea how it got there, other than that Madame Bowden must have placed it there while I was busy steam-cleaning the curtains or bleaching the bathroom. My curiosity won out and I got up to inspect the book. The spine read *A Place Called Lost* but the author was anonymous. I got back into bed and opened the beautiful old cloth-bound cover. It bore a picture of an antique shopfront with a stained-glass pattern in the window. I had to admit that, so far, it was very inviting.

I read the first line aloud: 'Once upon a time in an old town, in an old street, there stood a very old house.'

I hadn't told my employer of my issues with books or why I practically broke out in hives at the thought of reading them, so she wouldn't have known. But perhaps it was a gesture of some sort and it would've been rude not to accept it. I decided I should try to read it, in case she asked me about it. Besides, I had to break through this mental block if I had any hope of going back to university. I had to face my fears.

Chapter Eighteen

HENRY

I rehearsed what I would say all the way there, but when I tapped on her window, all of my lines fell away, like a novice actor on opening night.

'What are you doing here?' she asked, opening the window and somehow managing to heave herself out of it by climbing on a stool.

'Careful,' I said, setting down the coffees I'd brought. I took her arms but there was really no need – for a slight woman she was incredibly strong. Dressed in old jeans and a sweatshirt, with her hair roughly pulled into a bun, she looked even more attractive than I remembered and I struggled to keep my focus on the task at hand.

'I … I couldn't leave things the way they were.'

'It's fine—'

'No, look,' I interrupted, determined to be upfront and honest with her. It was the least she deserved after what she'd been through. 'I didn't get the chance to say it before and I want to say it now. What you told me … about your husband, I can't imagine the courage it took and I wanted to say thank you for trusting me with it.'

She looked at me, as though slightly relieved.

'And I should have told you about Isabelle. Honestly, I don't know why I didn't.' I said this although, at that moment, it was crystal clear to me why I hadn't wanted her to know. My feelings grew stronger every time I saw her, but there was nothing either of us could do about it. She was vulnerable and I had made commitments. The end.

'I hope we can carry on our friendship,' I said, sounding like something out of a Jane Austen novel. Yet it was the best I could do and I really meant it. Her friendship meant more to me than I realised and if I couldn't have anything else, it would have to be enough.

'Are they doughnuts?'

'What?' Of all the things I had imagined she might say, that was not one of them.

She hunkered down on the rough ground with its patchy grass and weeds, crossed her legs and opened the box of doughnuts I'd bought, whilst taking a large gulp of coffee.

'Of course we can be friends, you big eejit!' she said between bites, sugar all over her lips.

I sat down beside her and leaned my back against the gable wall. I couldn't think of anywhere I'd rather be.

'I mean, besides Madame Bowden, you're the only friend I've made since coming here.'

'Oh, I see, so it's more a lack of options thing?' I said, taking the lid off my coffee and blowing on the liquid, which was already stone cold.

'Beggars can't be choosers.' She shrugged and all but concealed a malevolent grin.

Banter. A safe harbour. I got stuck into a custard doughnut, grateful that we were back on a firm footing. I didn't know why she had confided in me and I wasn't sure why I had told her about the darkest times in my life, but perhaps the trick was not to question it. Not to put a label on it, as clichéd as it sounded.

'Any luck with the manuscript?'

I made a mental note that whenever I showed up at Martha's window, I should bring sugar. Her mood was positively upbeat.

'Um, no, not really. A colleague found something about her brother, Lyndon. He was a soldier – a general or something – in the war. It's strange,' I said, tearing a chocolate doughnut into two halves and offering her one. 'You'd think a woman like her who'd been rubbing shoulders with Hemingway and contacting one of the top book dealers in America would leave some sort of trace, wouldn't you?'

She took her time to think about it and once she had satisfactorily munched the last of the doughnut and wiped her hands on her jeans, she looked me square in the eye.

'You think it's strange that a woman has been silenced? Forgotten about? Written out of history? Henry, what have they been teaching you?'

'Okay, all right, that sounded completely stupid, but you know what I mean.'

'Well, maybe your problem is that you keep looking at Opaline from a man's point of view. Hemingway, her brother, the other guy—'

'Rosenbach.'

'Yeah, Rosenbach. Why don't you find out more about Sylvia and the bookshop in Paris?'

Why hadn't I thought of that?

'You know, you really are quite good at this.'

'What?'

'Research. What was it you were thinking of studying?'

Her whole demeanour deflated, like those inflatable men outside car dealerships when the air runs out.

'Ugh, let's not talk about it.' She checked the time on her phone and said she had to get back to work. With one leg halfway in the open window, she stalled for a moment. 'Madame Bowden told me something … a bit strange. About the bookshop.'

I felt the hairs on my arms standing straight up.

'Actually, forget I said anything, you'll think it's ridiculous.'

'Now, see, all you've done there is create a more captive audience. Spit it out—' I wanted to use her surname, but then realised I still didn't know what it was.

'The thing is, Madame Bowden tends to embellish a lot of her stories, so I guess you have to take it with a pinch of salt or whatever …'

'Just tell me.'

She pulled her leg back out of the window and stood beside me once again.

'One of her friends, who was probably very drunk at the time, claims that she saw the bookshop. Not only saw it, but walked inside.'

I said nothing. I couldn't risk opening my mouth to speak.

'It was back in the sixties, so, you know … hallucinogenic drugs and stuff. But I figured you'd want to know. Anyway, I really have to go.'

With that, she slipped back inside and shut the window behind her. I stayed on the patch of ground where the bookshop should have been and walked slowly around in circles until my legs stopped feeling like jelly. I wanted to tell her, but just as she had said, it sounded ridiculous. My first night in Ireland, following a few too many G&Ts on the Ryanair flight, I took a taxi straight to Ha'penny Lane. I was fully expecting to find a bookshop, and that is exactly what I found. Even the taxi driver must have seen it. I think. I remember getting out of the car, handing him the money and walking up to the door. The lights were on inside and there was a golden glow from within, dispersed through the stained-glass windows. It was warm and comfortable inside, with that distinct bookshop smell of old musty covers and something spicy, like cinnamon. The walls were lined with shelves full of colourful book covers and I felt the tips of my fingers itching to touch them. But I wanted to speak to the owner first – show them the letter I had found and see if they could shed any light on its contents. I heard the bell ringing over the door and as I turned to see who had walked in behind me, I found myself outside on the pavement again. Just like that. I hadn't moved my feet and yet there I was.

I turned back to where the shop had been and found nothing but the darkness of night, as though it had swallowed the shop whole. For some reason I patted myself down, maybe to see if I was still there when the shop I was just standing in so clearly wasn't. I did that ridiculous thing where you turn around and around on the spot, like a dog chasing its tail, in case the thing you lost is right behind you. But how could anyone lose a bookshop? The only logical explanation was that I had been very, very drunk. That is what I kept telling myself. A drunken haze, and the shop was a mirage. But I had been drunk many times before that and never conjured up a building, let alone walked into one. Now I had a corroborator. Someone else had seen the shop.

The question now was: what had caused it to disappear and how could I get it back?

Chapter Nineteen

OPALINE

Dublin, 1922

My first few weeks at Mr Fitzpatrick's Nostalgia Shop were punctuated by a string of strange occurrences. It seemed the building itself did not exactly welcome me with open arms, but I was determined to prove myself a worthy custodian. I ventured up the spiral staircase that led to the attic, where he had kept the overflow from the shop. At the top was a tiny door that required me to bend a little and when I pushed against it, I found that the wood seemed to push back. I stood back in order to take something of a run at it and on the third go I burst through and fell flat on my face.

'I see,' I said aloud. 'Like that, is it?'

I got up and dusted myself down, trying not to take the idiosyncrasies of an old building personally. A tiny window with a circular pane, opaque with green lichen, was the only source of light. I found a Victrola gramophone and immediately set it aside to bring downstairs. At first glance, it looked like an old museum with glinting treasure peeking out from under dustsheets. There was a telescope in the far corner behind bits of old furniture and lots of boxes. On a shelf I spotted a pair of workman's trousers and looked down at my impractical skirt, covered in dust and worn in places. Decision made, I slipped it off and pulled on the tan-coloured trousers. They weren't a bad fit and I pulled the belt through the loops, securing it around my waist. Mr Fitzpatrick must have been a rather slender man, as well as being a conscientious one, as they were neat as a new pin. Slightly too long in the leg, though, so I turned up the hem once and then twice, until I could see the heel of my boot. Catching sight of myself in a cheval mirror, which was amusingly strung with feather boas, I smiled at my reflection.

'Hello, Miss Carlisle,' I said, turning from side to side. I ran my hands through my hair and held it back, giving myself an androgynous look. My blouse looked remarkably well, tucked into the trousers, and I only wished I had a cravat to finish off the look, like the Parisian author, Colette. Perhaps I could also be known purely by my Christian name and conceal my identity. Opaline, however, was not a very common name. 'Hello, Miss …' I spotted a book lying on the dusty floor. *The Picture of Dorian Gray*. 'Hello, Miss Gray.' Not bad.

Keen to investigate the rare book dealers in Dublin city and see what could be picked up, I set out and walked across the humpbacked Ha'penny Bridge, like the spine of a whale decorated with lamps, to visit Webb's bookshop on the quays. Sylvia had mentioned the name to me before I left, and the only way I could retain the information was to picture a spider's web. I took a moment to lean against the iron railing and looked up at the green domes of the cathedral and the Four Courts. My eyes followed the River Liffey as it flowed down towards The Custom House, which had only recently been burned out by the Irish Republican Army. Joyce had neglected to mention that the country was in the middle of a civil war when he suggested I escape here. From the frying pan into the fire, as they say.

Wearing a man's trousers and using a pseudonym, I felt like I was playing the part of an actress. Mr Hanna was one of those rare types who took absolutely no notice of my appearance and instead filled a box with some popular titles to 'keep me ticking over', as he put it. At the mere mention of James Joyce, it seemed my good reputation was sealed. I had a quick scan through his Dickens collection, just in case my father's copy of *David Copperfield* was among them. It had become a little habit of mine, a way of keeping him close to my heart. It was a rare edition, and I could tell with a glance that it wasn't there. *No matter,* I said to myself. *I will find it one day.*

Armed with my new books and a list of distributors I could call on, I arrived back at Ha'penny Lane with renewed purpose. I looked around the shop, at the rich green walls and the little Tiffany lamps shedding their colourful glow on all the treasures that had held their breath, waiting for the doors to reopen after Mr Fitzpatrick's death. It almost felt like Sleeping Beauty's room in the tower and I needed to find the spell to waken her. I had insisted on keeping all of Mr Fitzpatrick's stock, for the shop would have looked bare with only my small bookcase of titles to furnish it, yet I had no idea how these two ideas would merge. I first looked at the window display, which hadn't changed in all the time the shop had been closed. If I wanted to entice customers inside, I had to use my imagination. There was a carousel with a winding mechanism which played a jolly fairground tune while the horses elegantly turned around and around. A string of pearls and other costume jewellery were draped artfully over a coffret, and overhead, various multi-coloured hot-air balloons with baskets were strung from the ceiling. That was when inspiration struck.

I opened the box of books from Mr Hanna and found just what

I was looking for: the Oz books by L. Frank Baum. They were utterly magical and would fit perfectly with the hot-air balloons. I would use Mr Fitzpatrick's curiosities to create a visual storyline for the books. I was so pleased with myself that I hardly noticed the hours passing by, as I played what felt like a parlour game of matching books with their props. I had received several Beatrix Potter books, which were always so popular with children, and magically found two little velvet rabbits with bows at their necks. The window now had the enticing look of a treasure chest – albeit slightly skewed towards a younger clientele. No matter, I thought. They were the true pioneers of every family and would lead their parents through any street or thicket to chase their hearts' desires. In any case, I set up a little trestle table outside with some cheap second-hand books, which could always tempt the passer-by.

It was just missing one thing: a sign. I searched for a piece of card, which of course I found in the stationery section, a rich cream vellum, and spied a beautiful calligraphy pen held on a piece of marble. That was when I realised that I had no desk. I found the perfect specimen – a rich walnut console table, which was currently displaying an alarmingly large collection of ceramic frogs in all shapes, sizes and poses. That was the amusing thing about collecting: you never knew what would hold value, nor to whom. Were we all preconditioned to love certain things? A moment in childhood, lost to memory but indelibly marked on our souls? To me, the promise of finding what I did not know I was looking for was the lure of the game.

I dragged the desk over to the corner by the window, so I had good light and a full view of the shop. I found a sturdy carver chair, also in dark wood and upholstered with a deep red and gold brocade. Rather unconsciously, I found myself modelling my surroundings on those of Shakespeare and Company. The memory made my heart lurch and I wished I could speak to Sylvia, ask her advice. But I knew what she would say, to trust my gut. And my gut was telling me that it was all well and good dreaming of printing my first catalogue of rare books, but I had to get some customers first. Let people know I was open for business.

And so I sat at my desk for the first time, placed the card in front of me and, with the pen suspended in mid-air, realised I hadn't even come up with a name for the shop.

'Gray Books?' I said aloud to no one but myself. It sounded terribly dull. 'Please, step inside and buy some grey books!' I chattered to myself, realising that my new pseudonym wouldn't do at all. I tried to think of my favourite book titles.

'Wuthering Books?' Again, such dreary names would never attract customers. I immediately thought of Emily Brontë's pseudonym – Ellis Bell. Bell Books? Or Belle Books, to add a little French flair?

'Perfect!' I said, congratulating myself, and in my best handwriting wrote the new name and 'Rare and Used Books for Sale' in smaller writing underneath. I put it in the window and nodded my head with satisfaction. No matter what came, I had my books, and in the quiet morning air, I could hear their breathing, patient and steady. Like the resonance of a piano note held in the air long after it's been played.

~

I jumped when the bell above the door rang shrilly and turned to see my first customer.

'I've come to buy a book, if that's all right.'

It was Matthew. I blushed momentarily at the memory of my outburst and how he had held me in his arms. I hadn't seen him since, despite the fact that he lived next door.

'Well, you've certainly come to the right place!' I said, a little redundantly. He moved about the shop, noting the changes I had made with a nod of his head. He was a tall man with piercing blue eyes and blonde hair that seemed to curl at the ends. He held the brim of his hat between his fingers, as though he were afraid to leave it down. That if he did, he might wish to stay.

'What books do you generally like to read?' I asked, busying myself with rearranging some stationery.

'Oh, non-fiction generally,' he said, turning briefly to face me before noticing my attire. 'Are … are they my father's work trousers?'

I blushed. I didn't think he'd notice. Not the fact that I was wearing trousers (everyone who came into the shop noticed that) but that they didn't belong to me.

'I found them in the attic. I hope you don't mind.'

'Not at all,' he said, failing to hide a bemused look.

'I have some new non-fiction over here if you'd like …' I began, changing the subject.

'Oh, it's not for me, it's for my son. Ollie.'

I had to prise information from him; not because he was unwilling to give it, but because he seemed to think I wouldn't be interested. Was I interested? I felt as though I should be. Women were supposed to be interested in children, after all. Yet it struck me that being a woman was akin to a performance, with its cues and lines that had to be learned. I knew how I was supposed to act and what I was supposed to say, I just wasn't exactly sure if I wanted to.

'He has a vivid imagination,' he said, keeping his sentences short yet heavy with implication.

'You say that as though it's a bad thing, Mr Fitzpatrick.'

'Matthew, please.'

'Has he read any of the Oz books?'

I went to the window and took the first in the series down from the shelf.

'What are they about?'

'Well, they're about a great wizard who lives in an emerald city—'

'I don't think so, Miss ...'

'Opaline, please.'

'Opaline. His mother wishes him to follow the family business.'

I panicked for a moment, thinking I would become unemployed and homeless yet again.

'*Her* father's business. Banking.'

'Ah,' I said, looking around the shop for anything that would suit a young banker. Nothing. The silence made me feel uncomfortable until the cuckoo clock announced the hour and made us both jump.

'Would you like some tea?' I wasn't sure why I said it. Possibly because I was certain he would refuse, but he surprised us both by saying yes. I went downstairs and put some things on a tray.

'So, is it going well?' he called down the stairs.

I wasn't sure if he was concerned about the business or my ability to pay the rent.

'Well enough,' I called back.

'I see you've managed to incorporate my father's antiques with your books. Very clever.'

I peeped out from the door and saw him standing by the maritime section I had created, with *Moby-Dick* and *Robinson Crusoe* floating on a blue muslin sea with mermaids and boats sailing in impossibly tiny bottles. I even had a copy of *Peter Pan* there, with a toy crocodile snapping at the corners.

'This is truly fantastic,' he said, finally coming to life. 'The shop seems ... bigger somehow.'

I went back to the kitchen and turned on the tap, but no water was forthcoming. The pipes gurgled and belched like someone with bad indigestion. I let it run until it spluttered and clanged and then was silent. I stood back and put my hands on my hips. It didn't make any sense, just like the attic door or the copy of *Dracula* falling from the shelf. I climbed the stairs, the kettle still in my hand.

'Are you wearing your landlord hat today?' I asked, holding up the kettle. 'I'm afraid I might need a plumber.'

'I'll have a look,' he said, in the way that men do, assuming the problem is something straightforward enough for them to fix. Before I knew it, he had his jacket off and was down on the floor, wrangling with pipes under the sink. I didn't even know there was a spanner and it seemed highly unlikely that he would carry one around with him. I almost asked him if he was quite sure what he was doing, but instead asked if he knew what the problem was.

'Probably a blockage of some sort,' he said, his voice straining. 'I'll have it fixed in no time. I'll just switch off the—'

Before he finished his sentence, the tap flew off the top of the pipe and water began gushing like a geyser. I ran to it and shoved an old rag into the hole where the tap used to be, stemming the tide until he managed to turn off the mains.

'Perhaps I should have called the plumber,' he gasped, getting up from the floor and brushing his wet hair from his forehead.

We looked at each other and realised we were both soaking wet. I could feel a giggle slowly erupting from my ribcage but tried to suppress it … until I saw him wringing water out of the ends of his shirt. He looked so ridiculous, my shoulders began to shake with laughter. He looked up at me then, his cross expression melting into a broad smile.

'Amusing you, am I?' he said, as I bent over with laughter.

'I-I'm sorry,' I said, turning my back to him so that I might stop. When I turned around he was taking the wet shirt off and wringing it properly into the sink. He had a vest underneath, which was also wet through.

'Might I hang this in front of the stove for a while?'

'Of course,' I said, and quickly added more wood to the fire. I hung his shirt on the back of the chair and moved it closer to the heat. He could have simply returned home, he only lived next door, but there was a silent understanding that the explanation that would have been required was too complicated. My clothes were wet also, but I couldn't change while he was there, so I merely wrapped a shawl around my shoulders and stood beside him, watching the flames.

'I'll have someone come and fix it first thing tomorrow.'

His tone of voice had changed again. I knew I wasn't imagining it, this closeness that he would temporarily allow, an intimacy, before pulling up the drawbridge again. I had to snap myself out of this silly attraction. It was some jumble of homesickness and loneliness – a misplaced focus for all of my mixed-up feelings. He was kind to me at a time when I needed comfort, but I knew this was dangerous and had to stop.

'Thank you, Mr Fitzpatrick.'

A moment passed and as though he had heard some distant noise calling him, he grabbed his still damp shirt and put it on. I responded and jumped to action, picking up his jacket from the floor and handing it to him. Our fingertips brushed as he took it from my hands. I did not look him in the eye but kept my head level with the hollow where his neck met his chest. I did not think about touching him but found my hand was already on his chest, above his heart. The rise and fall of his breathing grew heavier and in one movement, he pulled me close to him and our lips collided – clumsily at first, then passionately, desperately. His mouth was soft and yet eager. The sudden realisation of how he felt about me set fireworks off behind my eyelids. Knowing that it shouldn't, couldn't ever happen again, neither of us wanted it to end. I don't know how long we stood like that, buried in our embrace. We did not speak. Occasionally his hands would caress the back of my neck, but for the most part, he simply held me, enveloping me closer and tighter. I didn't want to move. Or think. Or wonder what it meant. The intimacy was all I craved. And then, it was over. I wasn't sure how or who had pulled away, but we were no longer touching. He thrust his arms into his jacket and buttoned it up. His eyes met mine briefly and the look was one of fear.

'I'm sorry.'

I tried to respond but found I had no words. My mouth formed the word 'I', but no sound came forth. Then he was gone, the bell ringing with his departure. I sat at my little table, shivering. What was I doing? Matthew was a married man with children. I could not, would not, be that other woman. But there was something between us and I wasn't sure how we could carry on suppressing it.

When I was in Paris, I had known Armand would break my heart, but Matthew – he would break my resolve, which was much, much worse.

~

The solution came with the postman the following morning. A letter with a return address printed on a gold label on the back of the envelope filled me with excitement – Honresfield Library. I had written requesting access to their vast collection of papers, manuscripts and letters, specifically those pertaining to the Brontë sisters. The owners, Alfred and William Law, were two self-made industrialist brothers, who grew up near the Brontë family home and had acquired some of their manuscripts from a literary dealer. I was taking my first tentative steps as a literary sleuth – thanks to Sylvia igniting the passion for a second Emily Brontë novel at Shakespeare and Company. There was just one problem: I would have to return to England to investigate further.

It was a risk, but now it seemed even more of a risk to stay. I had to put some distance between myself and Matthew. Besides, did I want to pour all of my energy into another doomed liaison, or concentrate on my work? I nodded in the affirmative. *My work.* That was where my true passion was to be found. I considered the logistics; The Honresfield Library was in Rochdale, near the Laws' factory. That was over two hundred miles away from London, so I was unlikely to run into anyone I knew. I thought of Emily's poem 'No Coward Soul Is Mine' and, without realising it, had already made up my mind to go.

I finally felt as though I were leaving Opaline Carlisle, the girl, behind. Miss Gray would become the woman I always wanted to be. As I glanced out into the street, I noticed that the stained-glass patterns had shifted and were now the shape of a vast and rolling moorland with a path leading up to a grand farmhouse.

'*Wuthering Heights*,' I whispered to myself.

Chapter Twenty

MARTHA

I began to read the book at night. There was something sacred about those quiet, dark hours that made it feel special. I lit some candles (despite Madame Bowden's repeated warnings against it) and arranged some cushions on the floor. It felt a bit like a seance at times because the strange noises in the walls wouldn't stop until I settled down to read. The branches spreading across the wall were now freeing themselves from the plaster and I half expected to find leaves growing. Instead, a new book appeared. *Normal People* by Sally Rooney, the book I had seen at the library.

It was Madame Bowden. I didn't know how she was doing it, but with her theatrical background, anything was possible. It was quite sweet actually, her quirky ways of encouraging me to read. If only she knew that I was carrying someone else's story on my skin. Another line had come to me that morning while I was polishing the floors. I knew my mind wouldn't rest until it was inked on my skin permanently. I had no idea what the story meant, how long it would be or whose words they were but the biggest mystery was why they were being told to me. I could never tell anyone; hearing voices was definitely still frowned upon, as far as I knew. But that was just it, I wasn't hearing a voice as such, the words just showed up.

A Place Called Lost was a much simpler story to understand and it seemed to be written for children, which suited me fine. At least in children's books nothing terrible happened, and if it did, it always got fixed by the end. It told the story of an old library in a remote Italian village. It was so remote, in fact, that it was said only people who wandered off the beaten track and became hopelessly lost could find it. A charming wooden building, it held ancient volumes stacked from the floor to the ceiling, arranged without apparent order. The guardian of the library was so old that no one could remember a time when he had not been there.

Yet one day, as he locked the outer gate at the end of the day, a violent storm blew up out of nowhere and the poor old man was hit by lightning. However, that was not the end of the story. Still wayward travellers would stumble across the faraway library and, despite the guardian's absence, would find themselves drawn to a certain book and, upon reading it, find the course of their lives completely changed. It was as though the library itself, the very fabric of its being, could intuit which book would help a lost soul to find their true path. But the locals feared what they did not understand and wanted the library destroyed. They believed that the building was haunted and that spirits were trapped within the pages of the books, waiting for a reader to set them free. And so it was that the books were taken out and dispersed across the land; but before the building was knocked down, a young man on his honeymoon arrived with a proposal. He would take the wood to build his own shop. In Ireland.

I knew this story was no mere coincidence. In fact, sometimes when I slowly read the enchanting lines on each page I felt as though my entire life was an elaborate plot line that would now somehow make sense, in this context, in this place and with these people. Person. Henry. I could already feel my ability to read him fading and I knew what that meant. My judgement was becoming clouded with that one emotion I could no longer afford to have. Love.

Before I blew out the candle, I read a line that made up my mind. In the story, there was a young woman who came to the library, miles away from her true home. She read a story about a girl who had come to a fork in the road and was so afraid of making the wrong decision that she stayed where she was, huddled in the hollow of a tree. After several days, an old woman came along and told her a riddle. She asked, 'What is something you create, even if you do nothing?' The answer was a choice. Choosing not to do something was still a choice.

I was choosing not to register for college because I was too scared. What I hadn't realised was that I was actively choosing to stay stuck where I was, which scared me even more.

~

The following morning I rang the admissions office and arranged an interview for the very next day. I felt empowered, strong, terrified and excited. There was no going back now, I assured myself, and hardly thought anything of it when the doorbell rang after I'd served Madame Bowden her breakfast. I opened the door with a spontaneous smile on my face, which fell the moment I saw him standing there.

It was too late to run. Besides, he had that look about him. The remorseful one, where he would promise me a brand-new start. I spotted the crumpled bouquet of flowers in his hand – even they looked brittle and half-hearted. I knew the routine; we had been through it so many times before. I felt my body becoming heavier as I came closer to him, the weight of being around him already crushing me.

'Howareya,' he said, bashfully, head lowered. All innocence.

'What are you doing here, Shane?'

He opened his mouth to speak, but then an overriding thought came to me. 'How did you find me?'

'A mate of mine was up for the day, shopping with the missus. He spotted you.'

'Where?'

'On Grafton Street.'

'So—' I was trying to calculate it in my head. 'How did he know I lived here? Did–did he follow me? Was it Mitch?' I didn't even have to ask. I knew it was Mitch. He was Shane's best friend and would have thought nothing of spying on me.

'Look,' he said, taking a step closer, which caused me to step back. He seemed visibly upset by this, as though my fear of him was an overreaction on my part entirely. 'Martha, does it matter how I found you?'

'It does actually. Do you think it's normal to have your goons following me around?'

'Mitch isn't a goon. Jesus.'

A couple walked past and gave us a wary glance.

'Can we go inside?' he asked. 'I just want to talk.'

I didn't answer. I wanted to say, *No, go away, leave and never come back, forget about me, pretend I never existed,* but nothing came out. I just turned away, looking at the street.

'Your mother hasn't been well.'

My head spun around to look at him.

'That's why I came. She wants you to come home.'

'What's wrong with her? Is it serious?'

'Serious enough, she's in hospital.'

'Jesus Christ.' My hand flew to my chest. It was as though all of the oxygen had left my body. I felt woozy, like nothing was real any more. Not the buildings or the street or my flimsy life here in Dublin. He took my arm and I no longer flinched. It was Shane. He knew me and I knew him. Regardless of what had happened between us, he was here to help me. I looked in his eyes and I could see the sadness that was there when his father died. He knew how I felt. He wanted to help.

'Okay, come in,' I said. I walked down the hall towards the stairs leading to the basement, but when I turned around, he wasn't following. 'I live in the flat down here,' I said, pointing to the stairs.

'Jeez, it's a nice place, isn't it?' he said, putting the flowers down on the console table and wandering into the front room.

'You can't go in there.'

He stepped out of my eyeline. After a few moments I followed him in. Madame Bowden was out, so I figured there wasn't any harm.

'Was it an accident, or is she sick?' I asked.

'What? Oh, it's cancer.'

My legs went weak and I sank back on the sofa. I couldn't believe it. It felt like a waking nightmare.

'Why didn't she tell me?' I didn't expect him to answer; I was simply trying to make sense of it.

'How could she? None of us knew where you were. You didn't even leave a note, Martha. I was so worried about you.'

'Were you?' I knew I shouldn't have said it. I could read his face like the weather and that comment made him angry. A flash of him beating me with the head of a mop came unbidden. My arms wrapped around my ribs instinctively. He turned his back on me and he walked slowly around the room.

'You've done all right for yourself though. I can see why you might have forgotten your family.'

'It's not like that.'

This was so twisted. I felt myself needing to prove that I still loved him, just to keep things civil. But I didn't love him. I fucking hated him. I stood up and walked towards the door that led to the hall.

'Where are you going?'

'I'd better pack a few things. What hospital is she in?'

'The Regional.'

He had delayed just a beat, but enough to raise some doubts.

'Who are you?' I heard Madame Bowden's imperious voice from behind us. She was standing in the doorway that led back to the parlour. I hadn't heard her come in and I had to fight the urge to hug her for her impeccable timing. She held her walking stick more like a weapon waiting to be wielded than a support.

'Another *friend* of yours?'

Oh God, don't say it like that.

'Th-this is my husband, Madame Bowden.' I was shivering all over. I didn't think anything bad would happen while she was there, but I couldn't be sure.

'Husband? Good grief, you kept that quiet!'

I wished she would shut up. She was making everything worse. I was immobilised. The past and the present were colliding in the front room and no one seemed to understand how terrifying that was. They continued to exchange barbed pleasantries and I just stood there, my mind racing to nowhere. I found myself wishing that Henry was here.

'Well, we'd best be off,' Shane said, walking towards me and taking me by the arm. I remembered this. How it looked normal because no one could see him digging his fingers into my skin.

'Oh, where are you off to? Somewhere nice? Bewleys do a lovely lunch menu—'

'Back to Sligo. Martha's mother is in the hospital, so I'm taking her home.'

Madame Bowden looked genuinely sad, although I couldn't tell if it was sympathy for me, or for the fact that she would have to make her own breakfast. She was unpredictable in her moods at the best of times – kind and gentle one minute, cold and uncaring the next. I couldn't rely on her to get me out of this.

'Well, I'm sorry to hear that,' she said, her eyes lowering to where his hand grasped my arm.

'I have to pack some things first,' I croaked, my voice breaking.

'There's no time for that now, we have to beat the traffic.'

'I said I'm sorry to hear that because Martha can't possibly leave today. No, I'm afraid I have a very important supper this evening and I cannot do without her. I'm quite sure she can make her own way there in the morning. We have a very reliable public transport system,' she added, enjoying how he visibly squirmed at her interference.

'Her mother is seriously ill, I think that's more important than your supper or whatever.'

I looked from one to the other. I didn't know what to do.

'I would like to hear Martha's opinion on the matter, if you don't mind.'

She was giving me breathing space and I had to grasp it, at least until I could find out for myself what was going on.

'Um, I'd better stay here for tonight anyway,' I said, despising the pleading tone in my voice. Five minutes with Shane and I was already back to the frightened girl hiding in a wardrobe. I hated him for making me this way, but I hated myself too. Why couldn't I be stronger?

He shook his head and widened his eyes in disbelief. 'Nice to see where your priorities lie.'

'It is my job, Shane. I'll call home tonight and be on the first bus down in the morning.'

'There, you have your answer,' Madame Bowden said, stepping in front of me.

'Don't call the house, there's no one home, obviously.' It seemed as though he was giving up. What else could he do with her there? He took one last look around the place, then filled his mouth with saliva and spat on the floor before walking out and slamming the front door. My lungs exhaled and I realised I'd been holding my breath for who knows how long. The relief of his absence was spoiled only by the embarrassment I felt in front of my employer.

'I'll clean that,' I said, reaching into my apron pocket for a cloth and walking away quickly so I could hide my tears.

'Martha Winter, you'll do no such thing!' she commanded. 'I think it's time you told me what exactly is going on.'

Chapter Twenty-One

HENRY

'I'm following a new lead.'

The sigh on the other end of the line was not open to interpretation.

'I'm just wondering, is all of this really worth it?' said Isabelle.

I gave my own version of the frustrated sigh. She had no idea. How could she? I'd been cryptic about my research for so long that she'd lost interest in asking.

'It's worth it to me.'

'Fine. Well, I suppose there's no point in me saying that I miss you, it hardly seems relevant to you.'

'Of course it's relevant, I really miss you too, Issy.' And there it was. My first lie. Or rather, the first lie that I was blindingly aware of, like staring into the sun and seeing the worst part of yourself eclipsed. I didn't want to be the kind of person who simply told someone what they wanted to hear, but I didn't know what the truth was any more. Or maybe I did but I didn't know what to do about it. I was stalling. Did that make me a bad person?

'Your mother called.'

'What? My mother called you?'

'Yes, Henry. She is going to be my future mother-in-law. If we ever get married, that is.'

I gulped.

'She said your father's checked himself into rehab.'

I'm not sure how many seconds passed by.

'Henry? Are you there?'

I cleared my throat. It felt thick with something I was determined to suppress.

'Yep, I'm still here.'

'Well, aren't you going to say anything?'

This was typical of my mother – using someone else to deliver the news she should have told me herself. I hated her and pitied her at the same time. She was always hiding behind someone or something. Perhaps she was ashamed of the whole thing. I know I was.

'What is there to say? Am I supposed to be impressed? He'll sober up for a fortnight, maybe three weeks at a stretch, then just when we're starting to believe that he's changed, he won't come home one night and that'll be the last we hear of him for another few years. It's always the same.'

'Oh, okay. I'm sorry.'

I made a fist of my hand and smacked my forehead. What was I thinking, saying this stuff to her?

'No, I'm sorry. You shouldn't be caught in the middle of this. I'll have a word with Mum. And I'll be home soon. I promise.'

I spent twenty minutes trying to schmooze the archivist at Princeton University on the phone. (My definition of schmoozing was leaning heavily on my British accent and hoping that made me sound important.) As it turned out, my schmoozing skills were either rusty from lack of use or highly overestimated. By me.

'Sir, you are welcome to visit the reading rooms here. Simply make an appointment—'

'Yes, I understand that, it's just not fiscally feasible to make that kind of journey at the moment,' I said for the third time. As much as I would have loved a trip to New York, I could hardly afford the bed and breakfast as it was. 'Is there any chance you could, you know, have a little look through Sylvia Beach's letters for any correspondence with an Opaline Carlisle?'

'So you want me to drop everything I'm doing and do your research for you, is that correct, Mr Field?'

'Now when you say it like that—'

'As I said, you can submit an online request – like everybody else – to consult the special collections.'

'Yes, but time is of the essence.'

'It is, Mr Field. *My* time is of the essence, and I have spent as much as I am willing to on this phone call. Goodbye.'

I stared at my phone. 'I think that went rather well,' I told myself and grabbed my wallet off the bed.

When I got to the front gate of the university, I saw her.

'Fancy meeting you here!' I said and wished I'd thought of anything more original to say. Thankfully she didn't notice. Her face looked paler than usual and her eyes were bloodshot. Had she been crying?

'Is everything okay?'

'Um, yeah. Fine.'

People were bumping into us as she stood motionless before the entrance.

'Are you going in?'

Her eyes darted about nervously, then she shook her head. 'I don't know what I'm doing, to be honest.'

'Well, let's just step out of the way,' I suggested, hooking my arm through hers and guiding her to a quiet corner inside the quadrangle.

'I don't know what I'm doing here. I think I've changed my mind,' she said, looking around with wide eyes, like a trapped animal.

'Can I help at all?'

It was clear that she wasn't even listening to me. Her mind was elsewhere.

'I thought my mother was ill. I can't speak to her on the phone and my father won't answer my calls, not since—' She broke off.

Not since she left her abusive husband? What kind of family would do that?

'I texted my brother. He said she was fine. Must've been a misunderstanding.'

'That's good news.'

I couldn't understand what was going on, but she was clearly upset about it.

'Fancy a walk? You'd be saving me from a boring afternoon in the library.'

This was a blatant lie. Libraries were anything but boring to me, but I knew it's what people said sometimes, and to my relief she nodded. I didn't really know where we were going, but sensed that it mattered little to her. As long as it was quiet. We wandered off the main thoroughfare and down the quieter streets with independent shops and honest cafés. I found the holy grail – a second-hand bookshop with a tea room upstairs called *Tomes & Tea.* I waited until she had a pot of tea and a scone with extra jam in front of her before I spoke again.

'We're friends, right?'

She nodded noncommittally, towering a spoon of light cream on top of her scone.

'And friends can tell each other stuff. No judgement.'

'Henry, I—'

'But they can also *not* tell each other stuff but still lean on the other person. If they want to. So what I'm saying, in the most ham-fisted manner ever recorded in history is, whether you want to tell me or not, that's up to you. But I'm here, either way.'

'Until you find your manuscript.'

'Yes, well ...' She could see right through me. I had nothing to offer her; even this olive branch of friendship was a flimsy substitute for how I really felt.

'If we're being honest, I can't understand why you would propose to someone and then immediately hop on a flight to another country searching for something that probably doesn't even exist.'

That was not the kind of honesty I had in mind.

'You're hardly in any position to lecture me on my love life,' I flung back, then immediately regretted it. 'I didn't mean—'

Her chair screeched on the floor as she got up. Her eyes were burning with hurt and maybe even hatred. I hated myself. What a stupid comment. I ran down the stairs behind her, quietly asking her to wait without wanting to attract attention. Walking through the bookshop, she happened to step into an anteroom by mistake and it was just us two, alone.

'Please, Martha, I'm so sorry. I wasn't thinking, it was a stupid throwaway comment.'

She was looking towards the ceiling, trying to stop the tears from falling.

'It doesn't matter, I shouldn't have said those things, I was being unkind.'

'You were right,' I said, stepping closer. 'I did run away from Isabelle. Not consciously, perhaps, but I found a way to not be there. I don't know,' I said, raking my hand through my hair. 'I thought it was what I wanted and then I just freaked out.'

The shelves of books around us muffled the outside world.

Wisps of blond hair fell about her face and her red cheeks glowed with the turmoil of emotion.

She bit her lip and leaned back against a bookshelf, considering her words. 'Love is scary.'

'Someone should write that book.'

She smiled and looked directly into my eyes as though trying to decide something. 'Are you in love?'

Such a simple question, but coming from her, in this context, I didn't know what the answer was. Did I know what love was supposed to feel like? Had I ever been in love? There was the initial attraction, then a kind of comfortableness followed by a sense of ... what? Unease. Like I knew all along that I had chosen the most sensible path and now resented every step I took upon it. As though I'd signed up for the wrong course in university and with each passing day was feeling more and more trapped. Looking over my shoulder for the life I should have had and never really being present in my own life.

She gave up waiting for an answer.

'I'm starting to think maybe love isn't supposed to be scary. Maybe I didn't love Shane at all. I thought I did, but that's the trap, isn't it? Fooling yourself into believing that it's your fault for not doing it right. But if I'd known it wasn't really love, I would have left sooner.'

She wasn't talking to me any more, although her words rang true for me. It sounded like a conversation she'd had many times with herself.

'I thought that's what love was – sticking by someone, no matter what. Waiting for the person I'd fallen in love with at the start to come back.'

I wanted to reach out to her, hold her, but I wasn't sure if it was the right thing to do.

'How could he hurt you?' I whispered, seeing the little girl inside of her that just wanted to be loved. Not beaten black and blue. She looked up at me with an expression that was completely unguarded. I didn't overthink this time and reached out to touch her cheek, brushing the tears away. She let her face be held and I could feel her melting into me. Before I knew it, she was in my arms, her head buried in the space between my shoulder and my chest. We didn't speak any more words. It felt as though the books were protecting us and I hoped the moment would go on forever, my fingers lost in tangles of her hair as I caressed the back of her neck.

'Christ,' I said eventually, unsure if I had spoken aloud or not, until she pulled back and looked up at me.

'What is it?'

I searched for words that wouldn't scare her off or make me sound like an idiot. 'I really like you. Like, a lot. And I don't know what to do about it.'

Her solemn expression slowly broke into a smile and then she laughed.

'Oh, thanks. Thanks for that,' I said sarcastically, still with my arms around her.

'I think I like you a lot too. And I don't know what to do about it either.'

That turned out to be untrue, because she did, in fact, know what to do about it. She slowly tilted her head upwards and, looking into my eyes all the while, moved her head closer to mine until our lips touched. To say that I saw fireworks would have been an exaggeration, but to say that I *felt* fireworks in my entire network of blood vessels would have been one hundred per cent accurate. I bent my head and kissed her as though it was the first time I had ever kissed anyone. It felt brand-new. We fit perfectly together. Her fingertips skated from my chest up along my jawline and then through my hair. I pulled her hips closer to mine and heard her sigh.

I stopped for a moment and spoke, my own voice hardly

recognisable as it had dropped to the husky octave of Barry White. 'Is this okay?'

She nodded and then her lips were back on mine. I don't know how long we stood there, it could have been twenty minutes or twenty seconds, before a customer came in and cleared his throat loudly. While silently vowing to murder him in his sleep, I found Martha's hand and curled mine around it.

'Do you want to come back to mine?'

'There's something I have to do first,' she said and she dragged me out of the shop, making a run for it.

'Where are we going?'

'Trinity. I have five minutes left to register for my course!'

Chapter Twenty-Two

OPALINE

England, 1922

My trip began as planned, with a visit to the Brontë Society. Merely to stand where the Brontë sisters had stood, to look out at the moors that inspired Emily's writing, was such a touching experience. The house itself stood like a fortress, its grey brick tempered by the large sash windows. I tried to imagine what it would have been like to live there, daughters of a fervently religious man, pressed up against the wilds of such an unyielding landscape. Young women, spinsters like myself, ignored by the world of men and literature, pouring their heart and passion into their writing and taking on the male pseudonyms of Currer, Ellis and Acton Bell. I stood there in Mr Fitzpatrick's trousers and a long overcoat, similarly at odds with the constraints of our gender. It was also a disguise, in case Lyndon had his spies out.

After Patrick Brontë's death, the entire contents of the house were either auctioned off or gifted to those who worked at Haworth. The Society was fortunate enough to have acquired much of these effects and their archives were quite impressive. I came across poems by Emily, annotated by elder sister Charlotte, immediately giving me the impression of a sibling power struggle, albeit a loving one. It was common knowledge that Charlotte was critical of her younger sister's masterpiece. In the preface to the 1850 edition of *Wuthering Heights*, where Emily's authorship was finally recognised, Charlotte wrote:

> *Whether it is right or advisable to create beings like Heathcliff, I do not know: I scarcely think it is.* Wuthering Heights *was hewn in a wild workshop, with simple tools, out of homely materials.*

Charlotte was the only one of the sisters to marry. She married Arthur Bell Nicholls, a curate who worked with her father and was not particularly liked in the village. I read that he inherited all of her belongings after her death, just nine months after their marriage. Perhaps marriage didn't suit her after all. He later moved back to his native Ireland and married his cousin. The Honresfield library acquired many of the manuscripts and effects in his possession, so that gave me a spark of hope that I might find some clue there on my visit the following day.

I decided to dine at the inn, which was only a short walk from my lodgings. I ordered a hearty shepherd's pie and sat by the window, drinking a small glass of gin as an aperitif. I spoke briefly to the landlord, who seemed well versed on all things Brontë. They were starting to make quite a bit of money out of visitors to the parsonage and saw it as their civic duty to fill tourists in on whatever the museum's curator left out. I sat there, reading Elizabeth Gaskell's biography of Charlotte Brontë. Unfortunately all that was known about Emily could scarcely fill a page. There was, however, mention of a Martha Brown – the maid who worked at the parsonage. As the landlord's son cleared my dish and wiped down the table, I ordered another drink and asked if he knew anything about her family, being from the area.

'Oh aye, the sexton's daughter. She never married,' he said, in a way that sounded so desperately forlorn.

I gulped a mouthful of gin. Why was marriage always seen as the key to happiness?

'So there was no family to look after her when she got sick.' He continued in his relentless character assassination of the unmarried woman. 'I think she died alone in a small cottage.'

I took another gulp of gin. My future suddenly looked quite grim.

'It says here in my book that she inherited quite a bit of the Brontë family memorabilia. I wonder if she had any other relatives she might have passed it on to?'

'My uncle John went to school with one of her nephews, as it happens.'

I clapped my hands. It felt like I was on a trail.

'Can I speak with him, your uncle?'

'He died this past year.'

'Oh, I am very sorry to hear that,' I said, keeping my hands clasped as though in prayer for his soul.

'I do remember him saying that the two brothers had a bookshop down in London. One of them still lives there. Maybe you could enquire there?'

'Oh, wonderful, do you have the name?'

He looked heavenward for inspiration.

'Brown's bookshop?'

'Quite,' I said, handing him some coins for my meal before walking back to my accommodation.

~

My appointment was at 9 a.m. to study the collection at Honresfield. Mr Law was away on business, so his assistant, a very diligent young woman by the name of Miss Pritchett, welcomed me. While the estate was vast and his wealth evident, the house retained a practical atmosphere. One wing was entirely devoted to their remarkable collection of British literature, with manuscripts by Robert Burns, Sir Walter Scott and Jane Austen.

'Your letter stated that you have an interest in the Brontë collection?' Miss Pritchett said, opening the large wooden doors to a smaller anteroom. 'I believe you'll find everything you need here,' she said, handing me a catalogue of the library and a pair of soft white gloves. 'Mr Law asks that every visitor wear these. We must preserve the integrity of the paper.'

'Of course,' I agreed, my eyes darting round the walls of shelves containing all sorts of riches, waiting to be discovered. First editions of *Pride and Prejudice* and *Northanger Abbey*, no doubt with a fascinating provenance, yet I had to pull my focus to the task at hand. With great care, I eased a first edition of *Wuthering Heights* from the shelf. I brought it to the table, which had a kind of easel to rest the book on. In its original cloth cover, it was in pristine condition. On the first page, I was intrigued to discover that it was inscribed by the Rev. Patrick Brontë to none other than Martha Brown, the family housekeeper and arguably a much-valued member of the household. My senses were fizzing with connections – what else might she have been bequeathed and where might it have ended up, if not sold at auction?

There were many boxes containing entertaining yet inconsequential letters between the sisters and Ellen Nussey, along with more interesting correspondence between Charlotte and her erstwhile biographer Elizabeth Gaskell. Then things became more interesting. I found a letter from Charlotte to her own publishers, complaining about Thomas Cautley Newby, the man who published *Wuthering Heights* and *Agnes Grey*. He was a bit of a scoundrel by all accounts, demanding the sisters pay £50 upfront and capitalising on the confusion surrounding the Bell name. The theory at the time was that all three books were authored by one man. Of course, it could not have been further from the truth, as Charlotte and Anne travelled to London to confirm: *We are three sisters*. Yet Emily remained at home and seemed to prefer the anonymity of a nom de plume. Unlike her sisters, she did not seek recognition from the London literary set, nor did she seem perturbed by Cautley's greedy character. Perhaps she understood that he was true to his nature, as she was to hers.

I noticed a letter without any address and scanned it rather quickly, as my stomach rumbled, yearning for food. The words caused time itself to stop.

London,

15 February 1848

Dear Sir,

I am much obliged by your kind note and shall have great pleasure in making arrangements for your next novel. I would not hurry its completion, for I think you are quite right not to let it go before the world until well satisfied with it, for much depends on your new work: if it be an improvement on your first you will have established yourself as a first-rate novelist, but if it falls short the Critics will be too apt to say that you have expended your talent in your first novel. I shall, therefore, have pleasure in accepting it upon the understanding that its completion be at your own time.

Believe me,
My dear Sir
Yrs sincerely
T C Newby

I sat there, blinking at the words in front of me. *Your next novel.* Here it was, irrefutable proof that Emily, or Ellis Bell, had begun working on a second manuscript. There was no record of the 'kind note' she had sent, but there was evidently some hesitation on her part in rushing its publication. Perhaps she was already unwell and felt herself unequal to the task? Or was it more likely that, being a perfectionist, she wished to take more time to complete it? My head buzzed with excitement.

I looked at the entry in the catalogue for further explanation.

Letter from T.C. Newby found in Emily's writing desk with an accompanying envelope addressed simply to Acton Bell.

But I knew it couldn't have been meant for Anne, for her second novel had already been submitted for publication. No, this was a correspondence with Emily regarding her follow-up to *Wuthering Heights*. I knew it! I sat back in my chair and looked out the long sash windows to the garden. If Charlotte had destroyed Emily's papers following her death, I would never find the manuscript. My hopes rose and fell with each contradictory argument.

Then I saw something I never would have predicted in a million years. Walking up the drive to the house was a man I was sure I would not see again. Armand Hassan.

~

'What on earth are you doing here?' I said, standing in the entrance hall and blocking Miss Pritchett's way.

'Opaline.'

He simply said my name and it all came flooding back. Paris, his apartment, the touch of his lips on my skin, the scent of his hair wax. It was intoxicating. He looked deeply into my eyes until I broke my gaze. I thought I had put my feelings for him far behind me, but seeing him again, I realised that I had merely hidden them. All of the longing and the hurt were still there, as strong as ever. He took my hand and kissed my wrist, then, still holding it, moved closer and kissed me on each cheek.

Miss Pritchett began to clear her throat behind me.

'Mr Hassan, is it?' she asked. 'I have the books you wished to view set up in the drawing room.'

I stood back and let them discuss their business. I couldn't help but watch him; he was dressed impeccably, as always, in cream linen trousers and a navy sports jacket. His skin was rich and darker now, thanks to his travels, no doubt. His hair shone like onyx and it was all I could do not to reach out and touch it.

'I'm here to view some illustrations for a client. However, I am attending an auction in Sotheby's tomorrow afternoon if that is of interest to you.'

'Sotheby's!' I repeated, failing to keep the excitement from my voice. I couldn't possibly go. It was too risky to go to London. My smile crumpled.

'No, I must return to Ireland.'

He looked at me as though he was searching for memories in my eyes. I looked away.

'You still wear my necklace, I see.'

My hand instinctively went to touch the golden hamsa pendant he had given me on my departure from Paris. A brief smile came to my lips unbidden.

Of course, I should have refused him. But I told myself that I needed news of Paris and Sylvia. That he was one of the few friends I had left, that without his help I would probably be back in London now and trapped in an arranged marriage.

'Well, maybe it wouldn't hurt,' I said.

How wrong I was.

He held open the door of a gleaming black car. If I didn't know better, I would say that he had come into some money, but it was too vulgar to ask.

'My client,' he said, replying to my unspoken question. 'She is quite generous.'

She. I looked out of the window, concealing the prickle of jealousy that pierced me. It had been several months since our time together in Paris; how could I still feel this way?

'I am so very glad to see you, Opaline. Many times I have wondered about you.'

And yet he had never sent a letter.

'Are you still in Dublin?'

'Of course,' I replied, quite terse. Where else would I be? Did he expect me to have travelled the world, finding a lover in every port, like him? I sulked for much of the journey and wondered why I had bothered to go at all.

We pulled up on a busy and grimy street full of eighteenth-century houses and shops, with trams trundling past at one end and the buses of High Holborn at the other.

'I thought we were going to Sotheby's,' I said, looking around and pulling my cap down to hide my face. I had decided to dress head to toe in men's clothing, with my giant overcoat concealing my form.

'Just a quick stop, I think you'll enjoy it.'

'Are you always so enigmatic?' I asked, as if I wasn't charmed by it. He knew how to reel people in. Women, more specifically.

We stood in front of a tiny bookshop, with the usual dusty barrows of unsellable stock outside. Next door to a junkshop, it had an old-style window divided into tiny square panes. There I spotted a sign:

THESE ARE THE ONLY DIRTY BOOKS WE HAVE.
PLEASE DO NOT WASTE TIME ASKING FOR OTHERS.

'What in heaven's—'

I looked up and saw the name printed above the door: The Progressive Bookshop, 68 Red Lion Street.

'Shall we?' Armand held the door open for me.

I wasn't sure what kind of den of iniquity we were entering, but I had a wonderful sense that we were going to find something out of the ordinary.

A nervous-looking fellow of similar vintage to ourselves was kneeling on the floor with his head halfway inside a cardboard box, quietly muttering expletives as he searched for something within.

'I understand you are distributing works that breach the British obscenity law,' Armand said in what was quite a passable London accent.

The man jumped up and propelled his wiry frame towards us with such haste that I took a step backwards (which was quite a feat in itself, as the shop left little room to manoeuvre).

'Armand Hassan, you bastard!' he cried, which caused Armand to smile broadly and then both men hugged like long-lost brothers reunited.

'I knew it was you,' he said with a slight German accent, laughing.

'Herr Lahr, may I present my colleague, Mademoiselle Opaline—'

'Gray,' I interrupted. 'Miss Gray,' and I proffered my hand.

'*Freut mich*,' he said, which I interpreted as a good thing.

He offered to make us some coffee, but Armand declined, saying that we didn't have much time before the auction.

'I have your copy here. Price as agreed – I must cover myself for any legal repercussions, you understand.'

'Of course,' said Armand. 'My client is very eager to have it.'

My curiosity was almost a fourth presence in the room! When he handed over the small rectangle wrapped in brown paper and Armand began to count out the notes, I asked if I might open it.

'Why not?' Armand replied.

I unwrapped it slowly, tantalisingly, and saw the title, *Lady Chatterley's Lover*.

'D.H. Lawrence,' Armand confirmed.

'The man is a literary genius and yet we must sell his books illegally like this,' Herr Lahr opined.

I wanted a copy very badly. I wanted twenty. Yet I was aware of how selling such controversial literature might bring unwelcome attention to my little shop. But I simply had to read it and so I negotiated a price with him for a copy of my own before we drove to Sotheby's carrying our prohibited literature on the back seat.

~

Through Sotheby's dark passages an excited throng tumbled into the large auction gallery, sweeping us both along with them. Armand took my hand and led me to a little alcove at the side of the room, where we stood pressed up against each other and the wall. For one heady moment, I inhaled his scent and again was transported back to that night and the heat of his body. I coughed several times and tried to count the number of people in the room to distract myself.

'Gosh, what a scene! I wonder what is up for auction.'

'You did not see the catalogue? It is the original manuscript of Lewis Carroll's *Alice in Wonderland*.'

'Good grief!'

Armand borrowed a leaflet from a man who was seated beside us and handed it to me.

'A Christmas Gift to a Dear Child in Memory of a Summer Day.' I had simply adored his book as a child and was surprised to learn

that Charles Dodgson (Lewis Carroll), a mathematician at Oxford, had lovingly penned and illustrated the little book in 1864 as a gift to the Liddell family. The story went that on a boat trip down the Thames, he first told his surreal story to the daughters of the dean, Henry Liddell. Eventually, he was persuaded to publish the work and the rest was history.

'This is fascinating!' I said, having completely forgotten my ardent thoughts of a moment earlier.

'There are rumours that the bidding could exceed ten thousand pounds.'

Barely noticed in the crowd was a small, elderly woman in a black dress. Armand pointed her out as Alice Liddell Hargreaves.

I turned to him and said, 'You don't mean … it couldn't be!'

He nodded, gratified by being the one in the know.

'She is the original "Alice". She held on to the manuscript all this time, but since the death of her husband, she has been drowning in tax bills.'

'Not Reginald Hargreaves, the cricketer?' They were a high-profile couple in London society. It must have pained her greatly to put the manuscript up for auction. She sat at the very front, her head erect and her pride intact.

The bidding began hesitantly, as it often does, while the buyers get the measure of each other. There's a certain amount of poker playing in the auction room and no one wished to show their hand too soon.

'Eight thousand, five hundred to the man in the alcove,' announced the auctioneer, as I felt Armand's hand go up.

'You never said you were bidding,' I whispered.

'On behalf of a client,' he said, always with that mysterious air. Another wealthy client; he seemed to collect them like snowdrops in springtime.

As the bidding rose higher and higher, attention focused on a short, well-dressed man with an unmistakable air of authority.

'Fifteen thousand pounds,' he announced, in a strong American accent, as though to bring this charade to a close.

'Who's that?' I asked.

'*Merde*! That, my dear Opaline, is the Terror of the Auction Room.'

The gavel came down with a decisive bang and the tense silence shattered into a cacophony of voices. Some in wonderment, most aghast that such a quintessential English work was now lost to an American. The man wiped his glasses, as some bidders went to congratulate him.

'He has outbid me at every auction this year,' Armand said, in a thorny tone that suggested begrudging admiration for the man. As we passed by him on our way out of the room, the two men nodded to each other.

'Mr Hassan, tell the baroness she will have to do better next time.'

Armand bristled at his gloating and attempted to bustle me out of the room.

'And who is your companion? Are you not going to introduce us?'

'Abe Rosenbach, may I present Mademoiselle—'

'Gray,' I interrupted him again. 'I am a book dealer from Ireland,' I said, loving how that sounded.

'Is that so? Here, let me give you my card,' he said, procuring one from his pocket. 'You never know when we might do business together.' He had a smile heavily laden with innuendo that I tried to ignore.

'Congratulations on your acquisition, Mr Rosenbach.'

'Thank you, Miss Gray, but this is not simply an acquisition. I have wanted this manuscript for a very long time. You see, it was the book my dear departed mother read to me when I lay ill in bed with chickenpox. I suppose, with my fever, I had a fancy that she was telling me a story about her childhood. I thought she *was*

Alice. She died shortly afterwards and I've read this book every night since.'

I was almost moved to tears by his story. Even Armand seemed affected.

'Hah! Don't be ridiculous,' Rosenbach bellowed. 'Never trust a book dealer who lets sentimentality get in the way. I had to own it because there is only one of it in the world – that's all there is to it. If I own it, then no one else can. I have known men to hazard their fortunes, go long journeys halfway about the world, forget friendships, even lie, cheat, and steal, all for the gain of a book.'

'Mr Rosenbach, you had me completely fooled!' I said, annoyed at having been lured in by his tale.

'Apologies my dear, I couldn't resist. After love, book collecting is the most exhilarating sport of all.'

'What a cad,' I whispered to Armand as we left the auction room, but he did not answer. They were made of the same stuff, Rosenbach and he. They felt no guilt, no remorse, and would do whatever it took to get what they wanted. It frightened and fascinated me in equal measure, like standing too close to a flame and hoping that I would not be consumed by its heat.

Chapter Twenty-Three

MARTHA

'What has you looking like the cat who got the cream?' Madame Bowden asked while I dressed her bed. It kept happening – I'd be in the middle of the most mundane task and I'd think about Henry kissing me and my cheeks would hurt from smiling so much.

'Just happy, I guess,' I replied.

'Nonsense. The only reason a woman blushes like that is a man. It's the scholar, isn't it?'

After the bookshop, he had taken me back to his B&B, but it turned out that it was the landlady's birthday and the house was full to bursting with a surprise party.

'Maybe.'

He walked me home after but I didn't invite him in. Things were still a bit new and I took the birthday party fiasco as a sign not to rush into anything. I did kiss him goodbye though. When I thought of that kiss, that's when my cheeks hurt the most because it was the most romantic kiss of my life. Under a streetlamp, his hands in the pocket of my coat, mine under his sweater, his lips slowly finding their way down my neck and to my collar bone. I'd never been kissed like that, with a tempting kind of tenderness, like he was telling me there was much more to come. That tickling sensation in my lower belly was threatening to unglue me completely. I had to focus on something mundane.

'Do you have anything for washing?' I asked, realising that she had been staring at me with a wicked grin on her face the entire time.

I gathered up the laundry and took it down to the utility room just off the kitchen. Separating the whites from the darks, my thoughts turned to my mother. In a house full of spoiled men, we always did the housework together. That's when I would practise my sign-language with her and my people-reading. But she didn't like me reading her too much. She said it wasn't right for a daughter to know too much about her mother's life. I never even asked why, but when I got older I tried to break that rule. Unlike everyone else I met, though, my mother was prepared for this kind of intrusion and kept herself guarded. There was something she was hiding from me, that was for sure. And so I began to hide things from her too. By the time I met Shane, our relationship had become distant and there was a different kind of silence between us. She told me I was making a mistake, that she didn't trust him, but by then it was too late. As if I was trying to prove a point, or punish her (or myself), I sleepwalked into my marriage like stepping out into oncoming traffic. And I had no one to blame but myself.

~

I was setting the fire in the living room when I thought I saw a movement at the window. I immediately thought it might be Henry and rushed, then slowed, to the front door. As I was opening it, I realised that Henry would never come to the front door, he always tapped on the basement window. The thought came too late. Before I had time to react I felt the hard blow against my cheekbone and it knocked me sideways against the wall. Shane. As I looked up, he threw a scrap of paper into the street before slamming the door shut behind him. I touched my face and felt the wetness, then saw the blood. His hard expression and clenched jaw told me everything I needed to know. He was in charge now.

'You must be losing your memory, Martha.'

'W-what?'

'Forgotten you're a married woman.'

'I don't—'

'I fucking saw you.'

'What are you talking about?'

'Last night. All over that guy like a slut. Is that how you repay me?'

Repay him? For what? I could smell the drink on him. There was no predicting what he'd do now. I began calculating the safest option; if I went with him now and took whatever punishment was coming my way, I could try and escape again. If I was still able. How was I back in this situation? He kicked my legs out of the way and walked into the hallway. Suddenly, I could see a future of this careful planning, weighing up the least dangerous ways of living a life with this man. My life was reduced to surviving Shane's violence.

'If Mitch hadn't been with me last night when I saw him kissing you, I would have murdered that guy with my own bare hands.'

'Henry? Please say you didn't hurt him!' I had visions of Shane attacking him on his way home last night.

'Henry? What the fuck sort of name is that?'

He grabbed my arm and tried to pull me up, but I stayed on the floor.

'You're my wife, Martha. You belong to me!'

'I belong to myself,' I said, tired of placating him. What did it matter anyway? Whatever I said, he would always be this angry person. I could see now that I wasn't the cause of it.

'I don't remember inviting you in,' came a voice from behind us. Oh Jesus, Madame Bowden. I wanted to die rather than have her see me like this. A victim.

'I told you already, her mother has cancer and wants her home.'

'You damn liar!' I found my voice again. 'How could you lie about something like that? And even if my mother was on her deathbed, I wouldn't go back there.'

He hesitated but only for a moment.

'I'm taking you home, now.'

'She's not a potted plant,' Madame Bowden said with a sarcasm that hardly fitted the situation. She would get both of us killed.

'I'm not going with you,' I said, scurrying backwards on the floor and shielding Madame Bowden. I didn't trust my legs to hold me upright.

Shane shook his head in disbelief.

'You ungrateful bitch ... I've given you everything.' He stepped towards me and began pulling me by my hair, but I grabbed on to the bannister of the stairs.

'Why are you doing this, Shane? Why do you want me back? We're not happy together – if we were you wouldn't hurt me like this,' I said, pointing to the blood on my face.

I'd never asked him before. Never had the courage. My voice sounded detached from my body. It must have worked, because he stopped for a moment, his hands still gripped around my wrists.

'You push me, Martha, you know you do.'

I was the scapegoat for everything that had gone wrong in his life. So he never had to face up to anything. Even now, he was blaming me, calling me everything under the sun. I turned my head towards Madame Bowden, but she was no longer behind me.

'You just keep pushing—'

And then something did push him. Something pushed him so hard that he broke through the wooden spindles of the bannister that led to the basement flat. The sound of wood breaking was like a volley of gunshots, followed by a sickening thump and crack.

'What happened?' I asked. The hallway was dark around and I had the sudden feeling that I was alone. The silence was terrifying. I couldn't move. My vision grew blurry.

'Is he dead?' My hand flew to cover my mouth once the words were spoken.

Finally, I heard the sound of her walking stick against the floorboards. She looked down into the stairwell for a long time, then turned around and asked me if I were all right. I felt as though I were in a dream. The noise of people outside told me that the world was still turning, but I felt like it had ended. I crept up behind her and looked over her shoulder. Down, down, down and there he was. Splayed on the floor with one of his legs trapped underneath him at an impossible angle. The bone was sticking out of his skin. I thought I would vomit and so kept my hand over my mouth. Letting my eyes reach his, it became clear that his head wasn't right either. Something was wrong, but I couldn't make sense of it.

'I want you to get your coat and go down to the shops for me.'

'W-what? What are you talking about?'

Madame Bowden looked unnervingly calm.

'I'll need a round roast for this evening and a nice bottle of that French Beaujolais I like.'

'Are you serious? Have you seen what's happened?'

I looked back down at Shane. It was strange to have our roles reversed like this, me standing over his injured body. I looked for some glimmer of recognition in his eyes – maybe he was still alive. But there was nothing. I began to shake all over.

'Martha,' she repeated, placing her hand on my shoulder. 'I want you to leave the house and do as I ask. All will be well on your return.'

~

I walked down the street unseeing. Outside, I could almost believe that it hadn't happened. I'd had some kind of episode and imagined the whole thing. I did exactly as she asked. I went to the butcher and asked for a round roast. I went to the off-licence and found the wine she liked. And yet all the while, the same words swam around in my head. *Had she pushed him*?

I walked up and down Ha'penny Lane a dozen times with the handles of my shopping bags digging into my fingers. How could I go back in there? And what did Madame Bowden mean by 'All will be well'? Was she calling a doctor or an ambulance? There was no sign of anything on the street. I could just leave, I thought to myself. I could just walk away now and never come back. But what about Henry? I had to get my phone and see if he was okay, and my phone was in the house.

I used my keys and let myself back in. The hallway was brighter now. The flowers in the vase were in full bloom and the broken stairway had been repaired. I left the shopping bags on the floor and forced myself to look over the edge. Shane was gone.

~

'I'm afraid your husband was pulled from the river last night.' A detective was standing in front of me, his small black notebook open, pen poised. 'His mother had declared him missing over a week ago. Did you have any contact with him during this time, Mrs Winter?'

'No.' I was no actress. I was still in a state of complete shock.

'Am I right in saying that you have been separated for some time?'

I nodded and bit my lips to stop them from trembling.

'I see.' He looked past me into the hallway. 'And can I ask you your whereabouts on the afternoon of Thursday last?'

'Yes, um, Thursday afternoon is when I do the shopping.'

'Anyone who may have seen you?'

'Of course, yes.' I gave him the names and addresses of every shop I'd gone to that day.

I caught sight of myself in the hall mirror. I'd put thick makeup on my cheek, but I didn't know how long it would hold.

'I have to call home, let them know what happened,' I said and he mercifully closed his notebook.

I shut the door firmly behind him and walked back into the living room to where she was waiting for me. I leaned against the doorframe and looked her squarely in the eye.

'What did you do?'

'I didn't *do* anything. I simply arranged to have the matter taken care of. And I suggest you take the accusatory tone out of your voice.'

'We've broken the law! I think.'

'Which law? The one that says you cannot take a violent man's dead body out of your basement and place it elsewhere? I've saved us both a lot of bother. It wouldn't hurt you to show some gratitude.'

'Is this what happened to all of your husbands?' I shouted, no longer sure who or what I was angry at.

'Emotions are running high,' Madame Bowden said, slowly getting up from her chair. 'I will pretend I didn't hear that.' With that, she made her way up the stairs and to her bedroom.

I slumped down on the couch. Ever since that day she had taken care of me. She had prepared my meals and encouraged me to eat when I felt I couldn't. She had reassured me that what happened to Shane was not my fault. It was an accident. Convinced me that telling the police the truth would only raise suspicion and make me a suspect with motive.

'We were both here,' she said, patting my hand. 'We both know what happened. It was an accident.'

'Yes, an accident,' I kept repeating after her. 'We were both there.'

Chapter Twenty-Four

HENRY

I thought I'd never get out of Heathrow. Travellers from every corner of the globe seemed intent on slowing me down, or perhaps I was moving with more purpose than I was accustomed to. Sitting on the tube, I thought about Isabelle and what I would say when I got there. It was like thinking about an old acquaintance, not the woman I had planned on spending the rest of my life with just a few weeks ago. How had that happened? All I knew was I had to end things and I had to do it face to face. Kissing Martha had left me without any doubts. I wrote her a letter explaining everything and left it in an envelope on the doorstep, beside the milk bottles. It was too early to wake her and besides, it was easier to pour my heart out on paper. I couldn't know what the future held, but I was clear that Isabelle and I were not right for each other. Not now I'd felt the emotion I'd spent my whole life longing for yet was too scared to pursue.

I heard the announcement for Pimlico and rushed up the steps of the station to street level. The streets were quieter now, with rush hour over, and the parks were playing host to parents watching their toddlers test their independence on climbing frames. I was testing something too. Trusting my gut. I arrived at Denbigh Street, where a terraced row of highly ornate houses with balustrades on the first floor and soft yellow London stock brick on the upper two floors. I felt a churning nausea at the pit of my stomach as I rang the doorbell.

A light flicked on and I could hear her footsteps before she opened the door.

'Henry!'

She pulled me into an embrace and I wasn't sure what to do. She wouldn't want to hug me after I'd told her what I came to say.

'Why didn't you say you were coming? I invited Cassie and James over for drinks. You don't mind, do you?' She was a manicured vision of beauty. Her silky auburn hair tucked expertly into a bun, a cream satin dress falling just so from her athletic frame.

'Um, I need to speak with you. Alone.'

My expression was unmistakable.

'What is it? Is everything okay?'

I was still on the doorstep. Christ, my whole life seemed to be lived on the doorstep. Never fully in or out, never feeling as though I belonged anywhere. She pulled the door behind her and stepped outside.

'You'll get cold,' I said.

'It doesn't matter. I have a feeling this conversation won't take very long.'

I looked up at her. She was always more intuitive than me. She was the smartest woman I'd ever met. There was no point trying to find the 'right' words because they simply did not exist.

'You're an amazing woman—'

'Oh God.'

'What?'

'Anything but the *"It's not you, it's me"* speech. It's humiliating, Henry.'

'But it's true! It's me, I'm the problem.'

'I know that. So why are you leaving me?'

Fuck. This was why people lied. It's far easier to lie to someone than to watch them bear the hurt of your careless words.

'Because I thought I knew what love was. I thought it was something I could ... manage. You and I, we knew how to rub along together. We had a good partnership. But if you're honest I know you'll think the same thing. We weren't'—I searched the sky for inspiration—'fireworks.'

'Wow.' She wiped a stray tear from her eye.

'You must have had your doubts too, Issy.' Stupidly, I thought she would agree with me.

'Don't expect me to make this easier for you, Henry. You see the thing is, I do love you. Very much, as it happens. And I thought we had fireworks.'

I felt ten stone heavier. Her arms were folded tightly around her. What could I say to make it better?

'I'm so sorry, Isabelle. I truly am. I never wanted to hurt you.'

She said nothing; wouldn't even meet my eyes.

'I feel terrible,' I said.

'You feel terrible? Try being dumped on the doorstep by your fiancée before we even had a chance to pick out a ring! This must be some kind of record.'

Nothing I said was coming out right.

'You're better off without me.'

'Finally, something we can agree on.'

With that, she walked back inside and slammed the door in my face. I buried my face in my hands and hardly noticed when the door opened again.

'And here is all your shit,' she said, handing me a black plastic bag. 'I hope she's worth it.' The door slammed again.

~

It was late by the time I returned home. There was scaffolding on the house next door, which, in the evening sunlight, made it look as though it were trapped in a gilded cage. I walked up our driveway and noticed an e-bike parked where my mother's old VW Golf used to be. I turned my key in the door and was hit by the welcome scent of a roast chicken giving me an appetite for food that I thought I would never have again. Not after talking to Isabelle. I never felt more unsure of who I was, and that was saying something – for a man who lived his entire life in the shadow of other people's opinions. I felt empty.

'Henry!' my mother exclaimed from the kitchen, rushing into the hallway. She held me in a tight embrace and I found myself absently wondering why she was wearing a long white shirt covered in paint and a bandana in her hair. She was normally a pearls-and-twin-set type of person, keeping up the illusion that we still had money and that my father had not drunk it all.

'You look different,' I said.

'I've taken up life drawing! Annie next door goes to a class every Thursday and—'

'It's just so they can perv over young naked models,' came the unmistakable monotone voice of my sister. She and her husband, Neil, thumped their heavy Doc Martens boots down the stairs.

'Oh, Lucinda, honestly!' my mother cried, rolling her eyes in mock offence.

My sister's eyes were rimmed with black liner and while her jet-black hair reached almost to her lower back, she had cut her fringe in a very definite hard line that gave her a stern look. We all made an obstacle course out of getting ourselves from the hall into the kitchen. It was awkward but familiar and I was glad of that.

'Why didn't you say you were coming home? A phone call would have been nice,' Mum said, putting on some oven gloves and bending down to take out the chicken and roast potatoes. I set the table while Lucinda and Neil carried on kissing each other as though we weren't there.

'It was a last-minute thing.'

'A surprise for Isabelle?'

I let the sound of plates and cutlery drown out whatever useless response I was attempting to conjure to that.

'Isabelle and I were a mistake,' I said eventually, having realised this for the first time. 'We both knew it. It's better this way.' There. No room for debate.

My mother stood like a statue for a moment, her mouth shaped in an 'o'.

'You young people today,' my sister said, punching my arm and slightly rescuing the situation.

'Gosh, you are incredibly pregnant,' I said, noticing the size of her bump.

'Yep, she really ballooned out these last couple of weeks,' Neil agreed, earning himself a kick on the shin.

'I'm not due for another fortnight,' she groaned, but it looked as though Neil was the one suffering.

~

Over dinner, I listened as they chatted animatedly about plans for the future and I realised that, during my short absence, things had changed at home. And for the better. My mother had become something of an eco-warrior slash militant cyclist and Lucinda seemed, well, happy.

'So, what was Ireland like?' Neil asked, his dark eyes peeping through a heavily back-combed mop of hair. 'Lu said you were researching an old bookshop. Sounds cool.'

I finished my last slug of wine before answering.

'It's proving elusive. But I may have found something else of interest,' I said, the smile forming on my lips.

'What?' my mother said, cutting the Viennetta into slices at the worktop. She loved a classic dessert.

'I've met someone. In Ireland. I'm going back as soon as I can get a flight.'

All of their faces turned towards me. I couldn't quite believe I'd said it. But that's how certain I was.

'Are you seriously leaving the country so you won't have to change a nappy?' my sister asked, slack-jawed.

'Bit extreme, mate,' Neil chimed in.

Mother cut another chunk of Viennetta. She decided this was a subject she alone should tackle.

'Henry, sweetheart, I know you were something of a late developer, but I don't want you turning into some kind of Lothario.'

I couldn't help but laugh. If only she knew.

'So you just came back to see Isabelle. What about Dad?'

Lucinda had always been his champion. She'd somehow managed to miss the worst of his drinking and he'd never taken his moods out on her.

'What about him?'

'Aren't you going to visit him? He's been asking about you.'

'You've seen him?'

'Of course,' she said, then flashed a look at my mother.

'You too?' I asked.

She shook her head.

'No. I'm moving on with my life. I have to put my own needs first now. You are both grown-ups and can make your own decisions. He'll always be your father, Henry, but it's up to you.'

If it had been up to me, he would have been a better father. It was never up to me. It was up to him.

Chapter Twenty-Five

OPALINE

England, 1922

I awoke the next morning to the sound of a milk truck making deliveries. The daylight had barely begun to breach the dusky pink curtains, but I could make out the line of his shoulder and his dark mop of hair on the pillow. Armand slept so soundly, it made me question my constant self-doubt. I doubted myself, my choices, my desires and my abilities all of the time. Oh, to be a man who is always sure of himself! And sure of his place in the world.

In becoming Miss Gray, I wasn't just hiding from Lyndon, I was hiding from everything and everyone. All of the expectations of my gender to be all of the things I no longer was – pure, timid, passive. I wished we were still in Paris, where being ordinary was frowned upon and breaking the rules was a rite of passage.

I hadn't slept well, or at all really. I found my thoughts returning to Matthew. He had visited the shop briefly before I left. I think he was embarrassed by what had happened, how we had held each other that night. I imagine he would not have come at all if he did not need to collect the rent, but his good manners precluded him from having a purely transactional visit and so he began to speak about the shop and his childhood dreams to become a magician.

'A magician?' I echoed in disbelief. As if to prove his point, he reached behind my ear and found a small glass ball. I reached out to take it from his palm, yet somehow it had disappeared into thin air.

'How did you do that?' I said, smiling brightly.

'Ah, now that would be telling.'

If only I could have made my feelings disappear so easily. On the days he came, everything was brighter, sunnier, happier. But when he left to return to his family, I felt wretched.

'*Mon Opale*,' Armand whispered, nuzzling into my neck.

I let him put his arms around me, chasing the loneliness away. I hadn't intended to come back to his rooms, but I suppose from the minute we set eyes on each other in Yorkshire, it was inevitable. Yet I couldn't help thinking that I held no place in his heart above any of the other women he bedded. Well, I wasn't going to let him think that I cared for him either. That way, I wouldn't get hurt. The reasoning of an idiot; but love, as they say, is blind.

'I must go,' I said eventually, kissing him lightly on his cheek.

'*Mais non, reste*.'

'I cannot. My boat leaves this evening and I have some business to attend to before then.'

'Business?' He propped himself up on his elbow and watched me dress. God, he was gorgeous! An Adonis. I had to turn my back on him while buttoning up my blouse.

'A book.'

'Of course it's a book. Tell me.'

I turned to look at him. Yes, he was beautiful and yes, he was a valuable connection in the book dealing world. He had also helped me to escape Paris. Yet, as I had realised in Sotheby's, he was cut from the same cloth as Rosenbach. Ruthless, single-minded and greedy. When it came to books, perhaps I was too, because in that moment I realised that while there may be honour amongst thieves, the same could not be said for book dealers.

'Perhaps I can stay a little longer,' I said, kneeling on the bed beside him and letting him unbutton my blouse again. Loneliness is not a discerning bedfellow. In fact, the more inappropriate the company, the more it suited my fatalistic outlook when it came to love. Something told me I would never find it, so why bother saving myself for it?

~

I didn't have much time. My ears echoed with the sound of my heels rushing along the pavement, as I scanned the numbers on the door. My search had led me to Soho and a small warren of alleyways tucked behind Regent Street. I stayed true to my word and told Armand nothing of my detective work regarding Emily Brontë's second novel. I made a decision that morning that I would stand by for the rest of my life: the work would always come first. However, I did ask him to suggest a dealer who might be familiar with bookshops that were no longer trading. Having spent an interesting morning in Mayfair, I was given the address of Brown's Bookshop.

It was now a solicitor's office, but I was reliably informed that the previous owners retained the flat above the shop. I knocked on the door for quite some time, before a middle-aged woman, dressed all in black, answered.

'Mrs Brown?' I hazarded a guess.

'Yes,' she replied, raising her head slightly to peer through the glasses that were sliding down her nose. 'Do I know you?'

'No, we are not acquainted and I am sorry to bother you, but I was hoping to speak to your husband. It's concerning his bookshop and his aunt, Martha Brown.'

She smiled in a sorrowful way. 'Oh, we haven't had one of these for a while, have we, Reginald?'

There was no one there, but I assumed Reginald was upstairs, as she looked skywards.

'One of what?'

'A Brontë fan. Do come in,' she invited, as it had begun to drizzle slightly. We climbed the stairs and came to a pretty little parlour room facing the street below. Every surface was covered with lace doilies but there wasn't a book in sight. It was not a good start. I took the seat she offered me at a small round table in front of the fire.

'We shall have tea,' she called out again to some invisible person. Within minutes a young girl with sullen features carried in a tray with cups and saucers and a silver teapot.

'Thank you,' I said but received no response.

'Well, she might look vexed. I will have to terminate her employment and go to live with my sister in Cornwall. I simply cannot afford to live here any longer,' Mrs Brown pointed out, sadly.

Once a polite amount of time had passed, I enquired about Mr Brown and whether or not I could speak with him.

'Oh but, my dear, you are a fortnight too late. My dearest Reginald passed away, in that very chair,' she said, pointing to an armchair in the corner. 'Hence the move to my sister's.'

'Ah, I see,' I said, ruing my terrible timing. 'I am very sorry for your loss, Mrs Brown, and I won't take up any more of your time with my silly detective work.'

She bade me stay a little longer, at least until the rain eased up, as it had now turned into a torrential downpour.

'Besides, I don't get to talk very much about our old bookshop any more. I used to enjoy working there.'

'Might I ask what happened to the stock? Did you sell everything?'

'Everything that would interest one such as yourself I'm afraid. Oh, there were many dealers back then, keen to get their hands on anything related to the Brontë family. Even a book of birds belonging to the family!' she cooed. 'I mean, honestly, there comes a point where you have to draw a line.'

She had no idea who she was talking to! When it came to book scouts, there was no line. Anything that might relate to an author or their life was of interest. 'Besides, if I had anything left to sell now, I would be only too happy to part with it. I will need all the funds I can muster at my age.'

Life was difficult for a woman on her own, I could appreciate that. I told her about my shop in Dublin and, as pathetic as it may sound, I revelled in her praise of my independence.

'But now I really must go, reluctantly, Mrs Brown,' I said, realising the time. I had to get the train back to Liverpool for the evening sailing.

'Oh, I am sorry, you've come all this way hoping to find something and I have been of no help,' she said, struggling up from her seat to see me out. 'Wait a minute, perhaps I do have something you might fancy,' she said, disappearing into another room. When she returned, she was carrying what looked like a little tin box.

'We had it in the bookshop, but it never sold,' she said, handing it to me.

'What is it?'

'An old sewing box, belonging to Charlotte.'

My eyes widened. I couldn't believe I was holding one of her humble yet personal possessions in my hands, something she would have used daily. I lifted the lid, which revealed a neat row of threads in dark hues and an embroidered pin cushion with needles lodged snugly in.

'According to my husband, who of course got it from Martha herself, it was Branwell who gifted it to Charlotte. Although Lord knows it wasn't much of a gift! He was fond of the odd tipple, that one.'

I knew from my research that he was fond of quite a bit more, having struggled with both alcohol and drug addiction during his lifetime. I often wondered if Hindley Earnshaw's chaotic descent into gambling and addiction in *Wuthering Heights* was based on Branwell, who often suffered delirium tremens while attempting to sober up.

'Two pounds and it's yours,' she said.

In any other situation, I would have required proof of the provenance of such an item, but I decided to take it on faith. Besides, I thought how amusing it would be if in fact she were a swindler, selling me her own sewing box and passing it off as a Brontë collectable!

I handed her the money, which she said would go towards her retirement pot, and I set out on my journey back home to the anonymity of Dublin. Perhaps it was hypervigilance on my part, but in London, I could not shake the sickening sense of being watched.

~

It had been three months since my trip to England and even though I had not expected to hear from Armand, having my thoughts confirmed by the postman every morning was a little stinging. Still, I found a sense of fulfilment in my achievements and the success of my wonderful little shop, which, despite the growing number of books I stocked it with, seemed to find room to accommodate them. I had long suspected that something just beyond my comprehension was afoot, as though Mr Fitzpatrick had put a spell over the place. At night, when sleep stole away from me like a vanishing point, I would make some cocoa and sit on the floor of the shop, wrapped in a blanket. I was immediately soothed by that breathing sound I had heard since I was a child: the stories settling between the pages. Only now I could hear another sound. I shuffled over to one of the walls and, feeling a little foolish, put my ear to it. A soft creaking, like the boughs of a tree bending slightly in the breeze. I smiled to myself and often fell asleep like that, cradled in the corner of the dark green walls, wooden shelves with fluttering book leaves shimmering overhead.

~

When I awoke, it was still dawn and a peach light filtered through the windows. I'd had the most vivid dream, the kind that leaves you drenched in a feeling you can't quite grasp the meaning behind. My father was listening to the books and smiling. Telling me to listen. I held one to my ear and heard a heartbeat. Then two; the second one lighter, quicker. And like an apple falling to the ground, understanding came to me all at once. I placed my hand on my stomach and felt a kick. I had not had my monthly courses since my return home and had put it down to travelling, or anything other than what it truly was. Now I felt the curve of my belly, it was real. A tear rolled down my cheek.

'This will not be easy,' I whispered, to myself or the shop. I wasn't sure which. But I could not deny the joy that bubbled up inside of me. A baby. A baby! Conflicting emotions rushed through me all at once: fear, excitement, anxiety, gratitude. I felt too young, too incapable of becoming a mother, but I simultaneously relished the idea of having a family of my own.

I completely lost track of time as I idealised a very different future for myself. I opened the shop quite late that day but it felt as though it were the first day of my life. Everything was gilded in optimism and grounded in meaning. I saw each customer as the child they once were or the parent they would become. I saw us as all being connected, a universal family. And in the quieter moments, I pictured the life growing inside of me like a little rosebud; an unparalleled beauty that would make the world a brighter place merely by her presence in it. It was only when night fell that my glowing heart began to doubt itself. Reality crossed my threshold in the form of Matthew, coming to collect the rent. I had to tell him. In another month or so he would see for himself. In another six months, there would be two of us living here. It all suddenly felt quite weighty. What would he think of me now?

I wished the shop could close in around us and keep us safe, keep the world outside. I wished we could hide within these walls for ever.

Chapter Twenty-Six

MARTHA

Once the autopsy was concluded, the body would be released for burial in a matter of weeks. It was decided that I would have to attend the funeral, to avoid any suspicion. These plans were not mine but Madame Bowden's. I really did start to wonder if she had, in fact, seen off her husbands, such was her calm approach. And I realised how forward-thinking she had been to ensure I had alibis to corroborate my whereabouts.

'Why are you doing this for me?' I asked her later that night when, despite my exhaustion, I could not sleep. Every time I closed my eyes, I would replay the scene.

'Doing what? I'm simply making sure that justice is done.'

'But, that's not how it happened.' I still couldn't say for sure what had happened. Had he been so drunk that he lost his footing and fell? Every time I replayed it in my head, I could still see him being pushed, but by whom or what? Some invisible force? Was there more to Madame Bowden than met the eye? I couldn't decide whether she was my guardian angel or a devil in disguise. Reading her was difficult; there were so many stories distracting me, too many for one lifetime. She told me once that, as an actor, she had to embody her characters. Perhaps they were all still living inside of her, like ghosts.

'Martha, the facts are that Shane arrived here drunk and abusive with ill-intent. He was the architect of his own demise and that is the only truth worth remembering of that day.'

She sounded so convincing that I tried to hold on to her words like flotation devices every time I felt like I was drowning in the darkness. I wasn't sure how I was going to face the funeral. My family. Shane's parents. I thought about asking Henry to come with me, but it would have been wrong on so many levels. Besides, I still hadn't contacted him. The shock of Shane's death had paralysed my senses. I tried to text him, but what could I say? I had to see him in person.

~

I took the bus to Rialto and found the bed and breakfast he had taken me to. It felt like a lifetime ago now.

'Ah, howya love, looking for a room, is it?'

A short man with a comb-over answered the door, with his foot across the threshold as a barking dog attempted to make a dash for freedom.

'No, actually I'm looking for someone staying here. Henry Field? He's English.' I added the last bit when the name didn't seem to register.

'Oh, Henry, of course. No, love, he's gone back home.'

'Home?'

'To England.'

I staggered back a little, as though I'd been shot. I couldn't take it in.

'Are ya all right? You look a bit pale there, if you don't mind me sayin'.'

I nodded and tried to say something coherent. 'When did he leave?'

'Oh, it's a couple of days ago now.'

'I-I …'

'Sorry, love, the match is on the telly,' he said with a longing gaze back down the hall to where the sound of a team scoring a goal could be heard.

'Oh, no worries.'

The door was closed before I had time to say anything further. The shock gave way to another feeling. Humiliation. I checked my phone. There wasn't even a text from him. It was obvious now; he must have known after kissing me that it was a mistake. And now he regretted it. Of course he did. I pressed the heels of my hands into my eyes. Maybe he just felt sorry for me. That was it. He pitied me and I mistook it for something more. It probably meant nothing to him. Or else he realised too late that he'd made a mistake and now he didn't know how to tell me. My fingers trembled as I pulled up his contact details on screen. I tapped the block button before stuffing my phone back in my pocket.

I staggered back down the street. I hadn't expected it to hurt so much. I always knew he would leave, but I never thought he would be so cruel as to pack up without a word. I stopped and took a deep breath. I wasn't going to give another man the power to hurt me. If there was one thing I was good at, it was being alone. Nothing could harm me now.

~

Time passed erratically. I would lose entire days to flashbacks and memories, then find myself jolted forwards into a reality I could scarcely believe was happening. Being back in the village was a shock to the system. Being back in the village for my husband's funeral was another thing altogether. It felt surreal. People had always thought I was a bit 'off'. I tried to act like everyone else but I could never quite fit in like other people did. Never really felt like I belonged there.

Shane's mother ran the local supermarket on her own after his father's death and she was often described as a pillar of the community. She had always treated me well, if somewhat standoffishly. She knew there was something different about me too. Or maybe she knew their son better than she let on. Better than I did. Maybe she saw the bruises and wanted to keep me quiet. She couldn't have a scandal like that ruining her reputation or her trade. And I silently went along with it. I didn't want to disrupt things either and somehow believed that I was partly to blame for it all. I must have been doing something wrong. Reading her, all I could see was a woman who loved her family to the point of blindness.

Madame Bowden had offered to accompany me but I didn't want her there. I was embarrassed by the town and everyone in it. I just had to get through the day and it would all be over. At least that's what I told myself.

I was in a black car with Shane's mother.

'Well, I hope that job in Dublin was worth it.'

'Sorry?'

'What kind of a wife would put a job before her husband.' She had been staring straight ahead at the road, but now her red-rimmed eyes were trained on me.

'I didn't.'

'And my poor Shane, he'd never stand in the way of your dreams. Said he didn't mind if you were away for a few months. Oh, but he was so looking forward to bringing you home with him.'

He hadn't told her I'd left him. I took a deep breath in. Of course he didn't tell anyone. How would he explain it? Either she had no clue about the violence, or her mind wouldn't let her see what was staring her in the face. *Not my son.*

'If it hadn't been for the accident—' She broke off, swallowing her words in one big gulp and pressing a handkerchief to her nose. 'Why weren't you there, Martha?'

'I …' My voice cracked. 'I'm sorry.'

She took my hand in hers so tightly I thought my bones would crack.

'I know what people are saying, that it was a suicide, but I don't believe them.'

I nodded and felt the mixed sensations of guilt and relief shudder through my body. No one suspected anything.

The day passed by in flashes, like some kind of avant-garde movie. His uncle making a speech at the church. The open coffin. Shane's cold, white face that looked as innocent as a child's. The graveyard and the cries of his mother when the coffin was lowered into the ground. The hotel afterwards and his friends retelling the story of how Shane and I had first met. Love at first sight. My two brothers toasting pints, saying what a sound man he was. Always fixing their cars at mates' rates. Never missed his turn paying for a round of drinks. As though that was what made a good man. I never cried once. I worried that people might think it was odd, but the priest assured me that we all express our grief differently.

~

My parents offered to drive me back to the apartment I had shared with the man who almost tried to kill me. The man who was now dead and buried himself. *It was a terrible accident.* I had repeated that line so many times to myself, like a mantra. If you say something enough times, it becomes true. Or at least that was the plan. I turned the key in the lock, but as soon as I stepped inside, I knew I could never stay there again. Everywhere I looked, I could see all the times he threatened me, yelled at me, hit me. Short films, with no beginning and no end. I never knew where the arguments began. I would try to trace them back to some logical starting point, but there wasn't one. Anything could spark his anger and the more and more I tried to cut off the parts of me that seemed to annoy him, the less and less there was of me. I was only existing in his world, on his terms, just trying to survive this 'love at first sight'.

I turned to my mother and without even speaking the words, she understood what I was asking. I went home with them.

I didn't sleep. I just lay in my childhood bed wondering how I had ended up here. By the time the first rays of morning light came through the thin curtains, I had made some decisions. I would never come back to this town again. Regardless of how it had happened, I had been given a second chance to start over. I dressed quickly and tiptoed out to the back door. Just as I lifted the latch, I heard a voice from behind me that I hardly dared to believe.

'I'm glad he's dead,' she said.

I turned around to see my mother standing there in her old dressing gown, her arms wrapped tightly around herself. These were the first words I had ever heard her speak. Rusty and half-whispered, they confirmed what I had suspected all along – she had silenced herself. But why? That was when all of the unshed tears released from within me and we held each other for the longest time.

'Come with me,' I said eventually.

I knew she wouldn't leave my father. He was a good man. It's just that people have very different definitions of 'good'.

She signed that I should go, be free and enjoy my life. That was all she ever wanted for me.

'I should've saved you from him.'

Her face was white as a sheet. Only now could I see how much she blamed herself.

'You couldn't have. He isolated me from everyone, made me feel like it was all my fault. I couldn't tell anyone, I was so ashamed.'

'Oh love, I thought you were ashamed of *me*! So I kept my distance.'

I hugged her again, as tightly as I could. It was all so obvious now, how he'd manipulated me. I would never forgive him. Never.

Chapter Twenty-Seven

HENRY

Felicity Grace Field decided she was going to make her entrance into the world two weeks early. Lucinda had convinced me to stay in London for another few days to help Neil finish off decorating the nursery. At 3 a.m. I heard panicked voices outside my bedroom door – my mother shouting at Neil about the overnight bag, Neil shouting at himself for misplacing the car keys, my sister shouting at both of them to stop creating a stressful environment for the baby. I jumped out of bed and lunged into the hall, where Lucinda stood in a puddle of liquid in her bare feet.

'What's going on?' I said, stupidly.

'I'm having a baby,' she replied, still managing a sarcastic tone.

'Like, now?'

'Like, yeah,' she said, imitating my gormless voice.

Just then my mother arrived with slippers in hand and an overcoat. I stood there, immobile, watching as they both struggled to get her dressed for the hospital.

'Henry! You're either part of the solution or part of the problem,' my mother shouted and told me to help Neil look for the car keys. I obeyed and found them in full view on the kitchen table, as Neil walked past them unseeing for the umpteenth time.

'Jesus Christ,' Neil said, wide-eyed and panic-stricken. 'I don't think I'm ready for this.'

'Right. Okay, well, I'm not sure we can really factor that in at this stage.'

'How the fuck am I going to drive? I don't think I can even see properly, my eyesight's gone all foggy. Is that normal?'

I drove. Lucinda had Mum and Neil on either side of her, puffing out their cheeks and exhaling air through pursed lips like two demented blowfish. I'm not sure it was helping but I could see by Lucinda's face that she was just glad of the quiet. It was an improvement on all of the shouting. I was quietly congratulating myself for being the rock in the situation and pulled up outside A&E.

'Here we are,' I said, as though I were dropping them off at the airport for a fortnight on the Costa.

'This ... isn't ... maternity,' Lucinda said in a very low, threatening voice and then emitted what could only be described as something akin to a cow bellowing. I stamped my foot on the accelerator and followed the signs for maternity before once more pulling up at the door. After helping them out, I parked the car and, by the time I got back, everything was over.

'It's a girl,' my mother whispered through tears and I hugged her tightly under a broken fluorescent light that flickered overhead. I couldn't quite believe that we had arrived as four people and we would be going home as five. 'They're delivering the afterbirth now.'

'Mum, please, no details.'

'Oh, for God's sake,' she said, smacking me lightly on the arm. 'It'll be your turn one day.'

Would it? I wasn't sure I wanted to be a father. I didn't want to inflict what I had experienced on anyone else.

'You can come in now.' Neil popped his head around the door. He was wearing a plastic apron over his clothes, as though he had delivered the baby. He was crying. 'Happy tears,' he said and I couldn't help but put my arms around him. It was endearing to see him so vulnerable.

The room was buzzing with the sense that something important had just happened. Then I saw my sister, her dark fringe pushed back off her face with sweat, her nakedness covered with a sheet and a little dark-haired head resting in the crook of her arm.

'Felicity, it's time to meet your uncle Henry.'

And then I was crying. Which didn't seem to matter so much because the baby was crying now too. Then we all laughed and cried until the nurse told us to get out because she had to show Lu how to get Felicity to 'latch on'. She wasn't going to get any rest, that was for sure. Ever, probably.

~

We spent the night at the hospital together, none of us wanting to break the little bubble of joy we had created. Well, that Neil and Lu had created, to be precise. A new person had joined our family and, without saying as much, we all seemed to be united in the conviction that her experience would be better than our own. We would become better people for her. The process had already started. Perhaps this was why people referred to new life as a miracle, because it had the power to change everything.

I suddenly had an overwhelming longing to see Martha, to tell her everything that had happened. I wanted her here, to be with my family. To be a part of it. I went on a breakfast run and picked up some more things for Lu – basically an excuse so I could call Martha, but there wasn't even a dial tone. I told myself that her phone was switched off. Simple explanation. While waiting for the coffees, I sent a string of texts with baby emojis, which was so out of character, she might have assumed I had been kidnapped and it was an attempt to communicate my location. Yet as the hours passed and there was still no response, I started to feel like something was wrong. I had explained everything in the note I'd left, but maybe she'd changed her mind. Maybe I was coming on too strong. I was still second-guessing myself when I walked back into the delivery room and almost bumped into someone. A man. My father.

'What's he doing here?'

'Henry, it's okay,' Lu said.

It wasn't okay. It was very far from okay, but the thing about having just given birth to a human is that your feelings trump everyone else's.

'I'll wait outside,' I said, leaving the takeout behind me.

~

I walked in circles around the smoking area outside. Why had she called him? Why did she want him there? Every time I saw him, all of the old hurts came to the surface. *No son of mine is soft.* That's what he said the first time I fell off my bike and started crying. Then he gave me a thump that knocked me over again. *You need to toughen up in this world.* I certainly needed to toughen up with him as a father. What kind of a grandfather would he be? I wondered. Then that made me even angrier. He'd probably be the perfect grandfather – get everything right this time around, now that he'd made all his mistakes on me. Lu escaped the brunt of his behaviour, maybe because she was a girl. Sometimes I resented her, but mostly I was relieved that she didn't have to go through it.

I thought of Martha again. For so long I had hidden the parts of me that seemed broken beyond repair. But she had seen past my feeble attempts at being someone people would like, hiding the breaches within me that always caused me to fall short. I had learned nothing from my father, only how to feel inadequate all the time. I realised now that this was the hollow inheritance passed down through the men in my family. And we spent our lives doing whatever it took to look like a strong man. Like scaffolding around me, it was only ever meant to be temporary. Something was supposed to get fixed inside. Only it never did. And somehow, Martha saw that brokenness and made it okay to be there. She didn't expect perfection, just honesty. Kindness. After everything she had been through, she was still willing to see that in me. To have the bravery to care about someone again. I checked my phone again. Nothing. If I wanted to be with Martha, I had to make sure I was worthy of her first.

Chapter Twenty-Eight

OPALINE

Dublin, 1922

It was almost Christmas. Matthew arrived with some sprigs of holly to decorate the shop and little parcels with cooked ham, biscuits and cake. Whatever he bought for his own house, I knew he always set aside a little for me, and the kindness of this gesture made my heart ache. I was in no position to refuse his charity. Whilst my catalogue of books was selling well in Ireland and even in the States, money was still quite tight and I was trying to put small amounts aside for the future. No sooner had he stepped inside the door than the stained-glass windows began to bloom with mistletoe.

'Stop it at once!' I said.

'Stop what?' Matthew asked, holding a sprig of holly aloft.

'Oh, nothing.' I blushed. 'The baby is kicking.'

He placed the holly on the table and gave me a lopsided smile.

'I remember when Muriel was pregnant with little Ollie. He used to perform all of his gymnastics at night.'

The baby wasn't really kicking, I'd only said it as an excuse, but when Matthew took a step closer, he asked if he could touch my stomach. I wanted him to, but I couldn't even speak. I just nodded. As soon as he put his palm gently on the curve of my belly, she began to move.

'Ha! There she is.' He grinned. 'That's real magic.'

He hadn't judged me when I told him about the pregnancy. He didn't even ask for any explanation about who the father was, or where he was. He simply asked if there was anything he could do.

'Why didn't you take over the shop?' I asked. 'You must have wanted to, when you were younger.'

He took his hand away and I felt the absence keenly.

'I grew up,' was all he said, shrugging and looking over the place with misty eyes. 'Besides, it's in the right hands now.'

'I don't know,' I said, running my hands along the shelf, wondering if he could hear the spines creak and pages sigh as I did.

'My father was never a wealthy man, Opaline. At least not financially. Yet I remember when times were hard he would never doubt himself, he would simply say that perhaps the shop was waiting to become a library again. And seeing your books here now, I believe he was right. It didn't want to be a nostalgia shop or even a magic shop.' He reached out and patted the wooden walls. 'It has returned to its roots.'

When he left, I filled the silence with a seasonal recording of Tchaikovsky's *Nutcracker* on the Victrola and took down a copy of E.T.A. Hoffmann's *The Nutcracker and the Mouse King*, on which the ballet was based. I recalled a note from the library in Yorkshire, which remarked that he was one of Emily Brontë's favourite authors. If I remembered correctly, she had read his novel *The Sandman* in its original German. And it was this simple thread of thoughts that brought to mind a possession I had put away and given no further thought since my trip to London. The sewing box.

The little purchase I had made from Mrs Brown was so plain and uninteresting that I had never given it more than a cursory look. And since I also suspected it had never truly been a part of the Brontë household, I had carelessly dropped it in the bottom drawer of my bureau, untouched.

I leaned down and took it out, placing it in front of me on the desk. I let my fingers run across the surface and closed my eyes as if I could somehow divine its provenance. It wasn't even a proper sewing box, but an old tin cash box. Inside was a collection of bobbins, needles, thimbles and thread. I removed them all, one by one, as I had done the first time on the boat back from Liverpool. Perhaps I had missed something – a name scratched in the metal or a clue of some sort. Nothing.

I could hear thunder rumbling in the distance and when I looked up, fat drops of rain began to hit the windowpane. I stroked my belly. 'Don't worry, little one, the gods are playing games in the clouds,' I said gently. Normally I hated storms, but I was determined not to pass this on. Besides, there was a magical feel to the air, as though something exciting might happen.

I got up to close the shutters on the windows and wrapped a woollen shawl around my shoulders. I took the sewing box into my hands and again tried to feel the past somehow. I had read of people who could touch an object and have a vision of the previous owner. Silly, of course, but I closed my eyes and as I turned it over in my hands, I found something. I hardly dared to open my eyes, reluctant to prove my sense of touch incorrect, but there it was – an almost invisible groove at the base of the box. If anyone passing by the shop could see my face, I'm sure that I resembled a treasure hunter at the entrance to an ancient Egyptian tomb!

Slowly, I slid the outer cover back and out slipped a tiny black notebook, the size of a playing card. I gasped. What had I discovered? How long had it been secreted in this hidden compartment and who had put it there? All of the possibilities crashed into one another and for quite some time I was frozen into inaction. I hadn't even realised how my hand pressed hard over my beating heart while my head bent low to the desk, as if the notebook would somehow speak to me.

While I savoured that delicious moment just before the unknown becomes known, I could delay no longer. My curiosity was at its peak. I reached tentatively for the cover and began to carefully open it. It released a dry, woody smell. Immediately I imagined a young woman scribbling notes by the fireside – as though its fragrance was still imbued with the environment in which it was created.

1846

I have devoted an entire lifetime to escaping the confines of this wretched place, only to find myself further entangled in its gnarled roots and oppressed by its looming towers. I am now satisfied that no one born on this land can wipe the dust of it from one's heels.

I held my flushed cheeks with the palm of my hands. Was this it? What I had been searching for all of these years?

Wrenville Hall is a spectre that haunts us all from one generation to the next …

I was almost too afraid to touch the paper – I had some irrational fear that, having survived all these years, it might somehow crumble in my hands. I searched the drawer for a magnifying glass, as the script was so small and squashed on the page, it was difficult to make out. I brought my desk lamp closer and leaned over the little booklet. The black ink was messy and words were crossed out with new ones pushed out into what remained of the margins. Having viewed some of the sisters' original diary entries at Haworth, I felt sure that this was the penmanship of Emily, but I would need to have it authenticated. Unless …

That was when I spotted it – a minuscule signature. EJB.

It felt like fireworks exploding in my veins. The baby kicked, the air crackled and a whooshing sound went through my ears. Was this the second novel, or at least the drafting of it? My head felt light and my feet tapped a jig on the floorboards. I closed my eyes and traced the joy on my face with my fingertips and tried to commit it to memory. My heart was beating against my ribcage like a bird at the window. I read on.

With the death of my father and the forced liquidation of my debts to my creditors in London, I was now returning to the estate in Ireland. … an impervious gloom haunted every corner of its cursed country and a week of driving rain had soaked the ground and reduced it to mud. Famine ravaged the land …

The text became unreadable at this point and the next paragraph seemed to jump ahead of sequence.

This would be my penance, my banishment to this hellish place. I passed through two great pillars and entered the avenue that swept up to Wrenville Hall. Lined with towering yews, it held a singular tranquillity that was tinged with terror. On my one and only sojourn in this place as a child, I recalled the old house servant speaking of spectres and ghouls that lived in the woods beyond. The house stood strongly defined against the dark sky. The gargoyles that came into view at the front-facing aspect of the grey fortress of a house stared down through the afternoon mist in delightful horror …

'It was night and the candles were lit as I dined alone on a passable meal of turbot in the dining room. A ferocious storm raged outside, driving the rain in sheets against the window, when all of a sudden, lightning flashed and I saw her face at the window. I ran to it and loosened the latch. A flame-haired girl, soaked to the skin, wearing a plain white dress that clung to her fragile frame like a winding sheet. She was deathly pale and did not struggle when I pulled her through the window and we landed on the floor like two drowned pups. Her skin was translucent, white as a ghoul or a vampire, and yet her beauty was like nothing upon the face of God's creation.

Furious barking of a mastiff; my father's old dog bounded into the room and had her pinned to the floor, his eyes glowing and his fangs protruding.

'Helsig!'

The hound stood down at my command, but continued to bark fiercely at the girl.

'Who are you?' I asked. 'You are trespassing on private land.'

The remark served to inflame her passion more brightly. She spoke to me then in the native tongue, a curiously expressive and fierce-sounding speech that left me in no doubt as to the message, if not the exact meaning. She folded her arms then and with a haughtiness hardly warranted by her station in life, she took a seat by the fire.

Her cheeks grew red by the glow of the fire and weak as she was, she fell into a soft slumber. I sat there for a time, studying her features while she slept. For the first time since my exile from Paris, I ached to draw, to paint. Being tormented by a love of art but not possessing the talent to succeed at it, had yielded nothing more than a reduction in my pecuniary resources. Yet here, now, it felt as though her spirit was at work within me, challenging me to capture it on the page. In sleep, she surrendered her wild beauty, which, like the landscape that bore her, could be both heaven and hell. I grew frenzied in my attempts to capture her likeness more faithfully still. Every draft seemed to bring me closer to something I had been lacking in all my years at the easel. I was bewitched by her.

Harnessing my passion, the bristles of my brush scratched feverishly against the linen canvas. I decided that no matter how long it took, I would create my masterpiece while this longing to possess her tore at me. My body ached, the night turned to morning and night again until finally, I stood back and saw. I had my Rose, all in bloom on the canvas. It was then I saw that she was still as the grave. Running to her, not believing the horrible truth, I touched her face. Cold as marble. She was dead.

I realised I had been clutching my blouse tightly at my chest. It was real. I had found it. I jumped up from my seat and then sat down again. I let out a shriek, then immediately wondered if it could possibly be true. Was this an excerpt from Emily's novel? My heart felt as though it were a balloon about to burst! I clapped my hands over my mouth, breathing excitedly into them. It couldn't be, could it? Was I still in my little shop, reading what would be the greatest literary discovery of modern times? I placed one hand on my heart and tried to steady its beat before reading it again.

It was a rough outline of a story about an Anglo-Irish landowner, Egerton Talbot, who had fallen in love with one of his tenants, Rose, set against the backdrop of the Irish Famine. She was described as a '*malevolent, devious creature with all the malignancy of Satan*' by the land agent and that she had put his lordship under some kind of spell. '*Even in the act of the appalling, she enchants!*'

I was fascinated and beguiled and utterly stunned. I was still half-afraid to touch the paper in case I damaged it.

What had inspired Emily's tale? I knew her brother Branwell was something of a tortured artist; perhaps he provided the raw materials for this Egerton character? It was also he who around that time had visited Liverpool, which was thronged with starving victims fleeing the Famine. Their images, depicted in the *Illustrated London News*, starving scarecrows with a few rags on them, would have been known to Emily. Some scholars even argued that Heathcliff himself, 'a dirty, ragged, black-haired child', who spoke a kind of 'gibberish' was Irish and labelled a savage and a demon.

My head swam with images of Millais' *Ophelia* and how his muse, Elizabeth Siddall, almost perished while sitting for the portrait in a cold bath. Or Oscar Wilde's painting, which seemed to be a doorway between two worlds, death and youth. It seemed to me that the slightly deranged Egerton could not see that his muse was dying, just as the English aristocrats refused to see that Ireland was starving from the Famine.

I checked my notes and the dates, which seemed to correspond with the letter Emily had sent her publisher, Cautley. This was it – I had, quite inadvertently, solved one of the twentieth century's most important literary mysteries!

I couldn't wait to tell the world of my discovery. I went back to my desk and picked up the receiver and then quietly replaced it. This was a rare moment – nay, a once in a thousand lifetimes moment. And it was all *mine*. I wanted to savour it. So I sat back down and began to write out a copy of the manuscript. It was something I used to do as a child; I would write out entire passages from books that I loved, just to know what it would feel like to write those words. Besides, I wanted to keep my own copy once the original found its proper home – I hoped within the public walls of a museum. It was hard to imagine what kind of price it might fetch at auction.

I brought my thoughts back to the present. Fifteen pages scrawled upon a miniature notebook, translated to almost double that amount in my own handwriting. I wondered if she had visited Ireland herself? This discovery was presenting more questions than answers! Perhaps that was why scholars analysed her work so intensely, in a futile effort to get to the woman who wrote so passionately and violently – a courageous writer whose novel carried us to the very depths of the human heart and the outer reaches of the supernatural environment. I felt her presence on the page, full of vitality, as though she were communicating still. Some things defy explanation. Emily Brontë was one of them.

Chapter Twenty-Nine

MARTHA

'I don't want it. I don't want anything to do with it.'

It was a letter from the mortgage company. My mother had forwarded it. I was back in Dublin, cleaning out the kitchen cupboards while Madame Bowden watched me from a high stool, sipping an herbal tea that made her face wince every time she tasted it.

'But it's your home.'

'This is my home!' I hadn't meant to shout. 'I mean, as long as you're happy to have me.'

She smiled knowingly. What did she know? I read her face. She believed I would be here for the rest of my life. Well, I wasn't so sure about that.

'I don't care what happens to that apartment. The bank can keep it. Burn it down for all I care. I could never live there again.'

'My dear, the bank has quite enough wealth as it is. Why don't you sell it?'

I didn't want to have this conversation. I didn't want to think about Shane or what had happened.

'I don't know, maybe.'

'You might not think it matters now, but trust me, in time you'll wish you had taken what is rightfully yours. Think of it as compensation.' She said the final part as though it were a matter of fact.

It made my skin crawl. Nothing could ever compensate for what he did and nothing could erase the blame I carried for his death. But, right or wrong, whenever I thought of my mother's words – the first words I had ever heard her speak, *I'm glad he's dead* – I didn't feel so bad. I was finally free and Madame Bowden was right, I couldn't waste this chance.

~

Evenings were the hardest. The need to speak to Henry was such a strong physical urge, I had to leave the house and just keep walking until it stopped. Despite everything else that was going on, my thoughts still went back to him and how he had just left. Maybe it was a bit of a knee-jerk reaction, blocking his number, but it was self-preservation too. I didn't want to hear his reasons or have to listen while he let me down gently. I could no longer read him and that frightened me to death. It felt like walking a high wire with no safety net. I had fallen in love with him and no one knew better than I what a risk that was. I couldn't – *wouldn't* – let that happen again.

It didn't help that my feet took me past all of the places we had been together. I found myself standing outside Pen Corner and thought of his crooked smile, the sound of his voice when he spoke French, his warm breath on my neck. It was late and the shop was closed. I let my forehead touch the window as I looked at the display of pens and notebooks.

That was when it happened: in the golden glow of the window, all of the words came rushing to me. I could see them in my mind's eye – the smallest handwriting, neat like stitching in dark thread. All of the words, lines and lines of a strangely dark story pouring into my mind. I could hardly catch my breath. I was so excited I ran as fast as I could in the direction of the tattoo parlour.

~

'Look, best I can do is Tuesday,' she said.

A young guy with half a tiger blazing on his arm was sitting in the chair.

'I just, I feel like I need to do it now, as soon as possible.'

'I get it,' tiger man said. 'Sometimes you just gotta strike while the iron's hot.'

'Exactly,' I said, slightly out of breath. 'He gets it.'

'Okay, I could make a start when I'm finished here, but I won't be able to do the whole thing.'

I told her that was fine and grabbed a pen and paper while I waited, in case I forgot the words. But it didn't seem possible to forget this time. They were emblazoned on my brain. The sound of the needle carried on until it was my turn. I lifted my jumper to show her where the lines would go. She needed a magnifying glass – I wanted to keep the writing as small as it had appeared to me.

'Um, hang on, what did you say the final line was again?'

'*"Cold as marble. She was dead."*'

'It's already here.'

'What? It can't be.'

She brought me to a full-length mirror and gave me another smaller one to hold in my hand. My back was covered. The entire story was already inked on my skin.

'That's weird,' she said.

It wasn't weird. It was impossible. And yet there it was.

'It's a cool story.' She was trying to make the situation a little less weird by completely ignoring the look of shock on my face and focusing on what was real. I tried to do the same.

'Yeah.' That was all I could manage.

'Kind of gothic.'

She gently reminded me that she wanted to close up now and apparently I didn't need a tattoo after all.

I couldn't even remember walking home. I let myself in as quietly as possible. Madame Bowden was watching the TV she said she wouldn't use, at a volume that would wake the dead. Walking into my basement flat, I saw it with new eyes. Everything was brighter, clearer. As I took my jacket off and hung it on the hook, my body felt different. I felt physically stronger and freer, as though my muscles had been released from some invisible restraints. I looked at my neat little bed and the branches of the tree growing in an arch over it, the kitchenette with its pretty wall tiles, which I had thought were plain blue but were now patterned with little flowers. I realised that I loved living here and weirdly, just as I had read in Madame Bowden's face, I suddenly felt like I never wanted to leave. Like I *belonged* here. But why?

I put a saucepan of milk on the little stove and made myself a hot chocolate with two spoons of Nutella, an old trick my mother used to do for me when I was a child. I laid my quilt and pillows on the floor and tried to quieten my mind. Not an easy task after discovering the completed tattoo. Where had the story come from and what did it mean? It was very old, that was clear. The language was old-fashioned. And why had it come to me? These thoughts were interrupted by another question that I'd refused to address since I got back. Could my mother always speak? If so, why had she kept silent? I couldn't make sense of it. When I was young, she used to tell me that it was a special gift because she could hear things better.

I drank my hot chocolate and let the rich hazelnut flavours take me back in time. Again, I tried to quieten my thoughts and just listen. By now, I was used to the creaking and cracking of the branches stretching across the walls of my room. But there was another sound now, a kind of soft breathing … in and out. Maybe it was my own breath. Maybe not. There was something about this place. I couldn't explain it, but I felt like I was exactly where I was supposed to be.

I picked up my book, *A Place Called Lost.* The story continued with the man who had taken the old library all the way from Italy to Ireland. He had very little money, but he began building his shop with his bare hands on a small patch of forgotten land down a cobbled laneway. He was a man who believed that the imagination was the greatest tool of all. His clever wife believed that love trumped all, and together they built a shop of memories and dreams from the mysterious Italian library. In no time at all and in the way that often happens, the very things they had hoped to fill the shop with found their way to them. Treasures from all over the world began to fill the shelves that had once buckled under the weight of books. The building was pleased with its new surroundings, although it had not lost its innate desire to point visitors in the direction of their true north. Items would tumble off the shelves (a particular hazard in wintertime when Mr Fitzpatrick liked to stock an array of snowglobes).

Soon the couple welcomed their first child, a son. Mr Fitzpatrick imagined the day when he would take over the shop, but it was not to be. A woman with an English accent who wore trousers and a man's haircut was to become the unlikely custodian. She had no idea that she was joining a long line of specially chosen people to guard this portal of discovery.

Fortunately, she loved books and soon she and Mr Fitzpatrick's Nostalgia Shop got along extremely well indeed.

An Englishwoman with a love of books? The book was about this place, about Opaline. Henry had been right all along. What had drawn him to this place, to this story? I thought about the missing manuscript and the woman he had said owned a bookshop next door. Opaline. Like following a knitting pattern, I could see that everything was linked, but I had no idea how or why or what the end result would be.

Chapter Thirty

HENRY

He was living in Wales and had found a community of sorts. Seeing my father at the hospital was so unexpected, but I should have known he would want to see his grandchild. Even I couldn't deny him that. Yet Lucinda wouldn't let it go. She kept telling me how much he had changed, that he was really sticking to the programme this time because he was doing it for himself. He had already hit his rock bottom when my mother finally left him.

'It might do you good, you know?' she said, her index finger gripped tightly by Felicity while she rocked her gently in her arms.

'You look like you've been doing this your whole life.'

'I think I'm on some kind of hormonal high. At one with Mother Earth and all that. Don't worry, I'll be back to my bossy self soon enough.'

'I don't doubt it.'

We were sitting on my mother's couch, trying to get our heads around the fact that one minute we were kids building forts out of blankets and now here we were, grown-ups. The only thing was, I still felt like a kid. I hadn't a clue what I was doing with my life.

'I just don't think I can forgive him,' I said, taking advantage of this rare moment of openness between us.

'You don't have to forgive him, Henry. It's not even about him. This is for you, to help you move on.'

'What, are you saying I'm stuck in the past? Because I'm not. I hardly ever think about him.'

'Look. It's your choice, but I'm just saying that it's helped me to see him as he is now. It's the start of a process, or something. Acceptance, that's what my therapist calls it.'

'You're seeing a therapist?' I hadn't meant my voice to sound so shocked.

'So is Mum.'

'Oh.'

'I suppose we don't have that macho idea that we can handle everything ourselves.'

'Noted. Although I think that's the first time I've ever been referred to as macho.'

She rolled her eyes. She was a convincing little bugger. I had to give her that.

'What happened with Isabelle?'

'Oh, that.'

'I never thought you were right for each other.'

'Easy to say that now, isn't it?'

'Look,' she continued, switching the baby to her other arm, 'the woman you've met in Ireland, if you want it to work out, you've got to lose some of this baggage.'

'God, you make me sound like a real catch! I think this caring and sharing session has come to its natural conclusion.'

So I went to visit him and found myself in the middle of the Welsh countryside. My mother had given me the address of an old dilapidated manor, converted by some charitable organisation as a centre for recovering addicts. It was idyllic, vegetables growing in an allotment, a notice board with activities ranging from meditation to ceramics. It was not the kind of place I expected to find my father and perhaps that was why, when he trotted down the old stone stairs and into the front lawn to meet me, he looked so well. The bloated features and ruddy skin had mellowed into a healthier man, with a tan and the beginnings of a goatee.

'Henry, son,' he said, opening his arms to hug me, then thinking better of it. I offered my hand to shake. 'It's good to see you.'

I found, after a long train journey, years of resentment and a night of little or no sleep thanks to Felicity, I had nothing to say. Well, nothing amicable at any rate.

'This isn't a social call,' I said, following the pathway marked *River Contemplation*.

There were two simultaneous emotions battling underneath my cool countenance: relief that he was doing well and bitterness that he had not sorted his life out sooner. He seemed happy, which made me want to smash his face in and also buy him a cup of tea, find out how he had turned everything around.

'I'm going back to Ireland soon,' I said, as if he even knew I'd been out of the country. 'I'm chasing up a lead on a manuscript.'

'I remember you used to love collecting books when you were younger,' he said, as if this was some casual stroll down memory lane. As though, now that he had the time to reminisce, we could talk in a way we never had.

'I used to collect memorabilia too. Remember when I found that letter from Tolkien?' I couldn't help it. How dare he suddenly claim a role in my life that he had never played.

I looked across at him to find his head hung in shame. Well, he could play the victim all he liked, I wasn't going to get sucked in.

We had stopped walking and stood on the riverbank, both staring at the tranquil water moving slowly by. I could see the shadow of some fish treading water in the shallows. I sneaked a look at my father's profile and saw an expression, or rather an openness that allowed me to see the man and not the caricature he had become to me. Perhaps even to himself. He looked hurt. I knew that feeling well.

'There's nothing I can say that will change what I've done.'

This was unexpected and different. Normally he was trying to manipulate my feelings, pleading and making excuses. This sounded like someone who understood the impact of his actions.

'I am truly sorry that I wasn't the father you both needed. I'm ashamed of how I treated you all and that's what always drove me to drink again.'

'So what's different this time?' I kept looking at my shoes, as though willing them to carry me away. For some reason I seemed to be rooted to the spot.

'Honestly, Henry, I can't promise that this time is different. But I'm getting good help here. For the first time I can see that addiction is an illness. Just knowing that has helped, somehow.'

An illness. I had never seen it that way either. It just felt like he was having his kicks and we were the ones paying for it. Like he preferred the drink to his family.

'No alcoholic enjoys drinking,' he said, as though reading my thoughts. 'It's all you think about from the moment you open your eyes, but it's like swallowing poison.'

For the first time I could see that he was struggling too. He had become a monster in my eyes, but here he was, all human, and it took everything I had not to weep for everything we'd lost; beat his chest and tell him how much it hurt to lose him.

'I have no right to tell you this and clearly had no part in it, but you've grown into a fine man. Henry. Son.'

I nodded, acknowledging his words but not quite sure what to do with them. I couldn't stay any longer, it was overwhelming, and so I said I had a train to catch.

'Do you think you might visit again? Bring your sister and Felicity, perhaps?'

'Maybe. I'll ask.'

We shook hands and he said he wished me luck with the manuscript. Even the knowledge that he'd listened to me and was interested in my life was unsettling. It was like meeting my real father for the first time and realising that the tyrant I had grown up with was simply a fake or an impersonator who got all the lines wrong. This was the man I was meant to call Dad, but I hardly knew him. A familiar stranger. As I walked away I had the clear sense that my life was like a play of two parts and the audience were just polishing off their drinks in the lobby, returning for the second act.

~

I checked my phone for the millionth time. Still no response from Martha. However, there was an email from Princeton University. I clicked on it and scanned through the message, picking up phrases here and there like 'files relating to her personal life' and 'letter received shortly before her death'. But the words that made my heart race were 'Opaline Carlisle'. I opened the attachment to find a scan of a tea-coloured letter dated September 1963.

Dearest Sylvia,

How wonderful it was to see you in Dublin last month and to see that you are in good health. I know Mr Joyce would have been thrilled that you were chosen to open the museum at the Martello Tower and it did feel as though all our lives had come full circle ... To think that we were both incarcerated, albeit under very different circumstances. I'm sure you gave the Jerries what for!

Martha was right, I had been searching in all the wrong places. And not just for Opaline. Within a few clicks I had booked my flight back to Ireland.

Chapter Thirty-One

OPALINE

Dublin, 1923

I had arranged to meet Mr Hanna from Webb's bookshop at Bennett & Sons, Auctioneers, on 6 Upper Ormond Quay that afternoon. I walked through the bright red door into a building that was plain but bright, owing to the large Georgian windows that faced the River Liffey.

'First impressions?' Mr Hanna asked as a young man handed us a catalogue before we took our seats.

'Well, it's not Sotheby's,' I said in a pinched, imperial tone, as though I were Queen Mary.

'No, but the porter tastes better,' he said and winked.

He had suggested we make a round of all the auction rooms to see if there were any hidden gems going at a good price. I recognised one or two dealers over from London and for a moment I wondered if I would see Armand there. It was a silly idea. To my knowledge, he had never even been to Ireland and, not wanting to speak ill of my new home, I couldn't see that there would be anything to tempt someone with his eclectic tastes. A tall man with a magnificent white beard stood on the podium and welcomed us all. I immediately spotted something of interest in the catalogue and, as luck would have it, it was the first lot to come up.

'Lot number 527, a book on Armenian Grammar gifted by Lord Byron to Lady Blessington as a keepsake when they parted at Genoa on 2nd June 1823.'

The bearded man's assistant, a young woman with strawberry-coloured hair, held the book aloft in gloved hands to a rather subdued audience.

'A reminder of her most enduring literary work, *Conversations of Lord Byron with the Countess of Blessington*, 1834.'

I turned my head slightly to try and read the room. There didn't seem to be much interest.

'Who is Lady Blessington?' I asked Mr Hanna, nudging him with my elbow.

'I'm not an encyclopaedia,' he said, rolling his eyes playfully.

'Oh, don't pretend you don't know, you know everything,' I said, flattering him.

'It's a bit of a rags-to-riches story. She was born in Tipperary—'

'She's Irish?' I interrupted him.

'Why wouldn't she be?'

'I-I don't know.'

'Never presume,' he said sagely, as someone placed a bid of £5 for the book. 'Anyway, between one thing and another, she eventually married Charles Gardiner, the Earl of Blessington, and became inordinately rich and cultured. She wrote travelogues and novels and was quite famous for her literary salon at her home in Hyde Park.'

I stared at him wide-eyed, as another bidder put £7 on the book.

'How is it that I have never heard of this woman?'

'Ah, I suppose things go out of fashion.'

'Women, you mean. Women go out of fashion.'

'Do I hear eight pounds?' The auctioneer, perhaps taking an unconscious cue from Mr Hanna, spoke of Lady Blessington's famed Gore House, which had been knocked down to make way for The Royal Albert Hall. 'One of the leading literary and political salons; Dickens, Thackeray and Disraeli were frequent visitors.'

The following lots were ephemera: letters and locks of hair, ghastly portraits of long-dead people I did not know. A man took the seat beside me and nodded to myself and Mr Hanna. He did not have a catalogue and so I handed him mine. My interest had begun to wane until I heard the name Lady Sydney Morgan.

'And here we have a signed copy of her most well-known work, *The Wild Irish Girl*, gifted to the *Irish People* newspaper.'

I shifted forward on my seat so far that I was hardly sitting on it any more. The book itself was beautiful – red boards with a gilt-framed title, almost botanical in nature, with a swooping swallow descending from the top left, pretty ferns growing upwards and an illustrated butterfly on the bottom right. I had to have it.

'A passionately nationalistic novel,' the man continued, although I had already raised my hand – an auction room faux-pas! – 'and a founding text in the discourse of Irish nationalism. The novel proved so controversial in Ireland that Lady Morgan was put under surveillance by Dublin Castle.'

I didn't care how much it cost, I would own that book. Mr Hanna touched my arm in such a way as to calm my temper, but I was no longer open to advice. Besides, what was it the printer from Bath had said? *Women's literature was not as valuable as men's…*

'Six pounds to the young lady in the red hat.'

'Hah!' I punched the air and presumably made a display of myself, but I didn't care.

Mr Hanna clapped me on the back and I felt such a thrill as I had never known. Now I understood how Mr Rosenbach must have felt in Sotheby's.

'Congratulations, Mademoiselle,' came a voice from beside me that almost made me jump. I turned around to see a young man with bright eyes and fair hair. My heart fell back into its regular rhythm.

'*Merci,* Monsieur ...?'

'Ravel. You speak French?' he said, shaking my hand.

'Like the composer, Maurice! Just a little,' I replied. 'Do you have an interest in Irish literature?'

'*Certainement.* I am writing an article about the Irish vampire.' He delivered this with the most innocent smile, which was quite disconcerting.

'Good Lord.' I nudged Mr Hanna. 'I do hope there is no such thing.'

'Ah, that'll be our very own Bram Stoker.'

'Oh, yes, now that I am familiar with. What a fascinating book,' I added.

But the Frenchman shook his head. 'Not just Bram Stoker. Le Fanu also. But today, I am in search of an older book than that. In fact, it is said that Stoker was inspired by it.'

'Pray, which book? You must tell us!'

Just then, the bearded man called our attention to a dark-looking tome.

'And here we have a rare copy of *Melmoth the Wanderer* by Charles Maturin.'

'Ah, this is it!' he said.

I could not have been more excited if a vampire was in the room with us. That was the thing about books and writers and stories – you never knew where you would end up. I was so pleased when he won his trophy and also congratulated him.

'You said that Stoker was inspired by this Maturin fellow. How did you discover it?' I asked when the auction had ended and the sound of chairs scraping the floor filled the air.

'At Marsh's Library. It was the first public library in Ireland. *Mais*, why do I tell you this? I am certain you already know.'

I shook my head. I felt like a dunce that I had been in Dublin this long and still remained unforgivably ignorant of its literary heritage, beyond the standard Anglo-Irish authors whose writing was easily exported.

'But these are not Irish names, are they?' I turned again to Mr Hanna, the encyclopaedia.

'Huguenot, am I correct?' he replied.

'Yes, indeed,' the Frenchman agreed and before I knew it, he had invited me to visit Marsh's Library with him.

~

It was a fine day and it felt good to stretch my legs. Mr Hanna 'left us young ones to it' and we chatted enthusiastically as we crossed the Liffey and strolled down Fishamble Street. It turned out that Mr Ravel was from Paris and was studying Irish Literature at Trinity College. He was suitably impressed when I told him about my time working in Shakespeare and Company and we both wondered how it was that we hadn't met before.

'I used to go there all of the time! I took my coffee *juste en face.*'

'Isn't life queer?'

'I find the same in my research. For instance, I only just found out that Charles Maturin was in fact Oscar Wilde's great-uncle.'

'You cannot be serious?' I said, stopping just as we reached the imposing facade of St Patrick's Cathedral, its grey spires stretching towards a sky of the brightest blue.

'Yes, it's true. His niece was Jane Wilde, Oscar's mother. Of course, you must have read her works.'

'I'm afraid my academic knowledge of Irish literature is sorely lacking compared to yours, Mr Ravel, but I find this all so fascinating!'

'I must warn you that her writings are quite anti-British.'

I laughed as we carried on walking past the railings of the church grounds.

'I am not very easily offended on that score.'

He stopped at an iron gate and ushered me to take the steps ahead of him.

It looked like such a humble entrance for this, the oldest public library in Ireland. The building was equally modest – redbrick and inviting in its own way. No colonnades or grand statues, just a sign with the opening hours.

'It does belie the significance of what lies within,' he said, reading my thoughts.

I gasped as we got in and I had my first full view of the library. Row upon row of books housed in beautifully dark wooden shelves, ancient books, whispering like leaves on a breeze. There were benches in every alcove and the air was thick with knowledge. I was stunned into silence.

'Come, I will show you the cages,' he said, again with that sweet smile that jarred with his frightful words. 'Maturin lived quite close by and so he spent hours here, every day, voraciously reading books from the sixteenth century.'

We came to the 'cages', which were in fact little compartments with doors that were half wood, half metal grid. Inside, a private space walled in books for study.

'While it is a public library, it is not a lending library. The librarians noticed that many of their priceless manuscripts were being stolen from the library and—'

'Hence the cages. So, do they lock you in while you read, is that it?'

At that moment, I thought I heard someone calling my name. But I didn't turn around.

'Mon Opale.'

My body stiffened. I didn't dare hope.

'Bonjour,' Mr Ravel said to whoever stood behind us.

I turned around to see Armand, more handsome than my memory could ever do him justice, his dark features all the more beautiful here. It was all I could do not to fall into his arms and, but for the fact that Mr Ravel was beside me, I dare say I would have. Instead, we embraced and kissed on each cheek.

'Mr Ravel, may I introduce my ... fellow book dealer, Mr Hassan.'

The two men shook hands and I found myself at a complete loss as to how I should handle the situation. My hand cradled my belly instinctively. Here stood the father of my child, but social etiquette prevented me from uttering a word. Mr Ravel had been so kind and chivalrous, how could I tell him to leave?

'Mr Ravel, I beg your forgiveness, but I have a very important business matter to discuss with Mademoiselle—'

'Gray!' I shouted.

The two men looked at me.

'He always pronounces it incorrectly,' I stammered, feeling utterly stupid.

'Of course,' Mr Ravel bowed slightly in the most respectful way that I felt a pang of guilt at simply abandoning him.

'And do call in to my shop,' I said, hoping that he would.

He smiled kindly and was gone.

Armand took my hand and led me into one of the open cages. I let my body lean against the ladder that was placed there for reaching books on the higher shelf and he pressed himself against me, his mouth on my neck, like a vampire himself. We didn't speak; the only sound was our breathing and the occasional turn of a page from the readers outside.

'Wait, wait. Stop,' I said, panting slightly. 'What are you doing here?'

He looked up at me and smiled, his deep brown eyes lit by rays of the afternoon sun, revealing flecks of amber. I knew then I loved him. I loved him madly. But I wasn't sure if he ever could or would love me.

'I'm after a book, of course,' he grinned and pulled the top of my blouse down revealing the white curve of my breast.

Not for me, then. He kissed me and I forgot myself momentarily.

'No, I mean what are you doing in Ireland? Why didn't you send a telegram?'

He stepped back slightly and sat on the desk opposite, where some old books lay open. His body language changed; he picked up a pen and fidgeted with it. When he looked at me, there was an air of disappointment in his eyes that I had spoiled the moment with my question. I'm not sure I had ever observed him so keenly, but then, I was never carrying his child before. An uncomfortable truth formed first as a sick feeling in the pit of my stomach, and his lack of response confirmed it in my thoughts.

'You weren't going to tell me you were here, were you?'

He got up again, all charm.

'It's not that, Opaline. You know what it's like, following a lead. I had not planned to come here, but a collector requested a very specific manuscript—'

I'd heard enough. I straightened my blouse and was struggling with the doors of the cage when I felt his arms around me.

'Please, *Mon Opale,* there's no need for such hysteria. I'm here now. Let's not ruin it.'

I sighed deeply, then turned around to face him.

'I have something to tell you,' I said, unsure of how exactly I was going to do it.

'Marvellous, we shall meet tonight for dinner. But now I have work to do.'

He looked so pleased with himself and I realised how much I liked being the one to make him happy.

Perhaps he would want the baby after all.

~

I arranged that he should come to the shop for an aperitif. My excitement made me giddy and ditsy – I dropped a glass and scratched one of my favourite records while preparing the shop for his arrival. It was overwhelming, Armand being in Ireland. I wanted him to love it as much as I did, so everything had to be exactly right.

Not long after the cuckoo clock announced that it was eight o'clock, I heard the handle of the door opening and the sound of his shoes scuffing the tiles. Mother had always said that punctuality said a lot about a person. I smoothed my hair behind my ears and climbed the stairs to the shop.

'Opaline?'

'Yes, *j'arrive*.' I hadn't spoken French in so long, it sounded strange and I blushed. When I reached the top of the stairs I saw him standing there in a dark suit, his hair damp from the rain outside. 'Come in,' I said, even though he was already inside. I was so nervous and I began rushing around and generally fussing with drinks and chairs and frothy conversation about the books on the shelves and Mr Fitzpatrick's antiques. In a silly way, I suppose I wanted him to be proud of what I had accomplished.

Eventually he put his hand on mine and asked me to sit beside him. I immediately filled the silence with yet more casual conversation, as though we were two complete strangers.

'So where are you staying?'

'The Shelbourne.'

Of course. Only the best for Armand. Or rather his employers.

'What is it? You are not yourself.'

I took a deep breath. I could no longer put it off.

'There's something important I have to tell you and I just don't quite know how to put it.'

He smiled.

'With words, of course.'

I returned his smile, but my doubts grew.

'You know I had the impression you were hiding a great secret, ever since I met you in England.'

'Really? Oh, Armand.'

Did he already know? Perhaps he had come to Ireland for me after all.

'One can always tell,' he said assuredly.

'Can you?' I covered my stomach.

'Of course! You found the manuscript you were looking for, didn't you? It doesn't take a genius to work out why you were at Honresfield. It's something to do with the Brontës, is it not?'

My heart sank, but I kept the smile frozen on my face.

'Oh. Why, yes. You know me too well.'

I sat there, smiling inanely like an idiot while he smiled politely back.

'Well?'

'Well what?'

'Aren't you going to show it to me?'

Wasn't I going to show it to him? I repeated the words in my head. It was, after all, the discovery I had been simply dying to tell someone about. And here I was with one of Europe's greatest book scouts, one of a small, select group of people who could truly grasp the significance and sheer luck of my achievement, and yet I hesitated. In that second, my conscience revealed to me the truth I had been trying to not see, ever since we'd first met. I didn't trust him. And yet now, here I was, faced with a choice of telling him about the baby or the manuscript. I had to decide what I was willing to risk.

I chose the manuscript.

'Wait there,' I said, as I took the sewing box from the drawer. I insisted we both wear cotton gloves to handle it and while he examined the notebook, I told him the story of how I found Mrs Brown in London and that my last-minute decision to buy this piece of memorabilia resulted in the discovery of Emily's manuscript. He wasn't to know it, but his reaction would decide everything for me.

'*Non, mais c'est incroyable*!'

'I know,' I said, pulling my chair closer to him and delighting in this shared moment. 'Having studied their letters at Honresfield, I'm certain this is Emily's penmanship.'

'*Bien joué, ma belle*,' he said, kissing me on the lips and I felt as though I were sitting on a cloud.

I'd never been so happy. I would tell him. Right away.

'Armand—'

'You must let me handle this for you,' he said, cutting across me.

'I'm sorry?'

'I will approach some of my collectors. I also have good contacts at the auction houses. *Mon Dieu*, where to begin?' He laughed, he was so giddy with excitement.

I reached across and took the notebook and sewing box back from him.

'There's no need. I'm perfectly capable of making the arrangements.'

He looked at me rather quizzically.

'I have contacts in the rare book world too.' I had intended to say it lightly, but I noticed a slight edge to my voice.

'But this is of huge significance, *Mon Opale*. We must achieve the greatest price for this, it will secure our reputation for ever.'

It was astonishing how quickly he had begun to talk of 'we' and 'our'. The elusive Armand had suddenly found it very easy to commit. I stood up and put the box back in the desk drawer, locking it with a key I replaced in my trouser pocket. I finally understood what it meant to have the wind taken out of your sails.

'Thank you, Armand, but as you can see, I have been running a successful business for some time now. *I* found the manuscript and I will decide what is to be done with it. Besides, I'm not sure it belongs in private hands. It might be of greater value to a museum.'

'Oh please, you cannot equate this little shop with the real world of rare literary antiquities. Opaline, you must see sense. I did not want to be forced into saying this, but you give me no choice. No serious collector will deal with a woman. Coming from you, they will never believe the provenance of the item and even if they do, they will know they can undervalue it.'

Armand revealed all of his true colours in a dazzling display. He didn't think me capable or up to the task because of my gender.

'I thought we were equals,' I said.

He stood up and walked towards me, attempting to take my hands in his, but I pulled away.

'Now you are being ridiculous.'

'Ridiculous?'

'I am not questioning your ability, I am simply being realistic. It's the world we live in.'

'And you have no interest in changing it, do you? It suits you better to maintain the status quo. That way, you can take my success and pass it off as your own!' I was shouting now. He had suddenly become ugly to me. The man I had adored for all this time, even though I'd always suspected that he was using me somehow.

'Why did you come for me at the hotel that day? I can never quite work out why you went out of your way to help me.'

'What are you talking about?'

'I'm not sure you've ever done anything for anyone unless it somehow benefits you.'

He looked at me as though he wanted to strike me, and the woman inside of me that I was still in the process of becoming raised her chin to him. His eyes burned and his jaw tightened.

'Perhaps you thought I could be of value to you, another contact.'

For the first time, I could see how insecure he was, underneath that glossy veneer. 'Because deep down, you don't believe you're capable of achieving anything on your own, do you? That's why you charm people into giving away secrets, so you can steal them and make them your own.'

'*Ferme ta gueule, salope.*'

I wasn't terribly familiar with French slang, but I knew the word for whore. With that, he turned on his heels and walked out, never to return.

Chapter Thirty-Two

MARTHA

I woke before dawn. I had tossed and turned all night and it sounded like the house had too. Something caught my eye in the morning gloom. The ceiling. I reached over to turn on my bedside lamp and looked up. Where the light pendant used to be, at the centre of the room, were now roots. A knot of tiny tendrils was growing out of the hole in the ceiling, like a chandelier. I stared at them for a while, until all I could see was their intricate beauty. Each root was made up of tiny, smaller roots, which broke into smaller roots again. All playing a vital role. Suspended, they seemed to search the air for something of value to nourish them. I wanted to reach out and touch them but jumped when my alarm rang.

'I feel like I'm going to vomit.' I stood behind Madame Bowden, brushing her hair, as she sat regally at her dressing table.

The room was gloomy, as she kept the curtains closed to the cold, grey morning. Today would be my first day as a student in

Trinity (albeit an evening class in literature) and I was, frankly, shitting myself.

'Dry toast.'

'I thought that was for pregnancy?'

'Good God, you're not pregnant, are you?'

'Of course not!' I stole a glance at her reflection in the mirror. It's strange how people can look so different in a mirror – the features seem to shift around, like shadows as the sun passes overhead.

'Listen to me, Martha – if you're not scared, then you're not living.'

I wasn't sure I wanted a weird pep talk at that moment, but it was what I got. I pursed my lips, gave her a withering look and hurried downstairs to make us both some toast before I set off.

My mind was frazzled and full of doubts. What if I humiliated myself by not knowing anything? Would I make any friends or end up sitting alone for the entire term? What if, what if, what if … The thoughts were endless. Where had the feeling of strength from the other night disappeared to? Why did my life always feel like two steps forward and three back? I grabbed my jacket and my new backpack from the hook in the hallway and stopped short by the spot where Shane had tumbled over the bannister. I reached out and touched the wooden newel post. It felt smooth and solid under my hands. I tried to breathe deeply into my belly like that yoga girl on YouTube said. Apparently it helped to calm anxious thoughts.

I counted one … two … three.

The house creaked softly and I closed my eyes for a moment. I had an image of a cradle being gently rocked in a bough. Madame Bowden's words returned to me. *If you're not scared, you're not living*. Up to now, I had never associated fear with anything positive. But maybe there were different kinds of fear.

'There's only one way to find out.'

My eyes flew open wide. She was there, again, sneaking up on me.

'What?'

'You're going to miss your bus at this rate, now shoo!'

I didn't move and looked at her with pleading eyes. 'What if I can't do it? What if everyone else is smarter than me?'

'I don't recall you having any doubts about your abilities to work here – and, frankly, you were mediocre at the start.'

'Thanks. That really helps,' I replied flatly.

She pursed her lips and sighed heavily.

'Tell me, that book you've been reading in the kitchen when you think I'm not looking …'

'*Normal People*?'

'Yes, that one. Do you like it?'

I considered her question. It wasn't at all what I expected. I don't know if I liked it as such, but I couldn't stop reading it. Connell and Marianne had also come to feel like real people to me. I was completely invested in their lives.

'It's good because I feel like I'm a fly on the wall, watching everything happen. And I like that Connell is a country boy, applying to Trinity.' I smiled.

'So, the characters are relatable.'

'Yes! That's it. But I get so angry with Marianne. I mean, why would she let people treat her that way?'

'Maybe she thinks she deserves it.'

The realisation was cold and hard. Even I couldn't see why someone would feel so unlovable that they'd accept abuse. I'd been uncomfortable reading her story all along but at the same time I felt like I wasn't going through this alone. If it could happen to someone like Marianne, who was wealthy and intelligent, it could happen to anyone.

'I think it's easy to get confused about what love is when you're young. Even the title kind of suggests that we normalise bad behaviour in relationships, or assume that being normal is the most important thing, so we hide all of the ugly stuff that happens to us. I mean, who even is normal, anyway?'

'Congratulations. You've just delivered your first critical review of a book. Now off you go and no more of this nonsense.'

As I walked down the steps of 12 Ha'penny Lane, I looked back to see her fading reflection in the glass of the living-room window. That was how it was when I tried to read her; she was always obscured by the light, rather than illuminated by it. Like an overexposed photograph. She was unlike anyone I'd ever met and maybe that was a good thing.

Chapter Thirty-Three

HENRY

The air felt different somehow, as I got off the bus in O'Connell Street. They say you can never enter the same river twice and maybe the same was true of countries. The streets were busy, full of people with purpose. As was I.

Walking up the steps of number 12, I took a moment to straighten my jacket and gripped the envelope with the letter I'd printed out. I couldn't wait to tell her about Opaline, Sylvia, the book. I tapped the knocker with a firm but not overly assertive force. It's the little things.

'Oh.'

'Well, you did knock,' replied Madame Bowden. 'Shall I simply close the door again and we can pretend this never happened?'

'No, sorry, I just—'

'Yes?'

'I was expecting to see Martha, that's all.'

'Oh, were you? Despite the fact that you left without a word, you expected the girl to be awaiting your return? Perhaps with a hanky dabbing her moistened eyes?'

'No, of course not.' I was completely flustered.

'Well then, you can walk back the way you came and we'll say no more about it.'

'No, now hang on, I left a note. Didn't she get it?' I felt a bit panicked. 'She does still live here?'

The old lady sighed and rolled her eyes, as though I were a puppy soiling her carpet.

'Oh, I suppose you might as well come through. You're here now.'

She stood back and I stepped inside, slightly annoyed at – well, everything. This wasn't going how I'd planned.

'I'm afraid you'll have to fend for yourself if you want tea,' she said, arranging herself on the cream sofa, with sprays of flowers forming guard on side tables at each end. 'Of course we could always forgo the niceties and head straight for the brandy.' She nodded towards a little drinks caddy by the fireplace and I poured us two healthy measures of amber liquid.

'So, why have you returned?'

'Hang on, how do you know who I am?'

'Oh please, let's not delude ourselves. She told me about you. The scholar chasing after a lost bookshop. I wasn't sure what she saw in you, but now that I can see you in person,' she said, adjusting her spectacles, 'I suppose I can see a certain boyish charm. Is that what attracted your fiancée, Mr Field?'

God, she really had told her everything.

'Do men like you ever realise the hurt you cause, flitting in and out of people's lives? No, I suppose not. That would require some sort of intellect.'

It appeared that no response was required from me. I was simply to bear witness to my own character assassination by a woman I had just met – and the worst part was that she was terrifyingly accurate in her summation. Except for one thing.

'I love her.'

'How do you know?'

'Sorry?'

'What is it you love about Martha? Is it how she makes you feel about yourself? Does she boost your'—she let her eyes fall here—'flaccid ego? Is that it? Do you get some kind of pleasure out of having two women on the go? I know your type, Mr Field and let me tell you, my Martha is worth ten of you.'

'No, you see, that's what I've been trying to tell her. The night we kissed I knew I had to end things with Isabelle. But I owed her more than a phone call. I had to go back to London straightaway and explain.' I felt ridiculous explaining myself to a complete stranger. But I could see how much she cared for Martha and that gave us common ground. 'I've been trying to call Martha ever since but she must have disconnected her number. My sister just had a baby and that delayed my return here, but I got back as soon as I could.'

She seemed to be considering what I had said and it seemed like an age before she spoke again.

'Much has transpired since you last saw her. I'm not sure if she'll want to see you.'

'Please, Madame Bowden. You're right. I've never known or understood what it really means to love or be loved. I'm not going to blame my past, but we all have one and it follows us around like a prison, always keeping us from the person we truly wish to be. Martha is the bravest person I've ever met and she's inspired what little bravery I have inside to listen to my heart for once. I don't just love her for how she makes me feel, I love her because when she came into my life it was like the lights came on. Everything suddenly had meaning and I think, *I hope*, it was the same for her. We all have crap parts and good parts inside, but when you meet someone who makes you realise that it's all okay, you think, what in God's name did I do to deserve it? All of my life I've been searching for hidden treasure, fortunes outside of myself. But Martha, she found them in me. I'm not perfect, by any means, but I know I want to spend the rest of my life making her smile. So I'm damned if I will let her go without a fight.'

She swallowed audibly.

I was almost shaking with the conviction I felt in that moment. For the first time, I had heard myself speak the truth straight from my heart and it sounded as clear and bright as a bell.

After a pause, she raised her glass and, with a grin, clinked it against mine.

'You might just do, I suppose.'

'Thank you. I know Martha is still married but—'

The look on her face made me stall my glass mid-air.

'You might want to take a seat.'

Chapter Thirty-Four

OPALINE

Dublin, 1923

Secrets are all very well and good, but having a fake name, a hidden pregnancy, a forgotten manuscript and forbidden feelings were all making for a very complicated and lonely existence. What compounded my isolation was the constant background fear of Lyndon coming to take everything away from me. It felt as though I were only living a half-life, shrouded in subterfuge. Every time I looked at Emily's manuscript (which was often!) I ruminated over the unfairness of my situation. The most amazing moment in my life and I realised there wasn't a soul I could share it with. Perhaps I could trust Mr Hanna, but how could I be sure he wouldn't let it slip to the wrong person?

It was the loneliness I felt at that moment that spurred me to do something rash. I snatched a piece of paper from the drawer and wrote a hurried letter to Sylvia in Paris. I didn't want to take the usual precaution of sending it through Armand. It felt wonderful and exhilarating to relay my news and I knew she would not tell a soul without my consent. *I'm going to be a mother!* I wrote before signing off, knowing that this would not be as exciting to her as the Brontë find. I told her to respond immediately, jotting down my phone number. I sealed the envelope and left it on my desk until I found a chance to walk to the postbox. Just knowing the excitement that Sylvia would share in my news gave me the strength to carry on with my day as normal and delay my decision on what action to take.

~

I had a busy afternoon and found myself tiring easier than usual. A group of students stopped by looking for a publication by a pioneering new writer, Virginia Woolf. When I bent down to find a copy of *Night and Day* on the lower shelf, I felt faint.

The atmosphere was heavy and humid, yet it wasn't until I was about to close the shop that fat raindrops began to splash on the footpath outside, turning it from grey to black. I was replacing some books and tidying the shelves when I heard the bell go. I was surprised to see Mr Ravel standing at the door, his overcoat sparkling with raindrops.

'Mr Ravel, what a lovely surprise!'

It was a lovely surprise, but I couldn't help wishing it had been Armand. Despite everything, I still hoped he would come and find me; say it was all a big mistake and that he wanted us to be together after all. But here was a very nice man and I was determined to at least pretend that I was moving forward.

We kissed on both cheeks and he asked, rather redundantly, if it was all right that he had stopped by unannounced.

'Well, of course it's all right. If people didn't stop by unannounced I'd have no customers at all,' I said, ushering him inside.

He took a moment to breathe in the atmosphere of the shop, then turned to me with a meaningful look.

'Mademoiselle Gray, your shop is like a treasure chest.'

Normally I batted any kind of compliments aside – it didn't do to court approval. Yet his words meant very much to me at that moment on many different levels. I offered to make some tea and left him to browse the shelves.

As I carried the tray up the stairs from the kitchen, I called out to him.

'In fact your timing couldn't be more perfect, Mr Ravel. I'm celebrating some very exciting news.'

I thought perhaps we should be drinking champagne instead of tea and was about to ask his opinion when I realised that the door was wide open, rain pouring in and no trace of Mr Ravel. I put the tray down on my desk and went to look up and down the street, but he was nowhere to be seen. I closed the door and shook my head, mystified. Then I glanced towards the desk and my heartbeat slowed, then speeded up. The letter I had addressed to Sylvia was gone. I searched the floor in case it had fallen, but it was nowhere to be seen. I covered my mouth with my hand, my breath ragged against my fingers. What had I written? The book. The baby.

Who was Mr Ravel? Was no one to be trusted now? Were they all working for my brother?

I had to leave, and I had to do it quickly.

It is strange how seemingly inconsequential conversations suddenly take on the mantle of fate and destiny when cast in a new light. I had been exchanging delightful letters with Mabel Harper, a woman who wrote an amusing column for the newspapers about her and her husband's life and travels. Her husband just happened to be none other than Lathrop Colgate Harper – a successful rare book dealer and authority on medieval manuscripts. She had suggested on numerous occasions that I travel to New York and visit the infamous Book Row, and now that I had the money to do it, I decided to waste no time.

I rushed out to the travel agency on D'Olier Street and just made it before they closed. I booked my ticket for a crossing from Cobh to New York on the White Star Line two days hence. I would travel to Cork in the morning and stay overnight there, before taking the tender out to the steamship bound for America. My hand shook as I signed the cheque and the man behind the counter asked if I was quite well. I caught sight of my reflection in the window and saw a pale face with a hunted expression. I would not ignore my instincts this time. Lyndon had found me. Perhaps he had been intercepting my letters all along. After all, what use was Armand? He clearly had no loyalty to me. I left the office and headed straight for the bank.

~

'What's happened?' Matthew asked, dismissing his secretary and leading me into his office. I was so touched by his concern for me and the baby and felt once again that familiar pull towards him. His kindness was a stark contrast to all of the other men in my life. But I could no longer entertain any feelings of weakness hoping to be saved. I had to save myself.

'I want you to keep something safe for me.' I reached into my back and removed the sewing box – contents still intact.

'What is it?'

I wasn't sure whether he would be better off not knowing, but I couldn't help myself. I steadied my breath and spoke as slowly as I could.

'I don't have much time, but I believe that I have found'—

sharp inhale—'Emily Brontë's second novel. Well, not a novel, but a manuscript. Well, part of it at any rate.'

I stood there like a bow, waiting for the arrow to land. It did not.

'Did you hear what I said?'

'Yes, but I thought she only wrote one novel. *Wuthering Heights*, wasn't it?'

I sighed. It was always difficult to deal with civilians.

'Precisely, Matthew. That's what everyone *presumed*. But I now believe I have proof that she was writing a second. This could change the literary landscape as we know it!'

He finally began to understand the enormity of the discovery.

'Good Lord, Opaline, this is fascinating!'

'It is!' I agreed, shaking my head vigorously. 'You're the first person I've been able to tell. But there's something else …'

'Why are you giving it to me?' Matthew asked.

'I'm going away for a while and it's too valuable to leave it in the shop.'

'Oh, I see.' He gave me a concerned look, reading my expression, no doubt.

'You are the only person I can trust.'

'You're shaking,' he said, taking my hands in his.

'It's just the cold, nothing more.' I had to leave. Matthew had his own family to protect. I had to protect mine. I slipped my hands out of his and gave him my brightest smile.

'I'll be back for it soon, just keep it safe until then,' I said and rushed out of the office before I started to cry. I felt so lonely at that moment, but I had to be strong.

~

When I returned home, something still didn't feel right. My books were silent around me, as though holding their breath. I struggled down the stairs to my flat. Had it gotten narrower or was I simply becoming plumper? It felt as though the very fabric of the building was contracting around me. I needed to sleep. I was so very tired. But I still had to pack. I decided I would just lie down for a moment and drifted off whilst humming to the baby. I woke up to a bright light in my face.

Chapter Thirty-Five

MARTHA

First of February. St Brigid's Day. I wanted to get out of the house and get out of Dublin. One thing you miss in a big city is the big sky of the countryside. But what I missed most were the storms that would blow in off the Atlantic on the west coast and drown out all the painful voices in your head. It was no day for the beach. The weather was freezing, with actual frost on the window when I woke up, but I was determined. I brought a flask of hot chocolate with me and took the Dart out to Sandycove, a small horseshoe-shaped beach.

The sun was rising just as I walked past the Martello Tower, casting a pink glow all around. It was beautiful, but also bitterly cold. Thankfully there was no wind and the water's surface looked calm enough to walk upon. I used to swim in the sea at home, but I stopped when I married Shane. Like so many other parts of my life, it just fell away as though it didn't matter. As though I didn't matter.

There were a few other people who had the idea of welcoming the first day of spring with a baptism in the sea. At least, it was spring according to the Celtic calendar, marking the transition from one season to the next. I stood and watched for a while as some bathers walked purposefully into the water and never hesitated, while others inched their way slowly. I couldn't decide which approach was better. There was no way of avoiding the shock and the pain of the cold. Perhaps it was better to get the hard part over with quickly and reach the exhilaration of having mastered your own senses and the environment. That was why we were all doing this, I thought. To prove something to ourselves. That we could do something so physically uncomfortable in order to feel our own sense of power. Or something.

I should have felt more powerful, now that Shane was gone. But I didn't. I felt numb. I felt guilty. I didn't feel as though good had triumphed over evil. There were no winners, only wounded people picking up the pieces of their broken lives. I would never know why Shane came into my life; why I was fated to live that experience. I often wondered if there was something I had done wrong to deserve it. But in my book *A Place Called Lost* the author believed that every hardship in life was a key to some greater understanding, and it was up to you if you chose to use it to unlock the future or bolt the door.

I inhaled deeply and looked out towards the horizon. The tips of the grey clouds glowed peach and the freezing water was mercurial, save for a golden strip that sparkled in the sunlight. I didn't want to bolt the door. I wanted to open it.

I unbuttoned my coat and pushed off one boot and then the other. I kept undressing, as though hypnotised by the view, and I walked, like one of those purposeful people, straight into the freezing water. I never hesitated. I kept going, emitting occasional squeaks of disbelief. Could it really be *this* cold? *Squeak!* Am I really doing this? *Squeak!* Will I keep going? *Squeak!* When the water reached my bum I thought I would scream like a banshee, but somehow that squeak only happened internally.

The moment had come, the momentum carried me and I dove down into the blue, my arms powering through the water and my legs kicking. I didn't stop until my blood was pumping loudly in my ears and I felt a little less like dying.

'Wow!' I shouted eventually, spotting an older man swimming nearby.

'Yeah. Bit chilly,' he said with a wink.

'Just a bit.' I was treading water, looking back at the little cove where more people were arriving and undressing. One person in particular caught my eye. He was pushing his hair back off his face and stamping his feet to beat away the cold. I didn't hesitate. I began swimming back and strode out of the water to where he stood and walked straight into Henry's arms. He unzipped his jacket and pulled me in, wrapping me up tight. For the first time I could remember, I felt as though I was exactly where I wanted to be. I lifted my head and without even opening my eyes, my lips found his. The warmth of his mouth was so inviting and soft that I almost forgot we were on a public beach. I just wanted to be with him, then and there.

'You taste salty,' he said.

I just smiled at him and reached my hand up to his jaw, letting my fingers run along his stubble and the dimples in his cheek, as though I were mapping out the territory of my new home. I kissed him again and when I opened my eyes, it was snowing.

'I've never been on a beach when it's snowing,' I said, suddenly feeling the cold again. 'It's so beautiful.'

'Beautiful,' he said, never taking his eyes off me.

He held my towel around me while, with as much awkwardness as is possible for one human being, I tugged off my damp swimming costume and forced my arms and legs back into my clothes. I could feel him staring at my back, but he never said anything.

'How did you know where to find me?'

'Madame Bowden told me you were at Joyce's Tower.'

'Joyce's Tower?'

Henry pointed back towards the round tower behind us, the stone now turned grey with snowflakes all around.

'That's what I wanted to tell you – Sylvia Beach was here. There's a museum inside and she came to Dublin to open it. She met with Opaline.'

His excitement almost broke my heart. Was that the only reason he had come back? For Opaline and that damned manuscript?

I stepped back from him and shook my head in disbelief. How stupid I was to think that he was here for me. I stuffed my towel into my bag and sprinted towards the stone steps to get back to the train. One was just arriving and I jumped on it before he had a chance to catch up. I saw him shouting and waving as the train pulled away, but I couldn't understand, although I knew too well what rejection felt like.

Chapter Thirty-Six

HENRY

I got very, very drunk.

I was having a dream about Isabelle; she was extremely cross about something and kept shouting at me to wake up. I tried to ignore her. I didn't want to wake up. Then her accent changed to a thick Dublin brogue.

'Are ya all right there, love?' said the woman in front of me.

She was kneeling on the ground, which must have meant I was on the ground too. I rubbed my eyes wide. No, it wasn't a dream. I didn't recognise her. She had dark hair and was wearing a puffy jacket, which seemed strange. Had I fainted? That was when I became aware of the sound of the traffic. I was outside, on the street, lying in a heap of rubbish.

'Where am I?' I asked.

'Thank God, will I call ya an ambulance?'

'What? No, of course not.' I attempted to get to my feet, but as soon as I moved, I felt a splitting headache over my right eye. Instinctively, my hand went to touch it and when I felt a dampness on my fingertips, I realised I was bleeding.

'He looks fairly battered, doesn't he, Marie?'

Great. I had an audience. I tried to retrace my steps, but all I found were blank spaces. Why was I feeling so unbelievably ill?

I heaved myself upright against the steps beside me.

'The smell of drink off him,' I heard the woman say. 'Like a brewery.'

Oh God. That's when it all started coming back to me. The pub. The whiskey. The blokes who came in to celebrate their friend's last night as a bachelor. The bet that they could drink me under the table. The whiskey. The sing-song. Had I sung 'Molly Malone'? Standing on a chair? Oh God. Smoking a joint with someone outside on the street. Then some other people, they thought he owed them money. Me explaining I'd only just met this guy. Then the punch in the face, the rubbish bin being dumped on me, repeatedly.

'Thank you, ladies, I think I'll be perfectly fine in a minute. Just need to get my bearings,' I groaned, as I held on to the railings and stood swaying, adjusting to the daylight.

'Are ya sure, love?'

I wasn't really sure of anything. When I'd returned to the B&B, Nora's husband Barry had told me how Martha had called by, looking for me. He'd told her I had packed up and gone home to England. The idiot! If only his wife had been there, she would have told Martha I was coming back. And now she wanted nothing to do with me. I'd upended my entire life to be with her and now she wouldn't even see me.

I took a few tentative steps, wincing with the effort. I looked up and saw the street sign. Ha'penny Lane. I was right outside her house. I didn't know what to do. I couldn't show up looking like this and besides, she'd made her feelings abundantly clear. The decision was taken out of my hands when I saw her pulling the curtains at the front window. She looked out, disbelieving, and bent down to get a better look. Then her hand went to her mouth. I tried to wave with my good hand. She disappeared back into the shadows and reappeared at the front door.

'What in God's name has happened to you?'

'Um, I believe I had a disagreement of sorts.'

She gave me a look of pity, which, under these circumstances, I was willing to accept.

She brought me inside and down the steps to the kitchen at the back of the house. She pulled out a chair for me at the kitchen table and then searched in a cupboard for some first-aid paraphernalia.

'How did you end up here?'

'Honestly, I have no idea. I may have been slightly inebriated.'

She arrived back at the table with a bowl of warm water, cotton wool, a tub of some odd-smelling cream and plasters. Neither of us spoke while she went about her work. I let my eyes close and permitted myself, for these moments at least, to imagine that everything was okay. That she did still have feelings for me. That somehow, it would work out.

'Will I live?' I asked sheepishly as she began to clear the things away. It was torment to watch her lithe figure in simple leggings and a T-shirt, imagining how good it had felt when she was in my arms on the beach. I ached to hold her again.

She looked back at me from the sink with a welcome grin. 'I think so.'

'Thank you, for all of this,' I said.

'It's nothing. I've had … practice.'

I didn't know what to say about her husband's death. About any of it. So I did what we Field men did best. I changed the subject.

'You know, before you came, I used to stand out there for hours,' I said, gesturing up to the bare patch of land just visible from one of the kitchen windows. 'I used to think that maybe I'd find some kind of clue, an imprint of the building. Like when there's a drought in the summer and farmers find crop circles on the land. I dunno. I was just so sure.'

'I wonder if people are like that?' she said, sitting back down at the table.

I shook my head in bewilderment.

'Like, if you can still see the outline of who they were, you know, before?'

'Wow. I don't know. I hope so.'

I took her hand in mine and for a moment she let me hold it, before pulling it away.

'I'm sorry, Henry, but I just can't.'

'But if only you'd got my note, or if that idiot at the B&B had told you I was coming back—'

'It doesn't matter now. Madame Bowden explained about the note, but it's not even about that. I just, I can't risk *this*.' She pointed to the space between us. Whatever it was. 'I have to find my crop circles.'

I smiled. Only she could make breaking my heart sound so charming. I had to respect her wishes. God knows her husband hadn't. Yet, I didn't have the strength to get up and walk out of there without her.

'And I know you'll find your manuscript,' she said, with a sadness in her voice. 'You'll tell me if you do, won't you?'

'Of course,' I said, remembering that I still had a printout of the letter from Opaline in my pocket. 'Actually, I had wanted to show you this,' I said, taking it out. I explained how I had contacted Princeton to search through Sylvia Beach's archives, just as she had suggested. 'It's thanks to you really.'

I handed it to her.

She read the last paragraph aloud. '"Thank you once again for taking copies of my book with you – after all those days stocking the shelves at Shakespeare and Company, it's amusing to think that my book will be there now too. Maybe one day she will find me." She wrote a book?' she asked, after some moments had passed.

'Sounds like it. But the real question is, what happened to her?'

Chapter Thirty-Seven

OPALINE

Dublin, 1923

The journey seemed to go on for hours. We travelled unfamiliar roads that jolted the back of the car and me with it. I cradled my belly, instinctively protecting my little one within. It was dark when he'd pulled me from my bed and even though I knew what was happening, and had long been expecting it, it felt like an out-of-body experience. As though it were happening to someone else.

'Where are we going?' I asked again, and again Lyndon ignored the question. 'Are you taking me to see Mother?'

I assumed that, having found me in the family way, I would have to face the wrath of a formal excommunication from the family.

'In case you didn't notice, I have a business to run. Surely the man you had following me told you that? The one who stole the letter? Mr Ravel. I cannot leave the shop unattended and swan off to England.'

'We're not going to England.'

He spoke with a calmness I found even more disconcerting than if he had shouted at me. All I could see were the leather gloves he wore gripping the steering wheel and the side of his face. The bad side, that seemed to melt downwards. I thought perhaps we were driving south, to take the ferry from there. But now that I focused on the road signs, I realised we were driving west.

'Where are you taking me?' I asked again, turning and looking out the back window. 'Lyndon, stop the car now and let me out!'

Still, he made no sound.

'Lyndon!' I said and began shaking his arm.

I didn't anticipate his quick movements. He swung his arm back and elbowed me in the face. The pain rendered me silent. I cupped my nose as it began to bleed. I had no tissue and had to use my sleeve.

'We're almost there, at any rate,' he said, as though we were having a casual conversation.

I didn't speak again. Didn't trust my voice not to quiver. I wouldn't let him see that I was afraid. The landscape outside was dull and brown – bare trees, dying grass on the verges. And then, out of nowhere, two stone pillars and a wrought-iron gate. A man appeared from the trees, it seemed, and opened it. The car rattled over the cattle grid and sped up a short drive which led to a square grey building. It looked like a monastery, with a small church off to the left. There were two black cars parked near the entrance and Lyndon pulled up beside them.

He got out and opened my door for me. I did not move. After a moment he grabbed my arm and pulled me out. There was a woman in a nurse's uniform waiting for us at the door. I looked askance at Lyndon, who still had hold of my arm. I had heard about mother-and-baby homes in Ireland – a place where unmarried mothers were sent to have their babies in secret by their families. More often than not, the child was taken away and adopted by a respectable family. I pulled away from Lyndon, but the nurse saw this and grabbed my other arm.

'No, no!' I screamed. It was all I could say. A primal demand for escape.

I was bundled into a room. A man was sitting behind a giant mahogany desk. He looked friendly, or so I thought, and I began pleading with him immediately.

'Please, you must understand, I am a woman of means. I own my own business and the baby's father left an income,' I said. 'My brother has brought me here against my will.'

'Opaline, let's not entertain this charade any longer. Doctor, the bastard child was conceived out of wedlock and this husband she speaks of is a pure fabrication.'

I was stunned into silence. The man walked out from around his desk and shook my hand politely.

'Please, Miss Carlisle, just take a seat and rest. Polly, can you bring the Carlisles some tea? They must be tired after their journey.'

The nurse disappeared and Lyndon sat down in one of the straight-backed chairs. I wanted to run out of there, but I didn't stand a chance with two men blocking my way, and so I also took a seat.

'Your brother has informed me that you haven't been feeling well recently, not quite yourself. Would you agree?'

'Absolutely not. I have not seen my brother in years and his sole interest in my affairs is borne of malice and jealousy.'

'As you can see, Doctor, she is still suffering from these delusions,' said Lyndon in the most sympathetic tone I had ever heard him employ. 'It has been clear to me for some time that she is not capable of managing her own affairs and so I shall be taking over the little shop with immediate effect.'

My head whipped around and my eyes burned at the sight of him.

'You read about the manuscript in the letter, didn't you? You know its worth. That's why you've come for me now. You couldn't care less about the baby. You are a jealous, spiteful little man—' I turned back to the doctor. 'He is determined to destroy everything that I have worked for, to ruin my reputation and claim what's mine!' I spoke so fast that there was spittle at the corner of my mouth. I had to make this man understand who Lyndon truly was.

The two men merely exchanged knowing looks.

'Wait a moment, who are you and what is this place?'

'I am Dr Lynch and this is the Connacht District Lunatic Asylum.'

I was sure I had misheard.

'I don't understand … Lyndon?'

My brother stared straight ahead of him. Doctor Lynch leaned forward and put his elbows on the desk, making a steeple of his fingers and resting his chin on the tip.

'Your brother has brought you here because he is concerned for your welfare, Opaline. You seem to be suffering from what we term puerperal insanity – a type of psychosis that can develop in pregnant women causing them to become violent to themselves and others.'

'She tried to attack me in the car on the way here,' Lyndon said, looking every inch the victim.

'You lying bastard!' I screamed. I stood up to go, but the nurse had returned and, displaying extraordinary strength, restrained me in her arms and forced me back into the chair.

'Please, try not to upset yourself, Opaline.'

I tried to free myself but it was pointless. The woman had me in a vice-like grip. My breath was short and ragged, like a trapped animal. It was then that I realised Lyndon had set the entire thing up. He knew how I would react and that my anger would only serve his purpose – to make me look unhinged. An angry man was dominant. An angry woman, on the other hand, must have lost her grip on sanity. I vowed to keep quiet after that and focus on regaining my breath.

'Your sister does seem to be suffering from some type of persecution complex, as you stated in your letter.'

This was it; they had already begun talking as if I wasn't there. Any argument on my part would be seen as further evidence of a fraying mental state. My head lolled on to my chest as my body seemed to collapse in on itself. With one fell swoop, all of the energy left me.

'I'm sure you understand, Dr Lynch, my family can't risk this kind of scandal getting into the papers. Opaline's lifestyle has long been a source of embarrassment to our mother, but this'—Lyndon said, gesturing to my pregnant belly—'well, it really is too much to bear.'

'Indeed. It is this century's loss of morality that has led to so many ills,' the doctor agreed, in deference to my brother, the war hero. He assured Lyndon that a stay in their asylum would cure me of whatever it was they both found so distasteful in my character. 'Now, if you'll just sign this committal form and release the agreed-upon funds, we will give your sister the appropriate care.'

With a great will of effort, my breathing had slowed and I was able to connect with some deep, primal part of my being. There would be no escape today, that was certain. But I could use my wit and intellect to convince this doctor over the coming days that I did not belong in this place. I did not know then that half the women already incarcerated had attempted the same futile exercise. I should have realised, they did not listen to women. The female sex was a curio for them; something to be studied but not understood. A nuisance to be controlled.

The nurse led me away from the doctor's office and down the hall, a firm grip on my arm. Away from the public areas of the building, the aesthetics changed. What struck me immediately was the bareness of the place. Nothing on the walls, which were painted a sickly green, and the smell of bleach made me want to retch. I was taken to my room, although they might as well have called it what it was – a cell. Two iron-framed beds (it appeared I would not be alone for my incarceration, and I could not decide if this was a good or a bad thing) were the only things in the room. There was a high window that I would have to stand on the bed to see out, although I noted that there were bars on it, should any notion of escape cross my mind.

'I need the bathroom.'

'There's a basin under the bed,' the nurse said, still with a tight grip of my arm.

I didn't fight her off – in truth, I could not have stood without her aid. I felt nauseous and asked for some water.

'This isn't a hotel,' she replied, vexed at my audacity to speak. 'You'll hear the bell for supper and you can follow the other women down to the hall.' With that, she let go of my arm, unceremoniously shoved me into the room and slammed the door behind me.

I heard the key turn just as I slid down the wall, no longer able to stand.

~

I lay on the floor that night, as though climbing into bed would signal that I had accepted my fate. I must have fallen into an exhausted sleep at some point, because I woke to the sound of shrieks and whimpering coming from the other inmates. Or patients. Did it matter? I didn't belong here and I had to break free. But how could a pregnant woman escape a place like this? It was physically impossible. I whispered Matthew's name, over and over. He would come and find me, surely. Somehow. I knew he would. I couldn't stay here.

'Everything will look brighter in the morning,' I told my little bump, but this time I didn't believe it.

Chapter Thirty-Eight

MARTHA

The solicitors had sent over the contracts for signing. The sale had gone through quickly and after the bank and agent fees were paid, I was left with the guts of €20,000. The property market was booming again and I had sold at just the right time, according to the agent. I saw the figures on paper but couldn't believe that it would actually be mine – in my bank account. I would be able to afford a full-time course in university, if I wanted it.

I wasn't sure what I wanted. When you've always had nothing it's hard to know how to react when a windfall comes your way. I needed more time to decide and, while I did, I wanted to stay in the one place where I had felt safe since leaving Shane: in Ha'penny Lane.

~

I took Madame Bowden her afternoon tea in the garden. She had been looking a bit pale of late and said the air would do her good.

'Are you any good at card games?'

I groaned inwardly as she pulled a deck of cards from her pocket, as if by magic.

'Other than snap?'

'Your generation has no idea how to pass the time other than staring at your blasted phones.'

She was right. I had been staring at my phone a lot. Ever since I'd told Henry that I couldn't be with him, I'd taken to reading all of the old messages we'd sent each other. And when I wasn't doing that, I was daydreaming about the day we'd kissed. I was glad just knowing that he was back. Life had been so dull without him. Dull was okay. I knew how to deal with dull. But when you've had a taste of magic, it's hard to be satisfied with the ordinary again.

'Twenty-fives, that one's easy enough,' she said, dealing out five cards to each of us and turning the top one on the pack right side up. 'Now hearts are trumps.'

'Okay,' I said. They sure are.

As time passed and the sun slanted on different parts of the garden, highlighting plants I didn't know the names of, I wasn't much closer to figuring out the rules of the game. I just took her word for it and found that the physical act of shuffling and choosing cards to put down was sort of calming. My thoughts began to form around things I wouldn't normally let myself think about.

'God, I hated being back in that town,' I said, thinking back to the funeral and placing an ace on the table.'

'Oh, you've won!'

'Have I?' I looked down and felt a rare moment of joy for joy's sake. She marked it down on a piece of paper.

'I always felt like an outsider there,' I continued, shuffling the deck. 'I mean, people always thought I was a bit strange anyway. Me and my mother. The kids at school used to think we were witches – how we could communicate without words. And they definitely didn't like when I started reading them.'

'Whatever do you mean, *reading them*?'

I silently cursed myself. How had I let that slip? I'd got distracted by the silly card game. I looked up at her face, her countenance alert. She'd done this on purpose, tricked me into saying more than I'd meant to.

'Oh, you know, you just get a gut feeling about people.'

'Intuition, some might say,' she said, motioning that I should deal the cards again.

'Yes, something like that.'

'Hmm. Can you read me?'

I considered her for a moment. After our initial meeting, I thought I knew all I needed to know about Madame Bowden. All I wanted was safety and I knew she would not harm me. But her question jolted me and I wondered if perhaps she had been hiding something in plain sight all along.

'You are testing me for something, although I'm not sure what.'

'Well, that doesn't take a mind-reader. What else?'

I hesitated. How could I say this without hurting her feelings?

'Come on, I won't break!'

I blinked. Was she reading me?

'You are very, very old. Older than you seem. And you are afraid that you will be forgotten about. You're waiting for someone, aren't you? Someone to take care of …?'

'Yes, well, that's quite enough of that.'

She folded her hands on her lap and looked at a blackbird splashing in the bird bath.

'See? People don't like it when you tell them things that you shouldn't really know.'

She sighed heavily then cocked her head to one side. 'I underestimated you. I won't do that again.'

I supposed that was a compliment and I nodded.

'Being an outsider can be a good thing,' she said, returning to our previous conversation.

'You think? It seems to me it would have been much easier if we could've just fitted in.'

'Heaven forfend, Martha! Conformity is a death sentence. No, my dear, you must embrace what makes you stand out. That's what they despise. It's the circle of hell in this life – blaming children for being who they are, because we were blamed and our parents before us. If you're not harming anyone, why try to change who you are?'

'I don't know. I never thought of it that way. All I know is that I feel so angry with myself all the time. Like I'll never be good enough for them, so why even try?'

'Good enough for whom? For people who are trapped in a life that is not of their own making? Surely you can see that they merely want you to be trapped with them, so they will feel less alone in their emptiness. Be careful, Martha, you'll become blind to your own value if you keep looking through the eyes of the bourgeoisie!'

~

That night, after I showered and looked once more at the story inked on my back, I thought about what Madame Bowden had said. I knew it as soon as I arrived in Ha'penny Lane, but I kept trying to deny it. I could feel the very fibres of the building getting under my skin, filling my head with ideas of a future I would never have dared to dream about. Yet when I saw Opaline's letter to Sylvia, I knew that the book she referred to was the one that had been given to me. Was it all somehow linked to Madame Bowden? All I had were questions and the only person I could talk to about it was Henry. Could we be friends? The idea made me feel so sad. But I couldn't see any other way. I couldn't risk losing myself again, not when I'd fought so hard to rebuild my life.

As I lay in bed reading one of the books on my literature course, *Persuasion* by Jane Austen, I noticed more books lying flat on the branch that had flattened out as a shelf. The words emblazoned on their spines were almost golden in the lamplight. *Dear Reader* by Cathy Rentzenbrink, *Never Let Me Go* by Kazuo Ishiguro and *Flowers in the Attic* by V. C. Andrews. Gosh. Did Madame Bowden really think I could manage all of this extra reading? I looked back down at the page I was reading. I couldn't let myself get distracted, as I had to finish it before my next class. My curiosity wouldn't let me be and I looked up again, only this time, certain words seem to stand out more than others.

Dear Reader
Go
In The Attic

I held my breath and pressed the book I was reading to my chest. This was properly spooky. I looked at the clock. A minute past midnight. I looked back at the books and they seemed perfectly normal and harmless once again, no word more luminous than the rest. There was no secret message at all. I should just ignore it, I told myself, figuring my eyes were tired and seeing things that weren't there.

Intuition, Madame Bowden had called it. Maybe ignoring it had been the problem all along.

I slipped my feet into my sneakers and pulled around me the old cardigan that doubled as a dressing gown. I didn't want to turn on the hall light upstairs – I knew Madame Bowden was a light sleeper – and as a result I stubbed my toe on the last step to the top floor. I silently cried out in pain and at being gullible enough to believe the books were telling me something.

But was it gullible? I was wearing a tattoo on my back, half of which I didn't put there.

I came to a small door at the highest point of the building and had to crouch down. I pushed and pulled, but it wouldn't budge. I searched fruitlessly at the top of the architrave for a key, finding only dust. It was pointless. There was nothing I could do in the dark. I made my way a little more carefully down the stairs and as I trod softly past her bedroom door, the lady of the house called out.

'Is that you, Martha?'

'Yes, just …' Shit. What could I say? 'There's a spider in my toilet so I had to use the one up here. Sorry.'

I waited for a reply, but after a few seconds I kept on going. Just before I reached the ground floor, it came.

'You're a terrible liar, Martha!'

Chapter Thirty-Nine

HENRY

'Are you still there? Mr Field?'

I put the pillow over my head and shouted some obscenities into it before returning to the phone call.

'I just need a bit more time, that's all. You got the initial draft, right?'

'Yes, yes, indeed, and it's a very promising premise but the problem is—' Derrick, the head of department, was a decent bloke and he had tried to break it to me gently. The problem was I couldn't accept what he was telling me. 'The problem is that you've produced absolutely nothing to back it up, Henry.'

He was right. I knew he was right. An old letter discussing the *possibility* of a second Brontë novel was just hearsay. I had no real hard evidence.

'I'm sorry, Henry, but they've pulled your funding.'

'What?'

'Look, I tried to fight your corner, but this isn't the first wild goose chase you've been on, is it?'

Oh good, a healthy dose of humiliation to boot. I thanked him for calling and delivering the bad news himself, rather than in a letter. Then I shouted into the pillow some more.

I'd spent years chasing down leads, trying to find that one missing manuscript that would make my name. Yes, I had attributed short stories or essays written under pseudonyms to their rightful authors, uncovered interesting letters between significant players in the literary world and handled countless texts discovered by rare book specialists, but, as yet, I still had not achieved that one big discovery. This was my chance, I could feel it. I'd let myself become completely distracted by my emotions and this was the result. Martha had made her feelings on the subject perfectly clear and if I was to salvage what was left of my career, I was going to have to throw myself into this search one hundred per cent.

I took out my laptop and propped myself up in bed. Trance music always helped me to focus; something about the repetitive tones and beats made me feel like I was moving even when I was sitting still. I was going to get to the bottom of this mystery, one way or another. I had already contacted Rosenbach's estate for confirmation that the letter was not a forgery. They had employed a handwriting specialist and fobbed me off with delays. Either way, if he had obtained the manuscript, surely the whole world would know about it by now. No, I had to get back to Opaline and find out what happened to her and why she claimed to possess Emily Brontë's lost manuscript.

I heard a tap on the door and assumed that if I kept quiet enough, Nora would presume I had gone out.

'I can smell the drink from here,' she said.

I got up to open the door and saw her standing there with a tray carrying a steaming cup of tea and a toasted bacon sandwich.

'You truly are a remarkable woman.' I took the tray from her and brought it inside.

'What in God's name happened to your face?'

'Oh that, yes.' I'd almost forgotten, what with having my reputation broken and my heart smashed to pieces.

'Are ... are you okay, Henry?'

'Never better.'

'It's only, I'm worried about you.'

It really had come to something when a stranger had fears for your sanity. I had to get a grip. Fast. I assured her I'd be right as rain and, after tucking into the food, I returned to my laptop and began researching everything I could about the Carlisle family. The father was a civil servant who had married a wealthy heiress. Both children attended fine schools and there was ample information on Lyndon's career in the army. As before, all records of Opaline seemed to just stop, except for a small newspaper announcement of the wedding of Jane Burridge to Lord Findley. Opaline Carlisle was named as the maid of honour. As much as it pained me to think of Martha at all, I remembered what she said about getting to know Opaline by the women in her life. Surely they must have been friends.

I took a large mouthful of cold tea and turned up the volume of the music before deep-diving into the life and times of Lady Jane. This was my happy place: researching people who were long-dead and forgotten by the world at large, as though the very act of my shining a light on them would somehow bring them back to life for a fleeting moment. That's what had really inspired me to enter the world of rare books in the first place – uncovering the amazing lives and stories of the people who had gone before us; people who cared every bit as much about the day-to-day trivialities of life as we do; people living through some of the most amazing times whilst being wholly unaware of the significance. Something about piecing all of these things together calmed my mind. Maybe it was a comfort to know that my life was just a page in the great history book of human endeavour. It relieved some of the pressure to be someone or something of importance. That feeling would last until I saw one of my peers being awarded some bursary or other, or another who wrote a bestselling tome on the discoveries of some obscure collectors from the past. I was cursed with that most enduring of human desires – to make my mark.

After hours of trawling through births, deaths, charity events and social engagements, I found a letter to the editor of an Irish newspaper dated 1930.

Dear Sir,

I am writing out of a sense of desperation, as my entreaties to all and sundry on this issue have gone ignored. I wish to draw your attention to the deplorable state of the country's asylums. Women who are as sound of mind as you or I are being involuntarily committed to these institutions without proper examination and being kept in the most horrendous conditions that are far below the standards of common human decency. My dear friend is being held against her will in such a place in the province of Connacht and despite letters to the government, I have been prevented from having her examined by my own independent physician. We need a root and branch investigation into these establishments as a matter of urgency.

Yours,

Lady Jane Findley

It was so out of the ordinary for an English lady to write such a letter, and to an Irish newspaper to boot. Why would she have done it? It didn't mention who the friend was, but my senses were tingling. Opaline's letter to Sylvia Beach spoke of being incarcerated. Was it possible that she had been placed into an asylum? I would have to find records of how many asylums there were in Ireland at the time and where.

I needed coffee. I needed Martha. The coffee would have to do.

Chapter Forty

OPALINE

For those precious few seconds before I opened my eyes, I had forgotten where I was. My mind told me that I was at home in bed, but my body knew different. I was freezing, and the rough blanket around me was not my own. I opened my eyes and the horrible truth was confirmed. It hadn't been a bad dream. I was incarcerated at the hand of my brother.

I heard boot heels resounding heavily down the uncarpeted hallway, like a small army on the march, and my door clattered open.

'Six o'clock, time to get up,' a nurse announced, without looking me in the eye. She opened the window and let the freezing cold air in.

Rationally, I knew it was useless to plead my case with her, but emotionally I couldn't help but beg for my freedom.

'Please, I have to speak with Dr Lynch. This has all been a big mistake. You have to let me go!'

The nurse, who had jet-black, greasy hair, parted severely in the middle, and dark eyes that seemed both vacant and piercing, completely ignored me. It was as though I hadn't spoken at all.

'Down to the hall with you, breakfast is on the table.'

'Yes but—'

'You'll speak to his assistant, Dr Hughes, later, you can take it up with him.'

She handed me a horrible grey flannel dress and told me to put it on. After dressing, she bundled up my own clothes and took them away to a place I knew not where. I was shown to a washstand, where all the other patients were rubbing their faces with icy cold water. They didn't look particularly crazy to me. They looked tired and afraid.

The nurse, whose name I found out was Patricia, hurried us along like cattle and into what I assumed to be the dining room. There was a long wooden table with a bench either side and on it were enamel cups of some sort of broth and in the middle was a basket of hard bread. At a glance, I estimated that there were about sixty women in all. At the far end of the hall there was a separate table seating about ten women who seemed to be suffering from some kind of intellectual disability and two nurses keeping watch on them. I sat down and tried to spoon some of the broth into my mouth, but I couldn't stomach it. My throat locked and it refused to swallow. I tried dipping the bread into it when the old woman beside me grabbed my hand.

'Don't eat it, it's poisoned!'

I dropped the bread instantly and at this she began to laugh mercilessly. I couldn't tell if she was crazy or just plain cruel.

'Leave her alone, Agatha.'

I looked around to find the speaker of these words and was surprised to see a young woman, scarcely twenty by my reckoning, who spoke with an authority beyond her years. I nodded my thanks. It was hard to tell how old any of my cohabitants were, given their state of dress and the mental toll it took being in a place like this.

'My name is Mary,' she said, with a gentleness I hadn't expected. 'Why are you here?'

'My brother—' I found I could not finish the sentence for fear I would burst into tears.

At the sound of whimpering, I saw another grey-haired woman at the end of the table crying aimlessly, and the woman beside me began muttering to herself, a senseless conversation that seemed to have no end or beginning.

'Go out into the yard!' This yell from another nurse announced the end of breakfast and everyone was given a threadbare shawl to walk around an enclosed courtyard. It was midwinter and bitterly cold. Added to this, the yard was north-facing and would never see the sun. The thought was like a heavy anchor, pulling my heart southward. It was all too much to bear. I froze to the spot while the others shuffled around me.

'Get in line!'

I ignored the order. I was too weak to move.

'Carlisle, get a companion and walk.' I wasn't used to being given orders and refused to obey.

'How many times must I tell you!' To my utter shock, this order was administered with a slap on the ear.

Suddenly, my life force came flooding back with rage. I was about to hit back, when I felt an arm slip through mine and almost drag me forward.

'Best to do as they say,' a voice whispered softly.

I looked to my left and saw Mary, the young woman who had spoken up for me at the table.

'I shouldn't be here,' I said.

'Do you think any poor creature should end up here?'

I shook my head, but, honestly, I didn't care about anyone else in that moment. The other women frightened me, their naked faces, devoid of any normalcy. I pulled the shawl around me tightly. I was shivering so badly with cold that my teeth were chattering wildly. I could see the other women's lips turning purple with cold. It was inhumane.

'Carlisle, come here.'

It had been so long since I had used my real name that it took me a moment to realise that the nurse, Patricia, was speaking to me. *Thank God,* I thought to myself. They've realised that this is all a big mistake and will release me. I pulled my arm from Mary and thanked her for her kindness, feeling sure I would never see her again.

I followed the nurse apace and once back inside, she led me to a room where I was weighed, measured and then approached by another nurse with scissors who cut my nails to the quick.

'Why are you doing this?' I asked.

'You are to see Dr Hughes,' she answered.

I told myself that this made perfect sense – a final examination before letting me go. For administrative purposes. Surely that was all it was.

After this perfunctory physical exam, I was led to another room. There, in a white coat, sat a man who introduced himself as Dr Hughes. Now was my chance to speak up for myself, but I found I did not know where to start.

'Who are you?' he asked, opening a cream-coloured folder and taking the lid off his pen.

'I … my name is Opaline Gr—. I mean …'

'Oh, well, that's hardly an auspicious start, is it?' His ability to find humour in such desperate circumstances set me on edge.

'My name is Opaline Carlisle, but I have been living under the pseudonym of Opaline Gray in order to protect my identity from my brother, who is a violent maniac.'

There. I was clear, coherent and concise. Surely this man would see that I was sane.

'Where do you live?'

'Ha'penny Lane, Dublin. I run a small bookshop.'

He raised his eyebrows. 'And you are pregnant?'

'Yes.'

'How many men have you had intimate relations with?'

'I beg your pardon?'

'Sexual intercourse, Miss Carlisle.'

I felt a rage coursing through my body and took several deep breaths. This is what he wanted, to see me react.

'Just the one,' I replied coolly.

'Your brother informs me that you have led an immoral lifestyle, is that so?'

I wasn't sure what to respond, so I said nothing.

'Do you see faces on the wall?'

'Not at the present moment, no.'

He looked at me with a kind of scorn and I cursed myself for getting smart with him.

'Do you hear voices?'

'No, doctor, I do not hear voices. There is nothing wrong with me, you must see that. My brother has engineered this entire charade. He is angry with me because I refused to do his bidding and marry a man I hardly knew. This is his way of punishing me, don't you see?'

The room fell quiet, save for the sound of his pen scratching his thoughts on to clean, white paper. I wondered where my clothes were and if there was a bus that would take me back to Dublin.

'That will be all for now, nurse,' he said, calling for Patricia to come back inside.

'Can I go home now?'

'Oh, I'm afraid it will be quite some time before you are ready to re-enter society, Miss Carlisle. If ever.'

His words were like a scripted play, something I expected to hear an actor speak in a theatre. This could not be real life.

'You cannot be serious! This is the extent of your examination?

Asking me if I see faces on the wall? Dr Hughes, you must see that I am as sane as you are.'

'Your brother—'

'Forget my brother! Is his word more valuable than mine?'

He said nothing, but replaced the cap on his pen. I had my answer.

I pressed my hands flat on the desk between us.

'He is lying to you! I can prove it. I have discovered a very valuable manuscript and he wants to steal it, don't you see?'

The doctor smirked at the nurse who had taken hold of my arms and was half-dragging me from the room.

'Come on now, Carlisle, it's better if you don't struggle,' she said.

'Give me any test you like. I will prove that I'm not crazy!'

'Oh, I think we know all we need to on that score, Miss Carlisle.'

'No! Please! Where is Dr Lynch? Let me speak to him!' I was shouting myself hoarse, my useless screams echoing down the hallway. Another nurse was bringing a patient to the doctor's room and Patricia called to her, saying I'd have forgotten all of this in an hour. They truly believed me to be crazy and every reason I used to protest this fact only confirmed their beliefs.

I was thrown back into my filthy room and I curled myself into the corner and cried for what seemed like hours. As the room grew darker, I looked up and saw a woman sitting on the bed. How long had she been there?

'Best to get those tears out. They won't be much good to you in here.'

'Mary?'

I pushed myself up from the ground, a difficult task with my pregnant belly, and I sat on the bed beside her.

'Why are you here?' I asked her, looking at her properly for the first time. Her hair was wild and stuck out all sides, her eyes dark and deep, but her cupid's mouth spoke with a measured tone beyond her years.

'Hysteria. That's what they told me.'

Hysteria; it could have meant anything.

'And how does it, um, manifest itself?' I asked, realising now that we would be sharing this room.

'I become highly emotional when my father beats me.'

'Dear God.'

She gave me a little smile, as though humour was all she had left.

'When I fell pregnant, I told him it was the priest that done it to me. But he wouldn't believe me; said I was a filthy whore. He wanted me out of the house, so he told them I had demonic fevers. That my wounds were by my own hand.'

I buried my head in my hands. How had we ended up here? I had left home inspired by the suffragettes, the modern women who were going to achieve equality and the freedom to pursue their own happiness. With the stroke of a pen, we were locked up. Troublesome women with inconvenient ideas.

'How long have you been here? You look so young.'

'Three years. I'm twenty-two.'

My tears spilled forth once again. It all seemed so hopeless. She gave my hand a firm squeeze.

'You have to be strong for the baby,' she said, then got up and undressed before climbing into the other bed.

I lay down on the thin mattress and looked up at the moon shining between the bars on the window. Mary was right. I had to look after my little Rosebud. I would eat the food, go outside and breathe the fresh air into my lungs and keep as healthy as I could. If this was the way it had to be for now, then I would accept it. For her good. I couldn't let myself get worked up like I did today. I knew it wasn't good for her. So I would be calm and, when the time came, they would take me to a hospital to have my baby and that would be my chance to escape.

~

Two weeks passed, with every new day identical to the last. One could never have imagined the length of days when there is nothing to do, say or think. The most remarkable feature was the cold. I could see my own breath when I spoke. An elderly woman took a fit one morning at the breakfast table, shivering and convulsing with the cold. She was practically hopping off the bench, such was her suffering.

'Let her fall on the floor, it'll teach her a lesson,' said Nurse Patricia.

The nurses wore their overcoats and despite every fibre of my being instructing me to keep quiet, I simply had to speak out.

'Can you not see that she will perish with the cold in this place? Surely you can spare her some extra clothing?'

'She has the same as everyone else.'

And that was the end of that discussion. I gave the woman my cup of hot tea when it came. It wasn't a great loss, watery as it was and tasting peculiarly of copper.

A new woman arrived that day, which gave us all something to focus on. We welcomed her in as best we could and I could now understand the thirst for information that had greeted me when I first arrived. Everyone wanted to know why she was here, mostly to drown out the mind-numbing boredom. I hoped to be proved right by her story – another innocent victim. But we couldn't make any sense out of what she was saying and before long she was taken away to be treated, whatever that meant.

Word came back that she came direct from the courthouse where she had stood accused of drowning her child. She believed it was a changeling, that her real baby was taken by the fairies. I almost got physically sick when I heard. I knew I would go mad myself if I didn't get out of that place. People imagine that the worst thing about incarceration is the thought of being locked inside, but there is another trauma to endure. Whilst some of the women were simply anxious or depressed, I was now living with women suffering all types of physical and mental disability and not only that, was considered to be one of them. That has a profound impact on one's sense of self; of what is true.

~

That night, I thought my time for escape had come. The pains in my stomach felt as though I were going into labour and the water that wet my bed confirmed it. I called out to Mary and asked her to alert the nurse. She banged on the door and shouted, but no one answered for a very long time. Of course, it happened in the early hours of the morning, as these things often do, and there was only the elderly nun on duty. She thought I was exaggerating the agonising pain of labour and said she would not wake the poor doctor from his sleep to come and tend to a spoilt English brat like me.

'Stop your play-acting,' she said, through the grille in the door.

'I don't want you to call the doctor, I need to go to a hospital!' I was so excited at the thought of leaving, that I hardly noticed the pain.

'Hospital? Sure, didn't the cat have a fine litter the other week and managed it all on her own.'

That was her final word on the matter, and all I could hear were her footsteps fading away.

'They're not going to leave me here, are they?' I asked Mary, who now sat at the end of my bed, patting my back.

'Not to worry,' she said.

Another contraction came and I groaned my way through it,

twisting the ends of the blanket tight around my wrists. The night carried on that way and I must have slept in between contractions. Mary stayed with me all the while. Any time I asked a question, she would tell me again not to worry, in a way that made me very worried indeed. As though all hope was futile. At six o'clock, Nurse Patricia came to get us up and when she saw the state I was in, called for the doctor.

'Please,' I begged her, all pride forgotten. I was in agonising pain and hadn't had so much as a glass of water. 'Please get me to a hospital.'

'You don't need to go to hospital to give birth. Maybe that's how things are done in England, but not here. Childbirth is the most natural thing in the world,' she said, pulling my nightdress up and shoving her cold hand between my legs.

'Get your hands off of me!' I spat at her and she responded by slapping me across the face.

I'm not sure what would have happened if Dr Hughes hadn't arrived at that very moment. He took charge immediately and sent her to fetch towels and a basin of boiled water. Two hours of contractions which felt like I was being ripped apart and I no longer knew or cared whose hands were on me. They were shouting at me to push and I pushed. Someone kindly placed a cold flannel on my burning face. I screamed for my mother, even though I knew she wouldn't come. I begged Armand to come and rescue me. And then another push; different this time, the pressure released. Voices whispered and I saw a nurse carrying away a bundle.

'Where's my baby? Where are you taking her?' I couldn't be sure if anyone had heard me, my voice was weak and my throat raw. 'My baby? Please give me my baby!'

A man's voice and words that made no sense. The cord was wrapped around her neck. She suffocated. Born blue. I don't remember very much after that. I suspect I started to go mad.

Chapter Forty-One

MARTHA

'So, what aspect of Austen's theme has changed with this book, her last published before her death?'

The tutor was sitting on the edge of his desk, one leg swinging free as he held a copy of *Persuasion* in his hand. There was a young American woman who always sat at the front of the class and apparently knew everything about every book ever written. I figured she probably fancied our tutor, but he didn't seem to notice.

'I mean, it's still all about marriage and social standing,' she said. 'Anne judges people by their character, rather than their rank but in the end she still succumbs to Lady Russell's snobbery and turns down Wentworth's marriage proposal.'

'Great summary,' Logan said, slouching at the back of the room. 'Saves me reading it.'

I smiled at him. He was my kind of people. Although why he was taking a night course in literature and not reading the book was a bit odd.

'Okay, okay, maybe Austen isn't for everyone. But in a way, the reason her books are still so popular today is because the themes still matter to us. Love. Family loyalty. Pride. Societal pressure to conform. You may all think you're walking around exercising your free will in every situation, but you're not. You're constantly influenced by what your heart wants, what your head wants and how you want the world to see you.'

He was right. In all of these years, nothing had really changed.

'I think the main theme,' said Beverly, a retired dental nurse who always sat beside me, 'is about getting a second chance at love.'

I was trying not to read people any more, it didn't seem fair, but sometimes I did it without thinking. Her first love had been killed in a car crash and she'd never met anyone since. I hoped for her sake that Jane Austen was right.

'Exactly, Beverly. Anne is "persuaded" to give up her chance of love because Wentworth has no prospects, but instead of moving on with her life, she bitterly regrets her decision. Yet, in the end, she realises that the years apart have made her more appreciative of love when it comes back to her.'

~

As we packed up for the evening, the tutor asked if I had given any more thought to the degree course.

'Based on your written assignments I think you'd be a perfect candidate,' he said, 'although I would like a little more interaction in class. I think it would benefit you.'

I still found it so hard to speak up in front of people. I had only just overcome my issues with reading. After the night I found the tattoo completed on my back, it was as though a spell had been broken. Books no longer troubled me in the same way and the stories they held within had become invitations rather than warning signs. It was like I'd been given the key to a locked door.

'Here's some material for you, entry requirements and such.' I took them and packed them into my bag, feeling like I was living a completely different life, the life of someone who could do anything they wanted. Maybe there were second chances after all.

I never tired of walking through the grounds of Trinity and I felt more than a little pride in myself after every class I attended.

'Now you have to promise me that you won't become one of those Trinners people who always manage to get the fact they've gone to Trinity into a conversation,' Logan said, buttoning up his coat. He worked as a chef but his real desire was to write comics.

'Oh, I'm already working it into conversations,' I said, thinking to myself how I would do that if I had anyone other than my classmates and Madame Bowden to talk to.

'I'm thinking of doing the MA myself,' he said.

'Really?'

'No need to sound so surprised!'

I could see in him then a boy who grew up reading comics and wanted to write his own. But a teenage romance had led to a teenage pregnancy and a job as a kitchen porter to pay the rent. He was now a chef in one of the top Dublin hotels, but his heart was still in storytelling.

'Austen not your cup of tea?' I said.

'I'm more into graphic novels.'

'I didn't even know there were graphic novels.'

He looked at me with the wide eyes of someone who has been mortally wounded, but with just enough breath left to tell you why you were wrong to fire the shot.

'Oh my God, you've never heard of *Maus*? Art Spiegelman?'

I shook my head.

'Come on, Martha, you're killing me here! What about *Glass Town*? You're a Brontë fan, right?'

I was laughing and making a mental note to see if these books were in the library when, just as we rounded the corner, I spotted a familiar figure walking across the square. He was chatting happily on the phone and hadn't seen me, but something made him look my way. Henry.

'Hi,' I said and gave him a small, awkward wave.

He raised his head and gave a tight smile.

'How are you?' he mouthed and I gave him a thumbs-up.

He pointed to the phone and I motioned for him to carry on, I was on my way out anyway. And that was it. He disappeared into the building and Logan carried on talking about an idea for a character he had – a superchef who fights crime or something. I felt so cold all over. It was as though we meant nothing to each other now.

I couldn't help but think of a quote from *Persuasion*: 'Now they were as strangers; nay, worse than strangers, for they could never become acquainted. It was a perpetual estrangement.'

Chapter Forty-Two

HENRY

'So you'll come?' she repeated.

'I'm sorry, how did you get my number?'

'From Martha's phone, naturally. Now, she's invited some of her chums from university ...'

I didn't even know it was her birthday. There was still so much about Martha that was a complete mystery to me. She had built her defences so high, it made the rare occasions she had let me in all the more meaningful.

'So you'll come at seven,' she ordered.

'I'm not sure she'd want me there,' I replied, looking out of the window at Nora's husband pottering around the back garden. I still hadn't forgiven him for telling Martha I'd left the country for good. It was easier to blame him than to accept that maybe she just didn't want to be with someone like me. She certainly hadn't invited me and I wasn't sure why her employer was taking it upon herself to interfere.

'Tosh! She will want to see all of her friends. It's been something of an *annus horribilis* for Martha, wouldn't you say? So I don't think it's asking the earth for you to put your own insecurities aside for five minutes and come and eat some cake! Men, honestly.'

With that final damning indictment of my entire gender, she hung up.

~

The weather was mild for the time of year and as I walked along the canal, daffodils created a golden path into the heart of the city. Dublin had started to feel like home to me. It wasn't long ago that I had fully planned to move here. The thought embarrassed me. Love, in retrospect, makes one look utterly foolish. To make such sweeping plans based on nothing more than a feeling – a bunch of chemicals, to be technical about it – seemed nonsensical in the harsh light of day. But there was no denying that I had felt more alive and awake in those weeks with Martha than I had done in my entire life. I had the sense that I was sort of sleepwalking through my life until I met her, making decisions based on what I thought was expected of me. How was that method of plotting a course for one's life any more correct?

I recalled something Lucinda had said to me before I left; that it didn't matter whether the decision you made was right or wrong, as long as you made it. That's what moved you along in life. In fact she had used the word 'journey' because she was still in her earth mother phase.

~

Buying gifts was never exactly a forte of mine. A horrible panic always set in, followed by a gaping realisation that I knew absolutely nothing about the interior life of the person I was buying the present for. So I stuck to books as a rule. You couldn't go wrong with a book. That wasn't strictly true. I once bought my father a book about problem drinking, which he chose to use as kindling for the fire. But this time, I knew exactly what gift to get.

'Would you like it gift-wrapped?' the shop assistant asked.

I nodded and took my debit card from my wallet, slotting it into the handheld machine.

'Oh, can you just try popping it in again? Sometimes it does this,' he said graciously.

I popped it in again. Again it was declined.

'Actually, I think I'll put this on my credit card instead,' I said, as if it was a choice. They'd wasted no time in cutting my funding, I realised. But as I watched him wrap the box in black paper with gold flourishes, I knew I would have robbed a bank (well, metaphorically) to get her this.

~

I arrived at the house just after eight and, like I always did, I took a quick check around the side, just in case. *Just in case what, Henry? That the bookshop with the manuscript inside has suddenly reappeared?* I threw my eyes heavenward and shook my head.

'Utter fantasist,' I muttered to myself as I walked up the steps to the front door.

I stopped mid-stride as I saw movement in the window. It was Martha in a sapphire blue evening gown cut low at the back, framing the large tattoo on her skin. Her bright blonde hair was styled in a braid that she wore like a crown around her head.

I felt my knees weaken. It was no use. No matter how much I talked myself out of it when I was alone, as soon as I saw her, all of the feelings came flooding back. Then I saw him, the same guy I'd seen with her at Trinity. He was telling some anecdote that had everyone in stitches. He was older and balding, but clearly he had something I didn't.

'Reliability?' a voice said, reading my mind. I looked up to find

Madame Bowden standing in the front doorway, walking stick in one hand, cigarette in the other.

'How long have you been there?'

She didn't answer.

'Are you coming inside, Mr Field?'

'Actually, I don't think I can,' I said. 'I've just realised, um, I have a previous engagement. Perhaps you could give her this?' I asked, offering the wrapped gift.

'I beg your pardon? You seem to be mistaking me for some kind of courier! I am the lady of this house and if you were a gentleman, you would come inside and give it to her yourself.'

I exhaled heavily. *That woman.*

The house looked magnificent, twinkling with a terrific amount of fairy lights. I could hear light chatter and the sound of glasses clinking in the drawing room. I waited to let Madame Bowden enter ahead of me, but she'd acted out of character and made herself scarce. Walking through the open double doors, I saw the table was laid with hors d'oeuvres and a large iced cake. It seemed the old dear had really begun to take a shine to Martha, looking at the spread she had laid on. But then, who wouldn't? I said hello to a few people, then slowly made my way towards the birthday girl, resisting every step that took me closer to her. She looked up and gave me that blue-eyed stare I remembered from the first morning I met her, looking through the basement window. But now, like this, with her beautiful dress, the look was even more disarming.

'Happy birthday, Martha,' I said.

She stepped away from her group of friends and let her hand rest on my wrist before leaning in to kiss my cheek.

'Oh, Henry!'

Yes, exactly the kind of reaction you want when gatecrashing a party. *Oh, Henry.*

'I'm so glad you came,' she tacked on, giving me an awkward

hug. Or maybe I was just an awkward person to hug. The jury was out.

'Me too,' I said, as if swerving tonight had never crossed my mind. 'You look beautiful.'

She put her hand up to touch her hair.

'Thank you. Madame Bowden insisted that I borrow one of her old dresses. She had it altered by a dressmaker and everything,' she said, her eyes wide with disbelief.

I watched as she swished the silk skirt.

This was heartbreaking. I had to get out of there.

'Listen—' I began but was interrupted by music that struck up out of nowhere.

'A birthday dance!' said one of her friends and all but pushed Martha into my arms.

'Oh, I'm not sure that's necessary—'

'I don't even know how!' We both began to protest in unison, but the crowd had warmed to the idea and formed the dreaded circle around us.

'It is my song,' she said a little shyly.

I listened to the wonky piano notes and tried to recall what it was.

'Tom Waits. My mother named me after this song.'

How could I refuse?

'Well then, if it is your song ...' I put one arm around her waist and held her hand.

We didn't speak, just shuffled slowly to what was possibly the most forlorn song I'd ever heard in my life. Dancing in public was bad enough, but dancing in public with the woman who had just dumped you should have been the most excruciatingly awkward moment of my life. But something happened; it became strangely magical. We looked into each other's eyes, unable to keep from smiling at the situation. The guests stepped back to give us more floorspace, but in my mind they might as well have disappeared entirely. All I could see was her. She felt so right in my arms. I bizarrely found that I could dance – I don't know if it was her evening gown or the candlelight, but I became a bit of a Fred Astaire. Or else it just felt that way and if someone had replayed a video I might have looked like Frankenstein's monster. The song reached its slow, plinking-plonking crescendo …

Martha, Martha, I love you, can't you see?

I couldn't take it any more. I let her go and stepped backward.

'Sorry, I have to go.'

I tried to walk out of there with as much dignity as I could, which was to say, very little. I reached to pull the handle of the front door, but it wouldn't budge.

'For God's sake …' I muttered, pulling it with all my might.

'Henry!'

I turned around to see her standing there, her face full of pity. That was the last thing I needed. I felt completely exposed. The only way out was to pretend.

'You were right. About us, I mean. It never would've worked.'

'Oh.'

Her face was unreadable. I had to get out of there. I turned to try the handle again, but it still wouldn't budge.

'Leaving so soon?' Madame Bowden asked.

God, that woman was omnipresent!

'It's fine,' Martha said to her. 'Thank you for coming, I mean it.'

I nodded, shoving my hands into my pocket. That's when I felt the box.

'I forgot to give you this.'

She peeled back the paper and opened it. Her eyes widened and her hand went to her chest. 'I don't believe it.'

'What is it?' the old lady asked, struggling to put on her glasses.

'It's a Mont Blanc pen.'

'On ne voit bien qu'avec le cœur.'

'Henry, I can't accept it. It's too much!'

I just smiled and hoped she knew that she was worth so much more than she knew.

'I thought you'd need a good pen for university.'

She took it out and held it close to her chest. 'I love it. Thank you.'

'Now, I really must go,' I said, my voice breaking slightly, 'but your door seems to be stuck.'

Madame Bowden reached out her hand and opened it easily.

'Goodnight, Henry,' she said with a wink.

Chapter Forty-Three

OPALINE

Connacht District Lunatic Asylum, 1923

I don't know how long I lay on that bed, if it was cold or warm, or if I was alone or in company. All of my senses were dulled by one overwhelming urge – to hold my baby.

'Sure, why do you want to hold a dead baby?' the nurse snapped, probably not for the first time.

I hadn't the energy to answer, or cry. My only hope was that I would die too. Mary tried to bring me food but I wouldn't touch it. They came in and stripped the clothes off the bed, opened the window to the cold January air, but I did not move. They lifted me and brought me to the bathroom, washing away the dried blood between my legs. I didn't care any more who saw or touched me. I wanted to die and be with my baby.

Then it was night and I woke screaming from a nightmare – Lyndon was tying a noose around my baby's neck.

'What is it?' Mary was beside me, stroking my brow.

I grasped her hand. 'I can't do this. I can't live.'

'You have to.'

'You don't understand,' I said, turning away from her.

'Oh, but I do. He punched my baby out of me, and the guilt—' She stopped short. 'That's why he put me in here. He couldn't live with what he did either, so it was easier to blame me. Lock me away.'

I turned around to face her again. It was dark, but her features held a grace I could never have imagined possible in such dire circumstances.

'Mary, I'm so sorry.'

'I don't need your pity, Opaline. I need you to survive. We need each other if we're going to get out of here.'

She seemed so strong and independent, I hadn't thought that she needed me at all.

'Let me help you now and you will get stronger. You will survive this.'

'But what's the point?' I asked, raising myself up on my elbow. 'What kind of future can we hope for?'

'I don't know, but hope is all I have, and I felt my prayers were answered the day you came here.'

I laughed bitterly. 'I would advise you to pin your hopes on anyone else in this establishment; you will find in them more inspiration than you will ever find in me.'

'You feel that way now but—'

I sat up and was almost nose to nose with her. 'I will *always* feel this way.'

She went back to her own bed.

The next morning, however, she brought me a saucer of oatmeal. I knew the risk she took; taking food out of the hall was expressly forbidden and was punished with solitary confinement. I said nothing, but sat up in my bed and began to eat. Later that afternoon she came with a piece of unbuttered bread and an enamel cup with some tea. The following morning, I leaned on her and walked to the hall myself.

'Can you sew?' Mary asked.

I had watched as she mended the threadbare clothes of the other women. She was the only one trusted with the use of a needle in that place.

'Before I came to this place, I was a dressmaker. My mother taught me. You have to keep busy, Opaline.'

'I could try,' I agreed, never even having sewed a button in my life.

~

Dearest Jane,

I find myself in circumstances I can hardly believe myself and so I am at a loss as to how I should describe them to you, my closest friend in the world. In fact, just imagining our childhood together makes this seem like a dream. However, my time is short so I must rush these few words – I am resident in an asylum. I can assure you that I am sane and still in possession of my wits. Lyndon is behind it. I need say no more than that and I am sure you will understand. Also, I had a baby. She did not live. Please help me, if you can.

Your friend,

Opaline

~

A year had passed and any hope of escape seemed like a distant dream I couldn't quite recall.

Mary spoke less and less. She had developed a worrying cough and could not sleep at night, so I sat up with her, wrapping her in my blanket.

'Tell me about your life,' she asked one night, as we lay in the darkness. 'Before you came here.'

My life before. How could I even begin to describe a life that no longer felt like my own? I was worried that speaking about it would push me further away from it.

'I used to sell books.'

There was a silence while we both adjusted to the reality of those words.

'I've never read a book,' came the reply.

I was glad the darkness of the night hid my features, which were a mixture of shock and pity. Mary wouldn't want either of those. Then she became seized by a fit of coughing that lasted more than five minutes. The wheezing sound of her lungs affirmed to me that she was suffering from influenza. With no heat, threadbare rags for clothes and a diet of porridge and watery soup, I feared for her health.

'Can you tell me a story? From one of your books?'

At that moment I would have done anything to offer her comfort and so I began to recite Emily Brontë's manuscript, picturing the tiny handwriting in my mind's eye. The words came easily, as I had read them in a way that was distinct from all other books. I was the only one to have seen them since they had been secreted in Charlotte's sewing box and so they entered my soul in a way that no other writing had previously.

Mary was calmed by them and, just like a child, asked for the same story every night, as her condition deteriorated.

Chapter Forty-Four

MARTHA

I closed the book and felt the room settle around me. I turned it over and looked at the front cover again with its image of Mr Fitzpatrick's shop. I let my fingertips run over the title, tooled in gold leaf.

'*A Place Called Lost*,' I whispered to myself. There was no doubt in my mind now that Opaline Carlisle had written it. I was almost at the end and I was trying to ration it out, like saving squares of a chocolate bar as a kid to make it last longer. The feeling was bittersweet, as the one person I wanted to tell about it probably hated me. Henry.

I was in the library at Trinity, where I was supposed to be writing an essay on *Persuasion* with Logan. He was sneakily looking up new dishes on Instagram, so at least we were both procrastinating.

'What is it? You've been moping about since your birthday,' Logan observed. He was a very loud whisperer and I could see that the people around us did not appreciate his vibe.

'Nothing,' I said, carelessly minimising my own feelings. 'It's just, I need some help with something and the only person I can ask is ...'

'Shhh!'

I pulled my chair a little closer to his. 'You see, there's this guy—'

'Isn't there always?' he said, smiling.

'It's not like that. I just – I can't get into anything serious right now, so we stopped things before they started and now ...'

He scooched a little closer. 'What you have here, Martha, is your classic "situationship". Take it from me, you want to avoid them like the plague. You never know where you stand.'

He wasn't wrong. Dancing with Henry at my birthday party had been overwhelming. I felt like a princess; for the first time in my life I was in a beautiful house wearing a magical dress and floating in the arms of a prince. He was charming, funny and attractive, with that whole dark academia thing he has going on. Of all the bruises and broken bones I'd sustained over the years, the numbing disappointment and emotional scars, I had never felt my heart crack the way it did when he gave me the Petit Prince pen.

'It's just, we were both involved in some ... research and I kind of need his expertise.'

'My advice? Set your boundaries, make it clear from the outset that you're just friends and—'

'SHHHHHHH!'

Just friends. Exactly. I could do that. I mean, he wasn't to know I had checked his socials, which was utterly useless because he rarely posted. The last photo was of his newborn niece. It had made me smile when I saw it but then it also made me upset because I knew that I'd never be a part of his life.

Logan was right. After all, Henry wouldn't have come to my party if he didn't want to remain friends. Nothing had really changed; he would still go home after he'd found his manuscript and until then, for whatever reason, we were both being pulled in the same direction by the bookshop and by Opaline. Some outside forces had decided that our destiny was entwined, but we didn't necessarily need to be a couple in order to fulfil it.

'You're right,' I said, closing my laptop and stuffing it into my bag. 'It *is* the twenty-first century,' I repeated, as though that made everything clear.

'Wait a second,' he said, reaching up to the top of my head and extricating a bright green leaf from my hair.

'Oh, thanks,' I said, giving my whole scalp a good ruffle through in case there were any more.

'Spring is in the air,' he said.

It was also in my flat. The trunk had begun to separate from the wall at the top and the branches overhead now hung over my bed, creating a kind of canopy. Buds had begun to grow and unfurl. I no longer thought about telling Madame Bowden. I liked it and didn't want anyone to suggest cutting it. On a trestle table outside a second-hand bookshop I found a book on the hidden life of trees, which was interesting because it did feel like this tree was hiding in my basement. And because that was the kind of person I was now: the kind who picked up books on a whim.

~

Logan's words buoyed me along, all the way to the front door of Henry's bed and breakfast, but that was where I began to falter. Who was I kidding, really? Of course I still liked him and he'd know it straightaway. It was a stupid idea. Maybe I could find out more about Opaline myself – who needed someone with vast experience in this area anyway?

As I was thinking this all through and talking myself out of ringing the doorbell, I saw two little dogs hop up inside the net curtains of the front window and, on sight, begin barking furiously.

'Shhh!' I insisted, holding my hands up for some reason, as if they were armed. It didn't work. Next thing the front door opened.

'Hello, love, I've no vacancies tonight, I'm afraid,' said the slightly harried-looking woman. She took a deep drag of her cigarette and sharply told the dogs to shut up or they wouldn't get their treat, which weirdly worked.

'No, I'm not looking for a room. I was just seeing if Henry was in but he's probably out so I'll just—' I had stepped back off the kerb and was already making my exit.

'HENRY! COMPANY!' Her voice pierced the air like a foghorn and she invited me to step inside.

What could I do?

~

I was sat on a little velvet buttoned seat attached to a small desk with a landline phone on it in the hall when I saw his brown boots coming down the stairs. He looked puzzled to see me, as well he should have been.

'Hi,' I said. I also waved, even though he was right in front of me.

He said nothing, which was kind of weird and made me feel as though I shouldn't have come.

'No prizes for guessing why you came back from London so quickly,' the landlady said, in better humour now and winking at me.

Henry bent his head and rubbed the back of his neck with the palm of his hand. 'Do you want to come up to my room?' he asked.

'Now, now, Henry, you know the rules,' she giggled, having a good old laugh at our expense.

I wanted the ground to swallow me. I got up and tried to think of an excuse to leave. 'You know, this was probably more of an email thing, so I'll just email you. Later. Sorry to disturb,' I said, making a break for the front door.

'Actually, I was just on my way out so ...'

We walked down the street, exchanging pleasantries about the weather and both agreeing that global warming was terrible altogether. Strange how quickly you go from feeling like you can tell someone anything to feeling like two strangers meeting at a bus stop.

'I wasn't going to bother you again, you know, what with the way things are, but I was talking to my friend Logan and he said that, you know, it's the twenty-first century and people can be friends ...' Jesus, it was coming out in the most awkward way possible. I sounded like a five-year-old.

'Logan? He was the guy at your party?'

'Yes! He's become a good friend actually. We're in class together.' It still felt so cool, saying that.

'I'm really happy for you, genuinely. It's good to see you doing so well.' He stopped walking and kicked some imaginary dust on the ground with his boot. 'Thing is, I have to focus on my work now.'

'That's what I'm here to talk about. Opaline.'

'Oh?'

'The letter you showed me, to Sylvia. It mentioned a book. I think that maybe I have it.'

'What?'

'And I'm pretty sure Opaline wrote it.'

'Hang on, what? How?'

'I don't know, I can't explain everything, and I know it's not the actual manuscript you're looking for, so I wasn't even sure if I should tell you—'

'No, you absolutely should. I'm glad you did. I'm sorry if I'm being …' He trailed off.

'It's okay. It's weird for me too. But maybe it is possible for us to, you know, be friends?'

I stood there feeling a bit vulnerable and he took long enough with his answer, which wasn't the one I was expecting.

'Shit, I'm going to miss my bus.'

Chapter Forty-Five

HENRY

It was a terrible idea. I hadn't a clue what I was going to do when I got to St Agnes's and now I was going to have an audience. No word came from my companion, who was happily devouring the most foul-smelling packet of crisps, which threatened to pollute the entire bus.

I looked out the window at the rolling countryside. It was a dazzlingly bright day and every colour seemed to leap forth. I overheard someone say that Ireland would be a beautiful country if they could just put a roof on it. I had to agree. We were heading west and the coach had just pulled into some one-horse town for a toilet break and for Martha to procure these stinking crisps. I decided on a can of fizzy orange, which I was already regretting as now I needed the toilet.

'We might not even find anything. You need to adjust your expectations slightly. Usually in these kinds of situations, the information doesn't just drop into your hands.' I was irritable and not very good at hiding it.

Finding the manuscript was my only focus now. I told myself that if I didn't find it, then all of this was for nothing. My career would be in tatters but so, more importantly, would be my reputation. I had staked my professional standing on that one letter from Abe Rosenbach, which still hadn't even been verified properly. But then again, didn't all the books I'd read about the most successful book collectors, like Rostenberg and Stern in the US, or the Sinai Sisters from Scotland, point to the power of instinct and gut feelings?

'Don't worry, Henry. Something I could never be accused of is having great expectations.'

I smiled. 'I see what you did there.'

'It's on my course.'

She blushed slightly and it was all I could do not to brush her fringe away from her eyes. I had to distract myself.

'Do you know anything about this place?' I asked her.

'The asylum? Not really. But that's the idea, isn't it? To keep these places hidden in the shadows.'

'And the women. Conveniently.'

She turned her body towards me, as though she wanted me to go on and I decided this trip would be a lot less complicated if I could keep our minds centred on the issue at hand.

'I've been researching other women who were sectioned around that time. Did you know James Joyce's daughter, Lucia, was sectioned in 1932?'

She shook her head.

'Women were institutionalised by the men in their family for all sorts of reasons, but it was said she was diagnosed with schizophrenia. Apparently she was treated by Carl Jung at one point.'

'How long did they keep her there?'

'Her whole life. Almost fifty years.'

'Jesus!'

We sat in silence for a while, the gravity of what we were investigating becoming more real.

'She was a dancer. Before, you know. In Paris. There are some books that claim she became mentally unstable after her break-up with Beckett, but I suppose we'll never know. Her nephew burned all of her letters.'

Had the same fate befallen Opaline? Perhaps I'd never find the real truth.

'There are some scholars who suggest she may have even written a novel, but it's never been found.'

'What if it doesn't want to be found?'

'Of course it wants to be found. What kind of question is that? I mean, if we're assuming that inanimate objects have wants, which is a pretty bonkers assumption.'

She frowned, then looked out of the window. When she turned around she looked properly annoyed.

'So that's all it's about for you? Getting the glory—'

'No, it's more than that. It's about adding to our knowledge of history, rediscovering lost treasures so we can study them and, well, it's our cultural inheritance. It belongs to us.'

'But why should you get to decide what gets found and what remains lost?'

'What?'

I couldn't understand where this line of questioning was coming from or why it felt like we were arguing about it. She knew what my profession entailed. And she was the one who'd suggested coming along.

'It doesn't matter,' she said eventually.

'Eh, it clearly does. You "found" the book that you think was written by Opaline.'

'I didn't find it. It was … given to me.'

I looked at her askance.

'I don't want to talk about it.'

Neither did I. It was the main reason I had agreed to let her come with me – the lure of seeing this book at the end. Although why she wanted to come here at all was a mystery to me. Conversation was clearly at an end, so I did what all sensible people do when embarking on a long bus journey; I pretended to sleep so I wouldn't have to look at her.

'Henry.'

It would have helped greatly if she didn't say my name with that Irish accent of hers.

'Yes?'

'We're here.'

The bus chugged and rattled to a halt at what passed for a bus stop around here – a hard shoulder with a statue of the Virgin Mary inexplicably keeping watch. The engine made a whining noise as it pulled off again, leaving us in a cloud of dust.

'Is this it?' I asked, as I strained to look up the laneway beyond the wrought-iron gates.

'Looks like it,' Martha replied, pointing to the small sign that said *Saint Agnes's*.

'You're a natural.'

She gave me a withering look. I had to stop being such a dickhead. Was it possible I was just jealous? Who was Logan anyway? I dragged my thoughts back to the present. The laneway was lined with pine trees that had overgrown and merged into one thick, dark wall. As we walked along the curving drive, the building itself loomed into view around the corner. It was a dark grey block of a thing, hunkered down into the land. It could have passed for a stark kind of monastery, if it weren't for the bars on the windows.

I stopped walking.

'What is it?' she asked.

'It's just so … real.'

I'd never had a sensation like it. As though something heavy was pressing on my chest. It was one thing reading about these things on paper, but being here was entirely different. I hoped that my hunch was wrong and that Opaline had not been incarcerated here. Martha put her hand on my arm, as though to steady me and I came back to my senses. There were three old doorbells outside and it didn't look as though any of them worked. I pushed the buttons and waited.

'Have you thought about what you're going to say?'

'I'm going to ask if Opaline Carlisle was a, um, resident here.'

Martha shook her head, making it clear that this approach was utterly useless.

'You don't know much about Catholic Ireland, do you?'

'In what sense?'

'These kinds of places, they're not exactly known for offering up information.'

I decided to knock firmly on the door. After several minutes, there was still no answer.

'Right.' I smacked the palms of my hands together. The universal signal to leave. 'Let's go home.'

'But we came all this way!'

'Yes, and now we're leaving,' I said. 'What time is the next bus back to Dublin?'

'You can't leave now. What's the matter with you?'

'Because it's just another wild goose chase. It's not bringing me any closer to the manuscript, is it? People can waste their whole lives chasing shadows and I can't let myself become one of them.'

I refused to stand there arguing about it. I'd made my decision. I didn't owe her an explanation. I started walking briskly down the drive, assuming she would follow eventually.

'Can I help you?' A middle-aged woman held open the heavy wooden door and addressed us in a tone that left no doubt – the last thing she wanted to do was help. She had short, tight curls and wore a white nurse's uniform. I didn't blame her for being miserable, I would be too in a place like this.

'Yes, I would like to establish if a woman by the name of

Opaline Carlisle was a resident here at one point?' I said, rushing back.

'Do you have an appointment?'

No greeting, just direct animosity.

'No, but I—'

'You have to make an appointment.'

She was about to close the door when I stuck my boot in the door.

'Excuse me, what are you doing?'

I didn't know. I'd seen it done so many times on TV I just did it without thinking of a follow-up plan. I stammered something incoherent. I just wanted to pull my foot back out but I couldn't seem to move it.

'We're from the Department of Health and we're running a spot-check,' said Martha.

I couldn't even look at Martha. I knew if I did, I would give the game away. What the hell was she doing?

'I wasn't informed about this,' the woman replied, suspicion narrowing her gaze.

'It's a spot-check, that's the point.'

I didn't know who this person beside me was. For all I knew she *was* an undercover spot-checker for the Department of Health, such was her conviction.

The woman shifted her weight from one foot to another and she looked even more cross than she was when we'd first arrived.

'I'll need to see some identification.'

'Mr Field, show her your ID,' Martha said.

Was she talking to me? Where the fuck was I going to get ID? I finally looked across at her, trying to express my what-the-fuckness with my eyes. She widened hers as if to say just bloody do something. So I pulled out my ID card. The one from university. The one that said I was a rare manuscript specialist.

'Very well, Dr Field' she said and let us both inside. 'I hope this won't take long. We close at four o'clock.'

Doctor Field? That was what she took from my ID? Not that I was a PhD candidate?

The place was eerily quiet. Inside, it looked as though the building was slowly deconstructing itself and nobody had bothered to fix it. The walls, painted a sickly green, were peeling and there were damp patches everywhere. Black mould spread out from the windows and the lino on the floor was curling at the edges. The smell was toxic. A mix of bleach and boiled cabbage. It was old and uncared for – just like the residents, I imagined.

'We just need to check some records, isn't that right, Dr Field?'

'Um yes.' I cleared my throat. 'Pertaining to the Freedom of Information Act, we would like to look at how the records of past residents are, you know, filed.'

The woman glared at me. 'Oh. Aren't you going to inspect the ward?'

'The ward? You still have—' I stopped myself before saying the word 'inmates'.

'Another time,' said Martha. 'We wouldn't want to keep you, and this is something that the minister really wants to get on top of before the new legislation comes in.'

'New legislation?' the woman asked, falling for Martha's spiel.

'It's being put before the Dáil next year.'

I looked at Martha with new star-struck eyes. It was a revelation to see her so confident and unfazed whilst lying through her teeth. I was so impressed, I almost forgot why we were there.

We were led into a narrow office on the first floor with a thin brown carpet and a flickering light overhead. There were rows upon rows of steel-grey filing cabinets.

'Sharon normally takes care of the admin,' the woman

explained, immediately absolving herself and again checking her watch.

'Not to worry Ms …?'

'Mrs Hughes.'

'Mrs Hughes,' I said, 'this won't take long. Any chance of a cup of tea in the meantime?'

'No.'

With that, she left the room and we both waited until her footsteps were far enough down the hall.

'What the hell was that, Angela Lansbury?' I whisper-shouted.

'I don't know! It just … happened.'

'I can't believe it worked.'

'Nor can I.'

She was giddy with excitement. We didn't know how to celebrate so in the end we just high-fived.

'Okay, we better start looking.'

We didn't have much time and our task was daunting. Admissions files were categorised by date, but then some records were filed under the resident doctor's name and others still were filed under the patient's name. It was basically a mess. We agreed to begin at opposite ends of the room. I was searching the dates – mid-1920s onwards – and Martha was searching for Carlisle. We hardly spoke, apart from the occasional 'I still can't believe you did that' coming from me. I was pleasantly surprised by how much she wanted to help me. Or perhaps that was conceited. If what she said turned out to be the case and she had found herself in possession of Opaline's book, then it made sense that she had her own connection to this intriguing woman. After all, as I'd told her on the bus, you didn't need a qualification on paper to make a big discovery. Knowing my luck, she'd probably find the manuscript before me. The thought hit me like a sucker punch. I looked across at her and watched as her fingertips picked their way through the hanging manila files. Had I been played all along? Was she using me?

'Henry. What are you doing?'

'What?'

'We don't have much time,' she said.

'Right. Yes. Sorry.'

I pulled open another drawer and flicked through the files. They were all too recent. We were about to meet at the middle filing cabinet when I heard footsteps coming quickly down the hall.

'Shit!'

'Stall her,' Martha said.

I didn't think, I simply did what she said and met the woman just outside the doorway.

'I've been on to the department, and they've never heard of a Dr Field. In fact, they said there was no spot-check arranged. So now, would you care to tell me who you are and what you're doing here?'

'I would like to tell you, Mrs Hughes. But if I did, I'd have to kill you.'

'Excuse me?'

Jesus, what was I saying?

'Candid camera,' Martha smiled, coming out of the room. 'See, I have a camera in my bag,' she explained, pointing to what looked like a badge on her rucksack.

'I don't—'

'Oh, you've been such a good sport, hasn't she, Henry?'

'Yes, yes, absolutely,' I said. 'Thanks for taking part.'

'Oh, I—'

'Someone will be in touch shortly. Of course we'll need your consent before we can use the footage on our show, but there's a two hundred euro fee so just have a think about it, okay?'

Martha took my arm and we half-ran down the stairs. We kept

running until we reached the bus stop and I had to bend down with my hands on my knees for a good ten minutes, trying to get my breath back. She was still laughing when I looked up.

'You should be on stage. Honestly, how do you improvise like that?'

'I don't know, maybe Madame Bowden's rubbing off on me.'

The bus pulled in and we got back into the very same seats that we'd had on the way out.

'Well, that was an experience. Pity we didn't find the file,' I said.

'Oh, but we did.'

She pulled a folder out from her backpack and handed it to me. I was speechless.

Chapter Forty-Six

OPALINE

Connacht District Lunatic Asylum, 1941

A war has been raging overhead, or at least that was what I was told. At St Agnes's, all remained deathly still. The place was like a vacuum, sucking life away from the people who were trapped within. Food was scarce; we subsisted on vegetables that grew stunted and undernourished in the dry ground outside. I became numb over the years, unsure when that set in, like rot. My skin would itch and flake and I would scratch until I bled, just to feel something. Eventually, I felt nothing.

Our numbers shrank. The appetite for reforming women had dulled somewhat since a madman decided to reform Germany. War made everyone question the status quo. It appeared to me that men in particular seem to need a war to find meaning in what they already have. To feel that heady sway on the verge of losing everything before waking up and stepping back from the brink. Why was that?

I had become a competent seamstress thanks to Mary's instruction and it was the only thing that gave my day any semblance of order. I began stitching words from Emily Brontë's story of Wrenville Hall into my skirt. At first it was something I did to amuse myself, but then it became a way of remembering that I did have a life before this place. Some sections of the manuscript came clearly and intact, but I knew there was no way I could remember it by heart. The joints in my fingers ached as I strained to make my stitches as tiny as possible.

I have devoted an entire lifetime to escaping the confines of this wretched place, only to find myself further entangled in its gnarled roots and oppressed by its looming towers.

Only two nurses remained. Two more than necessary, in my opinion. The only one who did anything worthwhile was Daisy, a young local girl who thought a job in this place was a step up in life. God bless the child. She was innocence personified, yet no stranger to hardship. I concluded that she was the only beauty left in the world, and for her part, she never made me feel like a hideous, frightful woman to be feared. She said she enjoyed the place, that it was quieter than the racket of living with four brothers at home. We shared a strong dislike for brothers.

One bright morning, I heard shouting and laughter and footsteps rushing along the corridor. Daisy ran into my room; I was lying prone on my bed, my head empty of thoughts. At least I stopped calling them thoughts. All I had then were images of a past life that may or may not have happened. *Did I have a child?*

'I have a letter for you!' she said, as though it were the most wonderful thing to have ever happened, and she ran off again, zig-zagging like a spring lamb. I lifted myself off the pillow and looked out through the bars on my window. The frost had created beautiful patterns on the glass. I became aware of a letter in my hand. From Jane, of course. Dear Jane, she had never given up on me. Even though I rarely replied, if ever, she was not going to abandon our friendship.

I read it in the haphazard way my eyes worked then, reading up and down rather than side to side: *Your mother has passed away.*

My mother has passed away, I repeated internally. I was an orphan, I realised, in some abstract way. Childless. Motherless. The world at war. My eyes began to blink.

And suddenly, I was awake.

~

In all the years of my incarceration, my mother never once came to visit, never wrote. I excused her behaviour because I knew she was under Lyndon's influence and, even if by some miracle she had refused to believe his version of events, she would never openly defy him. Yet she was my mother. How could she abandon me in a way Jane could not? Her own daughter. Why hadn't she helped? In fact, she was the only one who could have overruled my brother. Why didn't my mother love me enough to risk everything? Those thoughts would forever haunt me. It was true that I had been closer to my father, and my mother was never affectionate towards me. But I had to assume that there was some love there. Not enough, clearly.

As I made my way to Dr Lynch's office with a purpose I had not felt in my bones for a very long time, I thanked my mother briefly for at least giving me an excuse to get out of this place. Surely they would not refuse my request to attend my own mother's funeral. And once I was back in the UK, I could work out my release, with Jane's help.

I sat patiently on a hard wooden chair facing Dr Lynch, who sat in a leather chair at his walnut desk. His glasses perched on the end of his nose, he was carefully peeling an apple with a knife, as though I were not even there. The nurse had gone out to attend to someone screaming bloody murder, to which I had grown entirely immune. Satisfied that he had managed to peel it all in one go, he finally looked up at me, almost surprised to find me sitting there.

'Miss Carlisle, you're not due for a check-up until next month.' He had a way of speaking that always made me feel as though I were an idiot. No matter what he said, simply his tone implied that I had all the intelligence of the piece of fruit on his plate. It was something I endured. Until today.

'I am not here for a check-up.' I told him that I had just been informed of my mother's death and that I wanted to attend her funeral.

'Ah yes, my condolences. Mr Carlisle wrote to inform us, oh, it must be a fortnight ago. Your mother has already been laid to rest, so you see, there's no reason for you to leave St Agnes's.'

'I-I ...' I was so confused. I reached into my pocket and pulled out Jane's letter. Checking the date, I saw that it was written over a week ago.

'Why wasn't I informed?'

'Oh, were you not? I'm sure I told Nurse Patricia to pass the message along.'

I looked down at the letter, the words swimming in front of me. My hands began to shake with a rage that boiled inside of me. Not for my mother, but my last chance of escape. I couldn't take it any more. I jumped up and grabbed the knife off the table, pressing it to the artery in my neck.

'What in God's name are you doing?' he said, scrambling to get out of his chair.

'Don't move or I'll kill myself, I swear!' I shouted.

He froze, halfway off the chair, and raised his hands in surrender.

'And don't shout for the nurse.'

He shook his head and kept showing me the palms of his hands as he sat back down on the chair.

'You see, the thing is, Dr Lynch, I no longer care if I live or die.' I surprised myself by meaning every word I said. It would have been a sweet relief to end it all. St Agnes's had been like entering a sort of purgatory, with no hope of redemption. All of my humanity had been stripped from me. And yet some part of me must have subconsciously kept up the search for a way out, for the words that came out of my mouth next sounded as though they had been waiting inside of me for a very long time.

'But I think you do.'

'Of course I care, Opaline, now put the knife down—'

'Yes, of course you care, because as long as I live, you receive a handsome stipend from my brother. Isn't that correct, Dr Lynch?'

'That is to pay for your care—'

I pointed the knife as sharply as I could bear it against my skin.

'Come now, doctor, it's just us here. We are half-starved and barely clothed, with no heat to speak of. You pocket that money for yourself, don't you?'

'I resent the implic—'

'Oh, shut up. SHUT UP!' I screamed at him. Standing there in a ragged, stained dress, unwashed hair sticking out from my head, dark circles around my eyes and a knife at my throat, I had never felt more clarity of mind. He was scared. I could see it.

'If I die, you stop receiving Lyndon's payments.'

He looked rattled and his eyes searched the room. I knew I didn't have much time to convince him.

'We can help each other. If you let me leave, right now, I will never tell Lyndon and you can keep getting your money. You will never hear from me again. I'll change my name, I'll go to Europe. I have friends there.'

I could see him thinking about it.

'No one ever has to find out.'

He wiped his face roughly with his hand, then started biting his lip. He was looking at the framed photograph on his desk of his wife and children. He looked back at me and I lifted my chin higher, showing him that I was not bluffing.

'If not, I will cut my own throat right now and bleed out all over this rug. Then you will have nothing.'

I had succeeded. He was willing to consider it. My freedom was tantalisingly close and I was suddenly aware that I was no longer quite so free about sticking a knife in my throat. Yet I had to keep it there.

'Oh, what does it matter now anyway?' he said, slowly getting up.

He opened another door on the opposite side of the room. It led directly to a short passageway with an exterior door. He shouldered it open and I could see the backyard, which must have been used by the staff to come and go, as it led straight on to the road rather than the long drive. I looked back at him.

'If your brother finds out—'

'He won't,' I said, unable to keep the tremble from my voice.

'Then get out.'

With that, I realised that he had known all along. I should never have been locked up here. It was all a lie.

A mixture of relief and revenge pulsated through me. I still had the knife in my hand. I wanted to slit his throat. Pictured it; blood spattering the walls. Whatever I lacked in physicality, I could make up for with the passion of my anger. He moved back and kept his hands aloft. I couldn't believe my freedom was finally in front of me. I dropped the knife and ran.

Chapter Forty-Seven

MARTHA

'You came!' I rushed into her arms. My mother never left her house, not even to go to the shops, so I never expected to see her on the doorstep of Ha'penny Lane. 'How did you? What happened?' I had so many questions.

'I found my voice.' The words came out slow but strong.

'Happy tears,' I said, as she wiped them away with her fingertips.

'I should have spoken up a long time ago, Martha. My precious girl.'

'I'm okay, Mom, really.'

'I know you are. You are such a capable young woman. I'm so very proud of you. I wanted to come here and tell you that, even if it's a little late in the day.'

'It's never too late,' came Madame Bowden's voice from behind me. She had a knack for just appearing in the middle of other people's conversations. 'Won't you come inside?'

It felt like a novelty having tea with my mother in the back kitchen of this grand old house. Madame Bowden suggested it as it was roomier than my flat and left us to it, thankfully. I thought she would poke her nose in, but she did have some sense of tact when it suited her. I talked cheerfully about my course in Trinity, the friends I'd made, my new-found interest in literature.

'You've made a lovely life for yourself here,' she said, placing her hand on mine.

'I'm happy, Mom. Even living here with Madame Bowden – it's not what I would have envisioned for myself as a young woman, but it kind of works. I think we're good for each other.'

'She sounds like a guardian angel.'

I wasn't sure if that's how I'd describe her. I poured some more tea from the pot. All my years at home, my father and my brothers took up all of the oxygen, but here, it was like we could finally breathe deeply. It's only in something's absence that you realise how much space it takes up.

'There's something I want to tell you, Martha.'

'You're leaving Dad?'

She gave me a double take.

'I'd be lying if I said I hadn't thought about it, but no. Your father is … well, he's not perfect. But he's dependable, and even though sometimes I wish I could change so many things about him, he has given me a home where I feel safe.'

I had never heard her speak about my father that way. Despite the fact that I still had a different opinion, I understood and respected hers.

'What is it then?'

'It's not something serious … what I mean is, it won't change anything, for you at least. But it might help you to understand the past. My past.'

She turned the teacup on the saucer, slowly choosing her words. It was strange for both of us to hear her voice like this, when we'd always communicated in silence.

'After Shane, I began to realise that the past isn't something we leave behind. It is living with us, every day. It isn't simply DNA that we inherit. I think there are other things passed down through the generations. Memories, perhaps.'

She was speaking from a place of deep pain, I could see that. I moved my chair closer to hers. The atmosphere in the kitchen took on an air of intense stillness, as though it too was waiting for her story.

'My mother was adopted as a baby.'

Of all of the things she could have said, I never would have anticipated that. Our family history was something I had seen as set in stone. How could I have been missing such a huge chunk of information?

'Why didn't you tell me before?'

'I suppose I didn't think it affected you ... and besides, mothers want to protect their daughters. My mother protected me, as much as she could, but my grandparents were not kind people. How they were ever allowed to adopt is something I'll never understand. You know that your grandmother died from pneumonia when I was three years old?'

I nodded.

'That's the story we told everyone. The truth is that she set off to Dublin to find her mother. I don't know all of the details; my father only told me from his hospital bed before he died. It was the sixties and she told him that having her own daughter made her desperate to find her real mother. I don't know why she thought she'd find her in Dublin, but either way, she never did find her. There was an accident and she slipped from the platform. The train hit her.'

'Jesus Christ, Mom, I'm so sorry.'

She kept her head down, as though she just wanted to get the story out.

'Well, my grandparents, the Clohessys, raised me after that. Reluctantly. My father had a job and men weren't expected to stay home back then. So they took me in and spent every day reminding me of their sacrifice. That was when I lost my voice.'

I grabbed her hand.

'It doesn't change anything, but it changes everything, doesn't it?' she asked.

I nodded, wiping her tears this time.

'Did you ever try to find them? Her biological parents?'

'No, but I thought about it. Many times. My grandparents wouldn't talk about it. They did not say it outright, but I got the impression that the adoption might not have been very official.'

'We could try now?'

She shook her head.

'It's too late. But I wanted you to know because it's your story, as well as mine.'

We sat there for hours talking, drinking more pots of tea and raiding the biscuit tin. It was only when it grew dark that I realised I should have been getting dinner ready.

'Will you stay?' I asked.

'No, I'd best be off now so I can catch the last train.'

As she put on her coat and we walked out to the hallway, she turned to look at me again.

'I should have told you every day what a wonderful young woman you were. I sometimes feel like I wasn't fully present, you know? Just going through the motions. That's what happens when you keep a part of yourself hidden. Anyway, I wanted to tell you now so you'd know, you were always enough, Martha. It's just the people around you were too wrapped up in their own pain to see it.'

We hugged tightly, right by the bannister where Shane had fallen. I began to cry. I didn't just cry, I sobbed in her arms. She held me and shushed away the bad memories, rocking me from side to side. The wooden staircase creaked like the bough of a tree beside us and I could hear a soft rustling.

'It sounds like this old house is trying to tell us something,' she said in a playful voice, as though she were telling a fairy tale to a child.

'It does, doesn't it?' I smiled, wiping my eyes with my sleeves. 'I think that too sometimes. Maybe next time you can stay for longer?'

'I'd like that,' she said, then turned to step down on to the pavement. She turned and waved again and called up to me. 'I'm looking forward to meeting Madame Bowden too!'

I waved and then registered the strangeness of what she had just said. She had already met Madame Bowden.

Chapter Forty-Eight

HENRY

'Are you aware that you have a great big bloody tree root growing out of your ceiling?'

'Yes.'

'And the branch sticking out of the gable?'

'That too.'

'Oh good. Not just me then.'

I'd decided to visit 12 Ha'penny Lane by my old entrance, the basement window, but found a very large branch growing out through one of the broken panes. We decided I should probably come through the front door instead. I held the folder with Opaline's papers aloft, theatrically making it clear that I had a proper reason for visiting.

'The lady of the residence is out having her hair set,' Martha said and I was relieved to hear it. She could be a bit overpowering, even if she was technically rooting for me.

'I think it's trying to tell me something,' she said, plucking one of the leaves from the branches that formed an arc over her bed. She seemed bizarrely unfazed by it.

'Yes, I think it is trying to tell you something very important about the unsound foundations of the house. You really need to have this looked at.'

She batted my concerns aside and put on the kettle for tea.

I moved in for a closer look at the tree. 'Did you do this?'

'What?'

'*What you seek is seeking you.*' It was carved on to the bark of the tree.

She stepped behind me and leaned over my shoulder.

'No?'

I turned around to see her face. She looked different, somehow. As though the shadows she carried inside of her had been replaced by an iridescent light. She looked happy. Despite the tree. Or perhaps because of it.

'What is it?' she asked.

'Nothing. You look well, that's all.'

She smiled and tilted her head to the side. It felt like a moment where one of us should say something, but neither of us could even begin putting our feelings into words.

'Tea?'

I nodded.

She brought two mugs over to the small table and grabbed an open packet of digestives from a shelf above us.

'So, what did you find out?'

I took a piece of paper out of the folder at random.

'Far more than I had expected,' I told her. 'It's put flesh on the bones – she's a real person for me now. In fact, it's thanks to you I've decided to change the angle of the paper I'm writing.'

She looked pleased but also confused. I handed her the letter and she began reading it aloud.

Dearest Jane,

I hope this letter reaches you. The young girl who works here promised to post it in secret, but one can never be sure. It's been snowing for a full five days now. There is something calming about it; how each snowflake falls weightlessly, without a sound. Every so often a slight breeze will cause a flurry of flakes to spin and swirl and lift over the walls of this place. A silent escape. How I long for the same. My only friend here, Mary, has died. I woke to find her lifeless in her bed this morning. From the cold. It has set into my bones so much that I cannot remember how it used to feel before. I received your letter in which you wrote that you hoped the gloves and shawl you'd sent were keeping out the chill. Oh, dearest Jane. If only you knew that anything of worth is taken away long before it reaches us inmates.

The physician is expected tomorrow. I think. My thoughts meander in a deep fog these days. Again I will ask to speak to my brother, again. I will request to be released for I am not mad, though I fear this place will render me so. The screams at night are unbearable. Why does Lyndon not answer my letters?

It does not surprise me that the doctors here have turned down your offer to bring a specialist from London. Having me assessed independently would prove that I have been wrongfully committed here, that I am sane. Although I fear it may be too late on that score. Losing the baby, and now Mary, in this place of unspeakable horrors, I would rather my sense leave me entirely. If I cannot escape this place physically, I must devise a way to do it mentally. To dissociate from this nightmare. Please do not write any more. Go and live your life. Consider your old friend no more. She no longer exists.

Opaline

'Bloody hell. This is horrific. I never thought—' She stopped suddenly.

'I know, it's all very real now.' I put the letter back and dunked a digestive into my tea. I hadn't eaten since lunch the day before. I'd been up all night going through the folder and taking notes. I held the biscuit in the tea for a second too long and it sank into the depths. I sucked my teeth.

'I'll make you another one,' she said and got up to refill the kettle. 'I wasn't sure if I'd see you again.'

'Why do you say that?'

She shrugged but I pressed for an answer.

'It's just – you have what you need now. Opaline's records.'

Wow. I'd really made quite the impression. Was that really what she thought? That all I cared about was the manuscript? I opened my mouth to say something, then thought better of it. What did it matter? I had to stop thinking that this could ever go anywhere. We were just friends.

'You didn't think I could leave without seeing her book, did you?'

She rolled her eyes and gave me a knowing look. It had been left on her bed and when she passed me to get it, I reached out for her hand, without thinking. She stopped and looked down at me.

'It wasn't all about the manuscript, you know. Not for me.'

I let her hand go but she didn't move. A slight smile formed at the corner of her lips.

'Thanks,' she said, almost in a whisper, then she retrieved the book from the bed and brought it to me. I hadn't expected it to look so elaborate. I had seen my fair share of rare editions and not many books made me gasp, but this one did. It was covered with a deep sapphire blue cloth, making the golden title jump off the front.

'*A Place Called Lost*,' I read aloud. There was a beautiful illustration of an old bookshop and I knew it was the one I had seen when I first arrived on Ha'penny Lane. I hadn't been drunk. It really was there. I felt completely overcome and my nose started itching with what could disastrously become tears. I cleared my throat.

'Where did you find it?' I asked.

'It sort of found me. Stories sometimes do. Like the one on my back.'

Her tattoo. I wanted to ask what it was, but before I said it, she asked about the rest of Opaline's papers and I was glad of the distraction. Thinking about the last time I saw her tattoo, dancing with her, holding her in my arms, it was too much.

'Oh, yes. There were bundles of letters written by Opaline that were never sent. It seems a bit sporadic, maybe some got through the gates and some didn't. They don't make for easy reading, I can tell you that. I don't know how she survived. But she must have – we have the letter to Sylvia which proves that.'

'And the book,' Martha said.

Even if I never found the manuscript, I had the makings of a very interesting paper on a woman who had been one of the most prominent book dealers in Ireland who was nevertheless locked up on the word of her brother. It didn't seem to matter how talented, intelligent or independent a woman was, she was still seen as the property of a man, to do with as he pleased.

'I'm afraid I have to get back to the library,' I said, rising rather abruptly and putting on my jacket.

There was a beat before Martha reacted. Had she wanted me to stay? I would never know and I wasn't going to make a fool of myself by asking.

'Could I take the book with me? I'm trying to finish the paper I've been working on. Hopefully I'll still be able to get some funding for it.'

She hesitated, so I suggested a trade. Opaline's papers for the book.

'Actually, there's a photo inside. Would you like to see?'

She nodded enthusiastically. It was endearing to see her enthusiasm for this woman she never knew. It was not a terribly flattering photo. There were several women lined up in front of a dining table, their hands clasped, no smiles. Perhaps it was taken for the families who paid for their keep? There was no writing on the back. Martha cocked her head to one side, then asked if I had a magnifying glass.

'Not on me, no,' I joked, but it went over her head. 'What is it?'

'Maybe nothing.'

'You can't say that!'

She squinted and held the photograph close to her face.

'It's her skirt. It looks like there's something written on it.'

'It's hard to tell,' I said, looking at the grainy black and white image. When I looked back at Martha her expression had changed.

'You look like you've seen a ghost.'

'Hmm? Oh, it's nothing, I've just realised the time, Madame Bowden will be back soon.'

With that she almost shoved me out of the door and I found myself back on Ha'penny Lane wondering what it was that I was missing.

Chapter Forty-Nine

OPALINE

Dublin, 1941

'*Guten Abend, Fräulein.*'

I didn't know how to respond, or why he was speaking in German. I wrapped the sliver of a shawl tightly around myself, as if it offered any protection. I thought I'd heard something and had come down from the attic to check.

Following my escape from St Agnes's, I had made my way back to Ha'penny and was relieved to find the shop still standing. It was like a dream, where things were both familiar and yet strange. Like Miss Havisham, the shop seemed to have halted the passing of time after I was taken away. the front door opened at my touch and even the brass handle felt like the soft muzzle of a long-lost family pet. Things had decayed and deteriorated and most of my belongings were missing. The windows of the shop were all boarded up. I had dragged my mattress up to the attic – the basement was far too cold – with only tap water to fill my belly. After the elation of gaining my freedom, a tremendous tiredness had come over me and I couldn't do anything to help myself. Days had passed with no human contact and now I was standing face to face with this man.

He reached into his pocket and took out a packet of cigarettes and proceeded to light one. He offered the packet to me, as if this situation were perfectly natural and I wasn't noticeably shivering with fear. Still, he said nothing, he simply leaned against the wall, casual and unhurried. He was a tall man, with dark blonde hair slicked back and piercing blue eyes. I could see now that he wore an army uniform, a khaki jacket with an eagle sewn on the breast.

'How did you get in here?' I asked, hardly trusting my voice, which croaked from neglect.

'The window in the basement. It is not locked.'

I had checked it myself. Either he was lying, or …

'Who are you?'

'Josef Wolffe. *Zu Ihren Diensten*.'

'I'm afraid I don't speak German,' I said.

'You are alone.'

It was more of a statement than a question. I didn't reply. Life continued on the street outside as we stood there, figuring one another out. Friend or foe?

'Whatever you're looking for, you won't find it here.'

Every muscle in my body was tense. He simply nodded, as though this entire situation were commonplace. He looked around the shop, taking his time, then looked me over. What did he see?

'I come here, sometimes. To read.' He nodded towards the small pile of books that still remained on the bottom shelf. My books.

'This is my home. You have no right to be here.' I didn't feel very commanding, standing there in old rags, emaciated from years of undernourishment and my hair falling out. 'I want you to leave.'

He nodded to himself, as if having come to some decision, then he unbolted the front door. I rushed over and locked it behind him. When I heard the engine of a motorbike fade away, I finally let out the breath I'd been holding.

I slowly climbed back upstairs, feeling my way in the darkness, my legs threatening to buckle beneath me. I collapsed on the floor of the attic with relief and tried to quieten my shallow breathing; listening for that old familiar sound, the reassuring presence of my books around me. Perhaps I imagined it, but I thought I could hear a soft wind and gentle pats, like snow falling against the window. In the gloom I spotted a book with *Little Women* on the spine. I closed my eyes and I was in Concord with Jo Marsh and her family and even the thought of it brought warmth to my skin. The words were working a magic spell to give me refuge and reawaken my soul – to the person I was before all the badness happened.

~

The next evening there was a knock at the front door. I Ignored it, yet the knocking persisted. No one knew I was here. I was weak with exhaustion and hunger, but I heaved myself up to the attic window and looked down on to the street. There was a motorbike and standing in front of my shop was Josef Wolffe, the German soldier, with what looked like a large pine branch and packages under his arms. He was stamping his feet, trying to stave off the cold. He couldn't see me inside, for all was dark, but I could see him clearly. The light stubble on his jawline, his eyes scanning the street.

I hesitated for a moment, then walked wearily down to the door and opened it.

'You should not be alone. *Es ist Heiligabend*. Christmas Eve.'

He stepped inside and left the packages and the giant tree branch in the middle of the floor, then went back outside. All I could do was watch, as he returned with a box and closed the door after him. He squatted down and, opening the box, took out candles and lit them. He looked for somewhere to place them and I gestured towards the stairs. I was too tired and hungry to argue. Then he opened another package which had food – bread, cheese, meat. I went and grabbed the bread out of his hand and began ripping pieces with my fingers and shoving it in my mouth. I was like a wild animal, my eyes wide, my jaws chewing rapidly. I sat on the last step, still wrapped in my blanket, and watched as he unwrapped more items. A bottle of wine. Apples.

Neither of us spoke a word. He wandered around the shop and found an empty crate, which he turned upside down and used as a seat beside the stove. He snapped the branch into small twigs against his knee and used the old paper to start a fire. The wood was too new to burn well, but the flames instantly made me feel warmer and the smell of pine was sweet and comforting.

He ate also, but sparingly. He peeled the skin off the apple and gave the carved flesh to me. He opened the bottle and handed it to me. I'm not sure how long it was before I spoke.

'Why are you here?'

He looked up from under his blonde hair.

'I am a prisoner of war,' he said with a flourish, as though he were announcing that he had royal blood. 'The Irish government are very kindly detaining us at one of their camps in Kildare.'

'But, if you're a prisoner …'

'Why am I not in prison? Because we are permitted to leave during the day. I am completing my studies at Trinity University.'

'You can't be serious?' I tried to laugh but the muscle was stiff from lack of use.

'Ireland is a neutral country. We are something of a nuisance for them.'

I ate some more cheese and helped myself to another cup of wine. He seemed pleased that I was accepting his charity.

'I didn't know it was Christmas Eve,' I said.

He was sitting quietly, carving something out of a piece of wood. He didn't look up. It was strange, being in someone's company yet not being required to talk. I leaned back against the wall and for the first time since I had arrived, looked at my old shop. What had gone on here since I left? Who had emptied it? Where was Matthew? What should I do now? I felt myself growing drowsy with the food and the warmth.

~

Sleep came quickly and deep. I dreamed of my father, taking me to Christmas Mass as a little girl, and the strains of 'Silent Night' filling the vaulted space of the church.

I woke up with a start. Music. There was a record playing. I scanned the room and saw that Josef was still there, the Victrola on the floor beside him playing the carol that was in my dream. He was leaning back against the wall, his eyes focusing on an invisible memory that softened his face. Perhaps he was dreaming of childhood too. Then, almost inaudibly, he began to sing. *Stille Nacht, heilige Nacht*. It was the most beautiful thing I had ever heard. His low voice, breaking in parts, was so full of tenderness that I thought I would cry. The crackling of the record was all that was left as the violins faded away.

'Happy Christmas,' I said, stirring him from his reverie.

His eyes widened briefly and when he looked at me, he gave me a half-smile. '*Frohe Weihnachten*.'

After a moment's pause, he got up and with a curt bow, turned to leave.

'Fog,' he said, his back turned to me.

'I'm sorry?'

'You are wondering how I ended up here. Fog. And engine problems.'

He turned back and lit another cigarette.

'We took off from Bordeaux. It was the end of the summer, last year. Six of us crew flying a Condor for weather reconnaissance.'

All of that time I was wasting away behind barred windows, the world had been at war.

'We had to ditch somewhere along the south coast. Policemen found us. Took us to the internment camp and I have stayed there since.'

'I see.'

'It's not so bad. You see, we have much freedoms.'

'You were fighting for that madman Hitler?'

He blew cigarette smoke skyward and grunted bitterly. 'You think we had a choice?'

I shook my head. I didn't know. I thought of Lyndon then. The rumours about the shootings for cowardice.

'I suppose all Germans were conscripted.'

'I am not German.'

A car drove by and the lights dazzled me. I got to my feet.

'Perhaps I should get back,' he said.

He bowed curtly before unbolting the door.

'I am Austrian. Good evening, Fräulein.'

~

Over the following weeks, Herr Wolffe began to leave little parcels of food and wood for fuel in the basement. I never saw him arrive or leave. I would simply see a package wrapped in brown paper with a large 'W' written on a blank note. There was even a package with some worn but perfectly functional clothing, wherever he had managed to source it.

As I regained my strength, my desire to reclaim my old life grew, the life that Lyndon had tried to take away from me. But that required finance, and the only thing I owned that was worth anything was the Brontë manuscript. And so I did something rash

– I wrote to Abe Rosenbach. I told him of the provenance and that there was no doubt in my mind, the manuscript was a draft of Emily's second novel. He was one of the most powerful men in the book world and the richest. He would take the risk.

So I dangled the opportunity in front of him with a carefully worded letter, before finding the courage to complete the second part of my task: finding Matthew and my manuscript.

~

'Can I help you?'

'Yes, I-I'm looking to speak with Mr Fitzpatrick. Matthew Fitzpatrick.'

'I'm afraid Mr Fitzpatrick no longer works here. Can someone else be of assistance?'

I fidgeted with my hands and then shoved them deep into my pockets. Matthew had been my one constant from the moment I arrived in Dublin. When I thought of him, I thought of things being right. Now everything felt wrong again.

'Madam? Can I help you with anything?'

'Where is he? I mean, when did he leave?'

'I'm not permitted to give out private information.'

My only friend from the past was no longer here, and what did that mean for my manuscript? I had to believe that Matthew would have kept it safe for me.

'It's just that he was keeping something of significant value for me and I've come to claim it.'

'I'm sorry. I probably shouldn't tell you this, but I suppose it doesn't make much difference now. Mr Fitzpatrick, Matthew, was killed just over a year ago.'

I could hardly speak.

'B-but that's not possible!' She was telling the wrong story. A story about somebody else. 'There must be some mistake ...'

'The Germans had just begun bombing London.'

'No, that can't be right. Matthew wasn't a soldier, he wasn't in the army—'

'I'm sorry, I know it's difficult. He was visiting family there. It was simply a case of being in the wrong place at the wrong time.'

I couldn't make sense out of it. All this time he was gone and I hadn't even known. My time at St Agnes's was still stealing things from me. I felt completely robbed of everything I'd known.

'If you could give me your name, I will check the records and see if there is anything outstanding in his files,' she suggested, softer now that she could see my distress.

'Um, yes. Opaline Carlisle. Or perhaps Gray, I'm not sure.'

She checked and rechecked. There was nothing. Wherever he had put my manuscript, he had not left a paper trail. It was as I would have wanted, total secrecy, but neither of us had known then what was to come. Now I had no way of getting it back and in that moment, I no longer cared.

~

Josef visited again and helped me to unpack what remained in the attic. I found more of my belongings, some boxes with my books neatly packed inside, and one of the old mechanical bird music boxes belonging to Mr Fitzpatrick. It was broken.

'There's nothing more sad than a tuneless bird,' I said and put it aside.

When I looked up he was staring at me, thoughtfully.

'You must open the shop again.'

The wooden shelves seemed to whine a plaintive sound. He might as well have suggested I fly to the moon.

'I couldn't possibly.'

'Why not?'

It was always so simple for men. Just do this or that, whatever you please.

'For one thing, no one is supposed to know I'm here. My prison is far stricter than yours and if anyone found out ... The thought of going back there ...'

I hadn't realised I was shaking. He put down what he was doing and came to me, putting his arms around me. I was a little stunned at the proximity, but it felt overwhelmingly good to have human contact again. Kindness. He broke away before I did.

'I am sorry.'

'Don't be.'

After a moment, we both smiled.

'It's a shame,' he continued, opening another box of books. 'It must have been a wonderful shop.'

'It was.'

I closed my eyes for a moment and tried to remember how it once looked. To feel the warmth of customers coming inside and finding the one thing they didn't know they were looking for. Could I do it? Could I afford *not* to? Without my manuscript to sell, I had no way of providing for myself. I couldn't keep relying on Josef's charity. It was sheer luck that he had helped me in the first place. He saved my life. Perhaps he was right. What was the point in gaining my freedom, only to remain locked inside?

'I would have to be careful,' I said, and his broad smile gave me a tickle of hope.

The shop began trading quietly and without fanfare. I simply opened the door and invariably people began to wander inside. I used the money from whatever sold to begin restocking the shop properly, as well as stocking my larder. I could even afford some essential items that now seemed like luxuries. I bought soap, undergarments and a brand-new pair of shoes. I began to see a way forward again. I suppressed my worries about being found out; as long as Lyndon believed I was still in St Agnes's and Dr Lynch kept receiving the money, they would have no reason to bother me. Little by little, I returned to myself. Bruised but still intact – and that was more than some.

Reliance is something that happens without you noticing it. In the weeks that followed the shop's reopening, I grew to lean on Josef and his quiet, dependable ways. He asked nothing of me and sometimes I couldn't quite work out why he returned, day after day, without ever questioning the past or the future. Perhaps it was because he was not one to discard broken things. I discovered that about him the day he arrived at the shop with the tiniest tools I had ever seen, rolled up in a satchel.

'Where did you get those?'

'From the clock repair man. Is not far from here.'

He said it as though it were perfectly obvious. That a prisoner of war could wander into town and borrow some tools from an horologist and fix an antique music box belonging to a woman who had just escaped a madhouse. I couldn't help but giggle, which utterly bemused him, though he didn't ask. He never asked. He just went about his work.

'Do you know what you're doing?' I asked him, before setting out for groceries, now that I had some money again.

'In Salzburg, I used to repair organs.'

I shook my head, unable to assimilate this new information.

'What do you mean?'

'For the church,' he said, gently unscrewing the casing from underneath the gold-plated box.

'You used to repair church organs?' I repeated and he nodded without making eye contact.

'As a boy. With my father. Then I studied mechanics at

Göttingen University. I like fixing things,' he said, a broad smile stealing across his face.

How had someone like him ended up on a Luftwaffe airplane, crash-landing in Ireland? Perhaps for the first time, I began to wonder if he had killed anyone. He had been stationed in occupied France. I watched his eyes flicker keenly over the minute workings inside the music box and how he gently removed the little automaton bird that sat on top. His hands were smooth; long fingers with clean, precisely cut fingernails. His blonde hair had grown long at the front and without the gel he once used, it slipped into his eyes, and he shook his head to dislodge it. Sitting in my shop, he looked perfectly at home. He had brought two old wooden chairs and a table from who knew where. Josef just had a knack for finding what was needed. Nothing ostentatious, but

simple and sufficient.

He made me laugh without meaning to. In fact, that was how he seemed to exist in the world. Just making it better, without meaning to.

Dublin, 1944

'I am to be repatriated.' Josef stood in the doorway, rigid from head to foot in his uniform.

'When?'

'Now.'

His voice betrayed no emotion. I nodded as if this information was perfectly fitting. Surely some part of me had expected this. Nothing lasted for ever and his precarious position here was clear to us both. And yet we had created a bubble of existence where the outside world and its changing winds could not penetrate, until now. I was holding a book that had constantly tumbled from its space on the shelf, no matter where I put it or how snugly it fit between its neighbours. *The Count of Monte Cristo* by Alexandre Dumas. I clung to it now, trying to find some kind of steadiness.

'Is there someone waiting for you? In Austria?'

I had never asked. Truth be told, I had not wanted the answer before now. But now it was time to face reality. Perhaps it would help me to let him go.

'My father. There is no one else.'

He looked at me and I could see in his eyes what his words meant. I ran to him, threw my arms around his neck and buried my face in his chest. It was the first time we had even touched and so it should have felt unfamiliar, but it didn't. It felt like the only place I ever wanted to be. He hesitated at first, but after a moment's pause, he encircled me with his arms and I could feel his warm breath on my neck.

I pulled back to look at his face. His eyes looked straight into mine and held all of my world within them.

'*Mein liebling*,' he said.

All of this time, we had kept our distance from one another. I suddenly realised that, at least for my part, it was purely out of fear of losing another person that I loved. I had fooled myself into thinking that if I didn't allow myself to get close to him, I wouldn't miss him if he left. Stupid, stupid woman. Intimacy is only one string on the bow. The instrument still plays the music.

He took my hands in his, turned my palms upwards, then lifted them to his face, one on each cheek. Then he took each one and kissed them. The sadness that always seemed to tug at the corners of his mouth was still there, but there was something else. A vulnerability he had not let me see before.

It felt like time had slowed, just for this moment, as if he wasn't being whisked away from my life. I tilted my head upwards and let my lips linger next to his. I could feel his breath and watched as he let his eyes close. I brushed my lips ever so lightly around his mouth, then kissed the corners that would curl in a smile when he thought I wasn't looking. His arm pressed tightly against my lower back and when I could no longer hold back, I let myself melt into him. We felt like one person and I knew that no matter what happened, I had met my true soulmate, and maybe that was enough. Just knowing he was out there, breathing, living, would have to be enough.

~

I couldn't watch him leave. It was only when the engine of his motorbike faded that I went back out on to the street. Empty once again.

Chapter Fifty

MARTHA

Have you read the end of the book?

I blinked at Henry' message on my phone. The sun wasn't even up yet. Had he spent all night reading it?

I texted back:

No

I mean, I'd peeked ahead. Everyone does that, don't they? But it's hard to make sense of an ending when you don't have all the facts. *A Place Called Lost* was the story of a building that may never have existed in real life and a potential custodian who was most likely a fictional character. The one thing it hadn't mentioned was the one thing Henry was desperate to find – the manuscript.

'The manuscript,' I whispered to myself. The leaves on the tree shimmered and shook as I said it. I stretched my arm up over my head and touched the wood, so familiar to me now. How could I even begin to explain it to him when I couldn't even explain it to myself?

We arranged to meet up later and speak in person. Another

bittersweet conversation where I would pretend that I hadn't fallen in love with him. I groaned loudly and got up to prepare Madame Bowden's breakfast. I took my frustration out in the kitchen, banging saucepans and plates, and brought a plate full of sausages and scrambled eggs to the dining-room table. I finally decided that I would tell her about Opaline's book and the documents we'd stolen from the asylum. I was glad Henry had given them to me, but he was right – it did not make for happy reading. To have lost her daughter in that awful place, she must have wanted revenge on her brother. I know I would have. I thought of Shane and his accident. Madame Bowden had hardly flinched.

Something was tugging at my mind and I wondered why she hadn't come down for breakfast yet. Every morning she was the one to wake me with her shrill voice and endless demands. What if there was something wrong with her? With every step I climbed I told myself I was being stupid and that she was just having a nice long lie in, but I didn't really believe it. I knocked on the door to her bedroom and, after a moment, let myself in. My eyes adjusted to the scene. Her bed had not been slept in and she herself was nowhere to be seen.

'Madame Bowden?' I called out. 'Are you there?'

The door to the ensuite was slightly ajar, but on further inspection, it was empty.

'Hello?' I called out on to the landing, but the house had such an air of stillness that I knew I was alone.

I checked downstairs for a note but there was nothing. Of course she did not have a mobile phone, so I couldn't call her. She refused to have her daily movements monitored by technology companies. I wasn't sure what to do and spent the morning wandering from room to room, looking out of the windows at the street outside every few minutes.

'Do you have any of her friends' numbers that you could call?'

my mother asked, when the worry became too much and I had to call someone.

'I can't remember any of their names and there's no address book or anything.' It was only now I realised that I knew so little about the woman. 'Should I call the police? What if she's wandered off somewhere and forgotten where she is?'

'Has she ever seemed forgetful?' my mother asked.

'Well, no, but you saw her when you were here, she is pretty old.'

'I didn't see her.'

Her answer seemed out of place – like trying to force a cube into a round hole.

'What are you saying? Of course you saw her. I introduced you both when you were here the other day.'

After a pause my mother spoke again. 'She wasn't there when I stopped by, remember?'

My flesh broke out in goosebumps. What the hell was going on? I almost jumped when I heard the doorbell ring.

'Maybe that's her now,' I said, rushing to open the door, but it was Henry.

'You may as well come in,' I said, then told my mother I would call her back.

He looked a bit fidgety, like something was bothering him. We both spoke at the same time.

'I found something out—'

'Madame Bowden is missing!'

His eyes flashed wide. 'Missing?'

'I went to wake her for breakfast and her bed hadn't been slept in.'

'Oh.'

His tone was annoyingly dismissive.

'What was it you wanted anyway?' I hadn't meant it to come out as sharp as it did.

'Doesn't matter now. Another time, perhaps.'

He reached into the breast pocket of his coat.

'I brought your book back,' he said, leaving it on the console table. He hovered in the hallway.

'You're really worried, aren't you?'

I shrugged. She'd become like family to me.

'I have to keep busy,' I said, pulling a pair of rubber gloves out of my back pocket like some kind of cleaning superhero. 'Sorry, I don't mean to be rude.'

I expected him to leave, but he began shaking himself out of his jacket.

'Okay, what are we doing?'

'What do you mean?'

'Well, I'm not going to leave you on your own, am I? Got any more of those?' he asked, looking at my gloves.

~

I took out all of the silver and laid it on the kitchen table, Henry at one end, me at the other. At quarter-hour intervals I would look up at the clock and feel my worry growing. We hardly spoke, until he offered to make some tea. I didn't notice him leaving the cup beside me and I knocked it off the table with my elbow. The sound of the china smashing on the tiled floor made me want to scream. I wanted him to get the hell out and leave me alone to cope. Having him around only reminded me of all the things I couldn't have. I got up to get a mop and a dustpan.

'It's okay, I'll do it,' he offered.

'I'll be quicker doing it myself,' I snapped.

He stepped backwards, holding his hands up in surrender. I attacked the spilt tea and broken crockery with all of my pent-up anger and managed to cut myself. Next thing I knew, he was bending down beside me.

'Here, let me help,' he said, attempting to wrap my hand.

'It's fine.'

He sat back on the floor.

'You can let people in sometimes, you know. You don't have to do everything on your own.'

I wasn't about to take advice on how to heal my trust issues from him, of all people. The man who'd run away from every relationship in his life. I got up and found a box of plasters in one of the cupboards before sitting back down at the table.

'You can talk to me, you know. We are friends, aren't we?' He was leaning against the fridge.

'I hate this job.'

'No, you don't.'

'I do. I hate this stupid job. I don't know why I ever came here. And I hate my night course and every reminder of what I missed out on—' I struggled to open the wrapper on the plaster but my thoughts kept running on. 'Just when I think I've got a handle on things, my life is turned upside down again. And I don't even understand what any of it means. Why that book appeared in my room and seems to be talking to me. How Shane died in this house, as if by accident, but it didn't make any sense. Then my mother beginning to speak again, only to tell me that her mother was adopted and so nothing is what I thought it was. And now Madame Bowden – I know you think I'm overreacting, but something doesn't feel right! None of this is normal,' I said, my hands shaking. I threw the plaster on the floor and gave up. 'But you know what I hate most?' I turned to look at Henry, who was just standing there, letting me throw out the jumbled contents of my head. 'I hate how hard I've had to fight against what I really want because I'm so scared of getting hurt again.'

There was a moment of silence, where I almost regretted saying everything out loud.

'What do you really want?'

I looked up at him, tears in my eyes.

'You.'

We collided as if our lives depended on it. He swept me up in his arms and kissed me in a way that held nothing back. My entire life focused down to this point – like adjusting the lens of a microscope to find the one thing that matters most. Love.

Chapter Fifty-One

HENRY

We lay in Martha's single bed, every inch of our skin touching. The wall between us had crumbled with every heart-sore word she spoke in the kitchen, like an exorcism of the past. The truth shall set you free, that's what they say. We were both laid bare now and I knew then and there that she was my destiny. Every stupid, seemingly pointless, difficult, lonely, challenging thing I had done in my life before this had led me here, to Ha'penny Lane.

'Are you okay?'

I felt her head nodding against my chest and I pulled her even closer into me. My heart felt ten times its usual size. I felt like I could lift a car, if I needed to. Probably best not to try, but the feeling was there nonetheless.

'There's something I never told you,' I said.

'Oh God, you're not engaged to somebody else, are you?'

'Very funny. I'll engage you in a minute if you're not careful.'

'If you're not careful, I might say yes.'

'Did we just get married?'

She laughed a little hoarsely, directly into my ear, which was ridiculously sexy.

'I might give the whole marriage thing a miss for a while, I think, if that's okay.'

'Same.'

She rested her chin on my chest, waiting for the thing I'd never told her. Here went nothing.

'I've been in the bookshop.'

'What bookshop?'

'THE bookshop. Next door.'

She shook her head slightly, trying to make sense of my words.

'It exists, Martha. Or at least it did, for a time. The night I arrived in Ireland.'

'You've seen it?'

I nodded.

'Why didn't you tell me?'

I pulled my 'why do you think' face.

'You already thought I was a weirdo.'

'That's not true!' she said, laughing again. 'I thought you were a perv.'

'Well, there you are. I didn't want to be a perv *and* a weirdo, might have blown my chances with you altogether.'

'Are you saying you fancied me right from the start?'

'Fishing for compliments?'

She rolled over and pretended she was going to get up. I hauled her back until she was lying on top of me and I felt a desire for her aching through my body.

'I think I knew from the minute I saw you.'

She kissed me softly and let her fingers run through my hair. It was like a dream I never wanted to wake from – after all of the times I'd had to leave this house knowing she would never be mine, it hardly seemed real.

'Wait a second,' she said, lifting herself up on her elbows and annoyingly removing her lips from mine. 'Why do you think the shop chose you to see it?'

'Um, I'm not sure it chose me ...' It was hard to think rationally while lying naked in bed with this woman. Besides, for the longest time, I'd thought it was a drunken mirage, if such a thing existed.

She sat up now and wrapped the sheet around her. It seemed we were taking a break.

'The book, *A Place Called Lost*. I just assumed Madame Bowden had put it in here.'

'Along with your tree.'

She made a face at me. My sarcastic tone was wearing thin.

'I told you, none of it makes sense. This might sound crazy—'

'Crazier than seeing a shop that doesn't exist?'

She looked at me with her head tilted, as though sizing me up. 'The manuscript. It's really important to you, isn't it?'

Was she still doubting my motivation here? I began to explain myself but she interrupted.

'No, I know that's not what this is, but I get that you wanted to prove something.'

Hearing those words, it all suddenly sounded so superficial. Trying to win the approval of other people, chasing achievements that weren't really achievements at all. It's not as if I wrote anything, I just stumbled across someone else's work and tried to find my own worth in some kind of second-hand glory. Maybe I had it all wrong. Maybe it was time I tried to earn my own respect instead of everybody else's.

'Finding the manuscript would have been'—I paused, searching for the right word—'immense. But in a strange way, uncovering the truth about Opaline and her bookshop and, last but not least, meeting the perfect partner with the kind of laugh that makes my heart race, has sort of surpassed that.'

'Are we partners?'

'I'd like to be.'

'Okay.'

With that, she turned her back to me.

'Um, what are we doing? Is this some kind of mating ritual? Do I turn my back?'

She was laughing again. 'The words, Henry!'

Her tattoo. Of course. I leaned closer but couldn't make out the writing.

'Shit.'

'What is it?'

'I think I might need glasses.'

She bent towards her nightstand and fished out a magnifying glass from the drawer. I tried not to feel like an ageing tortoise. The script began …

Wrenville Hall is a spectre that haunts us all from one generation to the next, crushing every dream, every aspiration in its path. This ground is cursed, as is the lineage of each and every child born here. I am born into darkness and no amount of atonement will grant me the saving light I have sought in her, my darling Rosaleen. Darkness will reign on this place until my last breath, and beyond.

I wasn't sure what I had expected since seeing Martha's tattoo the first time, but I know I had not expected this.

'Can you see the date?'

I searched with my magnifying glass and saw the numbers 1846.

'What is this?'

She turned around to look at me, her eyes wide and solemn.

'I've never told anyone about this. I never really understood it – I mean, why it was happening – until I saw that photograph of Opaline.' She reached back and grabbed her phone off the nightstand, pulling up an image of the old photograph we'd found of Opaline at St Agnes's before handing it to me.

'What am I looking for?' I asked, taking the phone.

'Look at her skirt.'

I zoomed in and saw something I had missed before. There were stitches on the material.

'Words,' she said, prompting my brain to kick into gear. 'A story. The same one that's on my skin, she sewed it into her clothes.'

'What the—'

I looked at her back again and saw the initials at the end.

EJB.

My scalp tingled and it felt like my hair was standing on end.

'Henry, I think this is Emily Brontë's manuscript.'

Chapter Fifty-Two

OPALINE

London, 1946

Inspired by *The Count of Monte Cristo*, I spent months searching for information and came across a newspaper article about a soldier's family who believed he had been wrongly executed for cowardice. They named the unit. It was my brother's. I had my lead, all I had to do was follow it.

I uncovered damning court martial papers from two trials held in Ypres, where fifty men had been sentenced to death by firing squad (or murdered, depending on your viewpoint). Just days before the Armistice was signed and in full knowledge that the Germans were about to surrender, my brother had ordered two more men to be shot. I took the papers to a Mr Turner, a journalist working with *The Times*, and he agreed to investigate further.

From the trial record, it was clear that they were suffering from shell-shock. In Lyndon's own hand, he wrote that shell-shock was a regrettable weakness, not found in good units. 'There is insufficient evidence for a conviction,' he'd written, yet he recommended a death sentence in order to send a message to the battalion, who had suffered great losses the day before. There was no mention that it was the general's military strategy that had led to these wasted lives. One was an Irish soldier, Frank O'Dowd, who was shot for refusing to put his hat on because it was wet through from the endless rain. He was drugged by a doctor to get him through the final hours in the death cells. Mr Turner had been able to contact the medic, who confirmed that O'Dowd was a volunteer soldier. 'They couldn't see brave men when they were standing there in front of them,' the medic had told him. He also confirmed that, once the firing squad had finished, my brother gave the Irishman the final coup de grâce, a bullet to the head.

I spent the night at the Great Western Royal Hotel in Paddington. Unlike so much of London, it had made it through the war relatively unscathed, with some minor air-raid damage to the roof. It was strange being back home. I no longer felt a part of the fabric and the people seemed strange to me, different somehow. The war had robbed them of so much. In that, I should have felt a kind of solidarity, but my war had been a very different one. I met with Mr Turner for lunch and he handed me a copy of the article they would print in the paper the following day.

I read the article. It was powerful. Turner was an exceptional journalist and, rather than making a pantomime villain out of my brother, or a monster capable of terrible evil, he presented him as a very real man who had chosen brutality over human decency. This somehow made him more real, more accountable for his crimes.

'No going back now,' he said, tipping his hat to me before disappearing into the crowd on the street.

'There is an old saying, *Before you set out on a journey of revenge, you must dig two graves,*' said a woman's voice, deepened by time and wisdom, yet unmistakably that of my old friend Jane.

'Jane!' I cried, embracing her tightly. I had written and asked if she would meet me in the hotel lobby.

'Confucius said that,' she warned, fearing the endeavour would somehow destroy me too. 'Are you sure you want to go through with this?'

'I need to own my story. To take back my power.' I realised now that I shared another commonality with the families of those dead soldiers. I was shamed into silence. Ashamed of what happened to me, of how I had somehow 'let' it happen to me and of how people would look on me now, as some sort of damaged woman. I felt tainted by it. Other than Josef's quiet and humble company, I had isolated myself from the world because of it. Was I ready to return? Maybe not, but then, does one ever feel truly ready? All I knew was that, in that moment, I had suffered enough in my silence. At least the pain of speaking out might bring me courage.

'The world needs to know who Lyndon Carlisle really is. I offered up my own story - *Commanding Officer Carlisle, The Reaper, had his own sister locked up in an asylum for the insane.*'

'Good grief! Will your editor print it?' Jane asked.

'It's something of an old boys' network at *The Times*. What Lyndon did to me doesn't count, apparently.'

'That's absurd!'

'Mr Turner was of the view that any hint of mental weakness could tarnish my reputation and detract from the "real story". His words.'

'Perhaps he has a point,' Jane mused, chewing her lip. 'Lyndon might use it to his advantage.'

'I suppose you're right. One last sacrifice to see justice done.'

I had set events in motion now; there was no turning back. Was

I scared? Of course I was. Yet the story had now become so much bigger than me, I felt responsible to act on behalf of all those who would never have the opportunity to get justice for what my brother did to them. I would restore some integrity to the Carlisle name. I felt it was what my father would have wanted also. The time had come. I had to confront him face to face.

~

As the evening grew dark, I made my way to my erstwhile family home. The air was still and quiet, my footsteps on the pavement the only sound, save for the blood pounding in my ears. I came to the front gate of the house. How much smaller everything looked.

I knocked on the door, and in the moments while I waited, I tried to imagine myself as a very tall, strong-rooted tree. I let the muscles in my shoulders release and focused all of my energy into the centre of my belly. That's where the fire burned, and I knew I would need to draw on it now, with precision and fierceness. A woman answered.

'Mr Carlisle,' I said, plainly.

'Is he expecting you?'

'If he is not, then he is a fool.'

The woman looked puzzled, then went to deliver the message. I didn't wait for an invitation into my own home. I closed the door behind me and followed her across the parquet hall to the parlour.

'Excuse me, Madam, you must wait here.'

'I've waited long enough,' I said, pushing past her with ease. He was having his supper at the table and almost choked on his soup when he saw me.

'What the devil—'

'Surprised to see me, Brother?'

He didn't speak another word. He hated being seen to be at a disadvantage. He would wait to see the lie of the land before planning his counter-attack. I was not prepared for how much older he would look – older than his years. He had become frail, his skin papery and thin and frightfully red around his scars. His hands were arthritic, curling into themselves, and he was practically bald.

'You're wondering why I am here and not in my cell at St Agnes's?'

He patted the corner of his mouth with a napkin and placed it on the table. The woman who had answered the door still hovered around me like a fly in summer until he waved her away.

'*How did she do it?* you must be thinking to yourself. And what of Dr Lynch? He still takes your money every month, does he not?'

He narrowed his eyes and stood up from the table. For all his weakness, he could still command himself like an officer. It took all of my will not to step back.

'How dare you show your face here.'

I could almost feel his breath on my skin, he stood so close to me.

'I am not afraid of you any more. What more could you do to me?'

'Shall we find out?'

I held his gaze. I wanted to strike out, but I had something greater than violence in my armoury.

'You wanted to erase me? That little girl, Father's favourite? Well, allow me to congratulate you. That girl no longer exists. The woman that stands before you now is a very different creature, one who is also bent on destruction. Namely yours.'

'Am I to be moved by this spectacle? Because I assure you, I am not.'

I paced around him like a lioness around her prey.

'Within hours, the whole world will know what you have done. The ink is soaking into the paper as we speak.'

'What paper? What are you talking about, woman?'

'*The Times*. They were very interested in your past. Especially your nickname, The Reaper.'

I saw a flicker of concern.

'Paper will take any ink, regardless of its veracity. And you will only reveal yourself as a dim-witted fool who belongs in a sanitorium.'

'Ah yes, you have me there. Unjust as it is, I knew my story alone wouldn't be enough to ruin your reputation. Tarnish it, perhaps, but not the annihilation I seek. No, Lyndon, the morning papers will be full of your crimes on the battlefield and those men you murdered under the guise of cowardice. Most of the records were destroyed, but I have gathered enough evidence of your despicable acts to make you a pariah in the eyes of everyone you know and an enemy to everyone else.'

His eyes widened momentarily.

'Those pitiful excuses for men did not deserve to wear the uniform. They were a disgrace to their families, to their country.'

'I have proof that the men you shot were not deserters. Witnesses who are prepared to go on record that you murdered those men. Their families deserve justice.'

'I gave them justice!' His voice boomed like a cannon from his ribcage.

'It's just as I suspected. You are truly mad.'

We were all just pieces on a chessboard to him. Inconsequential pieces to be moved around at his will.

'Well, it takes one to know one. Besides, they were conscripts, not real soldiers.'

I knew he was baiting me.

'Some of them were just boys, did you know that? So yes, perhaps they panicked in the face of all that death, but they were not deserters.'

'Oh, please, Opaline, do tell us more about your experience of life on the battlefield. Enlighten me with your knowledge of such matters.'

'I know that it is not my right to be judge and juror over someone else's life.'

'Shall I tell you of the thousands that died of exposure that winter? Still more from cholera. The indescribable suffering of millions of the Empire's best men, lying in those mud trenches for weeks, in rain, cold, wind – hungry and weary under the constant rain of the enemy's bullets. The terrible booming and slaughter that carried on ceaselessly. The dead and wounded cleared away for new soldiers to face an enemy better armed and better prepared. Showers of black mud raining down on the wild, primitive countryside. Twenty thousand men were killed on the first day at the Somme. It was as if the last day had come, and every man had to face it with only the comrade at his side for support. In the trenches they ate when food could reach them, starved when it could not. There they killed and were killed, were buried in shallow graves, half eaten by rats. And they were the lucky ones.'

I hadn't expected this. He had never spoken about the war before now and if he had, perhaps things could have been different.

'Still, it doesn't excuse—'

'None of us could escape the horror of it. We had to defend King and country. So I did what I had to do.'

'What? Killing your own soldiers before the enemy could?'

'By making an example of their cowardice. Armies are ruled by fear. Do you think those men that volunteered understood the carnage that lay ahead of them? Don't you think that every man out there wished with every fibre of their being that they could leave that hellish place? What do you think keeps men marching forward to their death?'

I didn't know.

'Duty. Honour. Those weasels that you now seem so bent on protecting had neither of those things. They were out-and-out cowards.'

'If you truly believe in honour, then you will know, somewhere in your heart, or if you do not possess one, which I doubt you do, then in your conscience, that you were wrong. The families of those men have carried the shame for too long and for what? Even if those men felt fear in the face of a formidable enemy, is it a crime punishable by death? You could have pardoned them. Most Commanding Officers did. But not you. Why must you crush anyone who does not meet your exacting standards? Why must you humiliate and torment—'

'Enough!'

He walked away from me and poured himself a drink from the crystal decanter. I tried to steady myself, although my legs were shaking and I longed for a drink also.

'It's always your pain, your suffering. You never think about anyone else.'

I didn't even bother replying. There was little point.

'Can't you imagine for a moment the suffering I have endured from this?' He pointed to the side of his body that was burned. He took various bottles of pills from his pockets and threw them on the table. 'They barely touch the surface,' he said, calmly now. 'I did my duty out there. I put my body on the line and what did I get in return?'

'They gave you medals, didn't they?'

'Hah! Medals. I wanted respect. I wanted a future. A family. No woman would come near me when she saw this. I could no longer provide a wife with children, in any case. A useless specimen. I had to beg for a job. Do you know how humiliating that was? The one thing I asked you to do.'

'Marry Bingley?' I asked.

'And there you were, flaunting your freedom in front of me. The freedom I paid for!'

'Lyndon, if only you had spoken of this before, I could have helped.'

'What could you have done? You were only good for one thing and you wouldn't even obey me in that.'

'Obey you?' I almost laughed at the thought. What right did he have? He always acted like he had authority over me and I suppose our age difference normalised his behaviour. Not any more. 'You make it sound as though I owe you something and believe me, Brother, I owe you nothing.'

'You owe me everything! You would be dead if it weren't for me.'

'What on earth are you talking about?'

'Your mother wouldn't keep you. To this day, I still can't be certain you're even mine. French slut.'

It was as though I had wandered into someone else's conversation. His words didn't make any sense to me.

'My mother?'

He walked to the sideboard, picked out a cigar from a silver box and lit it with a round marble lighter. His eyes narrowed as he sucked and eventually blew smoke into the still air.

'You may as well know, now Mother and Father are both dead. Your grandparents.'

I shook my head. None of this sounded right.

'I'm not going to listen to this madness,' I said, turning to leave.

'Not so keen on the truth now, eh?'

I stopped dead.

'I thought you were here to set the record straight, to bring all of my past transgressions into the light? Well, you may as well know all of it then.'

I felt nauseated. There was a sickening feeling creeping up my veins and into my chest. I realised I knew what he was going to say; had somehow always known somewhere deep inside of me, but never allowed myself to see it.

'And when that cheap rag of a newspaper prints your version of events tomorrow, you will know that you have betrayed your own father.'

I turned around and looked him dead in the eyes.

'No,' I said, shaking my head again. 'You can't be.'

'We were touring Europe, the summer of 1900. My grandmother – your great-grandmother – paid for the trip. I was with some friends from university, doing the Grand Tour, as was the custom for a young man. I was twenty years of age, much like yourself when you made your own escape to the continent.'

I hated that he was comparing us. I was nothing like him.

'We were visiting the French Riviera. She made herself available to me—'

'Shut up!' I covered my ears with my hands. It was too much. But he came towards me and pulled my arms down by my side.

'It's the natural order of things, Opaline. Young men must sow their wild oats. But girls like her, they know an opportunity when they see one. Before I left, she came to me, saying that she was pregnant and couldn't afford a child. I told her she would get nothing from me, but she had my name and must have found our address. A year later, she showed up at our door and left you like an unwanted gift on the doorstep.'

I was crying, but he kept on.

'I suggested an orphanage, but Father, being the weak-willed man that he was, insisted on keeping you. I wanted nothing to do with it. I had my career in the army. So they brought you up as their own and you have been the thorn in my side ever since.'

I had stopped struggling and so he let my arms go, then walked back to the sideboard and poured two large glasses of brandy from a decanter. When he handed it to me, I drank it down in two large gulps.

'Father wasn't my real father?'

We stood in silence for a time, the dust settling on our words.

'What was her name?'

'Who?'

'The woman. My … mother.'

'How the devil should I know? It's over forty years ago. Celine, or some such. Or was it Chantal?'

I threw the crystal glass at him, but it hit the sideboard and shattered.

'You really are despicable. You have no feelings for anyone but yourself. You locked me up in that … that place for all those years. Did Dr Lynch know that you were my father? My God, it all makes sense now.'

'I did you a favour. I could see you were heading the same way as your mother, getting pregnant without a ring on your finger. So I got rid of it for you. And what thanks do I get?'

I was so angry and overwhelmed that it took several moments before I could process what he was saying.

'How did you know I would lose the baby?'

'What's that?'

'The baby. She was stillborn. You said you got rid of her, but there's no way you could have known that would happen.'

He poured himself another drink.

'Lyndon, what have you done?'

'I should have put her in a bag and drowned her like the unwanted kitten she was.'

I felt a rage inside of me that almost blinded my sight. I dug my nails into the palms of my hands. I wanted to kill him.

'What in God's name are you talking about?' I said in a low voice I hardly recognised as my own.

'But she was worth more to me alive. A boy would of course have earned more, but as it was, she made a tidy sum.'

He looked up at me and smiled. Laughed at my ignorance. Just as he had when we were children and I, the younger sibling, always slower on the uptake.

'You had no idea, did you?' He took a swig of his drink, looking victorious. 'Good old Paddy kept that secret to himself.'

I grabbed a knife off the dresser and lunged for him.

'God help me, Lyndon, if you don't tell me the truth right now I will carve your eyes out.'

'Steady, old girl, you could injure someone with that.' He casually sat back down in his carver chair. 'I sold her. To a couple who were desperate for a child. Lynch arranged the whole thing. Done it before, apparently.'

'She's alive?' I could hardly breathe and leaned on the back of one of the dining chairs for support.

He made no reply. Something was not playing out as he had predicted.

'You sound relieved.'

'God, you really have no clue, do you?'

'About what?'

'About what it means to love!' I steadied myself for a moment, then realised the extent of his inhumanity. 'You sold your own granddaughter.'

I threw Mr Turner's copy of the article on the table, then turned to leave.

'Aren't you going to ask me where she is?'

'Would you tell me if I did?'

He smirked to himself.

'You know me well, little Opale.'

The term unsettled me. Only Armand had called me that.

'After tomorrow, everyone will know you for exactly what you are.'

I walked out of the room and somehow, kept myself upright. I passed the housekeeper in the hall, who gave me a queer look. I was lost in an endless maze of emotions and memories that no longer seemed to fit anywhere. My daughter was alive. That was all I needed to hold on to.

On reaching the front door, I heard the loud report of a gunshot. I halted. Then I heard a woman's scream. I didn't turn back. I commanded my feet to move, one in front of the other, until I was out in the street, taking the air into my lungs. I knew I had a choice. I could let this awful series of events become my new story – a story I would be condemned to carry with me for eternity – or I could let it die with him. It was a choice I would have to make every day for the rest of my life.

Chapter Fifty-Three

MARTHA

It had grown dark. I felt safe in our little cocoon. It felt like such a relief, letting Henry in, sharing all of the things I no longer wanted to carry on my own. We knew that we had both been drawn here for a reason – something special that gave a shimmering magic to every kiss, every caress. I could hardly believe that he was mine, that those eyes were for me only. He whispered silly things into my neck, searched my skin with his fingers and, most sweetly of all, fell asleep in my arms.

Madame Bowden had not returned, and with some strange prescience, I no longer expected her to. Call it intuition, but I guessed that she had always known more about this building than she had let on. She knew more about me, also. Who was she? What had she been testing me for? Had her friends from the dinner party been in on it? Was it all some sort of act? I did not have all of the pieces yet, but I could no longer delude myself that my arrival in Ha'penny Lane was purely happenstance.

I became aware of something else, something wonderful. I could read Henry again. His stories were as clear to me now as the day we met. Even in his sleep, I was reading the reunion he'd had with his father and despite the complicated emotions, how much it had meant to him. Maybe it wasn't love that blocked my ability at all. Maybe it was the opposite of love, for myself. To stay with Shane, in spite of how he treated me, I'd had to abandon myself in some way. Silence the inner voice that knew something was wrong, ignore the gut feeling that told me I did not deserve this. That my life held so much more potential than becoming someone else's punching bag. I lost my gift of reading Shane when I grew blind to myself and my own needs. Equally, I lost my gift with Henry when I refused to see how much I loved him. How much I needed him.

I felt him stirring beside me. His hair, slightly damp against his forehead, smelled of paper and an autumn breeze. I carefully snuck out of bed, trying not to wake him, and slipped upstairs to retrieve my book from the hall table. I sat in one of Madame Bowden's Queen Anne chairs and read the last few pages.

Lost is not a hopeless place to be. It is a place of patience, of waiting. Lost does not mean gone for ever. Lost is a bridge between worlds, where the pain of our past can be transformed into power. You have always held the key to this special place, but now you are ready to unlock the door.

Each person who finds themselves here brings a special gift that if you use it, you can transcend your fears. A story handed down through memory, lives that reveal themselves to you without words, books that breathe their knowledge softly in your ear, mechanical toys that spring to life under kind hands, nostalgia rescued and reborn into a new life – all of these things are the real magic within these walls. There is an energy here that can transform into anything it wants. It has remained hidden from all except the true believers, a tiny seed that still contains all that it once was and can be again.

Are you ready to cross the threshold and claim your birthright?

My body felt steady and grounded like a tree with deep roots, while my mind was light and flowing in the breeze. This was my journey. While I never would have chosen what happened with Shane, it had led me here in my search for something better. Opaline was right – I felt powerful. Not in an egotistical way, but in a calm, knowing sort of way. Like I was finally ready to take ownership of my life.

Then I remembered something Henry had said, or rather had held back. My instincts told me that it was significant. I was ready to know the full truth.

~

'What was it you came to tell me?' I asked, sitting on the bed beside him.

He stretched and yawned. 'What?'

'When you came here today, you said you'd found something?'

He rested on his elbow and blinked a few times, like a computer restarting. 'Oh yes, hang on.'

He swung his legs out of bed and pulled on his boxers before grabbing his jacket from upstairs. I felt chilled the instant he left and smiled to myself.

'It's okay,' I whispered. I had to reassure myself that it was safe to have these feelings. It would not be easy, learning to trust him. I was only starting to trust myself.

'Opaline's baby,' he said, bursting back into the flat. 'She didn't die at all. They just told her that.' He sat on the end of the bed and handed me the time-worn certificate. It was an unofficial adoption record for a baby girl. Her name was recorded as Rose.

'My God, how could they do that to her?'

'Money, I imagine. It was quite common at the time.'

Henry squeezed my hand and I felt so glad that he was there. I couldn't face this alone.

'My eyes are playing tricks. Can you read out what the name of the couple is?'

'Clohessy. Am I pronouncing that right?'

My teeth began chattering from the cold.

'Hey, what's up?' he asked, pulling me close and putting his arms around me.

'M-my grandmother was adopted by a couple called the Clohessys.'

Chapter Fifty-Four

HENRY

'How are you so calm? Your grandmother's name was Rose Clohessy. I mean, how many Rose Clohessys could have been born that year? It's a pretty big coincidence, right?' I realised how loud I was being, as I paced around her basement flat, in relation to her almost zen-like poise on the bed.

'I'm not sure if I'd describe what I'm feeling as calm, Henry,' she said, unflinching in the face of this monumental twist in her family ancestry.

'You're processing. Good. Right.'

Well, this was nuts. I had met the woman of my dreams only to find out that she carried the missing manuscript of Emily Brontë ON HER SKIN, and now, it seemed, was the great-granddaughter of Opaline Carlisle, one of the greatest book dealers of the twentieth century. A fact that, up to now, she had been completely unaware of.

Wait until I told the faculty about this – I finally had my thesis!

'That's what you're thinking about?'

'Huh? What? Wait, how did you—' I hadn't spoken that part aloud, had I?

She got up and pulled on her clothes with an urgency that suggested some activity other than my preferred one.

'Of course you should write about it. Everyone needs to know Opaline's story. And you're the one to tell it.'

'Okay, how did you know that's what I was …'

'It's a gift, Henry. And I don't plan on hiding it any more.'

I tried to pretend that this wasn't unnerving at all and then immediately tried to not think of anything, lest she pluck it from my brain. The branches of the tree fluttered in an imperceptible breeze and the door slowly swung open with a theatrical creak.

'As for Emily's manuscript, no one's going to believe it, are they?'

She was right. We had no proof that it was real. But *we* knew and that was enough. The realisation blew me sideways. The recognition didn't matter to me any more.

'You'll have to settle for being the only one who sees it,' she said, kissing me on the cheek.

'I think I'm okay with that.' I was very okay with that.

'Right, should we give it a try?' she asked, pulling on her shoes.

'Climbing Everest? Dinner at the new Asian place?' Apparently I did not share her gift.

She batted my arm and gave me that heart-melting smile. 'Finding the bookshop. You read the last page, didn't you?'

I tried to summon up the words in my minds' eye.

The soul of the night turned upside down …

'I'm not even sure what it means … the soul of the night?'

'Don't be so literal,' she said, with a new-found confidence I'd never seen. It looked good on her. 'If I am to be the custodian, and everything that has happened since I arrived here has been screaming to tell me that, I need to believe. I've been in denial for so long. I suppose I just never dared hope—'

She broke off, her voice thick with emotion. I put my arms around her waist and told her to slow down, take a breath.

'You are so special. Only you can't see it.' I bent my head and let my lips touch the softness of her mouth, feeling the sweet scent of her breath pulling me in. 'I'm just not sure where I fit in,' I said, reluctantly breaking away. Stupid thoughts.

'You're the only one who has seen the bookshop. That has to mean something.'

It was true. The search for the manuscript had led me here and now I'd found the treasure I never knew I was searching for. She took my hand and led me upstairs. No light was on, but the rooms were lit by an incredibly large moon shining through the windows.

'What about Madame Bowden?' I asked, as we rounded the ground floor and headed up to the first landing.

'I don't think she's coming back.'

Any hint of anxiety had left her voice. What was going on? She stopped for a moment and turned to face me.

'Would you think it strange—'

'Martha,' I said, taking her by the shoulders. 'I think the strange horse has bolted, don't you?'

She smiled and physically shook off whatever last doubts were holding her back.

'Apart from us, there isn't one other person who has actually met Madame Bowden. I asked my friends from college – none of them saw her that night at my birthday party. Not even my mother.'

'Right. Okay. That is strange.'

'Apart from Shane,' she added, her forehead creasing as she became lost in troubling memories of the past. 'Why was that?' she whispered almost inaudibly to herself.

I began to wish I hadn't seen her either. Was she a ghost?

'I don't think she's a ghost.'

'So you're just reading my thoughts at will now, is it? I don't know if I like this!'

Martha smiled and assured me her 'gift' wasn't that refined.

'I read people's stories, not every single thought. Although sometimes your thoughts are easily readable,' she said, stepping closer to me in the darkness. We kissed again because, well, any opportunity.

A small door at the end of the hall, which resembled something you might find at the front of a gnome's house, required both of us to contort ourselves in equally undignified fashion in order to gain entry. Your average attic, where Christmas lay in hiding for eleven months of the year, was illuminated by the milky glow of the moon through half-size windows. Dustsheets covered unknowable shapes, and a cheval mirror at the end of the room reflected another young couple entering the room from a similarly tiny door. I recalled a book I had found at the bottom of a bargain bin in a charity shop near Camden. Something about the memories of buildings and how the walls are infused with them. *They never forget, what we, as mere mortals, misplace.* I hadn't thought of it since, until now.

'There's a note,' Martha said, picking up an envelope with her name on it.

Martha,

I have played many different characters in other people's stories. Your story was my favourite and this chapter shall be your finest yet. In order for something to exist, you must first believe in it. Invite your heart to see what your eyes cannot. Follow your path and bring the scholar, I like having him around.

B.

'Is that her handwriting?' I asked.

'Her?'

'Yes. Madame Bowden.'

'I don't think Madame Bowden is the person we thought she was.'

'What do you mean by that?'

She put the letter down and breathed in deeply, before smiling to herself. 'You never left at all, did you?'

I waited for a moment and looked around the small attic space. Who was she speaking to?

Truth be told, I felt a mixture of things. Glad to be there with Martha/stupid for hoping that something otherworldly would happen/useless because I clearly had no idea what we were doing. I had done all of the research, but Martha seemed to be able to just feel her way, instinctively. It was like that song 'The Whole of the Moon'.

'I spoke about wings. You just flew.'

'Is that a poem?'

'No, it's a song,' I said, taking her hand. I could not be in the same room and not be close to her. 'It's about the moon and this guy who's an idiot and a girl who just … knows everything.'

'Sounds just like us!'

'Exactly. I knew you'd like it.'

She put her arms around my neck and we stood there, shuffling a dance with no music.

'This isn't all too weird for you, is it?' Her words came out muffled as she spoke into the shoulder of my woollen jumper.

'If it was, I would have said so when the tree started growing out of your flat.'

She snorted, which made us both laugh.

'I feel like I'm in a dream,' she said and I concurred. But dreams had a habit of ending. I decided, quietly, that our dream would be different.

'There's another door!' She broke free of my arms and rushed to the far end of the room.

On closer inspection, there was indeed another door. It was exactly where I thought the cheval mirror had stood, with our reflections inside. I blinked slowly. Nope, it was a door. No mistaking it.

'How are we supposed to see where we're going?' I asked, after about thirty seconds of following her blindly in the dark. We were inside what felt like the eaves of the house.

'You're not. You just have to trust me.'

'But you don't know where you're going either?' I panted, now half crouched as I'd just whacked my head on a roof beam.

'You once asked me to trust you and you don't see me moaning about it,' she needled.

I kept quiet for another minute or so, until it felt as though we were going upstairs.

'Just checking that you're aware of ascending, despite being in the attic.'

'I'm aware.'

She reached back and patted the side of my head. It did not help matters.

'You remember the book, how it talks about an upside-down stairway?'

I did remember it, but I thought it was some kind of sweet fairy tale for kids, not a map for … what exactly?

'Yes, but, you don't really believe we're going to find the bookshop?'

Her voice seemed to be getting farther away. 'You can't find something that was never lost!'

Great. Even Martha was speaking in riddles now. That was Madame Bowden's influence. And where the hell was she? There was no time to think logically, as the passage grew narrower and I could feel the skin on my hands being scratched.

'Is now a good time to mention that I'm claustrophobic?' I announced, as casually as I could, bravely omitting to comment on the fact that the stairs seemed to be taking us downward now, in a tight spiral.

'I think these are the roots of the tree. Don't you?'

Of course they are, I muttered to myself. I mean, it made perfect sense if you had just taken some sort of Class A drug. Or if your last name was Pevensie and you had just stumbled into a wardrobe full of fur coats. I suddenly became very aware of my own thoughts – this constant stream of ridicule. As Martha pointed out, wasn't I the one who had walked straight into the bookshop on my first night here? Yet I had immediately dismissed it as some kind of drunken mirage.

My mind wouldn't let me believe. Martha suffered no such resistance and I decided that if I could not necessarily believe, I could at least believe in her.

'The soul of the night turned upside down.'

'Sorry?'

'That line from the book. It said that you have to trust you will end up exactly where you're meant to be.'

'I feel like I already have,' I said, but I wasn't sure if she heard me. No sooner had I spoken the words than I saw a literal light at the end of the tunnel. My heart began to race.

Chapter Fifty-Five

OPALINE

Dublin, 1952

'Hope' is the thing with feathers –
That perches in the soul –
And sings the tune without the words –
And never stops – at all –

I let Emily Dickinson's poetry book fall on to my lap and spied the stained-glass windows of the shop, the colours of which now painted the image of a bird and an open cage. I made a kind of pact with the universe that if I kept the door to my heart open, one day my little girl would walk through it. In the meantime, I found an occupation that created the illusion of doing something to bring that day ever closer. I began writing a book. A children's book. *A Place Called Lost*. I knew there was a strange kind of magic in these walls. Maybe not the kind you'd find in travelling shows or under the big top, but something far subtler than that.

I began to switch off the lights, lingering over the task. I had an undefinable sense that something, or someone, was close. Someone I knew. Someone I loved. But I couldn't trust it. Wouldn't. Even when I heard the knock on the glass door, I didn't turn to look. Couldn't face the disappointment of being wrong. I placed my hands on the desk and let my weight lean against it, squeezing my eyes shut. My heart was disobeying my mind and without consciously making the decision, I turned around.

He was there.

Josef. The snow falling gently on his head and shoulders.

A sigh of relief escaped my lips and I could have sworn the books on the shelves sighed too. The bookshop had let him in when I had first escaped St Agnes's and needed him the most. Now he had returned, everything felt hopeful again. He stepped closer to the window and I followed. We were separated only by the thinnest pane of glass. My eyes searched his eyes, his lips, his entire frame. Was he real?

'Are you going to let me in?' he asked, a lopsided smile on his face. 'It's a little cold.'

I burst out laughing and it sounded like silver bells to my ears, bells that hadn't rung for years. I opened the door and we both stood at the threshold, the stained glass overhead blooming with flowers.

'Are you back for good?'

'My father passed away in the autumn.'

I placed my hand over my heart. 'I'm sorry.'

'I can repair some of the old music boxes that were in the attic. Anything that is broken—'

'You've already repaired what was broken in this place,' I said, rushing into his arms.

'So many nights I have dreamed of you and this place,' he said, holding me tightly, as though nothing would tear us apart again.

'This bookshop is rooted in my heart,' I said. 'I have to find a way to keep it alive. For my daughter.'

He pulled back and searched my face for answers.

'She's alive. My baby is alive.'

He opened his mouth to speak but no words came out. The joy in his eyes was enough.

'Please, come inside,' I said, finally.

All he carried was a large canvas duffle bag with a book poking out of the pocket at the front. Red leather, gilt-edged pages. It was so familiar to me, but so utterly incongruous that I hardly dared to hope.

'For you,' he said, following my eyeline and handed it to me. 'I found it in an old bookshop in Austria.'

I took the time-worn book into my hands and felt the magic of childhood rushing back to greet me. I searched for the inscription and gasped when I saw it. Alfred Carlisle. My *real* father.

'How did you—?'

'*Mein liebling*, I beg of you, stop speaking and kiss me.'

Chapter Fifty-Six

MARTHA

I had the strangest dreams that night. I was walking through an old Italian village, hot and dusty with summertime sunshine. I stepped inside a cool, dark building that was lined floor to ceiling with old books. There was a man there and he handed me a key, then as quick as lightning I was back in Ha'penny Lane. Everything was the same but different. There was a woman inside, a familiar stranger. She told me that she had been waiting for me. That the shop had been waiting for me also.

'Wake up,' she said. 'Wake up.'

In the morning light, I could see the light brown strands of Henry's hair on the pillow beside me. If he had been disappointed with not finding the bookshop, he hadn't let on. The narrow passageway led directly back to my flat. It wasn't a secret pathway to another dimension, it was just an old servants' tunnel or something. He took me back to bed and said that he had already found everything he wanted. I had found more than I had ever dreamed of, and yet something felt incomplete.

'The tree!'

'I'm awake, I'm awake,' Henry responded to my scream, one eye still shut, his hair standing on end.

'It's gone.'

'Okay. The very fact of the tree growing here was odd in the first place, but this is just … what are you doing?'

I was getting dressed. Fast.

'Well, aren't you coming?'

Henry blinked, then reluctantly pulled on his jeans. I ran up the stairs ahead of him.

'Martha? Were these words always here on the stairs? *Strange things are found …*' he shouted up, but I had found something stranger still.

I had expected to find the hallway of number 12 Ha'penny Lane at the top of the stairs, where it always was. Instead, I found myself standing in a place I had never fully believed existed up to that point – Opaline's Bookshop. Daylight streamed in through the glass shopfront, creating rays of sunshine, glittering with dust motes falling like confetti. I hardly dared breathe in case the whole thing would evaporate. Slowly, I let my eyes readjust to what was in front of me. There were wooden bookcases from floor to ceiling lined with soft green moss and with ivy creeping along the edges. Fallen leaves swept silently across the tiled floor, and floating overhead were toy hot-air balloons. It felt as though the place had just woken up from a long slumber, like Rip Van Winkle, and was shaking off the years of hibernation. I blinked, but it did not disappear. The scent of warm wood and paper filled the air, along with a sweetness like a golden September apple. It was full of brightly coloured antique books and curiosities, all waiting for our arrival.

I'd come home.

Henry bumped into me at the top of the stairs and then took in the view.

'Please tell me you're seeing this and I'm not having an episode.'

'It's real, Henry.' I turned to look at him and smiled.

'I'm seeing it, but I can't believe it,' he whispered. 'How is this possible?'

I took a long, deep breath and tried to think of the last lines in Opaline's book.

'Maybe it was I who was lost all along and not the bookshop.'

I reached out for Henry's hand and he clasped it tightly.

'We did it,' I said. 'We found the bookshop.'

His smile was beautiful and unguarded, like that of a little child.

'Look at this,' he said, pointing to the stained-glass panels at the top of the windows that were like nothing I'd ever seen and yet inexplicably familiar.

'Is that—?' Henry stepped closer and pointed to a design at the very edge. A woman, wearing a long coat and trousers, with very short hair, holding hands with a soldier.

Epilogue

The rain had eased off outside and the bank of grey clouds that had huddled over the city like a lumpy duvet was breaking apart and revealing small, irregular windows of blue sky.

'Is all of that really true?' asked the little boy, openly stuffing a teacake in his pocket for later.

'Every word,' said Martha. She began shuffling the envelopes and letters. It was time to get back to work.

'What happened to the house and the old lady?'

'Number 12? It's still there. But someone else lives there now.'

He nodded his head, as though this explanation were perfectly satisfactory.

'So the book told you that you'd become a bookseller?'

She thought for a moment. 'I suppose it did, in a way.'

His eyebrows scrunched up in concentration.

'What is it?'

'I wish I could find a book that would tell me what I'm supposed to do when I'm old.'

'Older,' she corrected. 'Besides, I think it's already found you.'

'What do you mean?'

'You already know what you want to become.'

'Do I?'

She nodded her head patiently. 'Didn't you feel your heart jump? At a certain point in the story, when I told you about Matthew Fitzpatrick?'

'Oh, *that*.'

'Yes. That!'

He slid off the stool and dragged his feet along the tiled floor, back to where his schoolbag was abandoned. He hefted it up on to his shoulder, as though it held all the worries of the world within it.

'Teacher says it's a silly notion.'

'They're the best kind to have, if you ask me.'

He gave her a curious look. It was almost as if she was challenging him. Grown-ups hardly ever listened to him, and when they did, they certainly didn't encourage him to believe in silly notions.

'The thing about books,' she said, 'is that they help you to imagine a life bigger and better than you could ever dream of.'

With that, the bell rang over the shop door and a tall man with hair falling into his eyes breezed into the shop. He went straight over to Martha and gave her an altogether prolonged smooch on the cheek, which the little boy thought was gross.

'Who do we have here?' he asked eventually.

'Shall we tell him?' Martha asked the little boy. 'Shall we tell him who you *really* are?'

He looked a little uncertain at first, then seemed to gain some confidence and puffed out his chest.

'I'm a magician!' he announced.

'Is that so?' Henry asked.

'Yes,' Martha said. 'And for his first trick, he is going to make that magic book he's been reading all morning disappear.' She nodded her head for him to retrieve it.

'For free?' the little boy asked.

'The first one is always free,' she replied, and within moments he had it stuffed into his schoolbag before charging out the front door with sparks at his heels and, in the strange morning light, what could have been mistaken for a cape flowing in his wake.

'You've done it again,' Henry said, sliding his arm around Martha's waist.

'Done what, Mr Field?'

'Made someone, very, very happy, Mrs Field.'

This time they kissed for so long that they had to close the shop.

~

And that is where the story ends. Although they never did find Emily Brontë's manuscript. To this day, it lies hidden inside the vault of an Irish bank, just waiting to become a part of someone else's story.

Author's Note

Dear Reader,

I hope you enjoyed escaping into the charming world of antiquarian books as much as I enjoyed writing it!

This story began, as they often do, with a few lines hastily captured on paper before they had a chance to fly away, and the image of a man standing in the space where a bookshop should be. Little did I know then, the journey that Opaline, Martha, and Henry would take me on! All I knew was that I wanted to write a story about a very unusual bookshop with its roots in the golden age of rare book dealing and a little bit of magic, mystery, and romance along the way.

There was so much research involved in writing this story, it would take another book to include everything that has inspired it. I read somewhere once that you have to love what you write about, as you'll be spending a lot of time together. And I can truly say this was a labour of love. The books, the characters and how they challenge, inspire and heal each other is the real magic in this story, but don't tell Madame Bowden I said that!

I love to write in parallel timelines as I'm always intrigued by how the past shapes our present. In *The Lost Bookshop*, one of the major themes is that of finding your purpose in the world, a theme that echoes down through the generations. In fact, all of my novels share that sense of self-discovery, of becoming and of belonging. I like to write about characters that don't always fit into the conventional ideals that society imposes on them, especially women, and Opaline was certainly unconventional for her time. I wanted to write a book that would encapsulate how I feel, as a woman, about the women who have been marginalised in the past and continue to be written out of their own stories, even today. Writing her gave me the opportunity to research amazing women who achieved wonderful things, women like the journalist Nellie Bly, and the literary sleuths, scholars, and book dealers who inspired the idea of finding Emily Brontë's second novel – Leona Rostenberg and Madeleine Stern.

At the heart of all my books is the universal experience – what makes us human, our shared desires to be loved, to be seen, and to manifest the expression of our own innate specialness. That is the key for me and why I choose to tell these stories in the way that I do. Magical realism allows us to step outside of our limitations of imagination – to show that anything is possible. As Martha says, *books help you to imagine a life bigger and better than you could ever dream of.*

Love,

Evie

Acknowledgments

Firstly, I want to thank my editor, Charlotte Ledger. Her enthusiasm for this book brought such a positive energy to the process and she has been a dream to work with. To the entire team at One More Chapter and Harper Collins UK, my continued appreciation for your passion and expertise in making this book a thing of beauty.

Thanks also to Gillian Green, who encouraged the early chapters of this book and to Sophie Hannah for her heartening feedback and coaching.

My deepest gratitude to my family, especially my parents whose love and generosity have been constant and unwavering. And to my sister, who as luck would have it is also a writer, for her inspiring thesis and endless belief in this book.

Finally to you, dear reader, I'm grateful for your belief, for stepping into the world of *The Lost Bookshop* and letting it come to life in your heart.

Read on for an exclusive extract from *The Story Collector,* an evocative and charming novel full of secrets and mystery, from the bestselling author of *The Lost Bookshop.*

Available to pre-order now.

The Story Collector: Extract

Thornwood House

Where Thornwood House now stands, was once ancient woodland. It is said that when Lord Hawley purchased the estate in 1882, as a marriage gift for his wife, he ordered the entire site to be cleared before building works could commence. However, in the middle of this site grew a gnarled old hawthorn tree; a fairy tree, and 'twas said that misfortune would befall any man who so much as scarred the twisted bark. A seeress from the locality warned the Master not to touch it, saying that The Good People would have their revenge on anyone who tampered with their dwelling place.

But Lord Hawley was an educated man from Surrey, England and held no truck with local superstition. The plans were drawn up for his mansion house and he paid the workers handsomely to get the job done. Yet the local men still refused to be a part of it, and Hawley was forced to employ workers from his own homeland to cut the tree down. The seeress foretold no end of misery, but for the first few years, everything in Thornwood House seemed perfectly content.

However, when Lady Hawley fell pregnant with twins, she did become mightily sick and there was a fear for her life. Mercifully, she and the babies survived, but the real horror was yet to come.

A few short weeks after they were born, the Mistress began to act very strangely and insisted that the children were not hers. The physician was sent for, and rumours spread that the woman was suffering from hysteria.

The seeress, on the other hand, knew that it was not Lady Hawley's mind that had weakened. She knew that when a mother did not recognise her own child, it could only mean one thing: a changeling. The Good People had finally exacted their revenge by taking the human children and replacing them with evil, sickly souls. If they did not perish immediately, they would live to become mischievous and destructive individuals, intent on creating bitterness and hate wherever they went.

Before the Hawley twins ever saw their first birthday, Lady Hawley threw herself from the top window of Thornwood House.

Chapter 1

25th December 2010, New York

Were it not for that tacky ceramic sheep in the gift shop, Sarah would never have even heard of Thornwood, much less got on a plane to Ireland and spent the Christmas holidays there.

'Have you got everything you need?' Jack had finally asked, after an hour of silently watching her reclaim all her worldly possessions.

'Um, yes I think that's it,' Sarah said, looking about her at all the empty spaces she was leaving behind. Most of her belongings were already boxed and shipped. 'Well at least now you can have that snooker table you always wanted in here,' she added, trying to sound cheery, but regretting it as soon as she heard it out loud. 'I'm sorry, I didn't mean—'

'It's okay,' he said, touching her lightly on the arm and giving her a crooked smile. 'I don't know what to say either, but you don't have to pretend, Sarah.'

The easiest thing would have been to fall into his arms and bury her pain somewhere neither of them could find it, but she'd tried that already and two years later, it still wasn't working. They were living in a house of unspoken needs and muffled emotions.

'Are you sure you want to leave today? I mean, it is Christmas after all,' he said, nodding towards the lacklustre tree that blinked optimistically in the corner. 'You could wait till New Year's…'

'What difference does it make, really? We'd just be delaying the inevitable. I have to leave now or I never will. Besides, your family's expecting you for the big Natale Zaparelli, so you better get a move on too.'

He exhaled a long and weary sigh, stuffing his hands in his pockets. Sarah wondered bitterly what bothered him more: her absence from the Zaparelli family Christmas or him having to explain it.

'I wish it didn't have to be like this.' Jack shifted from one foot to the other. He didn't know where to place himself and finally, like an unwanted object in his gallery, he leaned against the nearest wall.

'Come on Jack, it's taking all of my strength to do this. Please don't go soft on me now or I might just crack,' Sarah said, reaching for her purse and coat.

'All right then, beat it lady and don't let the door hit you on the way out! Better?' he asked, with a half-smile.

'Much.' She hugged him, briefly but fiercely and turned on her heel, dragging her suitcase behind her. 'I'll call to let you know I've landed safely,' she called behind her.

'Maybe just a text message,' he said, adding in almost a whisper, 'I don't trust myself not to beg you to come back.'

~

Newark airport had a sense of business as usual but with a half-hearted nod to the holidays. It reminded Sarah of when she was a child and spent Christmas in the hospital having her appendix removed. The worn-out decorations only served to remind her of where she wanted to be, but wasn't, and now the airport felt the same. Where were all these people going? Were they all leaving their husbands? Most of them probably didn't even observe Christmas. Was all of this really going on every year while Sarah tucked into her turkey, naively assuming that everyone else had the same traditions?

Her sister Meghan would probably be serving her famous Christmas pudding about now. She wished she didn't have to impose on their holidays, but you can't always choose the timing of a marriage breakdown. After three years of marriage, she had precious little to show for it. If anything, her life had shrunk since she met Jack. Her only option was to move back in with her parents or stay in her sister's spare room. It wasn't much of a choice: failed daughter or failed sister. Meghan's was the lesser of two evils.

Sarah absent-mindedly wandered through the gift shops, hoping to distract herself from the recurring thought of what Jack would be doing now. He was putting on a brave face, like herself, but she was sure he would be feeling as lost as she was. At least she could go back to Boston, remove herself from the familiar, everyday things that would bring memories of their life together flooding back. Feeling certain that her hometown would act as some sort of restorative power, she booked the flight like a homing pigeon.

Coming back to herself, she realised she was standing in front of a display of ceramic sheep, in varying shapes and sizes. She must have been staring at them for quite some time, for the shop assistant stepped forward, sensing the possibility of a sale.

'They're super cute, right?' said the young girl, with an overly painted face and nose ring.

'Uh, I suppose, if you like sheep,' Sarah replied, not wanting to offend. 'What shop is this?'

'The Emerald Isle Gift Store. You get a 10% discount with your Aer Lingus boarding pass,' she added, as if this would sway her decision. 'What part of Ireland are you going to?'

'Oh no, I'm not going to Ireland, just home to Boston,' Sarah assured her, deflecting the sales pitch. She grew up knowing that there was some Irish blood in her family tree (hardly a novelty in Boston) and had always promised herself that, if she ever had the money to do it, she would visit one day. Her honeymoon had seemed like the perfect opportunity, but Jack had argued that two weeks in the Maldives would be much more romantic than shivering in the damp and dreary Irish countryside. Perhaps he'd been right, but the mysticism and charm of the fairy tale castles she'd saved on her phone called to her in a way that aquamarine waters never did.

The young assistant sat back behind the counter and was now testing the stretchability of her chewing gum. Given the day, Sarah took pity on her and picked up a rather startled looking sheep and an Irish newspaper for good measure. She hardly registered tucking the half bottle of Irish whiskey under her arm.

'Thank you ma'am and Happy Holidays!' the girl smiled as Sarah took her gift bag and headed for the departure gates.

Grabbing a cup of coffee to go, Sarah sat apart from the other passengers by the window, where she could see the aeroplanes being refuelled. A light flurry of snow had begun, illuminated by the airport lights to look like flecks of gold dancing through the air. Looking at the screen, she could see that her flight was delayed by two hours. Opening the screw cap, she nonchalantly poured a healthy measure of whiskey into the paper cup. A medicinal measure. The coffee was bitter, but mixed with the whiskey it flushed her bloodstream with a reassuring warmth. It all felt so surreal. Knowing that you're going to leave your husband and actually going through with it are two very different things. Her emotions were only now beginning to catch up with the reality of the situation. She twisted off the cap again and refilled her cup.

She wasn't getting much sleep since 'The Big Bad Thing' as she now referred to it. Somehow it was easier than saying it that way, contained it somehow, so the feelings couldn't get out. Going to bed was like buying a lottery ticket; some nights you won and grabbed a few hours of sleep. Other nights, which were becoming more and more frequent, she woke in a blind panic, hardly able to breathe.

'You're suffering from an anxiety disorder,' said her doctor, with her perfectly coiffed hair and rather inappropriate high-heeled shoes. I mean, how could you attend an emergency in those heels, Sarah wondered, while the doctor's explanation washed over her. Giving it a name didn't help matters. Pills were offered and refused. Jack had a lot to say about that. He had a lot to say about everything and often drowned any thoughts Sarah tried to have of her own. She was advised to cut down on the drinking. She didn't tell Jack about that part and had somehow managed to convince herself that this was a generic piece of advice that didn't really apply to her. She just knew that if she could be on her own for a while, she could sort herself out. Except, she wouldn't be on her own in Boston. It was only now beginning to dawn on her that the price for familial support would be more interference. More well-meaning platitudes from people intent on 'fixing' her.

'Another coffee please,' Sarah said, when a young man in an apron came to wipe her table and clear her cup away. She tried not to meet his eyes, surely he could smell the whiskey. Not that it mattered, she was well over the legal age. But there was a feeling of guilt there that she couldn't explain. She wasn't drinking for fun or because she had a fear of flying. She was trying to forget. She busied herself with her bag and spotted the Irish newspaper inside it. She took it out, purely for something to look at, when a photo caught her attention on the back page. An image of a beautiful hawthorn tree, blooming with tiny white flowers, standing alone and beside a busy road in County Clare in Ireland. The headline read: THE FAIRY TREE THAT MOVED A MOTORWAY.

'Huh!' Sarah said a little loudly, then bent her head to focus on the words.

"Clare County Council finally bowed to local pressure to alter the proposed route of a major new motorway currently under construction, all in an effort to protect a very special hawthorn tree. Ned Delaney, a local folklorist and storyteller, placed an objection against the motorway being built in the area, saying that the hawthorn tree was "an important meeting place for the fairies". According to folklore, this is the spot where the Munster fairies would meet when planning a battle against the Connaught fairies, and Delaney (known locally as "The Fairy Whisperer") insisted that to cut down the tree would "vex" the little people and cause untold misfortune for the workers on the motorway and future users of the road."

Sarah felt as though she were suddenly back in her father's truck, as a teenager, driving through the country to gather bits of dead wood from the forest. He would let her drive on the quieter roads and it felt so freeing, just the two of them, the road ahead and the trees lining the route. They would spend hours together in his workshop making impossibly crooked birdhouses and desk tidies and anything else that could be fashioned from rough wood and a few rusty nails. He always encouraged her and even got her to start sketching plans on paper for more sophisticated projects like coat racks and shelving units. It was thanks to those early days in the workshop that she finally decided to go to college and study art. She had such high hopes when she graduated, but New York didn't exactly work out as planned, on any level. Her working class roots had always made her feel like an outsider in the galleries of New York, but now she felt like she didn't belong at home anymore either. Her stomach churned at the thought of setting up home in her sister's spare room. She turned her attention back to the newspaper.

'Locals were hesitant to admit that they actually believed in fairies, but one resident summed up the general feeling when she said, "It's better to be safe than sorry".

Sarah blinked and shook her head. Could this be possible, in this day and age? She flipped the paper over and double-checked that it was in fact a genuine newspaper and not some kind of joke. Then she began to smile to herself and thought again of her father and what a kick he would get out of it. Her mother, on the other hand, had no time for such trivialities. Her mother and Meghan were the practical ones, but Sarah and her father were the dreamers. Or at least she used to be. All of the magic seemed to seep out of her after The Big Bad Thing. Maybe Ireland was the place to find it again?

Glancing out over the concourse from her little table at Dunkin' Donuts and realised she had walked quite far from her departure gate. In fact, she found herself slap bang in front of the Aer Lingus departure lounge, with the flight number EI 401 bound for Shannon flashing on the screen. An advertisement on the near wall showed the striking image of the Cliffs of Moher, standing majestically above the wild Atlantic Ocean, with the tagline:

'Ireland: The land of a thousand welcomes'.

Something inside her shifted, then settled. The decision was made. It was made the moment she saw that silly sheep.

Chapter 2

Sarah woke with a jolt when the plane touched down on the tarmac. Peering out of the window, she couldn't tell if it was day or night, for the torrential rain lashed the window in such persistent bursts that it was impossible to see out.

'You're lucky you slept through that,' came a lyrical Irish accent close to her ear.

Turning around, Sarah saw her neighbour smiling kindly at her, while wrapping up what appeared to be a hooked needle and a large ball of wool.

'I dropped a few stitches, I don't mind telling you!' confided the lady. 'I thought the wind would flip us over, but you slept soundly all the way through, you lucky duck.'

Sarah tried to compose herself and covertly wipe any drool from her face. She felt completely dehydrated and her head felt like it was being drilled at the temples.

'Sorry I wasn't much company,' she said, flattening her wayward hair into what should have been a bob.

'Oh don't worry about that, you obviously needed the rest and besides, my crochet always keeps me company. In fact,' she said, digging back into her bag, 'Happy Christmas!' she enthused, handing her a hat. 'I crocheted eight of them during the flight.'

She pulled out a perfectly stitched beanie hat in a lovely berry shade and handed it to Sarah.

'You're kidding me, you've been knitting these the whole time?'

'Oh God yah, I couldn't go anywhere without my crochet. It keeps me calm and Lord knows I hate flying, so this passes the time nicely.'

Sarah tried on the hat and it fitted perfectly.

'Thank you so much, that's really very kind of you.' Sarah realised that she really wasn't in New York anymore. People hardly made eye contact there, much less offered handmade gifts.

'Listen, my brother-in-law is picking me up so if you need a ride anywhere…' Sarah said, feeling seasonably charitable.

'Not at all. I'll get the bus straight from Shannon into Ennis so I'll be fine dear,' she replied.

Sarah had no idea what the woman was talking about. Shannon and Ennis didn't sound familiar. But rather than get into a tiresome discussion, she just nodded politely and fished for some tissues in her bag.

The pilot calmly announced that it was 06:45 a.m. local time and a chilly three degrees Celsius (whatever that meant in Fahrenheit).

Rather oddly, he also mentioned something about Shannon.

'Holy shit!' she cried.

'Don't worry love, it can't be much colder than New York,' her companion assured her.

'Where are we?' she gasped, grabbing the woman's arm.

'What? We're in Ireland love, I told you, you slept right through!'

Sarah had that sickening feeling that was becoming all too familiar. The cold sweat and the uncanny sensation of popping candy in her bloodstream. It was starting to come back to her – the sheep; the whiskey; the doughnuts. And something about a tree?

'We're not in Boston, are we?'

'Do you not remember love? Well, I suppose you were a little worse for wear. I think the air hostess only let you on to shut you up!'

'Oh God.' Sarah squeezed her eyes shut, trying to force the lock on her lost memories. She remembered laughing, possibly wishing people 'Top of the morning', but that was it.

'How did I even get a ticket?' Sarah shook her head, but still no memories came loose.

'You told me you were flying standby. Sure, they were only delighted to fill up the seats, weren't they? It's half empty as it is.' The woman was packing up her knitting and taking all of her valuable information with her.

Looking out the window, all Sarah could see was darkness and the blurred lights of the airport through the rain. It was clearly not Logan International. She dug her cell phone out of her bag, powered it on and dialled Meghan's number immediately.

'I'm so sorry Meghan,' she began remorsefully.

'And so you should be. Poor Greg was stuck waiting at the airport for you for hours last night. On Christmas Day Sarah! What the hell happened to you? Didn't you get my messages? Are you staying with Jack?'

The plane finally came to a halt and the passengers began to unclick their seatbelts and open the overhead lockers. Sarah cupped her hand around her ear to block out the noise.

'No, I…' Sarah hesitated. She knew the least she owed her sister was an explanation, but she was almost embarrassed to admit what she had done. 'I'm not in New York,' was what she finally settled on.

'Well you're not in Boston either, I can vouch for that!' Meghan snapped.

Meanwhile, the hat lady joined the line of passengers queuing to exit the plane, giving Sarah a supportive thumbs up. She obviously had more faith in her than Sarah had in herself.

'Look Meghan, I really needed to get away. I thought it might be good to be on my own for a while, try and work things out in my own space.' This sounded good, Sarah assured herself. It sounded like a coherent plan.

'Well I wish you would have thought of that before I spent all of Christmas Eve getting your room ready and half of Christmas Day calling the airline. How could you be so thoughtless? It's not like you,' Meghan replied.

'Okay, you're right, I deserve that. I just… I acted on a whim. I didn't even know what I was doing myself until I was on the flight and then I fell asleep and…'

'So you did take a flight, to where?'

'Um, well I'm in Ireland.' The line went silent. 'If it makes you feel any better, I seem to have arrived in the middle of a hurricane,' she added, looking out at a stiffly horizontal windsock.

'Sarah, what are you doing?' came her measured reply.

'Well, this is just a rough guess, but I might be having a midlife crisis.'

'This isn't funny.'

'I disagree. It's the first truly funny thing that has happened in the last two years. In fact, it's hilarious. I've just arrived in a country where I know nothing and no one, and it's Christmas for God's sake. I haven't a clue where I'm going, or what I'm doing, and another thing…'

Sarah suddenly noticed that an air hostess was standing by her seat, giving her a weary smile. Sarah raised herself up and realised that the entire plane was empty, save for her and the remaining crew. 'Listen Meghan, I've got to disembark. I'll call you once I get settled.'

'Settled where?' Meghan shouted, exasperated.

'Well, in Ireland.'

'You mean you don't even know what part of Ireland you're in?' Meghan accused in a high-pitched voice.

'Sorry, you're breaking…' With that, she rang off to the sound of her sister saying how they were all so worried about her and she instantly knew she had done the right thing.

Inside the terminal, Sarah dragged her lone sky-blue suitcase across the concourse. She'd packed the rest of her worldly belongings in a removal company van, which would probably be arriving at Meghan's house about now.

'What am I doing?' she whispered under her breath.

The place was deserted, apart from two tired-looking men in high visibility jackets leaning against the customs counter. She hauled her suitcase off the carousel and headed for the exit.

'Anything to declare, Madam?' the larger one asked in a deep baritone voice.

Sarah couldn't think of anything to declare, except that she was now officially homeless, so decided to keep her mouth shut. As the sliding doors opened, she felt the disappointment like a physical blow to her gut. Even though she hadn't been expecting anyone to be there, the sadness of knowing that nobody cared whether she was here or not still hurt. 'What kind of oddball travels abroad on their own for Christmas?' she wondered bitterly to herself. Still, there was nothing to do but get on with it now. A nice warm hotel room with a hot bath and some delicious food would make everything seem better, she assured herself and began to search the concourse for an information desk.

After walking the length and breadth of Shannon airport (which took about two minutes) Sarah couldn't find any desk open. She could feel the panic beginning to rise; that feeling of inexplicable yet imminent dread. Her only option was to try to outrun it, which was not a great option considering she didn't know where she was running to. The only people who seemed to be working were two security guards who looked at her askance when she demanded assistance.

'Why is nothing open?' she gasped, her throat tightening. 'I need to book a hotel room.'

'It's Saint Stephen's Day, the girls at the information desk won't be in until nine at the earliest,' responded one.

'There's an airport hotel across the road if you're stuck,' offered the other.

'Saint who?' Sarah was already experiencing culture shock and she hadn't even left the airport yet. 'Fine, I suppose that'll do for now,' she conceded, as she fought the revolving door and finally met with her first breath of Irish air. The gust almost lifted her off her feet and threatened to part her from her coat and suitcase. She struggled to button her coat and pulled her newly acquired beanie hat down over her ears as she made her way across the concourse and towards the hotel. She swiftly blew into the reception and took a moment to steady herself before stepping up to the reception desk. To her relief, a tall, distinguished-looking gentleman sprang up to greet her with all the agility of Fred Astaire.

'You're very welcome to the Shannon Airport Hotel, how can I help you?' he rattled off with practised ease.

'Hey there, Marcus,' she said, reading his name badge. 'I just need a room for tonight please and if you can tell me where I can get some breakfast, that'd be great.'

'Ooh,' he said, sucking air through his teeth, 'unfortunately we don't have any rooms tonight, but I can offer you a twin room for tomorrow night?'

'You're kidding, right? How could you be booked up when this place is a ghost town?'

'Oh no, we're not booked up as such, but there's been a slight problem with the plumbing on two of the floors, so we've had to close up most of the bedrooms until we get it sorted,' he explained.

Sarah slumped into one of the leather tub chairs facing the view of the car park outside. Despite the fact that she had slept for most of the flight, she still felt like an emotional wreck. An emotional wreck with a raging hangover.

'I'm not normally…' she trailed off.

'Ah sure, it's the time of year, makes us all a bit funny, doesn't it?' He stepped out from behind the reception desk and made a swift appraisal of the situation. 'Right, follow me.'

'What? Where?' But he was already making great strides through the lobby and towards a door marked 'Dining Room'.

Once settled at a table with a large plate of bacon, sausage, egg and soda bread, Sarah began to relax a little. Marcus joined her with a large pot of tea and two cups on a tray.

'Marcus O'Brien, at your service,' he said, introducing himself formally.

'Sarah Harper,' she replied, offering her hand. 'Where is everyone?'

'Skeleton staff at Christmas,' Marcus said as he poured a liquid black as tar into her cup. 'Anyway, what brings you to the Banner on this Stephen's Day?'

'The Banner?' she echoed.

'Oh, it's a nickname really, UP THE BANNER!' he said, waving his gangly arms about. 'Never mind,' he said, on seeing her blank look.

'Would you believe me if I told you that it was a newspaper article about a fairy tree that brought me here?'

'The hawthorn, of course. Are you a journalist?' he quizzed excitedly.

Great, she thought, he did believe it. She had her cover story. Anything was better than the truth.

'Not exactly. This is delicious by the way, I've never tasted anything like this back home,' she said, buttering her soda bread. It was magically curing her hangover too.

'Well if you can't get a good Irish breakfast here, we may as well all pack up and go home!' He excused himself with efficient courtesy and left to sort out some hotel business, wiping his finger along the tables checking for dust as he went.

Sarah took a moment to gather her thoughts, which basically consisted of how relieved she felt to stumble into the path of a man like Marcus. Sometimes you just needed to be looked after, especially after a night drinking whiskey and buying a plane ticket to Ireland. She started to think that maybe this rash decision wasn't so bad after all. She could spend a week or two having a nice little holiday for herself; enjoying the country and its people (if they were all like Marcus), before returning home with a clear head.

'You're in luck,' Marcus said as he returned to the dining room. 'I've found you the perfect place to stay in the village,' he said, rubbing his hands together.

'The village?' Sarah wondered if he meant the New York or the Irish version.

'Thornwood. It's just a twenty-minute drive from here. It's what we would call in the business "a home away from home".'

All she could do was smile; a home away from home was just what she needed right now.

Breezing through a landscape of stone walls and green fields, Sarah couldn't help but smirk at Marcus's leather driving gloves. Everything he did was so correct and proper. To every task there was an order, a precision that made you feel as though you were in safe hands.

'You really didn't have to drive me, I could have taken a cab,' she said, as they glided around a roundabout.

'Not at all, we often send guests over here when the hotel is fully booked. It's a small village but it's also a popular spot for tourists, so we keep busy. And you said you were from Boston yourself?' he asked, shifting the gear stick with practised ease.

'Yep, although I've been living in Manhattan for a couple of years with my…' she stumbled, memories flooding back. 'With my husband Jack.'

Marcus O'Brien had not spent the last thirty-odd years working as a hotel manager and learned nothing. He casually steered the conversation onto safer ground and chatted easily about all manner of subjects. Sarah marvelled at his ability to hold an entire conversation on his own, with little or no need for input from her.

Marcus wasn't exaggerating about the distance or the size of Thornwood. As the car rolled over the humpbacked bridge into the village, Sarah was amazed to see that 'the village' was simply a cluster of houses; a shop and a pub, with a quaint little church overlooking the river. Instead of streetlamps, the village was lit by old-fashioned cast iron lanterns, which were all festively dressed in red bows. The whole place looked so well maintained and cared for, with brightly painted shopfronts and window boxes bursting with evergreens.

'I have to give it to you Marcus, this is one pretty little village,' she said finally.

'Well, we're very proud of it and we have a very successful Tidy Towns committee,' he replied.

'Let me guess, you must be president?' she joked genially.

'Vice president, but I've got my eye on the prize,' he said, tapping his nose.

'Now,' he announced, as they arrived at a pretty stone house, which was guarded by two bay trees lit up with fairy lights. 'It's not a hotel, but I'm hoping you'll be open-minded.'

'It looks lovely, is it a guest house?'

'Oh, this isn't where you'll be staying, no it's the owner who lives here,' he explained.

'The owner?' Nothing seemed to be straightforward in this place. You had to go from A to C, just to get to B, which probably wasn't the place you were looking for at all.

'Yes, Mr. Sweeney, he rents out a gem of a little cottage down the road,' he said, checking her reaction.

'Sounds... very... authentic!' she said, secretly hoping that it would be plumbed with hot water.

'Oh it is, full of all those "original features".'

It sounded like a euphemism for cold and damp, but Sarah kept her reservations to herself.

Marcus insisted on taking her to the front door, which was adorned with a beautiful holly wreath. Sarah noticed the twinkling lights of a Christmas tree in the front window and she hoped they weren't disturbing these people. The shape of a person appeared in the coloured glass at the side of the door and they were greeted by a towering, grey-haired man with a ruddy face and a strong nose.

'Marcus,' he acknowledged, reaching out to shake his hand.

'Hello Brian, how are you?' Marcus asked, but before the man had a chance to answer, he ploughed on. 'Listen, you're great to look after us at such short notice,' he said, touching Sarah's arm, 'and I'll leave ye to it now, you don't want to be overcrowded!'

Sarah marvelled at his ability to speak without pausing for breath and while she shook hands with Mr. Sweeney, Marcus had her suitcase out of the boot – insisting that no guest of his would carry their own luggage, not on his watch.

'You'll be alright now, won't you?' he asked, as though talking to a child. 'You will of course,' he said, answering his own question.

Rather abruptly, the vital force that was Marcus had

disappeared off back down the road, leaving Sarah and her new charge in an awkward silence.

'I'll just get the keys,' Mr. Sweeney said, lacking the vitality of her previous companion.

'I'm sorry, I'm interrupting your Christmas.'

'Ah sure, it's over now,' he said in a very practical way. 'It's not very far, but I'm sure you don't fancy lugging your suitcase down an old boreen.'

Brian Sweeney was the polar opposite to Marcus. He was calm and unhurried, using his words only sparingly. There was a reserve there that made even small talk challenging.

They sat in a decrepit-looking jeep, with mud and manure caked on the sides. After a sputtering start, the engine eventually agreed to turn over and they set off down the road, past the church and back over the humpback bridge. The road forked into two and he indicated to turn left onto the narrower road.

'Is this a one-way street?' Sarah asked, which earned her a hearty laugh from her driver. There were no road markings, just a barely visible ridge of tarmac that, over the years, had formed something of a spine in the centre of the road. Like a prehistoric animal, asleep for now. 'You can't be serious; how are two cars supposed to fit on this road?'

'They're not! One of you has to reverse until you come to a layby or an entrance to a field,' he said, reassuring Sarah that it was all perfectly normal in the country.

The car heater was blowing out hot air furiously, making Sarah feel drowsy and slightly queasy. Despite the bright sunshine, everything still glistened with a light whisper of frost. To the left, there was a large woodland, with the top of a hill peeking out above the conifers.

'What's up there?' Sarah asked, pointing up at the verdant hillside.

'That's Cnoc na Sí,' he said. 'It's a lovely spot for walking.'

'Canuck na Shee?' Sarah repeated, trying to form the strange Gaelic sounds.

'It means hill of the fairies,' he translated.

'Seriously?'

'I'm not codding you; "Cnoc" means hill and "Sí" is the Irish for fairies. Did you think it was something we just made up for the Yanks?' he said, winking at her. She was glad to see he was thawing out a little.

After a slight dip in the road, the countryside opened out in front of them once again. The little river from the village reappeared, almost leading the way to a solitary cottage standing proud and dignified on its own little patch of land bordered by a whitewashed stone wall. He glanced furtively at Sarah to gauge her reaction as he pulled up at the little blue gate.

'Welcome to Butler's cottage. It's just been newly thatched and you know, despite what people might think, thatched houses are very warm,' he pointed out.

Sarah, however, did not need convincing. The cottage was like something from a postcard. The single-storey home was painted white with a neatly trimmed thatched roof that boasted a beautifully scalloped design. They trod carefully up the frosty garden path that was made up of a jigsaw of flagstones and came to the matching light blue door. As he jiggled the key in the lock, Sarah noticed that the door seemed to be split into two sections.

'Oh yes, it's an authentic half door,' he explained, slipping into his role as tour guide. 'It was a great way to let air into the cottage, without any four-legged friends getting in.' On seeing Sarah's face he continued, 'You know they used to say that if you were stood leaning on the half door, you were passing time; but if you were stood leaning against an open doorway, you were wasting time!'

Marcus was right about the original features; it felt like stepping back in time.

'When was it built?'

'Oh probably in the mid-1800s. My son bought it back in the nineties, but we still call it Butler's cottage. That's just how it is around here; the Butlers built this house and worked the farm for over a century, so it'll always be Butler's. It's pretty much open plan,' he continued, 'but it should be enough for you.'

The ceiling had been knocked through to the rafters, giving the place a light and airy feel. Sarah was relieved to see a small but modern country kitchen with a sunken porcelain sink and on the opposite wall was a giant hearth with two cosy-looking armchairs upholstered in plaid. A toy-sized window with four little square panes looked out onto the back garden. The place was certainly working its charm.

'Now here's what we used to call the "back bedroom",' he continued, opening a door to the side of the hearth where Sarah could see a double bed dressed with a homely patchwork quilt. 'Can I afford this?' she asked, concerned that her budget might not stretch.

'I hope so,' he laughed, then saw the look on Sarah's face. 'Well it's low season anyhow, so I'm sure we can hash out a deal,' he assured her. 'But of course, it depends on how long you want to stay…?' he said, trailing off.

'Oh you know, maybe a week, or two. Just checking out the old family tree,' she said, cringing at the cliché.

'Right so; I'll leave you to it. My son dropped off a few essentials earlier on; tea and the like,' he said. Without much further ado, he was gone. The stillness he left in his wake was almost startling after the day's events.

'Hello Butler's cottage', Sarah whispered to herself, as she kicked off her boots and turned to look at her new home.

She couldn't recall the last time she had done something so impulsive and purely for herself. She kept expecting the panic to set in, but as she took in her new surroundings, all she felt was joy. 'Maybe,' she thought, 'this is what following your heart feels like.'

ONE MORE CHAPTER

The author and One More Chapter would like to thank everyone who contributed to the publication of this story...

Analytics
Emma Harvey
Maria Osa

Audio
Fionnuala Barrett
Ciara Briggs

Contracts
Georgina Hoffman
Florence Shepherd

Design
Lucy Bennett
Fiona Greenway
Holly Macdonald
Liane Payne
Dean Russell

Digital Sales
Laura Daley
Michael Davies
Georgina Ugen

Editorial
Michelle Griffin
Eleanor Goymer
Arsalan Isa
Charlotte Ledger
Laura McCallen
Jennie Rothwell
Tony Russell
Kimberley Young

International Sales
Bethan Moore

Marketing & Publicity
Chloe Cummings
Emma Petfield

Operations
Melissa Okusanya
Hannah Stamp

Production
Emily Chan
Denis Manson
Francesca Tuzzeo

Rights
Lana Beckwith
Rachel McCarron
Agnes Rigou
Hany Sheikh
Mohamed
Zoe Shine
Aisling Smyth

The HarperCollins Distribution Team

The HarperCollins Finance & Royalties Team

The HarperCollins Legal Team

The HarperCollins Technology Team

Trade Marketing
Ben Hurd

UK Sales
Yazmeen Akhtar
Laura Carpenter
Isabel Coburn
Jay Cochrane
Alice Gomer
Gemma Rayner
Erin White
Harriet Williams
Leah Woods

And every other essential link in the chain from delivery drivers to booksellers to librarians and beyond!

Acknowledgments

When I sat down to plan this second book in The Three Fry Sisters series, which was going to cover the interwar years of the 1920s, I knew I had to bring one of the sisters to Paris. Everyone who was everyone seemed to descend on Paris in those exuberant, live-in-the-moment years following the horrors and deprivations of the Great War and the Spanish Flu. Ernest Hemingway and F. Scott Fitzgerald were there, of course, as were other creative stars like Cole Porter, Igor Stravinsky, James Joyce, Coco Chanel, Josephine Baker, Isadora Duncan and Man Ray. So, who best to set amongst this group but beautiful, wayward, artistic Etta Fry Marinetti? Once I'd made that decision, the book opened up to me, with Celie forging a new life in the wheat fields of Alberta, Canada; Jessie running her health clinic in a volatile Cairo; and their mother, Christina, facing her past in London.

I dived into my research, including re-reads of *The Great Gatsby*, *The Sun Also Rises*, and Hemingway's memoir *A Movable Feast*, which was an invaluable and entertaining source of dates, names and places. Michael Reynolds's excellent biography *Hemingway: The Paris Years* (W.W. Norton & Company, 1999) was a constant companion, and I am an indebted to my brother-in-law, James Dodson, for letting me borrow liberally from his extensive library of Hemingway novels and biographies.

I owe my sister, Carolyn Chinn, a debt of gratitude for her insightful feedback through many drafts of this book. When I have been unable to see the forest for the trees, she has set me back on the path through the woods with perceptive observations, usually over a couple of glasses of Cabernet Sauvignon and Doritos.

Along with my wonderful and supportive family and friends around the world, I must give a shout-out to my thespian colleagues in *The Graduate* at The Burgess Hill Theatre Club who brought some much-appreciated fun and companionship to the months of otherwise solitary rewrites and editing. Carolyn Chinn, Robson Ternouth, Sophie Davies, Phil Hawkins, Laura Witham, Archie Tipple, Luisa Deas, Andy Squires, Gemma Masters, Pippa Jones – you're the best!

This book wouldn't have taken the shape it has without the advice and support of my amazing editor at One More Chapter, Charlotte Ledger; copyeditors extraordinaire Julia Williams, Laura Burge and Tony Russell; designer Lucy Bennett for the beautiful cover, and my agent Joanna Swainson for her encouragement and support.

Most of all, I want to thank you, my readers, for taking time out of your busy days to spend time with Celie, Jessie, Etta and Christina as they negotiate the changing world of the early 20th century.